Praise for *Fool Her Once*

"This one really stops the presses! This terrific thriller mixes blood and ink . . . [A] sizzling read that will leave you on the edge of your seat." —**Barry Levine, author of** *The Spider* **and** *All the President's Women*, **Pulitzer Prize-nominated veteran investigative reporter and editor, and** *Huffington Post* **"Game Changer" award winner**

"Joanna Elm has masterfully crafted a stunning thriller that has it all: a beautifully flawed protagonist who we can't help but root for; a complex antagonist with a tragic past; a setting alive with vivid details, and a gripping story with cascading tension that explodes in the well-earned climax. Well done, Elm." —**Gregory Lee Renz, author of** *Beneath the Flames*

"Full of stunning twists and surprises, and you won't see the ending coming. Read it!" —**R.G. Belsky, award-winning author of the Clare Carlson mystery series**

" [Joanna Elm's] writing intricately weaves lovers, both former and present, in such a way that any one of them could be suspect for murder." —**Lois Cahall, #1 bestselling author,** *Plan C: Just In Case*; **Founder, The Palm Beach Book Festival**

"*Fool Her Once* is timely in exploring the theme of nature vs. nurture in forming personality and behavior . . . a good diversion in our trying times." —*The Southampton Press*

FOOL

A NOVEL

HER

ONCE

FOOL HER ONCE

A NOVEL

JOANNA ELM

CamCat
Books

CamCat Publishing, LLC
Brentwood, Tennessee 37027
camcatpublishing.com

Hardcover ISBN 9780744304930
Paperback ISBN 9780744304893
Large-Print Paperback ISBN 9780744304923
eBook ISBN 9780744304817
Audiobook ISBN 9780744304794

Library of Congress Control Number: 2021947761

Book and cover design by Maryann Appel
Map illustration by Sateda

5   3   1   2   4

For my husband, Joe and my son, Daniel.
Always and forever, front and center in my thoughts.

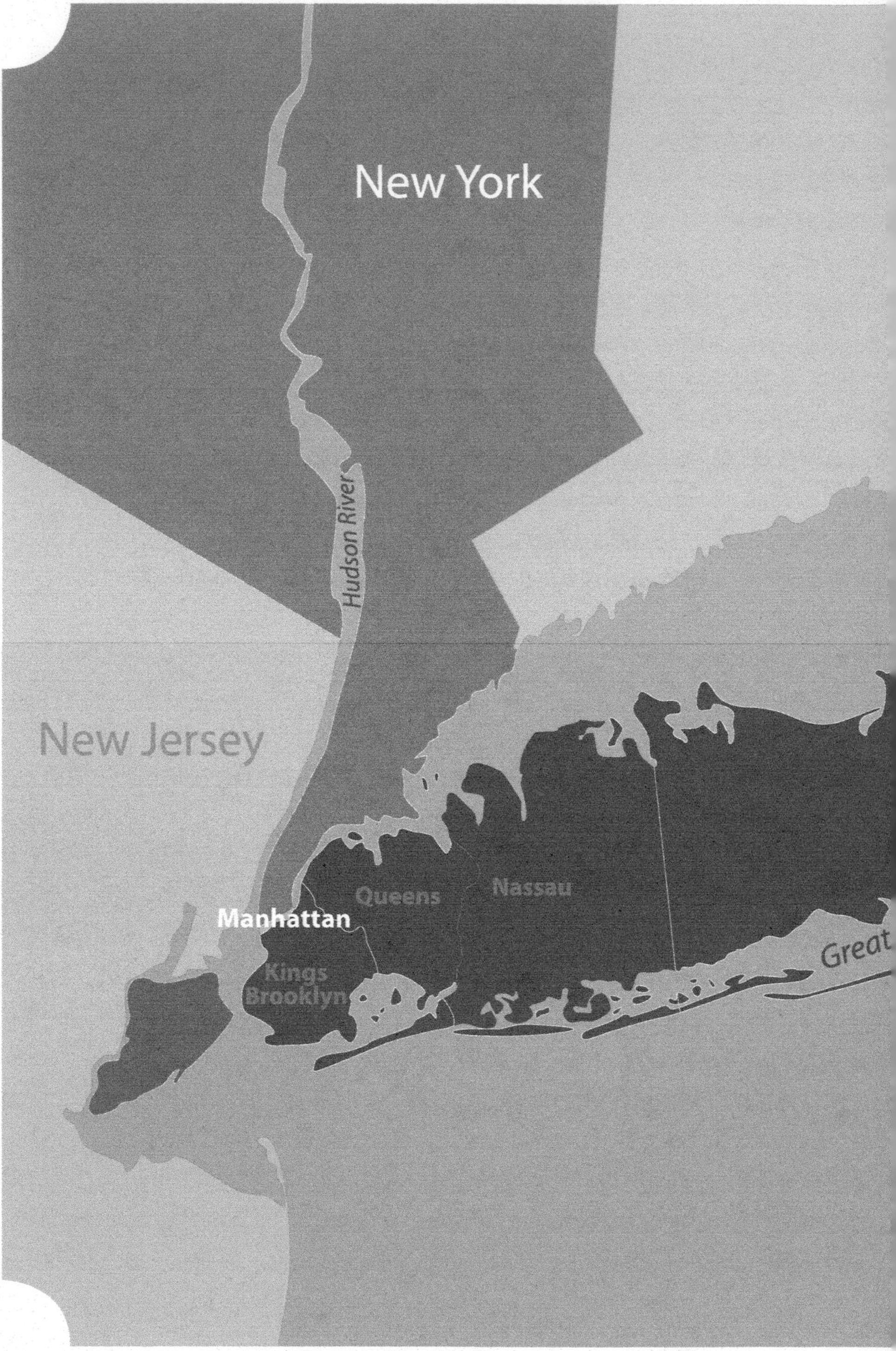
New York
Hudson River
New Jersey
Queens
Nassau
Manhattan
Kings
Brooklyn
Great

Connecticut

Long Island Sound

Block Island
Sound

North Fork

Orient

Greenport

Shelter Island

Cutchogue

Sag
Harbor

Montauk

Robins
Island

East
Hampton

Riverhead

Southampton

Shinnecock
Bay

South Fork

Atlantic Ocean

PART
ONE

Chapter One

June 2019
Week One: Thursday

I t took him four minutes to circle the block. He drove slowly, looking for a parking space on Jenna's street while keeping one eye out for surveillance cameras. He'd read somewhere that Midtown had more security cameras per block than any other neighborhood in the city. It made sense to know where they were located.

On his second go-round, he noticed the lights were still off in her apartment. He figured she'd have a light on if she was home. It wasn't dark out, but it was dark enough for a third-floor apartment in the shadow of the Fifty-Ninth Street Bridge. For sure, she wasn't sleeping. Not this early. Not in Manhattan.

It was only just coming up on nine.

Most likely she was out. Celebrating her big exposé in *City-Magazine* about uptown eateries in the Hamptons, the summer playground for the rich and famous. All in a tizzy now because of Jenna Sinclair's revelations of farm-to-table frauds like restaurants claiming their overpriced oysters were locally harvested, when in fact they'd been flown in from the Gulf. It was a big deal. She'd even been on TV talking about it. For sure, she'd come a long way from her rookie reporter days.

Deep in thought, he almost sailed past a spot opening up right across from her apartment building. But he slowed just in time and backed in, executing a perfect parallel park. He killed the engine, leaned back in his seat, and pushed his baseball cap around on his head. No one paid him the slightest attention. There were hardly any pedestrians around. This stretch of Sutton Place wasn't exactly busy since the Food Emporium on the corner had closed its doors.

That was good. He didn't want any witnesses when he confronted Jenna. He knew she wasn't going to like him turning up in her life like this. She wasn't going to like what he'd come to tell her. He hoped she wouldn't make a scene. He hoped things wouldn't get ugly. He really, truly, hoped not.

Chapter Two

Jenna Sinclair ignored the flashing neon-orange numbers of the crosswalk timer and picked up her pace across four lanes of traffic on Fifty-Seventh to arrive at Neary's feeling hot and sticky. Ryan was already seated at a corner table. His collar was open, his hair rumpled. He looked charmingly boyish—nothing like the distinguished, respected publisher he had become running *CityMagazine*. More like the Ryan she remembered from the old days. A Scotch sat on the table in front of him and he was scrolling through his iPhone. As she got closer, she noticed he was frowning. She hoped it wasn't because she was late. Her meeting at *My World* magazine had run longer than expected, and the Jimmy Choos she'd worn to impress the editors at her pitch session—*See guys, I'm going to fit right in with that swanky Monte Carlo crowd!*—had slowed her down as she raced across town. But it wouldn't hurt for Ryan to see her wearing killer heels—something to draw attention away from the hint of a muffin-top that had materialized when she'd pulled on her favorite skinny jeans this morning. Nothing that couldn't be fixed, she thought. Walking everywhere would melt those extra pounds right off. The energy of the city would work its magic.

Her cell phone rang as she arrived at the table. She recognized Zack's ringtone but she had no intention of answering. She was not going to let her husband—sorry, correction—her lying, cheating, soon-to-be ex-husband intrude on what had been a perfect day. She reached into her purse to mute the phone, but the sound had already caught Ryan's attention.

"Have you been waiting long?" she asked as he looked up, his frown turning instantly into a grin.

"Long enough—I'm trying to make up for lost time." He stood and reached for her hand, his fingers twining around hers as he drew her to sit beside him. "Work agrees with you, Sinclair. You're glowing."

"It's sweat," she laughed as a glass of chilled pinot grigio appeared in front of her. "I ran most of the way here." A slight exaggeration. She'd speed-walked, and only for the last couple of blocks, terrified that a heel would get stuck in a crack and send her sprawling facedown on the sidewalk.

Ryan was right, though. She was enjoying herself, setting up interviews and pitching to editors around town. Maybe reviving her reporting career was not going to be as difficult as she'd feared, what with everyone buzzing about her Hamptons restaurant exposé.

She sipped her wine and filled Ryan in on the highlights of her pitch session. "Gordon's very enthusiastic about the interview in

Monte Carlo. He says he'll try to get some advance expenses for me so I can spend a few days there."

"Well, I'm sure he can swing a couple of grand." Ryan grinned. "Your article is tailor-made for his magazine: glitz, glamor, dysfunctional families, the murder of the richest woman on the French Riviera. Her son-in-law has been convicted for conspiracy to murder, and you've landed an interview with his wife. What's not to love?"

Jenna nodded. It was Ryan who'd suggested she contact Gordon, the articles editor of *My World*, a publication that spread its net wider than Ryan's *CityMagazine*. But she was only half listening as Ryan's earlier greeting bounced around in her head.

Trying to make up for lost time. What did that mean? Lost time? Was he trying to tell her he'd made a mistake all those years ago when he'd let Teddi Conroy, the skinny, rich, blonde reporter-wannabe step—slither, one should say—into Jenna's shoes?

This was the third time Jenna and Ryan had met since her move back to the city. The *New York Post* had mentioned their first lunch as a one-line Sightings item. Only in New York City, and maybe L.A, Jenna had reflected, were the comings and goings of writers and editors and TV producers considered to be of any interest to the general public. Secretly, she was thrilled to see her name on Page Six. She hoped Zack had seen it too. It wouldn't hurt for him to think that she'd wasted no time in getting back together with her former lover.

At their second lunch, Ryan had told her he didn't care about gossip either. (Of course he didn't, otherwise he wouldn't have taken her to a restaurant where they would be noticed.) He and Teddi were separated, just like Zack and Jenna. Teddi had spent the past five months in Palm Beach generating gossip of her own.

Jenna knew all that. She'd heard it around town even before Ryan confirmed it for her.

Tonight, she wanted to hear more. She wanted to know what had happened between them. She wanted to know why he was wining and dining her at expensive restaurants. Was it just business because he saw her as a source for future articles?

Or was it more personal?

His greeting just now suggested it was the latter, but if he and Teddi were really through, why hadn't Ryan moved out of the townhouse they shared? Supposedly, he was living in the garden apartment of the townhouse and paying rent, but still. Why stick so close to an estranged wife?

However, as soon as the waitress placed their broiled lamb chop entrees in front of them, it was Ryan who jumped in with the questions. "What about the girl?" he asked. "How's she doing? Is she coming to live with you in the city?"

Jenna wondered why Ryan couldn't remember her daughter's name, and why, despite his apparent interest in Dollie, it sounded more as if he wanted to know how long he'd have Jenna to himself.

"Dollie's spending the summer in Maine," Jenna replied, aware of Ryan's thigh resting firmly against hers. She didn't move away. It felt good to be this close to him again.

"Maine?" Ryan arched an eyebrow. "That's a long way to go for summer camp, isn't it?"

She shrugged off the question. Ryan didn't need to hear about the difficulties of finding a summer camp for teenagers like Dollie. Then, she continued as if Ryan hadn't spoken. "It's good for her to be away from home. Zack and I need time to sort things out. I'm going to have to find a lawyer. . ."

"A divorce lawyer?"

"Yes."

"Because of . . ."

Jenna had mentioned the other woman's name at lunch two days before, but she certainly didn't expect Ryan to remember that name.

"Bethany," Jenna filled in the blank. "Bethany, the intern from the Culinary Institute. The one he took all the way to Maine when he was dropping off Dollie at summer camp."

"He's serious about her, then?"

"I guess he is." She shrugged. She really didn't know the answer. All she knew was that her husband had cheated on her with a woman who looked—and probably was—half Jenna's age.

But Ryan didn't appear to be waiting for any further explanation. He set down his knife and fork and sipped his Scotch. "Well, I'm really happy you're back, Sinclair," he said. "You don't belong all the way out there in the wilds of Long Island." He made a face she couldn't quite decipher, then said, "You were the best reporter the *Sun* ever had. You should never have quit."

Jenna shook her head abruptly to stop him from pursuing the subject. "You know why I couldn't stay."

"You weren't to blame for what happened, Sinclair. I told you a long time ago. You reported the facts, that's all."

Yeah, and a woman and her unborn baby died because of it. Jenna wanted to contradict but caught herself in time. She was not going to rehash old issues. She wasn't going to change Ryan's mind on this, just as he wasn't going to change hers. She regretted Ryan had raised the subject.

Apparently, so did Ryan. He swirled the ice cubes in his glass and looked around the room as if he was about to order another drink while she finished eating. "Another?" He gestured at her glass. "Or shall we finish with a nightcap at your place?"

Jenna's heart thudded against her rib cage. Ryan's suggestion of a nightcap at her apartment was how they had tumbled into bed together the very first time. Is that what he had in mind, now? For a moment she reveled in the thought that after all these years he still wanted her. It eased the hurt of Zack's betrayal and made her feel more desirable than she'd felt in a while.

But she wasn't going to jump into bed with Ryan just to get back at Zack. Was she? It had to mean more. If she and Ryan were going to revive their relationship, there was Dollie to think about, too. Her daughter might be forgiving of her father's philandering, but she would turn on Jenna in a heartbeat if she saw tweets or Snapchat messages about her mother cavorting with a former lover. Mothers had to be perfect.

She took a deep breath as Ryan signaled for a check, then put his arm around her, evidently taking her silence as consent. She checked her phone for any more missed calls or texts from Zack. But there was nothing.

"Are we good to go?" Ryan threw her a quizzical look.

"We're good." Leaving her phone muted, she dropped it into her purse as Ryan, hand at the small of her back, steered her out into the drizzle that was just starting to fall over Midtown.

Chapter Three

Week One: Late Thursday Night

He was afraid he'd doze off and miss her, but he was wide awake when she eventually strolled into view. With him. Arm in arm. Her and him. Together. Everything he had come to say to her suddenly vanished from his thoughts, evaporating in a haze of fury. The swig of water he'd taken a moment before they rounded the corner caught in his throat and he sputtered, the water dribbling down his chin.

He recognized McAllister immediately. He was the big-shot: the publisher, the editor-in-chief, the owner—whatever—of the magazine that had published her big exposé. The bastard's photo was in the gossip columns often enough these days.

Why was he surprised they were together? They were a team. Again. Just like the old days: digging up dirt, ruining lives.

He reached for his cell phone from the dashboard and held the camera on the pair of them trying to calm himself as they stood on the corner, talking to some scruffy guy pushing a shopping cart. Then he tossed the phone onto the passenger seat as they continued down the street toward her apartment building. He switched on the engine and prepared to pull out.

If he gunned it, the car would rocket toward them. It wouldn't take more than split seconds to slam into them before veering wildly away with screeching tires carrying him onto First Avenue and away before anyone realized what had happened. The surveillance camera below the building awning was fixed, pointing at the steps into the lobby. He'd had the last few hours to figure that one out. And there weren't any other pedestrians around for the moment. Just the building doorman, who wasn't paying attention, and the scruffy guy, who seemed to be mumbling to himself as he crossed the street.

His hands felt clammy on the wheel. A little voice at the back of his head was telling him to take it easy, to calm down, take a deep breath, count to ten—all the usual advice for moments of rage like this one. Besides, this really wasn't why he'd come this evening.

McAllister had changed the equation. Now he wanted to kill both of them.

He fixed his eyes on the traffic ahead on First Avenue. It was moving smoothly. Any moment, the lights would change in his favor, and if he timed it right, he could hit them and speed into the turn onto First, merging into the flow of traffic in seconds.

If he accelerated now. Right now.

Chapter Four

The buzzing of the intercom startled Jenna as she waited for the Bialetti to stop gurgling. Her head felt heavy, but her Fitbit told her she'd gotten almost six hours' sleep since Ryan had left the apartment. She moved the moka pot off the flames and walked into the hallway to the intercom.

It was Oscar, the day doorman. "Miss Sinclair, police here to see you. Coming up now."

She sat down abruptly on the narrow hallway bench. Dollie. Something had happened to Dollie. She felt ice cold as she opened the door to wait for the elevator to discharge the cops, who turned out to be plainclothes detectives. She tried to recall what someone—probably

Lola, her best friend who knew all about law enforcement—had once told her about cops always going in threes, not twos, to inform next of kin when there was a fatality. Was that still true? Maybe they'd downsized because of budget cuts. Or maybe the "three" rule did not apply in New York City.

Her heart was pounding, thudding against her chest, the blood roaring in her ears, as she beckoned them into the apartment. She barely heard as the taller, younger one said: "Miss Sinclair, we're sorry to disturb you, but we're wondering if you could answer some questions about yesterday evening? We're looking into an incident involving Mr. Ryan McAllister."

It took her more than a moment to refocus, and for the pounding of her heart to slow a little. They weren't here about Dollie.

"Incident?" She repeated the word, frowning.

They looked at each other. The taller, younger one was black with a shaved head and soft brown eyes. He introduced himself as Detective Jim Martins. His partner was older and shorter, with thinning hair. His face was slicked with perspiration, as if he'd walked up the three flights to her apartment rather than taking the elevator. Jenna immediately forgot his name.

Martins took a notebook out of his hip pocket but didn't look at it when he replied: "Mr. McAllister was found in the street, early this morning."

"What do you mean 'found'?" Her voice rose shrilly. "Is he dead?"

"No."

"Where was he found?" Jenna's heart was pounding again even as the memory from just a few hours ago flashed through her mind.

They had strolled back from Neary's; had stopped on the corner of her street while Ryan fished around for a loose bill to hand over to the homeless guy who hung out there.

She'd linked her arm through his as they walked into her building and to the elevator. They'd barely crossed the threshold into her apartment when Ryan had nudged her back against the door and brought his mouth to her lips, working down to the hollow of her throat, his fingers tugging at the straps of her cami. All thoughts of waiting, doing the right thing had evaporated in a millisecond. Instead, she had responded, clinging to him, thrilling to the thought that he wanted her.

They had moved as one into the living room, onto the couch, then down onto the hand-knotted wool Jaipur rug, Ryan pushing down her jeans and panties and flinging them over the couch.

"No. Wait." Jenna had sat up abruptly. "I can't."

The detective's reply jolted her back into the conversation. "Just a couple of hundred yards down the street from this building. You had dinner with him last night."

Jenna focused on Martins. He didn't sound as if he was asking. "Did Ryan tell you that?" She paused and repeated her first question. "What do you mean 'found'?" Jenna wished she could take a long gulp of espresso to get her brain working again.

"Let us ask the questions, Miss Sinclair, okay? We're just trying to figure out what happened."

Jenna didn't like the abrupt change in tone, and suddenly the detective's eyes didn't look so soft either. Did he think she'd done something wrong? She realized she sounded a little defensive. That was stupid.

There was nothing to hide.

"Yes, we had dinner," she said.

The other detective nodded, and she followed his gaze across the floor into the living area to where her white jeans lay crumpled under the chair. "We're just trying to establish a time line," he said. "We'd appreciate it if you could help us out. Give us some idea of what time he left here?"

"I don't remember when he left."

"He couldn't help us with the timing either."

Not hard to believe. The events of the night were wrapped in a mist floating around her head, but she remembered Ryan guiding her to the bed, sliding in beside her and holding her. "We don't have to rush," he'd said. "We don't have to do anything tonight. It's okay. We have all the time in the world."

"We don't know how long he was lying in the street," Martins mentioned casually. "He couldn't tell the paramedics what happened."

"Oh my God." The words came out as a whisper. The image of Ryan swaying drunkenly flashed before her eyes. "What happened? Did he fall? Did he pass out?"

"We don't know exactly."

"Is he injured?"

"We don't know the full extent of his injuries. They're checking him out now. He's at Lenox Hill Hospital."

Jenna had the feeling they weren't telling her everything. Why would detectives be investigating someone falling down drunk in the street?

Had he been hit by a car?

"Miss Sinclair? Can you give us an approximate time when you last saw him?"

She nodded quickly. "Sure, I'll try." She knew they could get a time from Nando, the night doorman, and she didn't want to appear uncooperative. "We had dinner at Neary's, round the corner," she said. "We came back here for a nightcap. We were discussing some writing projects I'm working on. I just finished one for his magazine."

"His magazine?"

Jenna nodded. "He's the publisher of *CityMagazine*. He bought the exposé I just wrote on restaurants in the Hamptons. We planned on working on some others together . . . I mean there were a couple of projects we discussed. We were talking, we lost track of time." She knew she was babbling. God only knew why she felt so guilty. She and Ryan had done nothing wrong. "It was probably around three." She paused. "I'm sorry. Yes, around three, maybe three thirty. That's when I saw him out."

"Did you part on friendly terms?"

Jenna stared at Martins. Had they already spoken to Nando? Had he told them he'd seen Jenna following Ryan down the street?

Just before leaving, Ryan had told her Teddi was returning, flying into La Guardia, and he had to go home, shower and change before picking her up. Jenna had been furious as she listened to the elevator carry Ryan down to the lobby.

She'd grabbed a T-shirt and sweat pants and headed for the stairs, arriving in the lobby in time to see Ryan walking out of the building, a little unsteady on his feet. She'd let him get to the corner before calling after him to stop.

"Miss Sinclair, did you have a fight?" Martins persisted.

"God, no!" Jenna's reply burst from her lips. No, Nando could not have seen her push Ryan. She was surely already out of the doorman's line of vision when she'd caught up with him.

"Okay." The detective gave her a curt nod and handed her his business card. "If you remember anything else, please call me." His partner opened the front door out into the hallway.

"You said he's at Lenox Hill?"

Martins looked over her shoulder and appeared to be staring at something in her living room. She hoped it was not at her discarded white jeans. "Yes. Lenox Hill." He nodded. "His wife is probably with him by now." He paused in the open doorway. "They have Mr. McAllister in the ICU," he added as he followed his partner to the front door.

The intensive care unit? It had to be serious.

"Did you say ICU?" She aimed the question at their backs, but the door had already closed.

Jenna returned to the kitchen. She was so parched it was making her dizzy. She stood at the faucet, cold water running into the sink as she cupped her hands and swigged from them, not caring that half of it was landing on the kitchen floor.

She poured herself a double espresso, carried the mug into the living room and sank into an armchair, looking around for her cell phone. Her eyes flickered round the room, noticing the mess the way the detectives would have seen it from the hallway. Through the door into the bedroom, she saw the empty glasses, the empty bottle of Jameson's on the nightstand. Blood rose to her face, she felt hot and cold and then hot again as she caught sight of her scrunched-up, bright white panties hanging off the middle shelf of her bookcase, where Ryan had tossed them.

She took a couple of deep breaths. The cops probably thought they had the whole picture: cheating husband, wife returning from a trip, girlfriend gets jealous, doesn't want to let him go.

They'd questioned her as if they thought she was the one who'd hurt him badly enough to put him into intensive care in the hospital.

She closed her eyes and tried to recall exactly what had happened when she'd finally caught up with Ryan.

Chapter Five

The hospital would not release any information because Jenna was not next of kin. She punched in the number of Ryan's cell phone and immediately hit the red button. No doubt Teddi would have the phone now, and Jenna didn't know what to say to her. Maybe she would call Ryan's assistant at *CityMagazine*, ask her what she'd heard, what she could find out. There was nothing online in the digital versions of the *New York Post* or the *Daily News*. She plugged in Ryan's name for a Google alert. If anyone got hold of the story, she'd know immediately.

Finishing her espresso, she retreated into the bathroom. She threw water on her face, brushed her teeth, ran a comb through her hair, and looked for her face cream on the counter. Then, she remembered how in a fit of reorganizing and cleaning, she'd stashed her lotions and face creams out of sight in the bathroom cabinet. And thank goodness. At least Ryan hadn't been exposed to all those tubes and bottles with "anti-aging" and "firming" stamped all over them.

She squirted an extra sliver of hydrating serum onto her fingertips before massaging it into her face and neck. Then, she threw on shorts, a tank top, and her running shoes. Grabbing her keys off the hallway table, she hurried out of her apartment.

Out on the street, she turned left, jogged to the corner, and stopped in the spot where she'd caught up with Ryan in the early hours of the morning. She stared down at the sidewalk, searching for any trace of an accident: loose change that might have rolled out of his pockets; tiny glass shards from a shattered iPhone, or a vehicle's black skid marks glancing off the curb, even a hint of a dried blood smear. She shuddered.

But there was nothing to see.

She stared across Fifty-Ninth, past the site of the old Food Emporium, and into the underpass between Fifty-Ninth and Sixtieth streets. Usually, two, sometimes three, homeless individuals were seeking a night's sleep on the sidewalk in there. Maybe one of them had mugged Ryan. Not likely, however. Despite most people's habit of ignoring the homeless on the streets, Ryan always handed them a dollar bill or five, often before they even asked. Perhaps one of them had seen what had happened.

She jogged in place for a minute before sprinting across the street toward the only body on the sidewalk, curled up with his back to the passing public, an unlaced black boot on his left foot and a knitted cap on his head. It was the same guy who'd stopped them on the street the previous night. She was sure of it. She recognized the big electric fan in his cart. She remembered wondering where he'd find an outlet to plug it into.

She stood for a moment, staring at the dirty, wrinkled hand clutching a stringy blanket under his chin. Then, she crouched down. "Excuse me. Sir, excuse me."

"Whaaa!" The body moved surprisingly swiftly into a sitting position. He shrank back from her against the wall of the underpass. His eyes darted from side to side.

"I'm sorry to wake you," she said softly. Before she could finish the thought, his leg jerked out, his stockinged right foot catching her across the shin. Jenna jumped up and back a couple of paces. The movement of his leg seemed involuntary. She didn't think he'd intended to kick her. Indeed, he was shrinking back against the wall again, covering his head and face with the stringy blanket and wheezing.

"Sir? Do you remember me? Last night, my friend and I . . ."

He broke into a frenzied bout of coughing, shaking his head violently. Jenna stared helplessly for a moment before reaching into her shorts pocket for some change. The dirty blanket stayed on his head and Jenna realized he wasn't about to tell her anything useful. She dropped the change into a can sitting in the shopping cart alongside the fan. Then, she turned and jogged back across Fifty-Ninth and past her building to continue up the street toward the tiny park on the East River. There she finally took a deep, long breath and slumped down on one of the park benches that afforded Sutton Place residents a panoramic vista across the river to Queens.

She continued to take deep breaths till her pulse slowed. Then, she let her thoughts loose, allowing all the unanswered questions to flood into her mind. She wondered how Teddi had gotten herself to the hospital. How had the cops known Ryan had spent the evening with

Jenna? If he was in the ICU, he likely wasn't in any condition to tell them anything. Then suddenly, the memory of what had happened when she'd caught up with Ryan on the corner forced itself into her mind.

He had tried to explain himself, swaying on the sidewalk. "Lovey, I can't leave Teddi stranded at La Guardia. Not with all that construction going on. She'll never get a cab."

"You should have mentioned it earlier," Jenna had blasted back. "Like before we returned to the apartment." Like, maybe even before we'd ordered dinner, she thought angrily. She'd felt betrayed and used. His words, "we've got all the time in the world," hammered in her head. A big, fat lie.

Their time had apparently run out, because Teddi was about to touch down at La Guardia.

"It's not what I want to do," he told her. "But she texted me from Palm Beach."

That's when Jenna had pushed Ryan away. Shoved him, really. With both hands. Then she had turned swiftly and headed back to her building without looking back.

Her thoughts raced now. Could she have pushed Ryan hard enough to knock him over? People died from simple slip-and-falls if they hit their heads hard enough. It didn't take very much if you hit the wrong spot.

And, if not her, then who? A random mugger? Or . . . ? She chewed on her bottom lip. Could it have been Zack? She hadn't given much thought to Zack turning up at the apartment. The only time he'd ever stayed there in all sixteen years of their marriage was for a week after Dollie was born. Zack hated the city.

But, perhaps he hated losing her more. "Don't just walk out like that, Jen. Let's talk. Please. We can resolve things," Zack had said as she stormed out of the inn, carrying two big totes, hurrying to leave before he tried to stop her.

But no, she shook off the thought. Even if Zack had driven the ninety miles into the city to resolve things, he would not have been lurking outside the building at two or three in the morning. If there was something he wanted to say to Jenna, he would have come straight up to the apartment and said it. He wasn't the type to beat around the bush, as he himself might have pointed out, with his usual flair for picking just the right hackneyed phrase.

She blinked and adjusted her shades. She had to find out what had happened to Ryan. She couldn't just sit around imagining the worst.

An hour later, having showered, and changed into a pair of clean jeans and T-shirt, she was in the lobby of Lenox Hill Hospital. Teddi picked up on the first ring of Ryan's cell phone, no doubt seeing Jenna's ID flash onto the little screen.

"Jenna." The hostility in Teddi's voice was unmistakable.

"I'm downstairs, Teddi." Jenna's words caught briefly in her throat. "I'm so sorry. The cops came to tell me about Ryan." Jenna hesitated, struggling for words. Of course Teddi's tone was hostile. Teddi would know all the embarrassing details by now; that Ryan had been found steps away from Jenna's apartment building in the early hours of the morning when he was supposed to be waiting for her at La Guardia. She would know that Jenna and Ryan had spent the night together. Jenna took a deep breath. "I'm really sorry, Teddi, I didn't know . . ." She paused again, aware she was making a total shambles of her apology. What exactly was it that she intended to say? That she didn't know that Teddi was coming home? That Ryan had misled Jenna about his marriage? She took another deep breath. "I just want to say, if there's anything at all I can do . . ."

"No." Teddi interrupted her. "You've done enough already."

Chapter Six

Nothing could have prepared Jenna for her first sight of Ryan in the ICU.

He was unrecognizable. Tufts of his hair stuck out from the bandages that swathed the top of his head and wound across one eye and around his chin. The other eye was closed. His lips were pale. Tubes came out of his nose and left arm and snaked into a machine that emitted beeping and whirring noises. His hands, lying lifelessly on top of the coverlet, looked bruised and swollen.

She glanced away, catching a snatch of conversation between Teddi and an older woman whom Jenna recognized as Teddi's mother, Ewa Conroy.

"*Co ona tu robi?*" Ewa directed the question to Teddi in her native Polish, then turned on Jenna. "What are you doing here?" Ewa's lips pursed as she waited for an answer.

"It's okay, Mama," Teddi replied. "I invited her up."

In fact, what Teddi had said, when Jenna had asked to see Ryan, was, "Sure, why not? You'll see exactly what happened to him on your street."

As if Jenna had lured Ryan to some crime-infested neighborhood in the Bronx.

Even in her distress, Teddi looked stunning. Jenna wondered if she had stopped at her townhouse to change, or if she'd stepped off her flight looking this stylish with her golden tan and her golden hair tousled just enough to seem sexy. Her crisp white cotton shirt was tucked into slim, patterned capri pants, and fashionable ballet flats rounded out what was, probably, the required, casual look in Palm Beach.

Jenna turned her attention back to Ryan. "How serious are his injuries?"

Teddi busied herself with smoothing down Ryan's bedding. "He's only just come out of surgery. They had to relieve the pressure on his brain. They've induced a coma to help the healing process. He was barely conscious when they found him."

"Do they have any idea what happened?"

"If anyone has any idea, I'd have thought you would," Teddi retorted, her blue eyes fixed on Jenna in a pointed stare. She looked across at her mother. "Mom why don't you go and grab a sandwich in the cafeteria?"

Watch out, Jenna thought as Ewa gathered up her giant Birkin handbag.

It looked like Teddi wanted privacy so she could grill Jenna about the events of the previous evening.

"Ryan and I had dinner," she told Teddi as soon as her mother was out of the room. "He walked me home from Neary's." She paused. "He came in for a nightcap."

"Do you think just because you've written one exposé for *City-Magazine*, the two of you are going to pick up where you left off? I saw the item on Page Six. You can get the *New York Post* in Palm Beach, you know."

Jenna was surprised that Teddi sounded so possessive—especially since it was she who'd left Ryan. But then, what did Jenna know? Teddi was a trust-fund kid. She moved in rarefied circles, flitting between Manhattan and the Hamptons and Palm Beach, thanks to her mother who had known enough as a Polish translator to sink her mitts into a New York billionaire during one of his visits to Warsaw. Ewa had accepted Jack Conroy's subsequent marriage proposal on condition that he provide for her in a prenup and set up a trust fund for her (fatherless) baby daughter whose unpronounceable Polish name had been whittled down over the years to the cuter-sounding Teddi.

Jenna blinked and wondered if Teddi was waiting for an answer. She didn't have one. It would be foolish to acknowledge that, yes, she had entertained some fuzzy thoughts about her and Ryan together again. She felt herself tearing up as she focused on the bruised fingers of Ryan's left hand.

She couldn't tell if they had been bruised in his fall or because of the needles that were stuck into the back of his hand. Two of his nails were turning black. A sudden graphic image of car wheels running over Ryan's fingers materialized in front of her eyes.

She could not reconcile his still form with the Ryan she knew. He'd never been one to stand or sit still. Jenna's first memories of him in the newsroom involved him always pacing, phone cradled between his ear and shoulder, back and forth at the news desk.

All the meaningful "firsts" in Jenna's adult life revolved around Ryan McAllister. He had hired her for her first newspaper job, had given Jenna her first byline, assigned her first scoop. He had been her first live-in lover and her first love.

A tear rolled down her cheek and onto Ryan's bed.

Teddi handed her a tissue. "The surgeon who operated on him thought he might have fallen," Teddi said, her tone a couple of notches softer. "Or that maybe he was hit over the head and mugged." She shrugged. "If it was a mugging, it wasn't very successful. He still had his wallet and Apple watch. And his phone. Thank God. One of the paramedics answered when I called from the airport." She shivered visibly at the memory.

Ryan's phone. Of course, thought Jenna, that's obviously how the cops had tracked her down. Ryan had never password-protected his phone. The cops would have seen the texts between her and Ryan and found Jenna's phone number and address in his contacts list.

She took a step closer to the bed and would have reached to touch his hand had Teddi not been watching her. Instead, she reached into her purse for her cell phone to text Lola. She needed her friend right now. She needed her advice on how to deal with the detectives if they came to interview her again.

Jenna was walking toward the door when a doctor entered the room and addressed her as Mrs. McAllister. Teddi, with a startled look on her face, crossed the room quickly. "I'm Mrs. McAllister."

"I'm sorry." The doctor cleared his throat. "I'm the chief radiologist, Dr. Stevens. I just wanted to update you on your husband's X-rays and MRI. We were able to ascertain before surgery that his skull was fractured in two places. Since then, we've taken another look . . ."

Jenna interrupted, unable to stop herself, "Because someone pushed him? Knocked him over?"

The doctor shook his head. "It was more than that. There are some abrasions and intradermal bruises that suggest someone aimed two very hard blows or kicks, one to each side of his head."

Jenna gasped loudly as the doctor continued, "These blows or kicks seem aimed precisely at his temples. Someone knew exactly what they were doing. So, yes, he may have been knocked down or pushed to the ground, but we believe he sustained his critical injuries because, in layman's language, someone kicked his head in. We've passed this latest information to the police. Sometimes they can follow up on the imprints left by a shoe or boot. It's not much, I know, but it may be all we have to go on if Mr. McAllister can't recall what happened or . . ." He stopped to take a deep breath.

"Or if he doesn't make it." Teddi's voice broke as the words came tumbling out.

The radiologist pursed his lips. "We can't really say that at this point, Mrs. McAllister. We just don't know."

Jenna backed out of the room before he finished speaking. She stood in the hallway, leaning against the plate-glass window that looked into Ryan's room, swallowing furiously to stop bile from rising in her throat.

Someone kicked his head in. The words spun around in her head like an out-of-control carousel. *Someone kicked his head in.*

She took a long, deep breath as her phone pinged with Lola's reply. "Come on down. Text me when you get here."

Jenna exhaled. Thank heaven. Lola would know what to make of this new information. "People get their heads kicked in all the time," she'd tell Jenna. "It's just a coincidence."

Lola would tell her to calm down and to stop imagining that monsters from the past were coming after Ryan. And after her.

Chapter Seven

Twenty-One Years Earlier: Summer 1998

Thud!

Jenna's fingers jumped off the keyboard as a bundle of newspapers landed on the edge of her desk. The *Sun*'s messenger boy winked at her as she surveyed the stack of out-of-town newspapers he'd just dumped on her. She figured it would take her a couple of hours to sift through them, looking for those "gems," as Ryan McAllister called them, that would turn a one-liner from a small local newspaper into a scoop for the *Sun*.

The weekly tabloid, which was sold at supermarket checkouts, was not the newspaper where she'd dreamed of working when she'd graduated from City College, but it was the only one that had offered her a job. It was also within walking distance of the Fifty-Ninth-Street apartment on which her parents had deposited a hefty down payment as a graduation present.

She glanced over to where Ryan stood at the news desk, phone glued to his ear as usual, and then she quickly picked up the top newspaper from the pile. Even in her second month at the *Sun* Ryan still scared her a little. He wasn't much older than she was, but he'd made his way up the ranks in the newsroom to the position of news editor very swiftly. He'd been working in newspapers since high school. He had grimaced when she told him about her journalism degree at her interview. "You can't learn how to be a reporter in a classroom," he'd said, and she caught the trace of a weird transatlantic accent, maybe British, maybe Australian. "And a college degree isn't going to get you more money," he added. "Not here, anyway."

A degree certainly hadn't led to an assignment out of the office yet; mostly she'd been given phone calls to make to add facts and quotes to articles written by other, more senior reporters. Then there was always the task of picking through out-of-town newspapers.

The first one she picked up in the new batch was a Connecticut newspaper that featured a "20 Years Ago Today" column on its front page. A lot of newspapers published similar columns. Jenna enjoyed those the most. They mentioned local news stories that had happened when she was just a baby and her parents were still alive. Sometimes the snippets would mention some movie that had been a super box-office hit at the time, or a song that had stayed at the top of the charts for weeks and weeks, and which Jenna remembered hearing on her mother's compact discs.

That day the Connecticut column caught her eye immediately. It was about the 1978 execution of Ed Haynes, a serial killer. Evil Ed, as the newspaper called him, was a New Yorker, but he had been caught in Connecticut with the body of one of his victims in the trunk of his car. A second victim had been killed and buried in Connecticut, but he had tortured and buried his other victims on the North and South Forks of Long Island. Haynes, the snippet informed her, was executed by lethal injection, the first to be executed after the death penalty was reinstated in Connecticut. The column also noted that at the time, *serial killer* was not yet a widely used expression, and that the execution was witnessed by Haynes's fiancée.

Jenna wondered where the fiancée was now, twenty years later? Had she married someone else? What had attracted her to a serial killer in the first place? Jenna thought an interview with the woman would make an interesting article.

She looked through the *Sun*'s archives before pitching the idea to Ryan.

It turned out that Ed Haynes had brutally assaulted, tortured, and killed six young women in all, and had raped about a dozen more. He had picked up most of them in bars on the South Fork, better known as the Hamptons. Most of his victims were imported summer labor from Ireland and Denmark. Their loved ones had not missed them till they failed to come home at the end of summer. Jenna had to remind herself that back then, in 1978, there had been no instant, easy ways to communicate—no emailing, nor even the capability to text like Jenna had on her bright orange Nokia.

The news clippings gave gruesome details about Haynes's trademark torture techniques and his habit of burying his victims in densely wooded areas. In one of the archived stories, she read that a childhood friend, Rosie Michaelson, had attended his trial. Jenna had a hunch that Rosie was the fiancée who'd witnessed the execution. She felt a shiver run up her spine as she wondered how on earth any woman could be attracted to a monster like Evil Ed.

Ryan was not enthusiastic about her pitch at first. "The fiancée is going to be one of those nutters who either couldn't find a boyfriend, or is some born-again do-gooder who believed in Evil Ed's redemption." Then, as Jenna turned away, trying to hide her downcast face, he relented. "But you never know. See if you can find her, Sinclair."

What Jenna found over the next couple of months was that she had a knack for tracking down people. She tried using a couple of search engines on her office computer. One of the other reporters suggested she use Altavista or Yahoo or Infoseek. Someone else recommended a new search engine, Google. But she couldn't find anything immediately useful in those searches. Instead, because Rosie had been described as a childhood friend, Jenna took a train to Ronkonkoma and then a cab to the school Ed Haynes had reportedly attended.

There she conducted a classic search. Among other things, she looked through school yearbooks for any mention of a Rosie or Rosemary or Roseanne. From there, she followed two leads, one of which brought her to Rosie's best friend in high school, who revealed that Rosie had married a corrections officer from the prison where Ed had been executed in Connecticut. "She's Rosie Miller now," the friend told Jenna. She also revealed that Rosie had had a major crush on Evil Ed when they were in school. "But he never gave her a second glance till she started visiting him in prison."

Unfortunately, Rosie's friend didn't have any information as to where Rosie lived with the corrections officer. As far as she knew, it was somewhere in Connecticut.

A series of phone calls to a local reporter in the Connecticut town where the prison was located produced a name for the corrections officer and a street address for him. But the reporter added that Norman Miller no longer worked at the prison. Nor was he living at the street address that a contact at the prison had provided. Undaunted,

Jenna tracked down some neighbors on Norm Miller's old street and discovered that Norm and wife Rosie had moved to a new address in Seaford, Long Island. Ryan looked impressed when she told him how much she had unearthed and signed a slip for a cash disbursement and a rental car.

"Don't get lost, Sinclair." He grinned at her stricken look. "And look out for all that weekend traffic on the LIE."

He had obviously sussed her out correctly as an all-city girl who had never spent much time—if any—outside of Manhattan.

"Don't worry." She waved a big Hagstrom atlas at him. "Got it all figured out," she added with much more confidence than she felt.

—◦◦◦— —◦◦◦—

Rosie Miller lived in a raised ranch on a quiet street that backed onto school playing fields. There was one car in the short concrete driveway, a Ford Taurus. Jenna didn't know anything about cars and would have had a difficult time identifying a Mercedes or even a Maserati, but she looked on the back, knowing it was the sort of detail that made stories sound authentic. Ryan liked that.

He preferred a story that described someone smoking a Marlboro rather than just a cigarette.

Rosie tried to close the door when Jenna identified herself.

"Please," Jenna put her hand on the door jamb. "My editor will fire me if I come back with nothing." Rosie's lips pursed but she opened the door wider, and let Jenna stand in the hallway.

"Please Mrs. Miller, it's taken me a long time to find you. I just want to chat. I won't identify where you live or even your last name."

"No. Please. My husband, Norm, died last year. But my son and his wife live with me. I don't want them to know anything about this."

"They won't need to," Jenna offered, moving a couple of steps farther into the house until Rosie had no option but to invite her into the living room.

"But you're going to have to leave soon," Rosie warned her. "I don't want you here when my son comes home."

Jenna nodded as she settled into one of the overstuffed armchairs. She noticed almost immediately that Rosie was a chain-smoker, tap-tapping her Virginia Slims into a big blue-glass ashtray. She tried to make the woman feel more at ease by telling her how lovely her necklace looked.

"Adele, Norm's daughter makes these," Rosie said. "That's his daughter from his first marriage. She lives in Arizona on a reservation. She's married to a Native American. Met him in college down there." There was a short silence and then, running out of small talk, Rosie answered Jenna's first question about where she'd met Ed Haynes. Her answers were short and clipped at first, but eventually came out in lengthy spurts as if she'd been waiting a long time to tell her story.

"I know most people won't understand what I could possibly have seen in Ed, but I knew him all my life. He lived two doors down, we went to the same schools. He was very good-looking back then, but he had a reputation as a bit of a juvenile delinquent. You know, graffiti, stealing bikes, destroying property. I was forbidden to talk to him, not that he ever took any notice of me. Only one time when a boy knocked an ice-cream cone out of my hand outside the ice-cream parlor. Ed saw it and laid the kid flat out on his back. I didn't really get to know him till after his trial. And it wasn't till after he was sentenced that I started writing to him."

"Didn't you believe that he had raped and tortured all those girls?"

Rosie shrugged. "He didn't deny it in the end, although he said the girls had led him on. But he stopped all his appeals. Said he preferred to be executed rather than castrated—which is what they talked about doing . . . I mean, chemically." Rosie shrugged, looking away from Jenna's horrified expression. "Don't ask me to explain that," she added. "It's just something I heard from Ed."

Rosie lit a fresh cigarette from the dying embers of the one she'd just finished.

"Weren't you afraid of him?" Jenna asked.

"Maybe a little to begin with. But Ed couldn't hurt me where he was. There were guards all around us all the time, and even when he was waiting, you know, on death row, when we were able to be in the same room, there was always someone outside the door."

"They left you alone together?"

Rosie nodded. "Norm did. He was the corrections officer who worked on death row. He understood those men. He tried to make it a little easier on them. He gave Ed and me time to be alone and close. He let us stay in the library where we could . . . you know . . ." She bit her lower lip.

"Make love?" Jenna prompted, hoping her voice did not betray her horror at the idea.

Rosie nodded. "That's what I mean, people won't understand. They won't be able to picture Ed as loving and gentle. He said he loved me and wished he had gotten to know me when we were still in school, before he started doing what he . . . He asked me to buy a ring for myself and he put it on my finger before he touched me."

Jenna felt a little wave of disgust—and disbelief—wash over her. Rosie was right. No one would be able to reconcile the image of Evil Ed putting a ring on Rosie's finger with the image of him as a depraved serial rapist and killer.

"You were able to enjoy having sex with a . . . a rapist while a guard was waiting outside the door?"

Rosie nodded, then abruptly looked away.

Hoping to erase the image of the woman sitting across from her having sex with a depraved maniac, Jenna turned her attention to Norman Miller.

"He was there on the day they executed Ed," Rosie said quietly. "He drove me home. I was shaking so badly I couldn't drive my own car. When we got to my apartment, he poured me a stiff drink and stayed till I was able to crawl into bed. Anyway, he started checking in with me to see how I was doing. I was living in the apartment I'd rented while Ed was on trial. I'd even gotten a part-time job in that town. I didn't move back to Long Island till after Norm and I got married a few years later, and he got transferred. He was a good man."

As she was leaving Rosie's house, Jenna noticed the framed photos in the display cabinet. One showed an older man with a small strawberry birthmark on his left cheek—Norm, she guessed. Another was of a pudgy-faced boy with straight, long brown hair flopping across his forehead and into his eyes as he blew out the candles on a cake with the numerals 2 and 0 in the center.

"Your son?"

Rosie nodded. "Yes. He turned twenty last month."

Jenna turned toward the door. Then, suddenly it hit her. The boy was twenty; born the same year that Evil Ed had been executed.

Jenna stopped and stared at Rosie. "Ed's son."

Rosie stared back, blinking rapidly as if she'd been caught in bright headlights. "Yes," she finally said. "That's why I have no regrets. My son is the best thing that ever happened to me."

Jenna wanted to retrace her steps back into the room, but Rosie was already opening the door. "Did Ed know about his son?" she asked.

Rosie nodded, now looking sad and miserable. "Of course. I was seven months pregnant when they executed him."

"How did he feel about it?"

"He was sorry."

"Sorry?"

"Yes."

—⟨⟩⟨⟩⟨⟩— —⟨⟩⟨⟩⟨⟩—

It took Jenna two days to write the story. She ended with Rosie's final quote: "He called his unborn son an unlucky little bastard spawn."

Then she hunkered down in her seat after hitting the send button on her keyboard. She did her best to look busy while keeping an eye on Ryan, hunched over at his computer screen. When he stood up and looked directly toward her desk, Jenna knew he had read her copy.

"Sinclair, over here," he beckoned and then redirected her to his private office. She thought he would have looked happier with her copy.

He had printed out her story. "What does this mean?" He read the last two lines aloud, and then said: "Are you kidding? You put that at the end of the story?" He sighed and tutted. "Listen to me and write this down."

Jenna grabbed a pad and pen off his desk.

"For the last two decades, Rosie M has lived with the horrendous secret that her only son is the "unlucky bastard spawn" of Evil Ed, one of the most depraved, sadistic serial killers this country has ever seen. Ed Haynes struck terror across the North and South Forks of Long Island when he tortured and brutalized six young women and then left them for dead in remote wooded areas on Long Island. After he was arrested, more than a dozen of his rape victims came forward. He was executed in 1978."

Jenna stopped.

"What are you waiting for, luv?" Ryan continued: "Rosie M's secret came to light in an interview during which Rosie, now forty-five, told me"—he grinned at her—"That's you. You're going to get a big byline on this one. Right, where was I? Oh, yeah, Rosie told me that thanks to the help of a kindly prison guard she was able to spend nights of love with the brutal serial killer. Quote: 'Eddie was a gentle lover,' said Rosie blah blah blah. Get it?"

Ryan opened his office door to yell for the photo editor. He tossed the copy to him. "Get one of your guys to doorstep this address. You're looking for a twenty-year-old goofy-looking kid with longish hair, and . . ." He turned to Jenna. "What's the kid's name?"

Jenna stood dumbstruck.

"You didn't ask?" Ryan shook his head. "Okay, find out, get more details about him, what he does, where he works, or goes to school, whatever."

Two days later, Ryan beckoned Jenna over to the art desk, where she saw a dozen photos and a layout for a double-page spread. She looked dumbfounded at the thick, black letters:

FOUND: SECRET "SPAWN" OF EVIL ED, SAVAGE SERIAL SLAYER

Ryan placed the loupe on the photos of a male outside Rosie's house, approaching the house, holding hands with a young woman. His wife, Jenna guessed.

"Here look at this," Ryan beckoned to Jenna. The loupe was on the woman, on her stomach. "That's not fat." Ryan grinned.

No, Jenna could see quite plainly that it was a baby bump.

She nodded unhappily.

"Grandson spawn of savage slayer. Coming next year." Ryan pretended to shudder. "Is that the kid you saw in the photo at the house?"

Jenna couldn't really tell. She'd spent more time looking at the birthday cake in the photo than the face. But the hair looked the same. She nodded.

"Did you get his name?"

She didn't answer. She had the name. She'd called Rosie immediately, had caught her off guard after Ryan had dictated the new lede to her story. But something warned her against handing it over to Ryan.

"Come on," Ryan urged her. "You got a couple of hours and then we're going to press."

Jenna returned to her desk, holding back tears even as Ryan materialized behind her. "Don't be so harsh on yourself," he said, his tone kinder now. "We don't really need his name."

"No, you don't. He's just a kid. It's not his fault."

"Screw him," Ryan replied. "You heard what Alan told you. That kid beat him up. Bit him on the hand and tried to grab his camera. Then, got him in a chokehold down on the ground, and kicked his head in. Kicked his head in with big, heavy work boots. The kid's a vicious punk like his dad. He's going to be in big trouble over this. Cops are charging him with assault."

"Ryan, people aren't going to like this story." Jenna didn't know where she had suddenly found the courage to speak to Ryan McAllister that way. "Do we need to focus on the son? None of this is his fault." A shudder ran right through her. "And that headline? It's horrible. It's awful."

Ryan held up his hands in mock surrender. "Please Jenna, don't blame me for the headline. You know that's Stan's job. I don't care much for it either, but Stan's got the last word."

She noticed the look in his eyes, as if he was surprised by her outburst but impressed that she'd stood up to him. He smiled at her. "Let's grab a drink later. We can talk about it then."

Jenna nodded, feeling miserable. She promised herself that as soon as the issue was off the newsstands, she would drive out to see Rosie Miller and tell her how sorry she was about the headline, and that she hoped the article hadn't upset her or her son too much.

Chapter Eight

June 2019
Week One: Friday Afternoon

Jenna saw her best friend striding across Foley Square. Her jacket was flapping open, her hair, a mass of tangled black curls, streamed behind her. Her heels clicked furiously on the pavement as she puffed away on a cigarette. Stick thin with high cheekbones and big, dark, almond-shaped eyes, Judge Lola Quintana turned heads wherever she went.

If Jenna had bumped into her on a subway or seen her on any Manhattan street, her first guess as to occupation would not have been judge, and certainly not a judge in criminal court in downtown Manhattan. She had looked so tiny the first time Jenna saw her on the bench, swathed in her black robe, reading glasses perched on her nose, directing a piercing stare at the young defendant who stood before her. She had addressed him in Spanish, in a kind tone.

Now, she grinned as she approached the bench where Jenna was waiting with a Starbucks latte grande. She took the proffered cup, sipped, flopped down on the bench, threw an arm around Jenna's shoulders and hugged her. "You look like shit. What's going on?"

"I texted you because I thought I might be in trouble and in need of legal advice." Jenna proceeded to recount her story starting with the visit of the cops to her apartment after finding Ryan outside her apartment building.

"Whoa!" Lola shook her head. "I'm not following this. Has any of it been in the news?" She took a long swig of her coffee. "I mean, I get the part about you seeing Ryan again, even though I had to read about it in a one-liner on Page Six." She turned to stare pointedly at Jenna. "But now, you totally lost me. What happened?"

Jenna took a deep breath. She and Lola had been best friends since graduating college in the city. They could go weeks, sometimes months without contact, but then picked up exactly where they'd left off, catching up on the highlights of their lives and filling in the gaps swiftly in half sentences and phrases that only the two of them could figure out.

Lola knew Jenna better than anyone else did. She knew Zack. She liked Zack. She knew Ryan. She'd liked Ryan till he had started messing around with Teddi. She was Dollie's godmother. She was the friend who had driven Jenna from the city to the North Fork for her wedding to Zack. So, Jenna knew she wouldn't have to give Lola a long explanation.

"Someone kicked the hell out of Ryan. Fractured his skull. Right outside my apartment building."

"And the cops think you did it?"

"Not sure. They asked a lot of questions. I doubt they knew the extent of his injuries when they came to see me."

"But you didn't tell them anything? Right?" During a stint as a defense attorney, Lola had reminded Jenna countless times to never volunteer any information to the cops. According to Lola, "I only had two beers (or two vodkas, or two Cosmopolitans), Officer," was the very worst thing you could ever say to a cop who pulled you over on the highway.

Jenna shook her head, "Nothing they couldn't find out from the doorman. Trust me."

"Hmm." Lola's tone was noncommittal.

"I was afraid that Nando might have seen us as Ryan was leaving. We had a little disagreement. I pushed him."

Lola laughed. "Pushed him hard enough to fracture his skull? Did you tell the cops about pushing him?"

"Of course not." Jenna gave her friend a weak smile. "Anyway, the doctors just told us they believe someone hurt Ryan intentionally. So, not an accident. Nor a random mugging."

Lola lit a fresh cigarette. "Someone was waiting for Ryan outside your apartment building?" It was a statement rather than a question, and she paused as if to think this through. "Well, I'd say both you and Ryan have made some real enemies recently. I can't imagine any of those chefs and restaurant owners in the Hamptons are very happy with your exposé, or happy with *CityMagazine* for publishing it. Your exposé is going to have some impact on their businesses."

Jenna mulled over this fresh insight from her friend. She hadn't even considered such a possibility. "The radiologist said someone kicked Ryan's head in; cracked his skull in two places." Jenna used both her index fingers to point to her temples. "Disgruntled chefs weren't my first thought."

"Have you ever seen Gordon Ramsay on TV?" Lola laughed. "He can get really steamed . . ."

"Gordon isn't one of the chefs in my exposé," Jenna interrupted her friend. "Anyway, the whole head-kicking scenario reminded me more of Alan's run-in with the spawn way back." Jenna used the fingers of both hands again to make air quotes as she enunciated *spawn*. She hated using the word. It embarrassed her, but it was the quickest way to refer to the story that had made such a splash twenty-one years earlier.

"Alan?"

"The photographer." Jenna was surprised she had to remind Lola of the story.

Lola exhaled a long stream of cigarette smoke. "Sure, I remember now." Then she added: "So, you think the spawn kicked Ryan's head in?"

Jenna shrugged. "I don't know what to think, but that MO made me think of the spawn immediately, although it does seem a little far-fetched after all these years. I mean, why wait till now to go after Ryan?"

"True. If I recall, he went after your photographer in the heat of the moment. Not a totally abnormal reaction when a paparazzi jumps out of the bushes at you." She cast a sideways glance at Jenna, who realized her friend was attempting to inject a little humor into their conversation. "And you're right. After all these years . . ."

Her reaction was reassuring; exactly what Jenna had hoped for. But the relief lasted only seconds.

"Unless, of course, it's you he's trying to hurt."

Jenna gasped. "Me? By hurting Ryan?"

Lola shrugged. "Who knows what goes on in the mind of someone like that? He's a serial killer's son. Think about it. He—whoever did this—was waiting outside your apartment building, not Ryan's. Ryan is a visible guy. Man-about-town. The spawn could have gone after him any time over these last twenty-or-so years. Whereas you're the one who pretty much dropped off the face of the earth after that story—quit your job on the *Sun*, fled the city, changed men, changed your name. You've only just now emerged, back in the spotlight with a byline in *CityMagazine*, using your professional name, with your article being talked about on TV."

Jenna's stomach cramped at the thought of someone waiting twenty years to take his revenge against her.

"So, he comes after you, waits outside your building, sees you with Ryan, then sees Ryan leave and decides he may as well go for him." Lola paused and shrugged. "If it's him."

"But I didn't drop off the face of the earth. I mean, I wasn't at the *Sun* anymore, but I was still here in the city with Ryan for a while. He had time to come after me before I disappeared to the North Fork."

Lola shrugged. "Even so, maybe he couldn't find you back then. Remember, Google wasn't the search engine it is today. There wasn't all that personal info on every citizen of the world out there on the internet. And maybe now that you're in the spotlight with another exposé, it's brought back all his anger and bad memories."

"You're saying his anger has been festering all this time, and he still wants to get even." Jenna took a deep breath. "So, he's going to hurt someone close to me because he still blames me for what happened to his wife and baby after my story was published."

"He could definitely be that unhinged if he inherited his father's deranged personality." Lola took a deep drag on her cigarette. "We've had classes on people like him in CLE. "

Jenna raised an eyebrow.

"Continuing Legal Education," Lola explained. "Judge school. Gotta take the classes, even judges have to learn new precedent, blah,

blah, blah. And stuff like this. Lots of talk these days about genes, evil genes, psycho genes, killer genes, warrior genes. Scientists have identified genes that increase aggressive traits and affect neurons in the brain that control empathy, which psychopaths don't have." Lola closed her eyes momentarily as if reciting something she'd memorized from a textbook. "That means psychological disorders can be inherited—passed on from mother, father, grandfather and so on."

Jenna nodded. "If you're born that way, if you get something like that passed down from your father, would that be some sort of defense in court?"

"Or the opposite," Lola smiled. "We did an exercise in one of our classes, and half the class voted to increase the sentence of someone with those types of genetic flaws on the grounds that if it's genetic and in the blood then the dude is always going to be a danger to society. So, a two-edged sword. But yes, it's possible he inherited bad genes from Daddy."

Jenna shivered. There was a moment of silence between them as Lola finished her latte and tossed the empty cup into a trash can beside the bench. She threw her head back and offered her face up momentarily to the rays of sun streaming through the buildings of lower Manhattan. Then, she stood to go. "Do you have any idea what happened to him?"

"The spawn?" Jenna shook her head. "No. None at all."

Lola nodded. She was walking away when she suddenly returned to Jenna's side. "You could share these ideas with the cops."

Jenna stared quizzically at her friend.

"I mean, if they ask if you can think of anyone who might have done this to Ryan? Tell them about the restaurants you exposed. And, about the spawn. They'll probably be able to track him down. Find out what he's been up to all this time."

Jenna exhaled nervously. "So, you do think he's a possible suspect?"

Lola adjusted her sunglasses. "I wouldn't rule out anything. Look, it's been a long time, sure. But you never know, maybe he's been sitting in jail, or in some psychiatric hospital, stewing and plotting." She leaned in to hug Jenna. "Anyway, keep an eye open. If it's you he's after, kicking Ryan senseless might not be enough for him. He could still be watching and waiting for his opportunity to come after you." Lola paused. "What's his name?"

"Dennison. It was Rosie's mother's name. His name is Denny Dennison."

"Okay," Lola said. "I'll make some inquiries on my end for a start. Check court records in the state; call around a few sheriff's departments. I'll let you know."

"I'll check Facebook and Twitter, and Google," Jenna said, but Lola was already striding away into the distance.

Jenna felt cold despite the warmth of the sun. The thought that so many people had motive for hurting her and Ryan, or that Denny Dennison could be out there still holding a grudge terrified her. She'd have to warn her building super and doormen to be on the lookout for strangers lurking outside the building. She'd call Zack and tell him not to give out any information about Dollie's whereabouts. To anyone. She was suddenly relieved that Dollie was hundreds of miles away in Maine.

Jenna stood, when suddenly her phone rang. She recognized Zack's ringtone and picked up. There was a pause at the other end, and Jenna felt the little hairs on her neck bristling before Zack spoke.

"You need to come home, Jen," he said. "Dollie's been in an accident."

Chapter Nine

"What happened?" Jenna's throat tightened. "Did someone hurt her?" Jenna was aware of inchoate, unformed thoughts about the spawn suddenly forcing themselves unbidden into her head. A fat face with long greasy hair materialized in front of her eyes.

Zack cleared his throat, and the pause before he spoke seemed to last forever. Jenna felt her knees buckling. She sat back down on the wooden park bench.

"No. She'll be okay," Zack finally spoke. "She was in a barn that caught fire. But she's okay. Everyone got out safely."

A chill ran up Jenna's spine.

"A fire? Oh, my God. When did this happen?" Feelings of guilt threatened to overwhelm her. Why had she and Zack banished Dollie all the way to Maine? Had they been too harsh on her? Had Jenna overreacted to Dollie's misbehavior?

"Yesterday." Zack's voice sounded even. "Dollie called me from the police station. They brought her to the precinct, and she called me."

"Wait, what?" Jenna interrupted. "She was brought to a police precinct? Why not the hospital? What's going on?"

Zack cleared his throat. "She and a couple of other kids snuck out of camp. Found the empty barn and broke into it to smoke pot." There was a long pause. "Somehow, the barn caught on fire. The police are considering charges of trespassing and, maybe malicious destruction of property." Zack laughed abruptly. "No charges for smoking pot, that's all lovely and legal up here, but apparently barns are a big deal. I've been with the juvenile corrections officer most of the morning trying to work things out. And I will. But she can't go back to summer camp. They told me she has to leave."

Jenna's thoughts were a jumble of concern and anger. With a sinking feeling, she realized Dollie had been told to leave a summer camp that supposedly had expertise in dealing with difficult kids.

"Why didn't you text me? Leave a voice mail? I would have had plenty of time to get there this morning. I could have asked Lola for some advice on handling this."

"I didn't have all the facts and I had to get myself up here, ASAP. Anyway, you didn't answer your phone."

"I was in a pitch meeting. I muted it."

"You must have seen the missed call, Jen."

But I'm not a mind reader, Jenna wanted to bite back. How could she have known he was calling about Dollie? Apparently, Zack had taken charge after Dollie's phone call, so the camp director had neglected to call Jenna, who was listed first on the emergency contact list.

"She's really sorry, Jen. First thing when she saw me, she asked where you were, why you didn't come. She thinks you'll never forgive her."

"Please put her on the phone, Zack."

"She's not here. She's getting her stuff together at the camp. I told her you'd be at home when we returned."

"Of course," Jenna heard herself saying. "I'm on my way."

"No. Don't rush. Dollie's pretty stressed out. I want her to calm down a bit. We'll probably spend the night somewhere along the coast."

Jenna couldn't stop the resentment that suddenly welled up inside her, or the memory of the Amex receipts she'd found; one for an expensive lobster dinner for two and the other for the Kennebunkport hotel suite after Zack had dropped Dollie off at camp. "Is Bethany with you?"

"Jeez, Jenna, of course not," Zack said. "Why on earth would you think that—"

"Don't give me that. You know perfectly well why I think so. You took Bethany with you to drop off Dollie at camp."

"And you know perfectly well that you and Dollie in a car for six hours would not have ended well. I merely thought your time was better spent working on your article than fighting with your daughter."

"That wasn't your decision to make. You wanted me out of the way so you could take Bethany along for the ride."

There was a long pause. "No, Jen. Not true." Then, an even longer pause. "Dollie's the one who asked if Bethany could come with us. C'mon, Jenna, you know they get along great."

Jenna's eyes filled with tears. Zack was the parent Dollie called when she was in trouble. That was bad enough. But what really hurt was that Dollie apparently couldn't stand her mother along for a car ride. She'd preferred Zack's intern.

Jenna wiped at her eyes. "Well, sure, Bethany's about her age, and obviously much more fun," she retorted hoarsely. "But you're a cliché, Zack, messing around with a girl young enough to be your daughter."

"Bethany's older than she looks," Zack replied, not exactly addressing Jenna's accusation. "Much older. She's not a child."

"But she's your intern, Zack. You're playing a dangerous game. Don't you read the newspapers? Do you want customers to boycott the inn after Bethany posts her #MeToo story on Twitter or Facebook?"

Zack was quiet at the other end for a moment. Then, he said: "Look, Jenna, I'm sorry. I'm sure you're busy with new assignments. So, I'm sorry Dollie's messed things up for you. But we can talk more . . . we can talk about everything when you get home," he said, emphasizing the word *everything*.

Jenna disconnected the call without responding. As she walked out of the park and toward the subway entrance, she wondered why she had misled Zack about muting her phone for a meeting. She'd muted it in Neary's for dinner with Ryan. She should have told Zack about the dinner. It might have conveyed the idea that Ryan was wooing her all over again now that Zack had discarded her for Bethany. That might have given Zack pause for thought.

Someone jostled her on the way down the steps into the subway, and her heart skipped. If anyone wanted to hurt her, pushing her down subway steps would be an easy way to do it. Or into the path of a train. No one would pay any attention.

The trains looked—and felt—as disgusting and dangerous as they'd appeared in Joaquin Phoenix's Joker movie that was set back in the bad old 1980s. The subway was definitely one part of city life she hadn't missed.

Oscar was still on duty when she arrived back at her apartment building. "Evening, Miss Sinclair." He greeted her and held up a hand, motioning for her to wait while he retrieved a package from the mailroom. He handed her a FedEx envelope. She glanced at the sender's name (which she didn't recognize) and at the origin address which turned out to be the 24-hour FedEx office about twenty blocks north on Lexington Avenue the one that guaranteed same-day city delivery, she thought idly as she ripped it open and withdrew two photos from the envelope.

The background of the first one was dark and showed her and Ryan arm in arm, on the corner of her street as they returned from Neary's. She flicked through to the second photo and exhaled suddenly and loudly. "What the . . . ?"

"Miss Sinclair, are you okay?" Oscar's concerned face peered over the top of the photos. She stared blankly at the doorman, then quickly stuffed both photos back in the FedEx envelope before rushing for the elevator.

Chapter Ten

Week One: Saturday Morning

J enna stared at the two photos on her coffee table. She'd input the tracking number on FedEx's website to discover that the envelope had left the FedEx office at four that morning. The sender could have walked it over to her building and saved the postage, she thought before laying the photos side by side and staring at them till she got bleary-eyed. Definitely the first was taken when Ryan and she were walking back from Neary's. The second, however, was taken several hours later, when Ryan was leaving her building and as Jenna had caught up with him.

Fortunately, for the photographer—unfortunately for Jenna— they'd stopped outside the front doors of the corner bistro. The bistro had closed for the night, but the light over its half awning was still shining, right in Jenna's face.

The photo showed her face and her fists. The photographer had caught her at the precise moment of pushing Ryan away with both her fists clenched against his chest.

So, someone had waited in the street for her, seen her and Ryan return to her apartment building, and then had waited for Ryan to leave. He or she had probably used the printers at the FedEx center to make copies of the photos to send to her. She wasn't sure exactly how that worked, but it was possible the photographer had had to use an email address or a credit card to access the printer. On the other hand, maybe he lived in the neighborhood and had used his own printer.

Jenna crossed the room to the thermostat to turn up the air-conditioning. She felt clammy even though she'd just showered before getting ready for her trip back to the North Fork. No doubt the photographer would be able produce a time stamp for the photo and it would place her at the scene, attacking Ryan just before he'd been found lying unconscious in the street.

You've made some enemies, Lola had said referring to the chefs and restaurant owners Jenna had exposed as farm-to-table frauds. Was it possible that one of them, or maybe a couple of them had gotten together and hired someone to make her and Ryan sorry? Clearly, someone had been following them, taking photos, documenting their comings and goings. And Jenna had played into his or her hands by causing a public scene with Ryan. What if whoever was out to get her and Ryan had then assaulted Ryan with the intention of pinning it on Jenna?

That sounded like something a psychopath might do. So, more Denny Dennison than chefs in the Hamptons. Maybe he'd already sent copies of the photos to the cops.

Jenna swept the two photos off the coffee table and into her tote before hurrying out to the elevator. She was halfway between her apartment building and the parking garage when she heard the footsteps behind her, and then a voice. "Miss Sinclair, wait!"

She turned around to see Detective Martins and his partner. She clutched her tote closer, her heart pounding at the thought that they'd seen the photos. She managed a weak smile at the one she recognized as Martins. He didn't return the smile, but simply nodded at her.

"We were just coming to see you," he said. "Do you prefer to be addressed as Miss Sinclair or Mrs. King? Last time we spoke, you didn't say."

"Miss Sinclair is fine," Jenna replied. Then took a deep breath. "I'm on my way out of the city. I have to pick up my car at the parking garage."

"We'll walk with you." Martins reached for a notebook in his hip pocket and flipped the pages. "So, this is the thing, Miss Sinclair. It looks like Mr. McAllister sustained his injuries as a result of an intentional assault, and obviously we have to ask about the situation between you and your husband and Mr. McAllister."

The question was so unexpected Jenna blinked in surprise. She'd been expecting them to produce the photos of her and Ryan. She recovered quickly. "There's no situation. My husband and I are separated."

Martins's partner (his name was Tuby; "rhymes with ruby," he'd said) asked, "How long have you been separated, Miss Sinclair?"

"A few weeks."

Out of the corner of her eye, Jenna saw what she could only describe as a "knowing" look pass between the two.

"Was Mr. McAllister the reason for your separation?"

Jenna shook her head. "No." Her answer was emphatic, and she didn't elaborate.

"So, then you have no idea where your husband was on Thursday night?"

"I think I do. He was in Maine picking up our daughter from summer camp?"

"You think he was picking her up from summer camp?" Martins ran his hand over his bald head, obviously puzzled by a pickup from camp when summer had barely started.

Jenna nodded. "Yes, my husband called me Thursday evening to tell me he was driving up to get her." Not quite the truth, Jenna thought, since she had not actually spoken to Zack that evening, but that's what his missed call had been about; she knew that now.

"Where in Maine?" Martins asked.

"Bethel."

"Driving from where?"

"Cutchogue. On the North Fork. He owns a marina and an inn there. The Kings Inn."

"How long a drive is that?"

Jenna had to think about it. "Well, you have to take the ferry from Orient Point, which is about as far east as you can go on the North Fork, go to New London, and then it's about a four or five hour drive from there to Bethel, depending on traffic."

She could almost hear them both doing the arithmetic in their heads. Tuby took his phone from his pocket and said: "We'll still need to talk to him at some point. How can we reach him, Miss Sinclair? We need his phone number."

She gave them the number at the inn figuring she'd be there before Zack and Dollie arrived. Then, she'd be able to explain to Zack why the cops wanted to talk to him.

"Miss Sinclair, did your husband know about your relationship with Mr. McAllister?"

Uh-oh, Jenna thought, staring at the duo. It seemed they were keen to establish that Ryan's assault was a crime of passion either committed by Jenna, because of Jenna's jealousy of Teddi, or by Zack, because of Zack's jealousy of Ryan.

She cleared her throat. "I was living with Mr. McAllister when I first met my husband, so I would say that yes, he knew."

Martins sighed. He looked like he wanted to admonish her for being uncooperative, but instead asked: "Did you separate amicably from your husband?"

Jenna shrugged. "We had words and I left." She was not going to elaborate that it was Zack's infidelity that had led to her leaving.

Tuby cleared his throat. "That's all? Words? You mean an argument? Did your husband get violent with you when you had these words?"

Jenna shook her head. "No."

"Has he ever been violent with you? Is he a violent person?" Tuby persisted.

Jenna shook her head again. "No." There it was again; the assumption that Zack had reacted badly to her affair with another man, when it was she who'd lost it after discovering that Zack had cheated with Bethany. It was she who had slammed her wineglass so hard on the kitchen counter the stem had snapped and sent red wine spilling all over the American Express receipts that were proof that Zack and his intern had spent the night together.

The truth was she had never seen Zack lose his temper, never mind get violent. In the beginning, she had wondered about it. She was used to being surrounded by highly strung creative types who would rant and rave and even throw telephones or ashtrays across the newsroom. She had never met anyone as even-tempered as Zack. She had waited in those early years for a display of temper, for him to lose his patience with something or someone, but it had never happened.

Except once. There was that one time when she had seen a totally different side of him, when she had ended up with bruises. Not the kind you could see, but big ugly welts on the insides of her thighs. But the solitary incident had happened years ago. And, of course, she wasn't going to tell the cops about any of it. Let them do the digging instead of jumping to conclusions.

She glanced at her watch and wondered how much longer the two detectives were going to quiz her. Then she remembered Lola's advice and directed her attention to Martins. "You should probably know," she told him, "that Mr. McAllister and I likely upset some people with the article I mentioned to you, yesterday, and . . ."

"What people?" Tuby interrupted.

"Chefs, restaurant owners out in the Hamptons." She saw the look pass again between them.

"Do you have any specific names?" asked Martins.

"I don't remember all the names," she replied. "But the article is in the current edition of *CityMagazine* on the newsstands and online."

"We'll be sure to check it out, Miss Sinclair," Tuby said in a way that suggested they didn't think much of her idea at all. She had a feeling they'd think even less of her idea that Denny Dennison was another possible suspect. No, thank you. She didn't want to explain why she thought some "kid" she'd written about twenty years ago was still holding a grudge against her and Ryan. It would look as if she was just desperately trying to divert their attention.

More important, there was always the possibility that she was entirely wrong about Denny Dennison. Suppose she set the cops on him, and it turned out he'd had nothing to do with Ryan's assault? She would be screwing up his life all over again. No, she couldn't let that happen. It would just be easier to make some preliminary inquiries herself. Since she was driving out east, she could swing by Rosie's house in Seaford and check things out. Maybe she wouldn't even have to ring the doorbell. Maybe she'd be able to catch sight of Rosie and/ or her son coming and going from the house. Maybe, her son had a whole new family by now.

"We'll be in touch, Miss Sinclair," Martins brushed the palm of his hand over his head.

Tuby nodded in assent, and Jenna watched them cross the street before she continued to the garage. Her stomach lurched at the thought of facing Rosie again. She wasn't even sure if she'd remember the way to Rosie's house once she got off at the Seaford exit. She'd only been there twice. More than twenty years ago. The first time when she'd landed the interview. And the second time a couple of months later, when she'd gone to reassure herself that she hadn't caused any trouble for Rosie.

Chapter Eleven

Traffic was already gridlocked on the Fifty-Ninth Street Bridge by the time Jenna retrieved her car from the parking garage. No surprise there. It was a glorious Saturday morning. Not that there was ever a good time for driving in the city, or on the Long Island Expressway. This Saturday, all the traffic seemed to be moving—or not moving—with her to the East End of Long Island. Of course, on a beautiful June day people were readying their summer homes in the Hamptons for the July fourth holiday, or looking for late rental bargains, or just driving out to look at the ocean.

It took her close to an hour to reach Exit 19. Seaford, at Exit 44, was probably another half hour. She remembered that Rosie's house backed onto an elementary school's playing fields, and the street name had something to do with water. She could always ask for directions to the elementary school and then "feel" her way to the house.

She did not have to meander long in Seaford, however. She recognized the street as soon as she turned onto it. As she pulled into a parking space across the street from Rosie's house, Jenna felt the same nausea she'd felt that horrendous morning after Rosie's revelation.

Twenty years later, the raised ranch looked unchanged, with the same dirty-looking cedar shakes—which were not really cedar but aluminum—and a brick facade on the lower level. Jenna's hands felt sweaty on the steering wheel. The thought of facing Rosie Miller made her heart pound with anxiety. She could imagine her—what would she be now? Sixty-five? Seventy?—slamming the door in her face. Then again, twenty years had passed. Maybe some of the shock and horror had dimmed with time.

She would tell Rosie that she'd never forgotten the tragic con-sequences of her story. (True.) She'd tell Rosie she'd never gone back to tabloid reporting. (Also true.) She'd tell Rosie she'd spent the last twenty years praying that her son had put his life back together. (Not really true because Jenna didn't pray.) But then what? Could she just come straight out with it and ask Rosie where her son was and what he was doing these days?

Jenna sat in the car, turning over her options in her mind. Maybe it would be better to go and ring the neighbor's doorbell first; pretend she wasn't sure if she had the right address for Rosie Miller. Was it number 16 or 18? You could get a lot of information from chatty neighbors.

She adjusted her sunglasses, swept her hair up under a baseball cap and willed herself out of the car and across the street on legs that felt decidedly shaky. She rang the neighbor's doorbell and listened.

Nothing. No sound of footsteps coming down the hallway. She rang again. Waited. Again, no sound. Her heart beating a little less fiercely, she stepped back down the concrete steps, and hesitated for just a couple of seconds before edging her way around the side of the house.

From there she could see into the neighbor's backyard and into Rosie's backyard too. She'd give anything to see a jungle gym or a trampoline on the lawn. She crossed her fingers. She so hoped that Rosie's son had found someone else, and made a life with someone new, and that Rosie was the grandmother she'd always wanted to be, and that neither Denny nor Rosie held a grudge against Jenna anymore.

But there was no evidence in the backyard of any kids, small or teenage. It was just as Jenna remembered: big and backing onto the school playing fields. Back then, the first time Jenna had seen it, coming from the city, it had looked huge and sprawling, and pretty with flowers edging the lawn. Now, there was just grass, a lawn of sorts, and not a very well-mown lawn either. And it was very quiet. All locked up. No windows or doors open anywhere. As if no one was home.

She took a deep breath and unlatched the gate into Rosie's backyard. She waited a moment to see if anyone would come running out of the house to demand what she was doing. But it was still quiet, so she walked to the wooden steps that led up to a deck which she recalled had run off the living and dining rooms. She could take a peek, she thought, just to see if it looked the same inside. She remembered that Rosie's living room had been furnished with rose-colored wall-to-wall carpet. At one end, she recalled, stood a big display cabinet with framed photographs on it. It was where Denny's photograph had caught her eye.

She trod carefully up the steps, crossed the deck to the sliding glass doors, where the drapes were open. The display cabinet was gone. In its place was an entertainment center. So, okay, people replaced furniture, but they kept their precious photos. She craned her neck to see further into the room.

Bam!

The doors suddenly shook, and the view into the room turned black. Jenna jumped back and immediately realized that her view was obscured by a person, a big, heavyset man, who was glaring at her through the glass as he reached for the lock on the door.

Jenna shrank back. "I am so sorry," she stuttered, clutching her purse close to her, her face flaming red from embarrassment over being caught snooping. "You frightened me."

The man laughed. "I think it's you who frightened me, lady. Who are you? What the hell do you want?"

He filled the doorway as Jenna eyed him, taking in his jowly, sleepy face and his fat belly straining against a stained sweatshirt. He looked to be in his forties, so about the right age, but if this was Denny he had aged badly.

"I'm looking for someone who lived here years ago. Her name is Rosie Miller?"

The man stared back at her, small eyes darting. His gaze swept over her body. She was relieved that she'd thrown a light sweatshirt over her skimpy yoga top

"You're not her son, are you?"

The man grinned, eyeing Jenna up and down with a little more interest.

"You mean Evil Ed's son?"

Jenna's heart pounded.

"Maybe I am," the man stood back from the door, beckoning her in. "Why don't you come in?" He stepped toward her and offered her his hand. "Please, come in. Then you can tell me why you want to know."

"I don't want to intrude," Jenna said, stepping back quickly out of his reach, and easing her way to the staircase. If this was Denny, she did not want to identify herself. It had been a stupid idea to come here—as stupid as it had been to come back to Rosie's house all those years ago, after her story was published.

Chapter Twelve

Twenty-One Years Earlier: September 1998

J enna rented a car the weekend after Labor Day for the drive to
Rosie's house in Seaford. She didn't tell Ryan she was going, but
she confided in Alan, the *Sun* photographer, just so that someone
at the tabloid was aware of her whereabouts. Alan's reaction was not
reassuring.

"You're nuts!" He exploded. "After what her psycho son did to
me?"

Six weeks after the publication of Jenna's scoop, Alan was still
wearing a big bandage around the top of his head. A tiny piece of his
right ear was missing where the spawn had aimed his boot at Alan's
head and caught the top of his ear. The ear had become infected and

doctors had removed the gangrenous tip. Most days, if asked about it, Alan, like a true paparazzi, would brag about the assault and how he'd escaped a murdering psycho.

"I have to do this," Jenna said. "I need to know that Rosie Miller is okay." She paused. "I feel guilty, Alan. No one was supposed to identify her or her son, or where they live."

"No one did," Alan replied. "Well, except for *Inside Edition*. Even then they didn't give out the full names or their address. Showing the outside of their house isn't exactly identifying them."

Jenna was still shocked by the frenzy her scoop had created among the tabloid TV shows. Even the city news tabloids had jumped all over the story and created follow-ups about the children of other serial killers.

Not that any of them had much information about such children, but where they lacked facts, they substituted hyperbole and lurid reenactments of serial killings, with psychiatric experts opining on genes and bad seeds.

"I need to explain how it all got out of hand."

"Don't complain. Don't explain," Alan chanted after her as she left the newsroom.

Thankfully, there wasn't a single camera crew or TV van in sight when Jenna pulled up outside Rosie's house a couple of hours later. But as soon as Rosie opened the door, Jenna realized that all was far from well. The anger in Rosie's eyes soon dissolved into tears rolling down her cheeks.

"What are you doing here?" Rosie demanded, shaking her head from side to side. "How dare you show up on my doorstep?"

Jenna was gripped with fear. "I wanted to say I'm sorry, and that I didn't write the headline." She took a step toward the woman. "Rosie, please, I'm . . ."

Rosie shooed her backward. "Don't come near me. You have no idea what you've done. You as good as killed Lisa and the baby yourself. How dare you come here?"

Jenna's stomach flip-flopped crazily as they stood in Rosie's hallway staring at each other. Lisa. Denny's wife. The pregnant woman in the photo that Alan had taken.

"What do you mean, Rosie?"

Rosie's shoulders started shaking, and for a moment Jenna did not know what to do. What had started with a sob became a low keening that within seconds turned into a wail punctuated by short, sharp intakes of breath.

Gently, she put her arm around Rosie's shoulders and was relieved when Rosie did not push her away.

"What happened, Rosie? Please tell me. I had no intention of hurting anyone. I kept your last names and address out of print just like you asked."

As Jenna looked for a tissue in her jacket pocket, Rosie dabbed at her eyes with her hands. "You think that made any difference? Oh no, Miss Sinclair. You think people around here didn't figure it out? Rosie married to a corrections officer named Norm, living on Long Island. Who do you think you are kidding? Everyone on this street guessed. And on the next street, and at the corner deli where they sell your garbage newspaper. Then someone tattled to the vultures in the rest of the newspapers and TV. They were camped out here for days!"

Jenna blinked rapidly. She hadn't thought beyond insisting to Ryan that Rosie and Norm's last name and address had to be omitted from the story. She certainly hadn't thought it through very well.

Tears rolled down Rosie's cheeks. "What did you think was going to happen when they started pointing fingers at my son and his wife and snickering behind their backs?" Jenna realized there was worse to come as Rosie brushed furiously at her eyes.

"I'll tell you what Lisa did. She went to have that baby aborted. And who could blame her? Who would want a baby fathered by a serial killer's spawn?" Rosie spat out the words. "And you know, she was more than five months pregnant, so guess what, Miss Sinclair? Her own doctor wouldn't do it. He tried to persuade her it would be all right. That she shouldn't worry. He reminded her how happy she was when she'd found out she was pregnant. But she'd made up her mind."

Jenna felt as if the blood really was draining from her face. Her stricken look must have given Rosie some measure of satisfaction.

"That's right, Miss Sinclair. She went and found another doctor. Not a very good one, but he got rid of my unborn grandson for her, and then a couple of weeks later she was gone herself. She died right here in this house. Can you imagine that, Miss Sinclair? She got an infection, something simple they said they could have treated if she'd gone for help immediately. But she didn't go; she wouldn't even admit what she'd done. Not to my son, or me. Until it was too late. The paramedics couldn't help her. They tried to save her. But the infection had gotten into her blood and killed her."

Rosie dabbed at her eyes. "You killed my family with your story."

Jenna felt nauseous. She put her hand to her mouth. She'd had no inkling of this horrible turn of events. No one had reported on the death of Denny's wife. Of course not. They'd camped out for a few days, and then moved on to new stories, new tragedies.

"Where's your son now, Rosie?"

Rosie looked as if she wanted to push Jenna right out of the door. "My son? Gone. Why would he stay here after that? He didn't even know who his father was until then. I told you that."

"I'm sorry, Rosie. I'm really sorry."

Rosie shook her head slowly, staring hard at Jenna as if she couldn't quite believe that all Jenna had to offer was a simple "sorry."

"I've lost my son, my grandchild, my whole family. None of this would have happened if I hadn't let you into my house that day." Rosie pursed her lips, her eyes hard black beads of regret as she moved to close the door. "How many papers did you sell, Miss Sinclair?" she said. "I hope it was worth it for you."

Jenna didn't know what else to say or do, but to step away. There were no words that could express how very sorry she felt or to put things back together the way they'd been for Rosie and her son before she'd tracked them down.

Ryan tried to comfort her later that evening when she admitted to her visit with Rosie. "Oh, luv, you shouldn't have gone," he said as tears filled Jenna's eyes. "Forget Rosie Miller. You can't blame yourself. You didn't tell her to screw around with a serial killer. You didn't tell her to give birth to a serial killer's bastard. C'mon luv, you didn't force her to give you the story. She spilled it to you. That's on her. You just reported the facts."

Jenna eventually stopped arguing. Other reporters at the *Sun* said pretty much the same thing. If you stopped to think how people would react to seeing their very own words in print, you might just as well give up and never write anything.

Which is what she should have done, thought Jenna. She should never have written the story. Whatever Ryan said, she knew the world would have survived without knowing about Evil Ed's secret son. It wasn't an exposé in the public interest. It didn't involve public figures or celebrities who sought the limelight. Her article wasn't an investigative report that had exposed a crooked politician or revealed a scam that hurt thousands of innocent people. The story had been published purely for its shock value, for the sole purpose of selling papers. She wished she'd never tracked down Rosie Miller. She couldn't imagine how she would interview anyone again without worrying about the consequences.

Chapter Thirteen

June 2019
Week One: Saturday Morning

J enna wanted to fall through a gap between the deck slats and just disappear.

"You're not intruding." The man smirked, watching Jenna through narrowed eyes.

What had possessed her to peer through windows?

"C'mon." The man encouraged her. "I won't bite."

Biting was not what Jenna was worried about.

She heard a car door closing in the distance, and then a door banging in the house, and then a woman's voice echoing through the living room out onto the deck. "C'mon, Sonny, where are you? Are you out of bed?"

"Don't worry," he directed his remark to Jenna. "I'm not Denny. But I was his best friend." Then, he turned back into the house. "I'm here, Ma. I was just leaving." The man responded to the questions just as a woman with long gray hair tied in a pony tail came through the living room weighed down with plastic bags from a supermarket. Sonny did not move to help her as she walked into the kitchen, but instead left the room.

Jenna realized immediately that the woman was not Rosie Miller. "I'm sorry I barged in," Jenna addressed her even as she stepped inside. "I was looking for Rosie Miller. She used to live here. I was looking for her son, really. Your son said he was a friend."

The woman appeared distracted with unpacking the plastic bags, taking out white sliced bread and rummaging in another plastic bag for deli-packaged ham and cheese. She retrieved a tub of margarine from the refrigerator along with some mustard and set about making a thick sandwich. She sliced the sandwich in two and stuffed it into a sandwich baggie.

"Excuse me." She brushed past Jenna and yelled. "Sonny, don't forget your sandwich, I made it fresh for you." Then she turned her attention to Jenna, holding out a bony hand. "I'm Sally." She shook her head. "Honestly, I swear, a grown man and he can't make his own sandwich. It's not as if he has to bake the ham or anything." She laughed. "My fault I suppose for letting him move back in, but what's a mother to do; there's no way he can afford rent on a stock boy's wages."

Sally cleaned off the counter as Jenna moved toward the kitchen. "Your son said he was a friend of Rosie Miller's son."

Sally shook her head firmly. "No, he wasn't. We rented in the neighborhood before buying this house. Sure, he heard about Rosie Miller and Evil Ed's son. Who hasn't around these parts? But it's old gossip."

"Did you ever meet Rosie?"

"Once. At the closing," Sally nodded. "That was about fifteen years ago."

It did not sound promising. "Do you know where Rosie lives now?" Jenna asked as Sally stared at her with what Jenna thought could be a suspicious look. "I'm looking for her son," Jenna added. "I knew him way back. I knew his wife. I never had time to offer him my condolences. I'd like to know that he's doing okay now . . ." Jenna let her explanation hang, adopting a sheepish expression. It was the best she could do. Fortunately, Sally nodded knowingly.

"I wish I could help you, hon. But I've no idea where he or Rosie are now."

Jenna took one last shot at it as Sally ushered her down the hall to the front door. "Why would your son say he was friends with Rosie's son? Are you sure they never met? Why would he lie?"

Sally looked quizzically at Jenna. "Really? You're asking me? Why does any man lie to a woman? Probably wanted to ask you out on a date." She laughed as if to acknowledge how ridiculous that sounded, then opened the front door to let Jenna out onto the stoop.

"Oh," Sally hesitated. "Carol two doors down knew Rosie quite well." Sally pointed left. "But she's not here today. She's away at Foxwoods. The casino."

"Do you have her phone number?"

"I have her cell number in case there's an emergency." Sally suddenly looked doubtful about giving Jenna the cell phone number. "I'll call her for you and leave a message."

Jenna took a Kings Inn business card out of her purse. She added her cell phone number. The inn name would make Jenna look respectable and upstanding, and not like some snoop. She followed Sally back down the hallway. She heard her dial, make contact and then some small talk before she said: "There's someone here about Rosie Miller."

Moments later Jenna was making plans to meet for a late lunch that afternoon—after Carol got off the ferry, which daily carried passengers across the Sound from the Foxwoods Casino in Connecticut to Orient Point at the tip of the East End of Long Island. From there it was a short drive to the restaurant where Jenna suggested they meet.

"That was fortunate," Sally pointed out. She had disappeared after handing the phone to Jenna and was now out of breath, having gone downstairs and back, heaving a big box with her up the stairs. "Oh, and I remembered this stuff. There might be something in there to help you find Rosie. We collected mail that still came here for her after she moved. She never left a forwarding address. Not with the real-estate attorney or even with Carol. I think they may have emailed or been on Facebook, but Carol always said she didn't have an address for Rosie Miller."

She dropped the box on the floor at Jenna's feet. "Sonny found it in his room after we moved in."

Jenna opened the flaps and saw some old folded newspapers on top. She picked one up. The headline was something about the children of serial killers. She showed it to Sally.

"Isn't this Sonny's? This one is quite recent. Since you moved into this house, anyway."

"Oh," Sally stared at the newspaper. "Yes, that. I guess Sonny added some stuff to the box. He was a little bit obsessed with Denny and his serial-killer father when we first moved in here."

"Then, this stuff is his. I shouldn't take it."

"No, go on. It was never good for Sonny to get so involved with those things." Sally pushed the box across to Jenna. "Please take all of this out of my house. I'm sure he won't even realize it's gone. I was going to throw out this old box, anyway, but I've just been forgetting about it." She chortled. "You know how it is, you start down the stairs and by the time you reach the bottom, you've forgotten why you were going down there."

Jenna smiled and picked up the box. It was too good a treasure trove to leave. Old mail was often useful for providing a decent lead or two.

She was heading North on the Seaford-Oyster Bay Expressway when she remembered the business card she'd handed over to Sally. She wished she hadn't left it; she hoped that Sonny didn't suddenly take it into his head to come after her looking for his stuff, but she couldn't very well go back to ask for it. She didn't have time. She'd have to wrap up lunch with Carol pretty swiftly as it was, to be home before Zack returned from Maine with Dollie.

She dreaded facing him.

They'd have to talk about Dollie, of course. They'd have to talk about Bethany too. He hadn't denied sleeping with Bethany. On the contrary, he'd sounded oddly unapologetic about taking her to Maine. So, maybe she had misread his parting shot as she was storming out of the inn almost a month ago—"Don't just walk out like that, Jen. Let's talk. Please. We can resolve things."

We can resolve things. At the time she'd thought he wanted to explain himself and to convince Jenna that she'd gotten it all wrong. Now she wasn't so sure. Maybe he'd wanted to discuss a divorce that night. Maybe he wanted to marry Bethany, and he was going to tell her that they were going to fight Jenna for custody of Dollie. Maybe the photographer outside her building was a private investigator hired by Zack to collect evidence to show what a bad mother she was.

Zack had often enough pointed out that he didn't have a way with words like some of her former colleagues and artsy friends. Jenna knew from experience that was just a blind. Once he decided what he wanted, Zack was always able to find the right words to get exactly what he had set his heart on.

Chapter Fourteen

Sixteen Years Earlier: April–September 2003

"He asked for you."

Jenna looked up at the sound of her assistant's voice to see her hovering in the doorway and pointing at the phone on Jenna's desk as she added. "He sounds nice."

"Hi, I'm Zack King," a young male voice said on the other end. "I own The Kings Inn and Marina on the North Fork." There was a pause before he added. "It's in Cutchogue, out on the East End of Long Island; on the not-Hamptons Fork."

"I know where the North Fork is," Jenna responded stiffly. The North Fork could have been on a different planet so far as most Manhattan residents were concerned. She'd never traveled that far, but as the chief research editor and fact-checker on *Hither & Yon*, a glossy upscale travel magazine, she'd certainly heard of a town that was within one hundred miles of the city.

"It's wine country," she added, not quite sure why she thought she had to impress a stranger with her knowledge, superficial as it was.

"I read your piece about that Hudson Valley bed and breakfast," he continued. "I thought it was awesome. If I didn't have my own inn, I'd have booked a weekend at that place."

Jenna had to smile. She occasionally wrote blurbs for the magazine on new restaurants or clubs that she and Ryan visited, but it wasn't exactly Pulitzer Prize-winning copy. She'd written up a couple of paragraphs on a B and B in the Hudson Valley after she and Ryan had stopped there for a night. She wondered now how quickly she could extricate herself from the conversation even as she roamed through the available search engines—Infospace, Altavista, and Google—on her desktop, looking for anything about the Kings Inn.

There was one article, about Zachariah King, owner of the Kings Inn and Marina, selling off eighty-five acres of an adjoining vineyard. The brief article also informed Jenna that the inn was "restored to former glory in 2000 by the late Jeremiah King who settled in Greenport in 1950 after he ran aground there in his sloop. Today, the inn and adjoining marina are run by grandson Zack and partner/chef Ana Watson." So, he had money—and a pedigree.

"I'd like to offer you an all-expenses-paid weekend on the North Fork. If you like my place, you could recommend it to your editor. We have access to the best golf, great sailing, vineyards, wine tasting, and all of that can be arranged through the Kings Inn."

Jenna laughed at the thought of Ryan on a golf course or a sailboat. Anyway, Ryan would never go on another trip out of the city so soon. He had complained for most of the drive up to Rhinebeck, and at one point had asked her, in all seriousness, if they had crossed the border into Canada. The trip, Jenna's idea of a romantic getaway to rekindle the spark, had been a big bust. She'd have done better checking them into a ritzy hotel in town.

"I can't accept a free junket," she said.

He was quiet for a moment. "Okay, I understand. How about our best spring rate? You won't be disappointed. The few celebrities and city hotshots who have discovered us rave about the inn. It's very secluded, they seem to like that . . ."

He stopped, as if realizing he'd said too much, and Jenna's interest immediately rose a couple of notches. True, she was no longer in the tabloid business, but living with Ryan, she knew he was always looking for gossip about "celebrities and city hotshots." Maybe she'd get to pry some worthwhile names out of Mr. Zack King if she made the trip.

And maybe separation from Ryan even for just the weekend—would work better than forced togetherness.

"Okay then," she heard herself say. "I'll come."

The ride was long. Around Smithtown, at Exit 55 on the Long Island Expressway, she thought of turning back. Dear God, it was another 18 exits to the end of the expressway, and then almost another whole Fork to go. At Exit 71, she slowed down and considered pulling into the Tanger Outlet Mall. She could pick up a couple of discounted purses at the Coach store and then head back to the city. But she had left a note for Ryan, and she did not want to return to the apartment to find that he had read it, but was really not surprised to see her back so soon. "Missed me already, did you, luv?"

Zack came to meet her in the village, and she followed him down a couple of winding roads where she would have gotten hopelessly lost on her own.

So, she couldn't size him up properly until he got out of his pickup at the front door of the inn. His tan told her he was someone who spent most of his time outdoors. He was tall, maybe an inch taller than Ryan, broadly built, with a flat stomach and tight abs visible through his white T-shirt. Cropped, sun-bleached hair and bright blue eyes completed the picture. He looked good enough to be the star of a gym commercial except for the faint but visible scar running from the corner of his mouth up his left cheek and across the corner of his left eye.

"I'm sorry," she said, realizing that she was staring.

"It's okay," he laughed, drawing his finger along the scar. "Accident on the water." He waved his hand at the bay, which she could see from the hallway of the inn. "Come on, let me take your bag. I've put you in the Miranda cottage. It's our best suite."

He suggested she unpack, and he would return for her in twenty-five minutes to give her the rest of the tour; to introduce her to Ana (an older woman who was obviously not Zack's love interest but appeared to run the inn and kitchen) and to Hank (who had run the marina while Zack's grandfather was still alive, which made him "older than dirt," according to Zack.)

"Bring a sweater or jacket, it might get windy on the boat," he told her.

Her face must have registered her apprehension.

"You don't like boats?"

She shrugged. Now was not the time to tell him her parents had perished on a ferry in the Mediterranean. Instead, she raised a finger to her face tracing a line from her eye to lip like his scar.

He laughed out loud. "Nothing's going to happen out there, today. Don't worry."

She was happy when they were back on land and enjoying drinks on the patio while Zack showed her photos of his mother, Miranda, as a beautiful teenager, as well as photos of the different stages of the inn renovation by Zack and his grandfather, Jeremiah. She asked to borrow some of the photos for the article in case her magazine decided to publish one.

As she was leaving, he asked her not to write about his mother, or any of the things he'd told Jenna about her. Like the fact that Jeremiah, her father, had kicked her out of the house for getting pregnant; how she had landed in a trailer park in Florida and how Zack had grown up there.

"But none of that has anything to do with the amenities of this inn," he added, looking wary.

She laughed. "I'm not looking for scandal or salacious gossip. Not my thing."

Anymore, she added silently to herself as she recalled that she hadn't even had the chance to ask him about the celebrities he'd mentioned during their first phone call.

Jenna called Zack two weeks and four days later to tell him she'd written a short piece about his inn, and she could ship his photos back to him if he gave her his zip code.

"I could do that, or you could drop them off. I can pick you up off the train in Ronkonkoma," he added, and she was impressed that he'd obviously remembered how much she'd disliked the drive from the city.

"Well, okay then, if you really will come to pick me up," she said not wanting to sound too eager, although she realized that's exactly what she was: eager and hungry for a little more attention than she was getting at home. Ryan had been staying at work later and later. It was difficult to ignore his constant references to the gorgeous, glamorous Teddi Conroy.

According to Ryan, Teddi was proving to be a never-ending source of tidbits and gossip, arriving in his office with dozens of items about the antics of trust-fund brats and tales of wild nights in the clubs and hotspots of the city. Ryan was talking about giving Teddi a job as a contributing editor.

"She doesn't know anything about journalism," Jenna objected. "She barely speaks the language."

Ryan had thrown her a pointed stare. "Not jealous are we, my love, *moja droga?*" he asked, adding the Polish translation, which he'd either picked up from Teddi or a Bobby Vinton song.

"I'll have to bring some work with me," she informed Zack while looking up the train times from Penn Station.

Zack asked her about her work on Saturday, after a lunch of a sumptuous Cobb salad, which he brought with a jug of Bloody Marys.

She wondered if he'd brought drinks to divert her from her work, but he set down the tray and was about to leave when she invited him to sit down. She was just checking some facts about the Maldives, she told him.

"Was that always your ambition? To be a fact-checker?" he asked.

She laughed out loud. Jenna could not imagine anyone ever having an ambition to be a fact-checker. "No, I wanted to be a reporter. In fact, I started as a reporter, but discovered I wasn't cut out for it," she admitted. "I just didn't have the stomach for the kind of cut-throat journalism they practiced at the *Sun*. So, I quit, but I did stick with the news editor—that's the guy I was with in Hudson Valley. We still live together. We've been together for almost five years."

Zack raised an eyebrow. "Doesn't he ask where you go weekends?"

"He's working on a big story. A first-person account of Ewa Conroy's battles with her stepchildren over her late husband's billion-dollar estate. It's not really her first-person account. It's her daughter, Teddi, who provides the juicy bits of Ewa's battles with her stepchildren."

"I guess I've heard Teddi's name. She's always in the gossip columns. I've seen her photo." He paused, then added: "I suppose it takes a lot of time to get a story like that."

Jenna stared at Zack, uncertain of whether there was some hidden meaning in his words. Was he telling her that he understood she was angry about Ryan spending time with a gorgeous woman like Teddi? But he didn't let her dwell on the thought. The next question came quickly on the heels of his observation.

"You love him. Am I right?"

Jenna didn't reply immediately. She thought maybe Zack was fishing around before he made a move on her. "Of course, I do," she said eventually. "I love him and love being with him. He's fun. He knows all the bigwigs in the city, knows everything that goes on." Then, in case Zack got the idea that she was totally shallow, she added: "He's kind, loving. He cares about me, and we're soul mates."

"Does he care that you're seeing another man?"

"Seeing another man?" She laughed. "Is that what I'm doing? I thought I was just bringing your photos back." Before Zack could follow up with another probing question, Jenna asked: "Don't you have someone who's waiting for you back there at the main house, wondering why you're taking such a long time to deliver lunch to a guest?"

"There's no one," he replied. "Not today, and not since I left Florida to come here."

Jenna was a little taken aback by his honesty, and by the hurt look that suddenly clouded his eyes. "Bad breakup?" she asked gently.

"Sad rather than bad," he replied. Then, before Jenna could say another word, he walked over to her chaise, sat down beside her, and asked: "What would you do if I kissed you right now?"

"You want to do that?" Jenna asked nervously.

"I wouldn't have mentioned it if I didn't."

Jenna laughed, and shyly tilted her face upward, letting his lips brush the corner of her mouth before she pulled away.

She wanted to tease him for using a line she'd just heard a couple of nights ago in a George Clooney film she'd watched with Lola. In *One Fine Day*, Clooney's character had said exactly those same words to Michelle Pfeiffer. But Zack looked so serious, she wasn't sure he'd appreciate her gentle ribbing—or even know who George Clooney was.

When she recounted the incident to Lola, her friend had tutted and said: "You're playing a dangerous game, my friend. He'll want more, mark my words."

"That's never going to happen," Jenna retorted immediately. "Never."

Jenna stopped talking to Lola about Zack as summer progressed and she continued with weekend trips to the inn. She certainly did not mention that Zack had expertly applied her sunscreen on the patio of the Miranda cottage on the third—or was it the fourth?— weekend she spent with him.

"It's a special service we offer here. If madam would allow me," Zack said slipping into the role of a solicitous innkeeper and picking up the tube of sunscreen that she'd placed on the little wooden table beside her chaise. "The sun does get very strong here."

Jenna let him work the sunscreen into her back, between her shoulder blades, his hands working in ever-widening circles. "It's really best to apply it all over." His fingers sneaked under her bikini top.

She felt a momentary alarm. "Don't know if the sun is going to get to that spot."

"It might, if madam decides to sunbathe topless. Many of our guests do. It's very private here."

"Do you always apply their sunscreen?"

"If they ask. It's part of the service."

Of course, she did not tell Lola that Zack had made her so horny that she had left the door of the cottage open when she went to bed that night so that Zack would see it when he made his rounds of the property later.

Instead, she explained her trips to the North Fork by saying she wanted Ryan to stop taking her for granted. "He needs to stop giving private journalism classes to that little Polish blonde, that's all."

Lola raised an eyebrow, and Jenna said no more to her friend until she came home to find Teddi and Ryan in her apartment. Not in bed, but lying on the floor with Teddi's head resting on Ryan's chest, her legs stretched out, her feet propped on the couch. They had looked so comfortable together, listening to something Edith Piaf-ish on the CD player. It was worse than if she'd found them in bed together.

Jenna packed up her projects a couple of days later and drove out to the North Fork, telling Ryan to get out of her apartment.

She spent her two weeks of vacation at the inn with Zack, who proved to be a perfect host. One afternoon he caught Jenna viciously ripping up the *New York Post* page that carried a photo of Teddi, the "Polish heiress," and "editor about town" McAllister arriving for dinner at '21'. Zack invited her out for the afternoon the following day.

He took her on the ferry from Greenport to Sag Harbor, and then into East Hampton for a movie and dinner and some window shopping along Main Street. When she sighed over a cream silk dress in the window of a hugely expensive-looking boutique, he suggested she go into the store and try it on even though she shrieked out loud when she saw the price tag.

Emerging from the changing room after trying on a half dozen other frilly—slightly cheaper—creations, she was stunned when the store assistant approached with the dress all wrapped for her to take out of the store.

"No, you can't give it back," Zack told her. "They're closing up. It will take too long to undo the payment." Then, he took her hand in his. "You can wear it to one of your posh events in the city." He paused. "Or for our wedding."

Before she could reply, he gripped her hand tightly and whispered: "Drinks, dinner, and a movie—for as long as we both shall live."

She had laughed out loud then. They'd both watched Tom Hanks deliver the line to Meg Ryan in *You've Got Mail* a couple of nights before.

But Zack shook his head. "I'm serious, Jenna. You've probably noticed I don't have a way with words, except if I borrow someone else's lines, but I want to marry you, and I think you must feel the same way. I don't know why else you'd drive all the way out here every weekend. I know you hate driving." He then added: "We're good together, Jen. You must know that—unless you've been faking it."

"Zack, no! Of course not." She fell silent. How could he think that? He was a wonderful, creative lover. She vaguely recalled Lola's warning about playing a dangerous game.

"Were you just toying with me, Jenna?" Zack asked, looking deflated and crushed as they drove back to the inn.

Jenna struggled to find words, to explain that she hadn't really been thinking about the future—certainly not a future where she'd have to give up her job, her home, and her friends.

"I'm not asking for you to do any of that," he countered, immediately blowing off every argument she made. She should keep her apartment, of course; she could work in the city, drive back for weekends, just as she'd been doing. They would make it work between them. Anyway, he added, fact-checking could be done anywhere, couldn't it? "You do it out here, now, on weekends."

She took the dress back to the city, hung it up in its plastic bag in the space where just days before, Ryan's suits had hung. Lola, ever the pragmatist, told her she should "go for it." She had not met Zack, but told Jenna he sounded like husband material—something Ryan definitely was not.

"C'mon, Jenna," Lola urged. "He doesn't want you to give up the city or your job, or your apartment or your friends. You'll have the best of both worlds."

But she wouldn't have Ryan, Jenna thought. Ryan had assured her that he liked Teddi "a lot" but that he loved Jenna so maybe she should give him another chance. As if reading Jenna's thoughts, Lola said, "Ryan McAllister is the sort of man you outgrow. He's lovable, and fun, but he's not husband material. With him it's always work first, then you. You're always going to be second—when you're not third," Lola added slyly.

She had a point. With Zack, on the other hand, Jenna always felt she was at the center of his attention.

On her next trip to the inn, she and Zack set a date. The wedding would take place on a late September Saturday afternoon on the beach.

There would be a small group of guests, mostly friends of Zack's from the North Fork. The ceremony would be performed by a local judge who was friendly with Fran, Zack's business attorney.

On the evening before her wedding day, Jenna invited just a few of her closest girlfriends to an impromptu bachelorette party at the bar around the corner from her apartment in the city. Even then, she'd been waiting for Ryan, willing him to walk into the bar, to beg her not to marry another man.

Then suddenly he was there, just as she'd envisioned it. He walked in as her bachelorette party was wrapping up. He waited at the end of the room till all her girlfriends dispersed and she could join him, walking slowly down the length of the bar to touch his hand to make sure he was real, and not just an apparition of her wishful thinking.

Chapter Fifteen

June 2019
Week One: Late Saturday Afternoon

Jenna wasn't sure why she had suggested to Rosie's former neighbor that they meet at Legends except that she knew she'd never bump into Zack or any of his close buddies there. Even though the sports bar was practically around the corner from the inn, Zack and his buddies preferred watching sports in the comfort of the TV room at the inn.

She was relieved that Carol was already waiting for her when she stepped inside the restaurant.

Carol was the only woman in the sports bar, seated alone, her fingers wrapped around a glass of water. There was a bottle of Pellegrino on the table in front of her. Jenna asked for the same as Carol, who was gazing at the dozen or so TV screens dotted around the bar area.

"Interesting place. Are you a regular?"

Jenna shook her head. "No. I just figured it would be a good place to meet," she said. "I stopped here on the morning before my wedding."

Carol smiled. "To calm your nerves?"

"Something like that." Then Jenna changed the subject quickly. "I didn't tell your neighbor that I wrote that story about Rosie all those years ago."

Carol took a long sip of her water. "I recognized your name when Sally called. I always wondered about you, Jenna. I wondered what sort of person writes that kind of an article."

Jenna also took a sip of her Pellegrino. "Rosie hated me, didn't she?"

Carol shrugged. "Let's just say she certainly regretted letting you into the house."

Jenna cleared her throat. "I tried to apologize to her. I had no idea what I wrote would have such terrible consequences."

Carol patted her hand. "I'm sure you didn't, honey."

Jenna looked around for their waiter so they could place their orders, and so that she could finally get some answers about Rosie and Denny and where they could be found. "So, have you kept in touch with Rosie?"

Carol gave her a blank stare. "Goodness, I haven't heard from Rosie in as many years as she's been gone from the street. I thought you had some information for *me*. When Sally told me you were there about Rosie, I thought you were coming to tell me she had passed . . . I guess I misunderstood."

Jenna sighed. "Sorry, I didn't mean to alarm you. I was hoping you could tell me where I could find her."

"No idea, hon. She said she was moving to Arizona to be with Norm's daughter, Adele. You know, Norm was the corrections officer who was there at Evil Ed's execution . . ." Carol's face reddened slightly. "Of course you know; you mentioned it in your story. Adele lived with Rosie and Norm and Denny before she settled in Arizona after graduating college and getting married. I think Rosie and Adele got along pretty well. Anyway, Rosie said she was going to help out with Adele's baby. Said she would write when she had found her own place, but she never did."

Carol stared out of the window, then turned back to Jenna. "After a while, I just figured she wanted a clean break in new surroundings where no one knew about her. I wasn't going to force the issue. Anyway, she never gave me an address, so . . ."

"So that was about fifteen years ago? That's when she sold the house?"

"That's right."

"Do you remember if she said where in Arizona she was going?"

"Of course." Carol laughed. "I remember looking it up. She said it was near Tempe."

Jenna thought Tempe sounded like one of those old Southwest towns where they sold tons of Native American silver and turquoise jewelry, the kind that Rosie was wearing the day Jenna met her— jewelry Rosie said was a gift from Norm's daughter. "She makes it," Rosie had told her.

"Do you know anything about Adele? Rosie said she made her own jewelry?"

Carol nodded. "Oh yes, it was quite lovely. That's why she stayed in Arizona after she graduated college. She married the son of a Native American chief. She's half Native American herself, you know, because of her mother, Norm's first wife. If I remember correctly, she was a Shinnecock."

There was a momentary silence as the waitress brought their orders. "Well," Jenna said as the waitress stepped away from their table, "maybe she's still in Arizona. I'd like to find her. Really, I'd like to find Denny."

Carol gave her a pointed look. "Doing a story on how the bad seed turned out?" Her tone suggested she did not think it was a good idea.

Jenna shook her head. "Of course not. I'm sorry for what I did, Carol. I quit my job after that story. I never went back to being a tabloid reporter." Jenna shook her head again as if to emphasize the truth of the matter. "I'm just curious how things turned out for him."

"I don't know that Rosie would be able to tell you that. You know, he took off after Lisa was buried. Went off to the islands, in the Caribbean. Came back once for Christmas, but I never saw him again after that. He and Rosie must have had a huge fight. If I ever mentioned his name, she'd just shake her head and say, 'He's gone.' I stopped asking after a while. I felt bad for her. And for Denny."

"You liked Denny?" Jenna threw out the question casually.

Carol nodded. "He was not an evil kid. That was a horrible headline in your newspaper, calling him a spawn."

"So, nothing like his father?"

Carol shrugged. "Not that I ever thought so before your story."

"You didn't know about Ed Haynes before then?"

Carol smiled thinly. "Would you have shared that with anyone? All I knew was that Norm married Rosie when Denny was two. Norm was very good with the boy. He took the trouble to make sure the boy got the attention he needed."

Carol took a sip of water. "I think Norm had some good ideas. He'd been around a lot of troubled individuals in various prisons where he'd worked, so he recognized some of the signs you or I might have missed . . . especially after the incident . . ." Carol hesitated, as

Jenna's interest perked. She let her beets and goat cheese salad sit on her plate while Carol picked at her quesadilla.

"Incident?"

"I was there. Norm and Rosie invited me over for a barbecue. I guess young Denny was about six at the time. He had one of his friends over to play. Adele was around too. It must have been Memorial Day or Fourth of July or something like that. Anyway, we were in the backyard when we heard Adele scream. Rosie dropped her glass. Thank heaven it was plastic. Anyway, she ran into the kitchen and I ran in right after her."

Carol swallowed and fanned her face with her hand. "Denny and his friend had taken one of Adele's goldfish out of the bowl and put it down on Rosie's cutting board and were slicing off its fins with a paring knife."

Jenna felt her stomach heaving. Carol shook her head as if also trying to erase the image. "It wasn't a pleasant sight. But, you know, as a kindergarten teacher I've seen kids do all sorts of weird things, so I didn't say anything. Denny blamed his friend and said they wanted to see if the fish had red blood. It wasn't till after your story came out in the newspaper that Rosie admitted that this was when Norm decided to get therapy for Denny. Of course, you just go back and see everything in a suspicious light."

"Like what?" Jenna asked.

Carol sighed. "Well, Denny always seemed polite and helpful, offering to look after my cat and to water the plants when I went on vacation. Then he became a teenager and I suspected that he was bringing back girls to my empty house, drinking liquor from my cabinet. He had a lot of different girls before Lisa."

Jenna shrugged. "Doesn't sound so different from a lot of normal teenagers."

"Perhaps not. But I know Rosie worried that he was going to be like his father. At one point, before the story came out, she'd told me Denny's father had been a womanizer with a real mean streak."

Jenna put a hand to her mouth to mask her soft snort of disbelief. It was one way of describing Evil Ed, she supposed. Carol didn't seem to notice her reaction.

"Looking back on it, I understand now that she was probably always worried about Denny. I think she was happy when Lisa got pregnant and they got married, and Denny seemed settled."

"And was he settled?"

"I think so." Carol laughed suddenly. "He stopped wanting to come over to water my plants. Said he didn't have the time now that he had his "own little flower" to look after. Those were his words. It was odd really. He seemed to take to married life just fine. He was just like a normal guy, you know."

Jenna pursed her lips. "Except when he kicked in my photographer's head."

"A lot of people didn't blame him for that. Not even the cops. Rosie told me they dropped the charges in the end."

Jenna shrugged and didn't bother explaining that the charges had been dropped because Alan had told the DA he wasn't going to help the prosecutor by giving him a statement. The public tended not to be sympathetic to paparazzi photographers, and Alan didn't want to stir up any more trouble for himself by testifying against someone he'd ambushed outside his own home.

"Anyway, the goldfish incident eventually became a bit of a family joke," Carol added as she pushed away her plate and wiped her mouth.

"A joke?" Jenna couldn't keep the shocked look off her face.

"Not funny ha-ha, just something Rosie eventually dismissed as Denny's first forays into the world of high-end cuisine. You know like that Bourdain fella who used to bite the heads off live fish in the ocean? She said it would probably make a good story when Denny became a celebrity chef himself."

Jenna stared blankly at her.

"Denny was signed up for culinary school when your story appeared." Carol paused. "Didn't you know that?"

Jenna shook her head, feeling totally disheartened. "No. I didn't really know anything about him except that his father was a serial killer."

Carol smiled. "Ah well, don't take it to heart now. I'm sure he's okay. Probably cooking up a storm somewhere in the islands." She patted Jenna's hand and reached for her purse. "That was delicious. Thank you." She got to her feet. "I should get going. If you find Rosie, would you please give her my phone number so I can get in touch? I miss her."

They walked out of the restaurant together and crossed the street to where they'd both parked overlooking the water. Carol hesitated a moment as she opened her car door. "I guess you got over your nerves . . . I mean on your wedding day," she added, evidently assuming that Jenna had already forgotten she'd told Carol about calming her wedding-day jitters at Legends. "I mean, you're here, so I'm guessing everything turned out just fine that day."

Jenna smiled. "Wasn't quite the fairy tale you might imagine, but not a total disaster," she replied. Carol evidently decided not to probe further and got into her car. Just as well.

As Jenna slid into the driver's seat of her Jeep, all she could see in front of her eyes was the big, ugly red stain soaked into the front of the beautiful, expensive dress Zack had bought for her to wear on their wedding day.

Chapter Sixteen

16 Years Earlier: September 2003

"You're not getting married."

Jenna heard Ryan's simple pronouncement as he intertwined his fingers with hers, and then the quizzical note in his voice as he added: "You're not really getting married are you, luv?"

He held on to her hand as they left the bar where minutes before she'd been surrounded by girlfriends toasting her with champagne. Lola had been the last to leave.

"I'll be banging down your door at six tomorrow morning. Be ready," she warned Jenna.

"Tell me the truth, Sinclair," Ryan persisted as they walked. "You're just messing with my head."

"Why would I mess with your head? Zack is more serious about me than you ever were."

"Not true, Jenna. I love you. I thought we were soul mates."

"What about Teddi?"

There was a long silence. "I'm fond of her. I admit. Would you rather I lied?"

That was the trouble. Ryan wanted to be soul mates with her, but he was also "fond" of Teddi, whatever that meant. Lola was right. He wasn't ready to commit to Jenna. Maybe he never would be.

Still, she let him walk her back to her apartment building, right to her apartment door, and then into the apartment so that she could show him her wedding dress, hanging on the back of the closet door.

"That's it. That's what I'm wearing tomorrow," she informed Ryan, her voice breaking as she stared at his downcast expression. But then, he grinned.

"That's not a wedding dress."

Jenna had to laugh out loud. "Did you think I was going to get married in a white gown and veil?"

"Can I see it? On you?"

Jenna's throat tightened, but she took the dress off its hanger and discarded the sundress she was wearing before slipping the exquisite, silk creation over her head. She stood impassively as Ryan stared at her for a while before moving to the kitchen, where she heard him pouring himself a drink. When he came back into the living room, he was holding a glass of Scotch and a glass of cabernet for her.

He handed Jenna the glass of cabernet and reached for the sales tag attached to the back zipper. He let out a low whistle. "Wow! Fancy price."

Jenna put down the glass and reached for the zipper to take it off, but Ryan stopped her, and put his arms around her. "You look fabulous, luv, like a million dollars. I hope you're going to be happy." Then, he hugged her more tightly than she ever remembered him doing.

—◦◦◦— —◦◦◦—

She woke with the gray early-morning light filtering in through the blinds and was startled to find herself on her bed, on top of the duvet with her dress hiked up around her waist. Ryan lay sprawled beside her. She slipped into the bathroom, turned on the water, looked up at her face in the mirror, and her eyes were immediately drawn to the wine stain that had soaked into the fabric of the dress, just under her left breast. Her shriek brought Ryan stumbling into the bathroom behind her.

"Oh, jeez. Sinclair," he gasped, a look of bewilderment on his face. "Did I do that?" Ryan snatched a facecloth off the countertop, held it under running water and reached out to dab at the stain.

"No! Don't! You can't do that to silk." Jenna shrank back as a groan escaped her. "The dress is ruined."

Lola was appalled when Jenna showed her the dress an hour later. "Jen! How did that happen?"

Jenna had to agree with her friend that the dress was irreparably damaged: a little tear could have been mended, creases could have been steamed or ironed out by the wonderful dry cleaners two doors down from her building, but a red wine stain? That would never, ever come out.

"I wore it to show Ryan. He hugged me. He wouldn't let me go. I'm not sure what happened after that."

"Did you ask him about Teddi?"

"He said he was fond of her; that she reminded him of me when I first joined the *Sun*."

Lola pursed her lips in disapproval. "See, he couldn't commit to you, even knowing he was going to lose you forever."

Lola didn't have to say it. It had become obvious that Ryan admired Teddi. She shared his killer instinct for getting a story. Still and all, he hadn't wanted to give up Jenna. He'd said so, hadn't he? Jenna started to cry.

"Don't," Lola admonished her. "Your face will puff up and you'll look like shit in all your wedding photos."

Jenna cried harder. She begged Lola to leave her alone. Let her stay in her apartment.

"I'll call Zack, tell him I can't go through with it. I'll tell him it's me, not him. That he's too good for me."

"Fine," Lola agreed. "But if that's what you want to say, you're going to tell him to his face. It's the very least you owe him."

By the time they pulled into the makeshift parking lot outside Legends with Jenna telling her friend she needed some Dutch courage—*damn right, Lola, I need a Bloody Mary, maybe even a straight-up vodka*—she had worked out exactly what she needed to say to Zack. She would show him the ruined wedding dress and tell him the truth about falling asleep in it. She probably wouldn't tell him the whole truth about Ryan falling asleep beside her. After all, nothing had happened, had it? Not that she could remember. So, no point in stirring up needless anger. She would tell Zack she was a bad person, and she'd tell him why she'd quit her reporting job; the whole story about her exposé, and what had happened to the spawn's wife and unborn child after her story was published. He would see that she had as good as killed a family. He would have to let her go. He wouldn't want her as his wife after he knew all that. Would he?

But Zack's reaction was not what she'd expected. As soon as she and Lola pulled up to the inn, Zack whisked her away to the loft above the garage, which he was turning into living quarters for them. The builders were almost finished, but she didn't want to see all the magnificent features. She was determined to confess every single last fault.

When she was finished, he took the wedding dress out of its garment bag. "I don't care about the dress," he said, tossing it across the floor. "I don't care what you wrote five years ago, or what happened to this 'spawn' and his family." Then he took a deep breath. "You can't go on beating yourself up forever for whatever happened back then. You've got to move on." He looked at her. "I know what it's like. I did it."

"What?" Jenna thought she'd misunderstood his meaning, but Zack nodded.

"That's right, I never told you all of my secrets either. I know I told you that my last relationship had a sad ending." He threw her a crooked smile. "But I didn't tell you why."

"No, you didn't."

Zack took a deep breath. "She died, just like the spawn's wife, and I didn't think I'd get over it. But then I met you, and I told myself that I deserved to be happy again."

Jenna didn't know what to say. She was torn. She didn't want to hurt Zack, but wouldn't she be hurting him by marrying him when she didn't feel sure that she was doing the right thing? She made a last attempt to extricate herself.

"But you didn't cause her death, and at least, you didn't kill an unborn baby."

"Well," he said. "We were actually on our way to the clinic. Lana thought she was pregnant. She didn't want it. We were arguing about it when the accident happened."

"Oh my God, Zack!" Jenna didn't know what else to say. She sat down in the middle of the unfinished concrete floor, her thoughts spinning. Just for a crazy second, she wondered if perhaps he was borrowing the scenario from some movie he'd seen, or just making it all up to persuade her that this was her chance to make up for everything that had gone before.

"No." She shook her head vehemently. "I don't want to hear any more, Zack. I can't."

Zack smiled at her, offered his hand to help her up. "Whatever you decide, Jenna, I'm not going to try to talk you into staying with me." He took her hand in his. "I'd like to stay friends, I'd like to say you're welcome to come and visit whenever you want. Treat the inn as if it was your home."

Jenna realized she was trembling probably from the relief that things weren't going to get ugly between her and Zack. "We should go downstairs and tell the guests . . ." she said softly.

"Screw 'em. They'll be fine. Ana's prepared a feast. They won't care if there's an actual wedding or not. You're my only concern right now." Then, he put his arms around her and hugged her so tightly she could hardly breathe.

Chapter Seventeen

June 2019
Week One: Saturday Evening

Oh, how young and sweet she was back then, thought Jenna, sitting in her car long after Carol had driven away. So reluctant to hurt anyone; thinking about everyone else's feelings rather than her own. But she was not that person anymore; not the young, gullible woman who had sat in this same spot sixteen years before, rehearsing what she was going to say before folding at the last minute because of—what? Guilt? Pity? Or because she hadn't truly known what she wanted and, in the end, it was just easier to go along with what Zack wanted for her. Not that she regretted eventually going ahead with the wedding. How could she, when her marriage to Zack had given her Dollie? This time however, she was going to lay it on the line for him. Whatever Zack planned to tell her, she was going to make it clear that he had hurt her badly by betraying her with someone who had wormed her way into their home and their business—and into Dollie's affections. They could go their separate ways, she'd say. But she wasn't going to let Bethany take her husband *and* her daughter.

She would talk calmly to Zack about Dollie, see what they could do about their daughter's run-in with the law in Maine, and then she'd suggest that Dollie return with her to the city. There was no need for either of them to turn the conversation into bitter recriminations.

She reached for her cell phone and clicked on Ryan's number, bracing herself for the sound of Teddi's voice. She'd probably be brusque and hostile to Jenna, but surely she'd understand Jenna's concern, wouldn't she? The phone went straight to voice mail, and something clutched at Jenna's heart when she heard Ryan's greeting. After the beep, she left a message for Teddi asking her, please, for an update on Ryan's condition.

Then, she switched on the ignition, glancing over at the box that she'd gotten from Rosie's old house sitting on the passenger seat beside her. She decided to move it out of sight, behind the car seats. If Zack was home and came out to the car when she pulled up, she didn't want him asking what was in it. Balancing it on one hip, she reached to open the back door when the box slipped and fell to the ground disgorging papers and envelopes. She gathered them up and reached for the last piece of paper, a photograph lying face up. Without her reading glasses, it appeared a little blurry. She looked closer. Even then, she wasn't sure she was seeing it correctly.

She reached into her pocket for her readers and adjusted them on her nose. The picture was clear now, and it made her stomach heave. It showed Dollie as a newborn in her stroller. The photo had been taken in the city; Jenna was sitting on one of the benches in Sutton

Place Park along the East River. Dollie was just a week old. Jenna had insisted that her child be born in Manhattan, like she herself had been. Zack had complained but suffered through their cramped stay at the apartment for a couple of weeks before bundling them into the SUV one glorious sunny day and driving them back to the inn.

The snapshot didn't tell Jenna very much. She looked for clues as to where Denny Dennison might have been standing when he'd taken it. He could have been anywhere in the park or even on the street. When she sat on the bench facing the East River, she'd always turned Dollie's stroller away from the rising sun, exposing the baby to anyone who wanted to snap away from the street.

The photo was fifteen years old, taken just before Rosie moved out of her house in Seaford. More to the point, this was six years after Jenna's big exposé on Denny.

Denny had known exactly where to find her. He'd stalked her and Dollie; was he still holding a grudge six years after her article? According to Carol, Denny had left home and taken off for the islands almost immediately after the story in the *Sun*. He had come home for one Christmas and had never been seen again. But did this picture, shot several years after that, mean that he'd returned from the islands without letting Rosie know, just to stalk Jenna in the city? Had he been planning to harm her all along? Hurt Dollie? Get his revenge by targeting her baby? Had she and Dollie escaped in the nick of time, back then?

PART TWO

Chapter Eighteen

Week One: Saturday Evening

Zack heard Jenna's car rolling down the driveway, but didn't stop hulling the strawberries he was preparing for dessert. Sound carried out on the point, and he heard the gravel crunching under her wheels as she pulled to a stop. He took a deep breath to calm himself. She'd certainly taken her sweet time. How the hell could it take longer to drive home from the city than it had taken him to drive with Dollie from Maine?

Stay cool, he told himself and took another deep breath. He knew how to keep calm around Jenna. He'd had years of practice. Sixteen, give or take. Going right back to that dress fiasco on their wedding day. He'd almost lost it when he saw what she'd done. Back then, the cost of the dress was as much profit as he took in from the inn and marina in a good month.

But he'd done that thing where he'd visualized doing something nice with the person you wanted to unload on. So, he'd shrugged, and forced himself to picture introducing Jenna as his wife to all the regulars at his buddy Jim's bar.

He'd masked his anger well back then. It was one stupid little stain on a frothy little dress. He'd get her another, he'd said. He'd mouthed all the right words, and made exactly the right moves so as not to screw up his chances of marrying Jenna Sinclair. Just as he wasn't going to screw up her homecoming now.

Sure, he and Jenna had been through a rough patch, rougher than the usual moody interludes he had to suffer through after Jenna saw a photo or gossip item about McAllister in the newspaper. He knew it always reminded her of the life she could have had, but usually, he could make her forget it.

This time, the fault had been his. But he was going to make her forget this latest hiccup too. He would explain everything. They would sit down at the table he'd set on the patio and enjoy lobsters and chilled chardonnay.

Then he would tell her that he loved her and that he was truly sorry he'd hurt her.

He turned on a smile for her as she walked into the kitchen. "Hi, Jen, you're home. Was traffic awful?"

"Where's Dollie?" Jenna asked, walking across the kitchen to get a bottle of water from the refrigerator.

"She asked to go to Cath's house. You weren't here."

The look on Jenna's face turned as cold as the water she was holding. "We were supposed to discuss things, the three of us. She should be here."

"The two of us should talk first." He stared at her, pausing in his hulling.

Jenna took a long swig from the water bottle and then a deep breath, seeming to calm herself. "So why did the camp ask her to leave? It can't have been just that one accident?"

"She and a couple of other kids snuck off the premises the first week they were there," Zack said. "And there were other incidents. Her counselors said she wasn't settling in the way they'd hoped."

"What about the barn burning?"

"Well, that matter is pending. They still have to decide whether to charge her."

"Who has to decide? Charge her? With what?" Jenna's questions came fast and furiously. He couldn't keep up when she was like this.

"Sorry, Jen. I'm not sure about all the details. But the JCCO, the juvenile community corrections officer, said it could all probably go away if she pays restitution."

"She? You mean, if we pay restitution," Jenna interrupted, then sighed. "It's always something."

Zack finished hulling the strawberries and reached for the cantaloupe, trying not to show his disappointment. Jenna always seemed to believe the worst about Dollie, as if Dollie's misbehavior was something their daughter had control over. He wished now that he had shared his concerns and fears about Dollie with Jenna long ago. There were times he'd never told her about the trouble Dollie had gotten into—especially if things happened when Jenna was on one of her trips into the city. There was no way he could have that conversation with Jenna now.

"You could have left a voice mail. Or texted. I could have asked Lola to look into it." He heard Jenna's tone soften. He knew she was trying to figure out the best solution even though she sounded angry.

"I didn't think you'd leave your phone on mute for so long."

Jenna paced around the kitchen. "I told you, I muted it for a meeting. I forgot about it when I went to dinner." She took another quick swig from the water bottle. "I was with Ryan McAllister."

"At the meeting or at dinner?" He focused on the cantaloupe, slicing through it, digging out the seeds and tossing them into the garbage disposal.

"At dinner."

He carried on digging out the seeds, avoiding Jenna's eyes. He didn't want her to suspect that he was getting just the smallest bit of satisfaction from the fact that she'd never mentioned being at dinner with McAllister when they'd spoken on the phone. He figured that meant she felt guilty about it—which, surely, meant she hadn't given up on their marriage.

He realized she was staring at him when he finally looked up. Then she cleared her throat. "Ryan was assaulted in the street outside the apartment building. Cops said they may want to talk to you. I had to give them the phone number here."

"To me? Why?" He sliced neatly between the fruit and the outer skin, tapped the knife on the cutting board and adopted a quizzical expression.

"You know cops. They'll always want to talk to the husband. Someone kicked the hell out of Ryan after our dinner. Put him in the hospital."

"You did tell them I was three hundred miles away in Maine picking up our daughter, didn't you?"

"I mentioned it, but I didn't know the details, did I?"

"What time did the mugging happen?"

"It was sometime after two in the morning." Jenna's voice dropped a notch. "Probably more like three."

He was not surprised that the cops wanted to talk to him. Anyone who watched *Law and Order* knew that the cops always looked at spouses first. They were probably searching through tapes and footage from CCTV cameras at the tunnel and the bridges right now, looking for his E-ZPass identification. Let them look.

He changed the subject abruptly. "I've got lobsters for dinner. We could relax, have a nice glass of wine. Then I'll go pick up Dollie."

Jenna shrank back, even though he hadn't come anywhere near her. "I'm sorry, Zack. There's a lot we need to talk about. I wasn't planning on an evening of relaxation with a nice glass of wine."

"Jenna, please." His voice rose a notch before he could stop himself. "You can't honestly think there was anything between me and Bethany? She hasn't even been here while you were away."

Jenna's disbelief was written all over her face. "I'm saying I want to know the truth, Zack, so that we can both move on."

And then, because her words probably sounded as harsh to her as they did to him, she softened her tone, and the hostility in her eyes seemed to fade as she added: "Okay, lobsters sound good. I am hungry. I'll go bring my stuff in."

Might be okay, after all, he told himself. They'd have dinner, a few glasses of wine. He'd charm her back the way he'd always done in the past.

Jenna dashed the hope before it was finished forming. "I'll take the Miranda cottage if there are no overnight guests."

He masked his disappointment with a shake of his head. "Sorry, honey. Miranda cottage has a leak in the kitchen pipes. I had to shut off the water."

"Then, which suite can I use?" She shook her head. "I'm sorry, Zack, but I can't sleep with you knowing you've probably been all over that girl while I've been in the city."

It was all he could do to stop himself from grabbing her by the shoulders and yelling at her. *Suite? You don't need a suite. What the hell is wrong with you, Jenna? I made one mistake, for heaven's sake!*

Instead, seeing her stubborn demeanor, he said: "You can use the Peconic suite."

He poured himself a stiff vodka and tonic as he heard the front door open, but her remark about moving on stung. Had he ever said she couldn't be a writer, or even an investigative journalist? No, he had not. Hadn't he tipped her off to the restaurant frauds? It was a good local story that she could investigate and write from home. All he'd ever said was that she could do all her writing just as easily from home.

It was obvious she was still furious that he'd taken Bethany along on the trip with Dollie. He wondered if what really made her furious was the thought of Dollie having fun with Bethany. Or did she really believe he'd had a wild night with his intern? Or was it because she was afraid that Bethany could cause trouble for him, and for the family, like all those #MeToo women in the news?

Just as he took a sip of his drink and went to retrieve a big pot and the lobsters from the kitchen sink, he heard voices in the hallway. He looked out the kitchen doorway to see Jenna followed by Brad Halsey from the local police department.

"Chief Brad is here," Jenna announced. "It's about Bethany." She raised an eyebrow, but then abruptly left the kitchen carrying a box in her arms and a tote slung over her shoulder.

Chapter Nineteen

Zack detested Brad Halsey, who was, in fact, only one of the deputies in the Southold Police Department. It was Jenna who insisted on addressing him as "Chief." She said it cost nothing and kept him sweet.

Better to be on the good side of law enforcement in town, she always said, which is why she usually welcomed him to the inn whenever he decided to pay a visit.

But Zack had Halsey's number. The deputy had been trying to bulldoze his way into their family since Dollie's birth. Whenever Halsey got the chance, he'd bend Jenna's ear about his long-ago relationship with Zack's mother, Miranda.

"You know, Zack's Mom and I had a thing going before she was kicked out of the house," he'd say, usually after a few drinks at the bar on the inn's patio. "It's possible I could be Zack's father. I could be Dollie's grandfather. Zack could take a DNA test. Then we'd all know for sure."

"Nope. No. Definitely N-O." Zack knew that Jenna had been alarmed by his vehemence the first time she heard him with Brad.

"What would it hurt?" she'd asked.

But Zack never wavered. "No. Don't need to be taken on as anyone's family now. It's too late to step up to the plate."

Even so, Halsey went out of his way to be helpful, like the time he'd brought Dollie back after finding her skinny-dipping and smoking weed with a group of classmates from the high school. "I'm watching out for her," he told Zack, puffing out his chest as if to show how important he was around town. "Good thing it wasn't any of the other cops."

And a good thing Jenna had been in the city when that incident occurred. There was something smarmy about Brad. Zack suspected that he had enjoyed himself spying on Dollie and her classmates for a while before breaking up the fun. That's the kind of psychopathic vibe he gave off. Zack wasn't surprised. It was common knowledge that there were certain professions that attracted psychos, just as it was well known that the police force had its fair share.

Now, in the kitchen, Zack offered the deputy a cold drink, reaching into the refrigerator for the jug of fresh, lemon-flavored iced tea Ana prepared every day. He poured out a generous glass as Jenna reappeared.

"So, Bethany Smithers." Brad cleared his throat. "She's that cute little thing working here part-time, right?"

"Yes, Bethany is an intern here," Zack responded.

"Well," Brad continued, as if Zack hadn't spoken. "Her room-mate in Riverhead says she's called and texted her, but has heard nothing since last week. She says she called the inn and Ana told her she hadn't seen or heard from her either. When was the last time you saw her?"

He directed the question at Zack, who remembered exactly when he'd last seen Bethany.

"Last Sunday," he said. "Yep, it was last Sunday . . . Wait . . . you're saying no one's seen her for a week."

"That's how it looks."

Zack opened the refrigerator and beckoned to Jenna, pointing to the iced tea. She shook her head no. "She's usually here from Friday afternoon through the weekend, the weeks she comes, that is," Zack explained to Brad, pouring himself a tall glass of the tea.

"But she's not here this weekend," Brad stated.

Zack shook his head. "She's an intern. She doesn't get paid, she gets credits for the culinary school. It's the end of the semester for her. Truth be told, I wasn't expecting her here. End of semester, they have all kinds of presentations."

Brad nodded, but his eyes narrowed. "You're sure she left on Sunday afternoon?"

"Yep. I'm positive."

"Only her friend says she got a text from her Sunday morning that Bethany was planning to stay here the week."

Zack shook his head again. "Bethany offered to stay because Jenna was on a work assignment in the city and she wanted to help out. It was sweet of her, but I told her school comes first. I was very firm about that."

"Did she drive back on Sunday?"

"She always takes the jitney to and from Riverhead."

Brad looked puzzled. "I didn't think the jitney was local transportation. Don't you have to go all the way to the city if you take it?"

Zack nodded. "Strictly speaking, yes. But you can get a ticket for the airport connection in Islip. They stop there. It's twenty-one bucks. We give her the money for that, and she makes a reservation and then just gets off earlier, at the Riverhead stop. It's a thirty-five-minute ride. No one on the bus cares."

"So, she picks up the jitney at their stop in town?"

Zack nodded.

"How does she get to the jitney from here?"

"One of us will drop her off at the stop. Me or Jenna or Ana."

Jenna was nodding now too. But added, "I wasn't here last Sunday."

Brad kept his eyes on Zack. "Did you see her get on the jitney?"

"Nope, Chief. I did not actually see her get on the jitney. She doesn't expect me to wait with her. The jitney's never on time Sundays in the summer."

Brad guzzled his iced tea before asking, "But didn't you expect her to call this weekend if she wasn't coming?"

"I haven't really had time to think about it. I had to drive to Maine to pick up Dollie from camp. I only just got back. Ana might know more." Zack sat down abruptly on one of the kitchen stools. "Shit! How can she be missing for a week, and no one notices?"

Jenna was staring at Brad. "Have you checked with the jitney? They'll have the list of passengers. They'll tell you whether she actually got on the bus. Have you checked her cell phone location?"

Brad shook his head. "Whoa! We only just got the call from her friend."

"She has a boyfriend." Zack jumped in with a nugget of information he suddenly remembered. "He's a bit older, she said, with a young son. He's divorced and has custody of the boy. I think he works in a Riverhead restaurant. Sorry, I don't know his name."

"What about her parents? Do you know where they live?" Brad took out a little notebook from his jacket pocket.

"They live in Ireland," Zack responded. "She came here years ago as a summer nanny on some sort of work visa and then decided to go to culinary school." He looked at Jenna, shrugging. "Didn't she tell us her parents disapproved of her living in the sin capital of the world?"

Jenna frowned. "Riverhead?"

"No, New York. I think her first nanny job was in the city."

"Sorry," Jenna looked embarrassed. "I don't remember that."

"This is awful." Zack pursed his lips. "We should know more about her."

Brad drained his glass. "It's okay. We'll find her. She's a girl. There's reasons they take off, and we don't git to know them for a while." He wiped his mouth on the paper coaster and looked like he was finally leaving. "Have a good evening, you young 'uns." Zack noticed that his grin was more of a leer at Jenna as he walked to the front door.

Jenna waited till they heard his cruiser pulling away down the driveway, then gave a big, exaggerated shudder. "You're right. He is a creep. And dumb along with it," she said, heading for the stairs.

"Where are you going?" Zack asked, not wanting to lose the sudden bond they appeared to be sharing in their joint disgust of Brad Halsey.

Jenna pointed to the top of the house. "You'd think he would have asked to look around Bethany's room."

Chapter Twenty

Jenna pushed open the door to the room Bethany used whenever she stayed overnight and gasped. It was stifling. There were only window air-conditioning units up here, and they were switched off. The air hung hot and dense. Jenna looked around for the floor fan. She flipped the switch and immediately the fan roared into action, stirring the stifling air around her.

The room was tiny. Just enough space for a single bed, a tiny dresser and a nightstand. An IKEA clothes rack blocked most of the light from the small dormer window. Jenna switched on the little lamp on the nightstand. She wasn't sure what she expected to find, but crossed to the clothes rack and checked the pockets of a couple of sundresses that hung from the white aluminum rod. She recognized two other outfits as favorites of Bethany's. Low scooped white blouses and floral peasant skirts. Jenna had described them as "serving wench" costumes, suspiciously eyeing Bethany's cleavage when she'd first appeared in them. She'd noticed Zack's eyes following Bethany around the kitchen although the girl herself had appeared oblivious. In the beginning.

Jenna wondered what had gone on between Bethany and Zack after Jenna had left for the city. Zack's explanation to Brad had not rung quite true. Why would he not have accepted her offer to stay and help?

She threw back the bedding and tossed it on the floor, eyeing the bottom sheet as if expecting to see evidence of Zack's infidelity staring her in the face from the middle of the small bed. It would have been a sweaty coupling up here, she thought, tearing off the bottom sheet and also tossing it on the floor. She heard a soft thud as the bottom sheet landed on the floorboards.

It took her a few seconds to pick through the bedding to find Bethany's cell phone. Without a doubt, it was hers. She remembered Bethany telling Dollie that the bright pink case was a Mophie that would recharge her phone without being plugged in. But she saw the phone was dead as she clicked several times on the home button. Jenna didn't like what she was seeing. She did not think Bethany would have left the inn without her cell phone. Who, these days, would go anywhere without making sure they had their cell phone with them?

She made her way down the stairs and into the kitchen where Zack was sprinkling what looked like lime zest and a spice into a little saucepan on the stove.

He looked up as she came into the kitchen. "Honey-lime syrup for the strawberries," he pointed to the saucepan. "Here, let me get you a drink. The syrup can cool for now."

Jenna held up Bethany's cell phone as Zack switched off the stove. "It's Bethany's," she said. "I found it in her bed."

Zack's eyes widened.

"It's dead now," Jenna nodded. "Didn't she realize she'd left without it? And how come she still hasn't realized? She's been without it for a week."

Jenna poked at the home button. Still no response. She looked across at Zack. "Wasn't she looking for it on the way to the bus stop?"

Jenna couldn't read the look on Zack's face. He hadn't moved away from the stovetop and was jiggling the little saucepan with the honey-lime syrup as if trying to look busy.

"Zack?" she walked across the kitchen to the island. "What's going on?"

He shook his head, then took a swig from his glass of water. "I didn't drive Bethany to the jitney last Sunday."

"So, she didn't go home?"

"I don't know where she went, Jen."

"What's that mean?" Jenna's words were clipped, and the hint of annoyance in her voice was unmistakable.

"Calm down." Zack took another swig from his glass. "I was working on the sailboat when she came to say she'd stay while you were gone. I told her no, she couldn't do that. That's the truth. I told her I'd be back at the house in twenty minutes, and I'd drive her to the jitney."

"And?"

"When I got back to the house, she wasn't here. She was gone. I thought maybe she called that friend, the one who works on Love Lane? But that one drove by later that evening looking for Bethany. So then, I figured she'd walked to the jitney."

"Jeez, that's a three-mile walk, Zack."

"Honestly, Jen, I had no idea at the time. I figured she was pissed off that I was making her go back to school, and she just took off without waiting for me. It didn't occur to me she would walk."

Jenna sat down abruptly on one of the kitchen stools. "You lied to Brad about dropping her off."

"No, I didn't. I told him I didn't see her board the jitney. I didn't actually say I'd driven her to the stop."

Jenna rolled her eyes as he continued. "Jen, you've got to believe me. You know I'd never have let her walk all that way alone. I mean, dear sweet Jesus . . . I'd have to be a real jerk. That's why I didn't tell Brad. I'm embarrassed. But I guess I should have mentioned it. Anything could have happened to her between here and the bus stop."

Jenna felt her heart hammering against her ribs. Of course Zack was embarrassed, but that was nothing compared to what was going through her own mind. Anyone seeing Bethany and Dollie together could have mistaken them for sisters—could have mistaken Bethany for their daughter.

Bethany had disappeared on Sunday, three weeks after Jenna's exposé on the Hamptons restaurants had appeared on the newsstands and online. Her bio had appeared at the very end of the article: "Jenna Sinclair lives with her family at the Kings Inn and Marina on the North Fork of Long Island, where her husband, Zack King, owns a restaurant."

Jenna had not wanted the bio to be that specific, but one of the copy editors at *CityMagazine* had suggested that it was needed in the interest of full disclosure. "If it comes out later that your husband owns a restaurant, it could look like you had an ulterior motive to badmouth other restaurant owners on the East End. Better put it out, upfront."

What's more, Bethany had disappeared just four days before Ryan was mugged and left for dead outside her apartment building. Jenna shuddered. She did not believe in coincidences. No. No such thing as coincidence. Girls around these parts didn't suddenly disappear unless they ran away from home. Whoever had assaulted Ryan could have taken Bethany, mistaking her for Dollie.

Panic rose in her chest. She got to her feet, pushing back the kitchen stool. It wobbled and would have fallen over if Zack hadn't been right there to steady it. And her.

She brushed off his hand. "I'm okay." She took a deep breath. No point in sharing her fears with Zack just yet. First, she'd charge up the phone and see if there was any clue to Bethany's whereabouts in her texts or voice mails. There could be a simple explanation, as Brad Halsey had suggested. Not that the phone would help anyone locate her present whereabouts, obviously. Nor would it help if Bethany had been picked up—God forbid—by Denny Dennison after she'd set out to walk to the jitney.

She'd call Brad and tell him they'd found Bethany's phone as soon it was charged up and she could ascertain if it was password protected. As soon as she could take a quick look to see if there was any other explanation for Bethany's absence.

For the moment, Jenna's attention was diverted to the little plate of grilled shrimp in front of her. She noticed they'd been prepared in her favorite coriander-lime marinade. She reached for one and popped it in her mouth. She was ravenously hungry. She popped another in her mouth and turned to Zack. "I'd really like for Dollie to be home, now." And then, because she didn't want to sound like a total nag, she added, "She's missing this fabulous spread. She should be here."

"On it," he gave her a half smile, getting his cell phone out of his pocket and speed dialing Dollie's cell phone.

Jenna listened to his side of the conversation, which was more a series of grunts of assent finishing with "Okay, sweetheart." Then he disconnected the call. "She says they're in the middle of dinner and then they want to watch a movie, and please, please, please, let her stay till tomorrow morning." He shrugged. "No real reason for her to come back now, is there?"

Jenna frowned. Zack never put his foot down with Dollie. But she supposed it was fine. Cath's parents lived in town. The girls would be fine at Cath's house. In fact, Dollie was probably safer in Cath's house than in her own. If Jenna's suspicions were right, then it was possible that Denny Dennison might come back for Dollie. After all, he'd surely realized by now that Bethany was not Jenna's daughter.

Chapter Twenty-One

Week One: Saturday Night / Sunday Morning

Jenna was not at all sleepy by the time she made her way to the suite on the second floor of the inn. Thankfully, Zack had made no further comments about her choice of sleeping arrangements, though he'd tried to convince her over dinner that there was nothing going on between him and Bethany. "Don't you think if there was something going on between us, I'd have agreed for her to stay after you left?"

Jenna didn't think that at all. For one, Zack could have insisted on playing it cool while things were in flux.

Now, in her suite, she unpacked her tote, plugged Bethany's phone into the charger, and plopped down on the floor beside the box she'd brought from Rosie's house. The photo of Dollie lay facedown on top of the other contents. She put it to one side without looking at it again. Then she dug deeper into the box to retrieve copies of what appeared to be microfiche from New York newspapers that had carried articles about Evil Ed Haynes at the time of his trial. They were stamped with dates, the way newspaper librarians stamped and filed clippings of newspaper stories back then. There were also copies of *True Detective*, *Startling Detective*, even a *Crime Beat* magazine double-page feature on serial killer Evil Ed, published a couple of years before her exposé. Denny would have had to write to the magazines for back copies.

One of them advertised a jailhouse interview with the headline THEY BEGGED ME FOR IT. In the article, Evil Ed claimed the girls who subsequently testified against him on the rape charges had all told him where they were rooming. One had been in the pool skinny-dipping when he arrived; one had accepted a ride when walking alone to the cottage she was sharing with four other girls, and one had left the door unlocked for him. "She wanted me to come to her room and get in her bed," he bragged, although the article also pointed out that evidence at trial had shown that Evil Ed had cut through the screen door which his victim had, in fact, locked.

The names of Ed's victims were circled in the stories from the trial, and Denny had obviously asked the Seaford Library for articles on each of the named victims. There were articles going back to the discovery of the bodies over a period of three summers, from 1969 to 1972, when Ed Haynes was finally caught.

Deeper down in the box, Jenna was startled to discover a roughly drawn map of the East End on which Denny had traced the area all around Peconic Bay along the northern edge of the South Fork, around the southern and northern shores of the North Fork, and across the Sound along the Connecticut shore, where Ed Haynes had buried his victims in the woods after torturing them. Denny had marked the locations where all the bodies were found. She noted that one of the bodies had been found in a copse on the grounds of the North Fork Country Club. Seeing the black initials "NFCC" penciled in on the page surprised her. The club and its fifty-acre golf course were located just a couple of miles from the inn.

There were also copies of articles from the *New York Times*. One was dated July 1998 (a month after Jenna's scoop) and was about a woman grifter and her son. Jenna saw that Denny had highlighted various sentences in the article about Kenny, the son. The first was a quote from a neighbor: "Basically, he just didn't care. I wouldn't say he was inconsiderate, but he wouldn't think of others when he would do things." Further down in the article, Denny had highlighted another sentence: "At college, Kenny's own violent streak surfaced."

Another article in Denny's box was the obituary of a serial killer who had died in prison. The highlighted sentence in this article was about the serial killer's son, Michael, aged thirteen at the time of his father's serial killings. "Almost as shocking as the crime's savagery was the participation of the boy under his father's guidance."

It looked to Jenna as if Denny had started gathering his own facts to find out how many children of criminals had followed in their fathers' or mothers' footsteps. She felt momentarily sorry that she was the one who'd driven him on such a horrible mission. How awful for any child to realize that they had someone as sick and violent in their family tree. No wonder Denny's wife had made the heartbreaking decision to abort their baby. What a shock to discover that gene pool when you were already pregnant.

It was well after midnight when she finally switched off the lights. Before slipping into bed, she double-checked the lock on the door leading to the outside staircase and made sure that the screen door was also locked. The next thing she knew, she was being jolted awake by the sound of footsteps on the staircase. She clicked on her Fitbit to see that it was just coming up on six in the morning. There was bright light streaming in through a narrow gap between the drapes.

Was Zack bringing her coffee? Breakfast? She slid out of bed and tossed the articles she'd left on the floor into the box, then dragged it over to the closet. She did not want Zack to see the box or any of the contents.

There was a soft tap at the door. She closed the closet door firmly and unplugged Bethany's cell phone from where she'd left it charging on the dresser, shoved it into the top drawer, and went to open the door.

Her daughter stood outside, holding a to-go cup out to her. It smelled like coffee.

"Dollie! You're back."

"Yep. I came back last night. Cath's dad dropped me off at the end of the driveway. He didn't want to wake anyone."

Jenna gasped. The driveway was long and meandered through a grove of high rhododendron bushes. She immediately visualized it as a perfect lurking spot. "Oh, Dollie! What was he thinking? He should have brought you right to the door."

Dollie's expression suggested that Jenna wasn't making any sense. Then, she rolled her eyes. "Yeah, and good morning to you too, Mom. I should have known I didn't need to hurry back."

She thrust the to-go cup into Jenna's hands, turned away, and hurried back down the staircase.

Chapter Twenty-Two

B y the time Jenna found her flip-flops under the bed, her daughter was already at the bottom of the steps.

"Dollie! Wait up! Please, hon!" Jenna hurried after her as Dollie skirted the swimming pool and patio and strode toward the bay. She was moving fast, as if propelled by her anger. Jenna caught up with her at the jetty where Zack's motorboat, the *Dollie Too*, was docked.

"Dollie! Please, stop!" Jenna grasped her daughter's hand.

"Don't." Dollie shook her off but didn't move away. Jenna blinked in the bright sunlight and stared at her daughter, the sight grabbing her by the throat. Dollie's thin shoulders, unwashed hair, and stained jeans made her feel guilty. What kind of a mother was she? Most other mothers would be spending the summer doing mother-daughter fun things like mani-pedis and window shopping in the new boutiques opening up in Greenport.

She wanted to hug Dollie, but the look in her daughter's eyes was cold and unwelcoming.

"Dad said you wanted to talk to me."

"I always want to talk to you," Jenna said.

"Cut the crap, Mom." Dollie fixed her with an unwavering stare. "I know you're going to grill me about what happened at camp. I know you're going to tell me I'm a huge disappointment."

Jenna shook her head. Part of her wanted to tell Dollie she wasn't a huge disappointment.

On the other hand, she wanted to take her to task and not let her get away with that sort of manipulation.

"I'm not going to grill you. I got the whole story from your father. You got into trouble. You snuck out of camp and apparently destroyed someone else's property. Now you've got to appear in court. Have I got most of it right?"

Dollie bit her bottom lip. "It was an accident."

"But why, Dollie?" Jenna prodded as gently as she knew how.

"Why did you make me go all the way up there? No, don't bother answering that. I know why." Dollie glowered at her. "Because. You. Freaked. Out. Mom."

Dollie jumped down onto the sand beneath the jetty, then waited for Jenna to join her.

True. Jenna had freaked out that day on the sailboat. So had Zack. "What did you expect, Dollie? You dove into freezing water and didn't come back up again. Your father and I both freaked, as you put it." It had been the last straw.

Dollie bit her lower lip.

"Do you have any idea how many times your father dove in to look for you? Do you have any idea what was going through our heads when we radioed for help?"

Dollie stared back at Jenna, a glum expression on her face.

"Do you have any idea what we were going through while we waited for the Coast Guard to arrive? I know, it was only about fifteen minutes, but it may just as well have been fifteen days."

Jenna squeezed her eyelids shut trying to eclipse that moment when even Zack had started sobbing as the Coast Guard divers entered the water, jumping off the swinging ladders.

"I went down to look, I don't get it," Zack had told them on the radio. "She swims like a fish; she's been swimming since she was two."

"But Mom, I called you immediately when I saw the chopper arrive." Dollie's voice broke into the vivid scene playing out in Jenna's head. She would probably never forget the moment, or Dollie's words when she answered her cell phone. "Honest, Mom. It's me. I'm on the beach. I can see you. Is all that stuff with the chopper and boats because of me? Look! Look across to the beach. Do you see me waving? I'm on Chrissy's phone."

Had she made too much of the incident? Jenna wondered.

She took off her flip-flops and walked ahead on the narrow strip of sand and rounded the rocks that separated their cove from the neighboring beach as Dollie followed.

They were both quiet for a moment as the gulls squawked above and the frothy, white-flecked waves of the bay lapped around their feet. On days like these, Jenna was hard-pressed to find fault with the North Fork. The water shimmered in the early morning sun under a sky of puffy white clouds. It was so clear, she could see the yacht moored just off Robins Island. It belonged to the owner of the private island, some billionaire hedge fund owner from Manhattan.

Zack knew him. Jenna had never met him. He didn't often visit. She noticed, however, that Zack's sailboat, the *Good Times*, was not on its mooring out in the bay.

"Where's your dad's sailboat?" she directed the question at Dollie in an effort to change the subject, but her daughter shrugged it off. She obviously had still more on her mind.

"Mom, I know I should have been more honest and told you I didn't want to go sailing, and that I wanted to picnic on the beach with my friends, but Dad was excited about taking the sailboat out, and I didn't want to hurt his feelings."

Jenna couldn't ignore the sudden sadness that welled up in her. Dollie was always so solicitous of Zack's feelings, never Jenna's. At least that's the way it seemed. Jenna had no idea what she could do about it, but as if realizing how hurtful her words might have been, Dollie slipped her hand into Jenna's.

"I'm really sorry, Mom," she said. "I had no idea you'd think I'd drowned."

The incident itself had been upsetting enough, but what had bothered Jenna even more eventually was that Dollie had seemed oblivious to the pain her prank had caused her parents. Even Zack agreed that a summer camp that included some "light therapy sessions" was probably a good idea for Dollie.

Which, obviously, it had not been, thought Jenna now, still holding Dollie's hand as they made their way back to the jetty. She was about to suggest that Dollie return with her to the city when Zack appeared, walking toward them, holding a big cooler.

"Good morning." His face creased into a broad smile, no doubt at the sight of Jenna and Dollie getting along. "Just to let you ladies know, I'm headed over to Shelter Island with the couple who stayed here last night. They want to motor around the bay, then meet up with friends for dinner at the Ram's Head Inn. So, we'll dock at Island Boatyard overnight. I'll be back tomorrow."

Jenna shrugged, but Dollie released her hand from Jenna's grip and sidled over closer to her father. "Dad, can I come? I could prepare the snacks and drinks on board?"

Zack and Dollie both eyed Jenna with what she could only describe as pleading looks. It wasn't really necessary. Jenna was already mulling over the request. Maybe it wouldn't be such a bad idea to keep Dollie away from the inn, where Denny Dennison—if he was looking—could easily find her. She sighed theatrically as if to say they'd talked her into it, and before she could say anything else, Dollie gave a whoop of joy and started running toward the inn.

"Get your bathing suit, sunscreen, and leave the cell phone home," Zack called after her, then turned back to face Jenna. "She might make herself useful on trips like these. You never know, she could run the family business one day."

Jenna had no response to that sort of suggestion, so instead she asked, "Where's the sailboat?"

"I took it over to Rick at the boatyard for some repairs."

Jenna nodded, not even really listening to Zack's reply as her thoughts raced on to a more important topic. She knew she had to share her fears with Zack before he and Dollie left. He had to know that Dollie was in danger.

"You realize Dollie walked home from the intersection last night," she said, opening the conversation.

"I know. She wanted to be here for you. Did you scold her for coming home so late?"

Jenna shook her head. "Not for being late home. I wasn't happy that she walked home alone." She paused. Then: "There's something you should know, Zack."

She hesitated, not knowing quite how to start. She hated the idea of reminding Zack of her big scoop. It was something they'd talked about once and never again, and now she was afraid that Zack would never let her return to the city with Dollie if she told him she suspected that Denny Dennison was stalking them.

"Okay," Zack stared at her with an expectant look on his face, then he nodded toward the boat. "Come on, we can talk while I unload this cooler."

Chapter Twenty-Three

Z ack watched Jenna board the *Dollie Too* and tried to hide his amusement. He wasn't being mean. It was just that, even after years of being around boats, Jenna still couldn't board one without clutching at any hard surface or railing as she did so. He offered her a hand, but she ignored it and sat down abruptly on the banquette nearest the steps.

"Go, unload the cooler. I'll wait," she said.

He didn't have a clue as to what was coming, but when he returned on deck, Jenna looked frightened, and suddenly she was making him promise not to let Dollie out of his sight, saying something about a stalker abducting Bethany, and that maybe he was coming after

Dollie. She was talking fast, telling him she was worried her past was catching up with her. He could hardly make any sense of it.

"Slow down," he said, sitting down on the banquette beside her. "Who is after Dollie?"

"Denny Dennison." She stared at him expectantly.

The name exploded in his head.

"You know, the kid I told you about years ago, the one the paper called the spawn?"

He'd never heard Jenna mention that name before. It had always been the "kid," the "boy" or the "spawn."

"Denny Dennison," he repeated the name just to see if he could wrap his tongue around it. Hearing the name now was like getting a bucket of ice water thrown over his head. It took him right back to the fateful trip he'd made up the coast of Florida twenty years ago when Zack King and Denny Dennison had set sail from Fort Lauderdale on the *Manny Boy*.

It was difficult to keep the shocked look off his face, although Jenna obviously misinterpreted his reaction.

"I know," she finally said, "it sounds like a stretch, but I think he might try to hurt Dollie. I wasn't going to say anything until I did a little more digging, but I'm scared, Zack."

He took a deep breath. It was the last thing he'd been expecting to hear. "I don't get it," he said.

Jenna sighed and then, speaking in a hushed tone, she pointed out that Ryan had gotten assaulted within a couple of days of Bethany's disappearance. "Don't you see, that's not a coincidence, Zack. I think he kidnapped Bethany, then came after Ryan and me in the city. By now, he must know he has the wrong girl, but it's obvious he still wants revenge," she added, her lower lip trembling. "I fucked up his life, and he's determined to get even."

"I still don't get it," he said quietly. "Revenge? After all this time? How do you figure that, Jen?" He reached for her hand. "You'd have to be a psycho to hold a grudge and plan revenge for such a long time."

Jenna's head snapped around and she stared at him with narrowed eyes. "That's not a stretch! He probably is a psycho, considering who his father was." Then: "I just found out he was stalking me for several years after that story, at least till Dollie was born, till we brought her here from the city."

"What?"

"Look, I know it sounds crazy, but Ryan got his head kicked in exactly in the same way that Alan, my photographer for the article, got his head kicked in. That's what got me thinking. So, I . . ." Jenna trailed off, looking embarrassed. "Well, on my way here, I stopped at the house where Denny lived with his mother, Rosie. Turns out, they moved a long time ago, but the new owner still had a box with some stuff and mail they'd left behind. She never got a forwarding address for Rosie, and she didn't just want to throw it away, and she forgot she had it until I turned up."

"What?" He knew he was repeating himself, but he had a bad feeling about where the conversation was heading.

"Yes," Jenna nodded. "I looked through it this morning. There was a whole bunch of old articles about Evil Ed, and about serial killers and their children. My exposé destroyed his life, Zack. No wonder he wants revenge. Oh, and there was a photo of Dollie in her stroller in that little park around the corner from my apartment."

"Shit!" He had to turn away and stare across at the water so Jenna couldn't see the horrified look on his face. He shivered. He was getting the heebie-jeebies, wondering what else Jenna was going to drop on him. He squeezed her hand. "But even so, this is almost sixteen years later. He'll surely have moved on by now. Didn't we have this conversation a long time ago, Jen, when you told me what happened to the spawn's wife and child?"

Jenna didn't seem to be listening to him. "It's too much of a coincidence, Zack. I'm thinking he probably saw Bethany walking from the inn to the jitney stop and figured she was Dollie. Four days later he kicks in Ryan's head."

"If he assumed Bethany was Dollie, and if you think he picked her up when she was walking into town, don't you think he would have found out pretty quickly that she's not our daughter? And, if he found out, then what's he done with her?"

"That's why I'm scared. I don't know what he's done with Bethany. But if he knows she's not our daughter, it means Dollie is still in danger."

Zack's thoughts raced. It was obvious Jenna was not going to be dissuaded from her idea of a vengeful Denny Dennison—unless he told her about their sailing trip and told her what had happened to Denny. He didn't have to tell her the whole story. He'd just have to explain that he'd never realized that Denny, his sailing buddy, was the spawn whom Jenna had talked about. He could remind her that she'd only ever called him the spawn, never Denny, and he could tell her that Denny hadn't really talked about his past—and why would he, with a past like that?

On the other hand, maybe he shouldn't say anything to Jenna about himself and Denny Dennison. Maybe, it wasn't entirely a bad idea for Jenna to mention Denny Dennison to Brad or the city cops. It would certainly take the pressure off him as a suspect in McAllister's assault if there appeared to be another person of interest in the mix.

"Why don't you tell all of this to shit-for-brains Brad?"

"Shit-for-brains Brad?" Jenna laughed. "You really don't think much of my idea, do you? Brad will never have a clue as to where to start. Besides, explain to Brad why I think this kid is out for revenge? I don't think so. I didn't tell the cops who are investigating Ryan's assault. I don't want to get Denny Dennison in trouble if I'm wrong. I couldn't do that to him again."

"I think you should just let the cops handle it."

Jenna took a deep breath. "Lola's going to check it out for me first; see if maybe he's got a record, or if he's been in prison or some institution. There's also a stepsister, Adele. I'd like to find her. She may know where Rosie is. And Zack, I do want to find Denny. I don't want to be looking over my shoulder all the time."

He nodded and sighed, as if to agree with her. He saw Dollie ambling down to the dock to the boat. She'd changed into clean shorts and T-shirt and it looked as if she'd washed her hair, but then he realized she was wearing her air pods. So, she was bringing her cell phone even though he'd told her not to. He could tell her to go back to her room and ditch the cell phone, but either way, he'd run out of time to discuss the subject further with Jenna.

"Really, Jen, if you ask me, I think you're wasting your time." It was the best shot he had at persuading her to dump everything on the cops. The way he figured it, Brad wouldn't have a clue as to where to start looking for Denny Dennison, and the city cops, likely, were not much smarter.

Jenna, however, was more resourceful—and tenacious—than the whole bunch of them put together. He did not want her nosing around, digging up old secrets about Denny Dennison and Zack King.

Chapter Twenty-Four

Jenna watched the *Dollie Too* pull away from the dock and felt a sense of deep unease. She wasn't sure if she'd convinced Zack to be as careful as she thought he needed to be. He had seemed doubtful about her theory, otherwise why had he suggested she mention it to "shit-for-brains Brad"? Well, Lola hadn't downplayed the idea, and Lola had a much better grasp on how deviant minds worked. So, Jenna was going to steam right ahead with her search for Denny, and finding his stepsister Adele would be a start.

How difficult could it be to find a jewelry designer in a little town like Tempe? These days, it was so much easier to find anything or anyone with Google. Not like when she'd had to track down Rosie in person. She opened her laptop, entered "jewelry stores, Tempe," and hit the search button.

She was surprised so many popped up. There had to be dozens of them. She tried to recall what Rosie and Carol had told her about Adele. Something about being in college in Arizona. Carol said she'd married the son of a Native American chief. Did that mean the jewelry shop was on a reservation?

"Idiot," Jenna berated herself abruptly. There was a better way. After all, Adele had a fairly distinctive profile: a New Yorker married to the son of a Native American chief. A story like that would have made the pages of some local newspapers, wouldn't it? It would be known among the locals, and most likely would be known by the university alumni association. And if Adele was designing jewelry, then surely she'd have a Facebook page and maybe Instagram and Twitter accounts.

But first Jenna needed to note down the search terms she'd already used to keep track of the searches as she went along, and then she needed to save the document to a flash drive to keep everything connected to her search for Denny off her laptop. If Zack ever got access to her laptop, he didn't need to know she was pursuing something he considered "a waste of her time."

She went looking for flash drives by way of the kitchen, where she greeted Ana. She helped herself to a slice of melon from a plate of assorted fruit before heading across the courtyard to the gray-shingled two-story loft over the garage where she, Zack, and Dollie had lived since Dollie's birth.

Their master suite was a duplex. She had loved the space. Zack had designated an area for her office off a dressing area with a hugely generous closet. Every room had high Palladian windows that looked out over the bay. On the clearest of days, she could sometimes catch glimpses of the ferries traveling between Shelter Island and Greenport. But she had no time for the view this afternoon.

She switched on the desktop computer that she and Zack had shared in their living quarters, and looked in the desk drawer for flash drives. She needed to find a blank one. She inserted the first one and saw a folder labeled INN, which held subfolders for recipes, reservations, menus, tax records, and receipts for purchases for the inn's kitchen. The folders were all copies of those Zack kept on his desktop computer in the inn's kitchen.

A second flash drive was a duplicate of all the same folders and subfolders.

Yes, that was Zack, Jenna thought, always copying and backing up, saving to flash drives and Dropbox. His fear—no, make that paranoia—was that he would lose something he needed to hand over for his tax returns. In the early days, Jenna had laughed at his meticulous record keeping. He was a stickler for filing away documents and scanning invoices, receipts, and any official communication.

"I don't intend to piss off the IRS," he'd say, ignoring her teasing. "Don't need that kind of grief."

She glanced in the folder labeled "Accounts" and saw separate folders for their joint account, a couple of savings accounts, the restaurant account, a marina bank account, and a "Caymans" account.

What? Jenna was about to click on that one—it could prove useful, she thought, when she and Zack got down to dividing up their assets in a divorce—when she noticed another folder titled "Dollie."

Curious, she clicked and realized it was a meticulous digital record of Dollie's vaccination certificates, report cards, attendance notes. Sure enough, the very last entry, a pdf, was titled "End of Year School Report 2019." Zack had scanned it in, circling in the comments section "has made friends. Is popular with most of the class."

Zack had penciled in a note below that: "Sounds NOT like anti-social personality."

Jenna paused before exiting the document. She wondered where Zack had gotten the phrase "antisocial personality." It sounded too clinical for him. Not something she'd have said about Dollie either. On the contrary, she thought Dollie had too many friends, and mostly of the wrong kind. She wondered who had even put the thought in Zack's mind.

Jenna focused on the screen in front of her and looked down the list of files in the "Dollie" folder. She scrolled up to the top, clicking her way through pdfs that were scanned-in entries from the *Baby's First Year* booklet handed out in pediatricians' offices. Zack had scanned in the notes of weight, length, record of vaccinations, ear infections, colds. Then there were entries for first tooth, sitting up, crawling, first words, first steps.

Jenna smiled. Typically, they were listed in strict chronological order. She had seen them, of course. She had made most of the entries in the actual "Baby Book" herself at the weigh-ins. But the next document was a stand-alone Word document that she had never seen before. It was titled "Sleeping @ 6 months."

Jenna glanced at the text: *Asked the nurse at doctor's office about what we should do if Dollie wakes in the night and cries. J does not like getting up. She says her mother told her when J was a baby, she let her cry herself to sleep. Not sure with everything else that's a good combination. First big disagreement with J over Dollie.*

Jenna puzzled over the phrase "everything else." What did that mean? Was that a criticism of her mothering abilities? But there was no use puzzling over the phrase. Zack was not a writer, and the phrase did not seem to belong to any other train of thought on the page. It was no use trying to decipher what "everything else" encompassed, and certainly not worth feeling aggrieved over the fact that her name was abbreviated to "J" throughout, whereas Dollie's was written out in full. Jenna clicked out of the document, glanced down the list in the folder, scrolling down to the next stand-alone pdf: "Kindergarten Interview November 9, 2008. Dollie (4 yrs 5 mos):"

> *Dollie failed her entrance exam to nursery school today. Totally messed it up. J's words, which she hissed at me. OMG. Dollie spilled some tea. Some of it went on the skirt of the dragon who was doing the interview. Dollie said it was an accident. J didn't seem to believe her.*
>
> *But Dollie was nervous because J was nervous. It meant a lot to J to get Dollie into this school. Said she had to work in the city more days a week. She said it would be good for Dollie to go to school in the city; she'd meet lots of different types of kids. I was so sorry for Dollie. J pulled her out of the room. I don't know if J is right that Dollie did it on purpose. Accidents do happen.*

Jenna clicked angrily out of the file. She caught sight of more folders on the list, but she'd seen enough. There were probably more notes about her and how demanding she was of Dollie. She yanked the flash drive out of the port immediately, getting a prompt about how ejecting incorrectly could damage files.

She didn't care. Zack probably had another dozen backups of his Dollie diary.

Why was he even keeping an account of things like her lack of mothering skills? The thought niggled at her, but she had no time to dwell on it as the phone rang. It was Brad. He'd gotten her message, he could stop to pick up the phone in an hour or so on his way home from the station.

"Of course, it's probably password protected anyway," he said, then added: "On second thought, I'll stop by in the morning."

Jenna rolled her eyes. There was not a whit of urgency in Brad Halsey's voice. It sounded as if he'd already decided that examining Bethany's cell phone was going to be a fruitless task. Well, that was okay with her. It would give her time to scan Bethany's texts and phone calls herself. She'd probably do a much better job of it than Chief Brad.

She retrieved the phone from the drawer where she'd tossed it earlier that morning. Thankfully, the phone was not password protected. She clicked on the phone icon and scrolled through Bethany's contacts, then through her recent calls. There were nine missed calls, six from someone by the name of Sara at a Suffolk County number, with the area code 631.

Jenna hit the messages icon and saw Sara's name at the top of the list. She clicked on the name and arrived at the last one from Sara to Bethany:

Where r u, Betts? need to know ur ok.

Jenna scrolled up through the texts, noting there were fifteen texts from Sara with no replies from Bethany.

She stopped at the one that was dated on the Sunday Bethany had disappeared. From Sara:

You must be having fun. I'll cover 4 u in class. Have u moved into the MBR yet?

Jenna continued the upward scroll through dates that went back another month. She bit her lower lip as the words materialized and took shape in front of her eyes. There were more than a dozen texts between the two women before Bethany's disappearance.

One was dated the day after Jenna had left for the city.

Ding dong, the witch is gone, Bethany had texted.

Then, scrolling upward to the week Zack had driven Dollie to the summer camp in Maine:

Can't believe it. Best time EVER. So cool when u have all nite. Will tell all when I c u. Cover 4 me.

Scrolling even further upward, Jenna stopped at a text that read:

He says SHE isn't interested in him anymore.

Sara had texted back:

All husbands say that.

Bethany had not replied.

Jenna stared at the words for a while. *Best time EVER.* So, not just the one time. *So cool when u have all nite.* As opposed to what? thought Jenna. A quick grope in the car? No wonder Zack had volunteered so eagerly to drive Bethany to the jitney stop on Sundays.

He was lying. It was obvious there was more going on between them than just one night in a Maine B and B. So, maybe that's why Zack hadn't seemed very concerned about Bethany's disappearance, or Jenna's fear that Dollie might be in danger. Maybe he knew exactly where Bethany was and why he'd concocted a story about Bethany leaving the inn in a hissy fit.

Jenna looked across from her balcony to the bay to the spot where Zack's sailboat, the *Good Times*, should have been moored. She now realized that Zack's reply about repairs at the Island Boatyard on Shelter Island hadn't made much sense. Hank in their own marina was pretty handy when it came to sailboat repairs, so why take it to Rick's?

She wondered if Zack had moved the boat to the Island Boatyard so that Bethany could live on board until Jenna was out of the way again.

So, maybe Jenna was on the wrong track. Maybe Bethany's disappearance had nothing to do with Ryan being assaulted. Maybe

Bethany was safe and sound on Zack's sailboat. Maybe nobody was after her or Dollie.

She had to take a deep breath, and then another to calm down.

Of course, if Bethany was safe and sound, there was no need for Brad to know anything about Zack and Bethany. Jenna could check out that angle all by herself when Zack returned from his trip with the Smiths and there was no danger of bumping into him at the Island Boatyard. It would be embarrassing if they ran into each other while she was snooping around.

She hit edit and checked off all the texts between Sara and Bethany. For a second, she hesitated. But no, if Bethany was sitting on the sailboat waiting for Jenna to leave, then she hadn't disappeared and Brad certainly didn't need to know about these texts; if she had been taken by Denny, then none of these texts would be of any help to Brad in finding her anyway.

She hit the little trash can icon, erasing all "evidence" of an affair between Bethany and Zack.

She took another deep breath. Even if Denny had not abducted Bethany, there was still the question of who had beaten Ryan half to death. She needed to track down Denny, if only to answer that question one way or the other. It was the least she could do for Ryan.

She picked up her own cell phone and clicked on Ryan's name. She knew her call would probably go to voice mail again, but she needed to hear his voice—even if only on his recorded greeting.

Chapter Twenty-Five

20 Years Earlier: August 1999

They were both on deck on the *Manny Boy* when the squall came up. One minute they were sailing along in blue skies and sunshine. Then, almost in the blink of an eye, the wind shifted direction, and the clouds came speeding at them. Ugly, dark, flat-bottomed clouds with gray streaks underneath that for sure meant a slab of rain was going to blast them any moment. Like most squalls, it seemed to come from nowhere as a single, sudden thirty-five-knot blast that set the sails flogging wildly as the boat rounded up.

Denny, with less experience than Zack, knew enough to realize they were seriously over-canvassed. He started to drop all the sails just as Zack barked the order to do so.

He hooked his safety harness to the jackline and looked around to make sure everything on the deck and in the cockpit was secured. Only Zack remained unsecured, but there was no point in saying anything to him.

Denny knew he wouldn't listen.

Zack had explained his views on safety harnesses a dozen times. "Are you kidding, dude?" He'd laughed at Denny. "Tether myself to a boat so I can get dragged along or under? No thanks." At least he was wearing his inflatable flotation device, Denny observed.

Just then the sailboat turned into the wind and the boom swung across the boat, hitting Zack squarely in the head and sweeping him toward the railings. The last thing Denny saw of his buddy was Zack's deck shoes flying off his feet as he sailed up in the air and overboard.

It was over in seconds. Spray flew over the bow, and then the rain arrived. A torrential downpour that obscured everything. Denny couldn't see a thing.

He moved unsteadily toward the spot where he'd thought he'd seen Zack go up and over. He saw nothing in the water. He just couldn't see a thing through the sheet of rain cascading down onto the boat, but he grabbed a couple of life preservers and hurled them over the side.

He recalled being told that the first gusts of a squall were always the strongest, and though the rain was still coming down like crazy, suddenly the boat stopped bucking like a wild bronco. And then, the rain eased up enough for Denny to spot his buddy about thirty feet from the boat's starboard side.

His heart sank as he saw Zack floating facedown. "C'mon," Denny urged silently, watching for any sign of Zack's attempt to right himself into a faceup position as the wind died down. "C'mon, buddy, let's see your face."

Denny gave it less than thirty seconds before he made his way to the cockpit and picked up the radio transmitter to make the Mayday call. They were out of the squall zone and apparently not that far offshore when the first Coast Guard vessel arrived not more than a half hour later. Two coast guards boarded the *Manny Boy*, while the crew remaining in the vessel pivoted in ever-widening circles to pick up Zack.

It took them almost thirty minutes before they brought him back to the *Manny Boy*. By that time the squall had departed and the skies were blue again. The coast guards who'd boarded had taken control of the sailboat and calmed Denny down. He was surprised to see that the one who was examining his face was a woman, something he noticed only when she opened a first-aid kit. "My name's Rachel," she told him, adding that his left cheek needed "a bit of attention." He'd barely noticed any pain when a line had come loose during the strongest of the winds and whipped across his face.

"You may need stitches," Rachel said.

Denny nodded and averted his eyes from Zack lying bedraggled on the deck. The coast guards who'd brought him back were still working to revive him.

"Come," Rachel beckoned him over to one of banquettes on deck. "Why don't you tell me what happened?"

Denny shook his head and swallowed hard as she handed him a flask of water. "I don't get it. Why did he stay facedown?" he asked Rachel. "I was waiting for him to right himself. I should have gone in . . ."

Rachel placed a hand on his forearm. "It wouldn't have helped. You were better off calling for us. Unfortunately the flotation devices you have on this boat aren't the type that automatically turn someone in the water faceup. Is it your boat?"

Denny shook his head. "We're sailing it from Fort Lauderdale to Block Island for the owner."

Rachel nodded. "So, we'll take the boat into the Lake Worth Inlet, to the town marina, where they'll check it out for damage, and we'll get the EMS to meet us there."

She reached into her breast pocket for a notebook and pencil. "But let me get down a few details here." She opened the notebook. "Let's start with names."

"Sure." He nodded, glancing over at Zack, lying still on the deck. "Denny Dennison."

"That's two *N*s in both first and last names?"

Denny nodded as Rachel looked across to where one of the coast guards with Zack was getting to his feet, shaking his head "no" at her.

She put her hand on Denny's arm. "I'm sorry. There's nothing more they can do." Then, in a gentler voice she asked, "Do you know who his next of kin is?"

Denny blinked. And, then blinked again. "Next of kin?"

"Yes," Rachel nodded. "Denny's next of kin?"

It took him maybe five seconds, maybe less to realize that she'd assumed he'd given her his buddy's name first. It took him maybe another five seconds to let it ride. Maybe not even five.

"Yeah." He nodded. "Yes, of course I know Denny's next of kin." He looked again across the deck at his sailing buddy's body now being covered by a black tarp. Then he looked at Rachel. "You're sure he's gone? You can't do anything? At all?"

Rachel shook her head. "I'm really sorry."

Denny buried his face in his hands for a moment, then he said. "It's his mom. His next of kin is his mom. Her name is Rosie Miller. She lives on Long Island." He took a long, deep breath. "I've met his mom. I know her. Do you mind if I call her first before you guys call?

It might be easier if I break the news to her. She'll want to know I was with him."

———◊◊◊——— ———◊◊◊———

Hours later, after the medical examiner had driven away with Zack's body, after the marina staff looked over the *Manny Boy* and declared no damage done, after he asked them to find him a new crew member so he could complete his trip to Block Island, Denny returned to the sailboat and sank into the captain's chair, letting the soft rocking of the boat lull him into a half sleep.

There was still time to correct his lie, he told himself. Tell them that it was Zack who'd drowned, not Denny Dennison. But did he really need to do it?

Why not let it ride? Zack King was a much better name than Denny Dennison. Zack King may have lived in a trailer park with a mother who sounded half batty, but that was still better than going through life as the "spawn" of a sadistic serial killer. Look where that had gotten him with Lisa.

He shook himself awake and went below to open the only bottle of liquor in the galley, a bottle of Jack Daniels. He poured himself a glass and sat down to make mental notes of what he knew about Zack King.

He and Zack had known each other for almost a year, since they'd met in the Islands and Zack had signed him on as a mate on a sailing trip to deliver a boat from St. Thomas to Miami. They'd sailed together since then, and partied together between deliveries of boats to rich old coots who then sat on their decks at the ends of their jetties without going anywhere. They'd been wildly successful—especially in picking up women. Sometimes they were mistaken for brothers, once even for twins—though the woman who'd made that guess had been sloppily drunk. Still, they'd spent enough time together for Denny to know almost everything he needed to know about Zack King.

While Denny, naturally, had chosen to keep his life story to himself, Zack had regaled him with his stories of a hardscrabble life growing up in a trailer—albeit in a trailer park on the ocean—with a mother who'd tried to do her best for him. His mother had owned the trailer so Zack owned it now. He recalled Zack telling him he was going to rent it out.

Bye-bye, trailer park, Zack had said when they'd gone together to clear out the trailer. Denny had heard that story many times: how Miranda had been thrown out of the house by her father, Jeremiah, when he discovered she was pregnant; how Zack felt bitter because Miranda had died young. She'd had a hard life, he said. He blamed his grandfather. She'd also apparently drunk like a fish and, in between the drinking and her "batty" episodes, she had threatened to kill her son if he ever spoke to his grandfather. Once she was dead though, he told Denny, there was nothing to stop him sailing north and introducing himself to the old fogey. It sounded like his grandfather had some serious assets.

Denny always listened because, really, he hadn't had any choice when they were trapped together on a boat. He'd heard the whole story. More than once. Zack was excited about his rich grandfather. He told Denny he was going to quit sailing to live the good life with his grandfather on the North Fork of Long Island.

So, what was to stop Denny from sliding into Zack King's shoes and living the good life with a grandfather who'd never set eyes on his grandson? What would be the harm in checking out the lay of the land? And, if things got a little uncomfortable with the old man, Denny would just take off. No harm done. On the other hand, if things turned out okay, he could bury Denny forever and never have to worry about his screwed-up past again.

In the meantime, he needed to square things away with his mother. He needed Rosie to fly down to make the formal identification of her "son." Maybe then, they could both move on with their lives. She would understand. He knew she would. She would help him bury Denny Dennison forever. He'd never again have to answer to any name but Zack King.

Chapter Twenty-Six

Week Two: Monday Morning

He woke to the smell of sizzling bacon wafting in from the galley but didn't move. He lay under the sheets thinking about Jenna. For a couple of seconds, he entertained a fantasy that she had decided to surprise him and Dollie. Eggs and bacon were Jenna's specialty. Especially scrambled eggs. He'd taught her to cook, and now she made them light and fluffy with chopped fresh chives and just a hint of grated Vermont cheddar cheese. She could easily have driven to Greenport and gotten the ferry over to the marina. But he knew he was deluding himself. Jenna didn't want to be with him; she didn't want to be on a boat. He punched at his pillow and groaned. Jenna was off on her wild goose chase, trying to track down

Denny. What had seemed like a good idea yesterday, to suggest that Jenna tell the cops about Denny, suddenly didn't seem like a good idea at all.

What if, by some incredible stroke of genius or luck, Jenna or the cops managed to track "Denny" down to Florida? What if she discovered, according to all official records, that he'd drowned back in 1999? Then, naturally, she'd want to know who had taken the photo of Dollie five years later.

Dear God, what kind of dumb luck was it that Jenna had found a photo of Dollie that he'd given his mother all those years ago? He'd always been afraid his mother would somehow give the game away before she moved out of that house. But he'd had to tell her what he'd done. He couldn't have just shut her out of his new life. Not after everything she'd been through. And while she'd been very understanding about what he'd done, she'd drawn the line at announcing to all her friends that her son had drowned. There was no way she could pull off playing a distraught mother, she'd said. The best she could do was suggest they'd had a falling out, and then she could tell everybody, "He's gone."

What sheer dumb luck that the new owners of the Seaford house had kept the box with all that crap his mother had left behind. Jenna had gotten that wrong too. The newspaper clippings were not clippings he had collected. It was Lisa who'd gotten hysterical and asked her cousin who worked in a library to get her all the old newspaper articles about Evil Ed. She'd wanted to know everything about him, and then she'd seen the TV shows about other serial killers' children. She'd gone on and on about how it didn't prove anything that Denny himself was as fine and normal as the next guy. Like red hair, bad genes could skip a generation, she'd said, and she'd convinced herself that their son would be born as twisted as his grandfather.

Finally, she'd lost it altogether and decided she had to get rid of the baby.

That had all been on Lisa. He'd been relieved to be rid of her by the time he'd spent some months in the islands, where no one had heard anything about him or his father. Almost like a new life. He'd never blamed Jenna for Lisa's death, or the baby's. Not for any of it. He'd never had any thoughts of revenge. By the time he was on the North Fork with Jeremiah King, he had no regrets whatsoever about the turn his life had taken.

But if Jenna somehow discovered that "Denny Dennison" had drowned twenty years ago, she'd dig deeper. He knew how she investigated stories. She was relentless. She'd want to know who had taken the photo of Dollie, and somewhere along the way she'd find out Zack King had been the skipper of the *Manny Boy*. And then what?

"Daaad!" Dollie's voice rose above the slapping of water against the hull. "Dad, breakfast's almost ready! Come and get it."

Her voice brightened his mood, and he immediately shut down his terrifying train of thought. He slid out of bed and stumbled into the main cabin, eyeing the undercooked bacon stacked on his plate. "Oh, yummy." He grabbed the top slice and chewed diligently. "Toast?"

"Yep. Coming right—" Dollie shrieked as wisps of smoke rose from the toaster. "Shit. Oh shit!"

He laughed, reaching for two more slices and swapping them out for the burnt offerings. "We got plenty of bread."

"But not that many eggs," she countered, pointing to the congealed mess on his plate. "I made them all. Eat."

After they'd dropped off the Smiths at the dock in Coecles Harbor the previous day, they'd gotten a ride over to the village store to buy some farm-fresh provisions, honey, and eggs, but there'd only been a half carton left.

"Dad?" Dollie was staring hard at him as he chewed. "Why did you ask someone to take the sailboat to Florida?'"

The question caught him off guard. He didn't think she'd been listening when he told Rick he'd hired a couple of kids to deliver the sailboat, the *Good Times*, to Key Biscayne after Rick finished with the repairs.

"That's where you want to be?" Rick asked. "Hurricane season is just starting."

"I know."

Dollie was still staring at him, waiting for an answer.

"I want it in place for the winter," he said. "I'd like to take your mother down to somewhere warm when the snow starts."

Dollie laughed. "Mom won't go. She hates the boat, and she hates the sun."

He shrugged and grabbed a slice of burnt toast, ignoring Dollie's puzzled expression. "Are you ready to cast off?" he asked.

"Will be as soon as I've cleaned up in here."

Zack stepped out of the sliding doors onto the deck and immediately found himself worrying again about Jenna and her search for Denny.

Sure, all these years he'd had no reason to say anything. Jenna had never actually mentioned Denny Dennison by name so, okay, why would he have admitted that, as Zack King, he knew, or that he'd met the serial killer's spawn?

But now that the name had come out in the open, shouldn't he have had some reaction like, hey, that name sounds familiar; that was the name of a sailing buddy I met down in the islands; and oh yeah, he drowned on one of our sailing trips.

He could have even helpfully suggested that it was the "spawn's" mother—mad with grief over losing her son—who had stalked Jenna and Dollie and taken the photo.

But then, inevitably, Jenna would have circled back to the tricky question. He could hear her zeroing in on it in that way she had of making everything sound like an interrogation.

So, she would say, Denny never told you he was a serial killer's son. I get that. And he never told you he was running from an exposé that called him a spawn. I get that, too. I understand why he might not have mentioned that the newspaper exposé had led to the deaths of his wife and unborn baby. So, I can see how you didn't put it all together when I told you about my article on the "spawn." But, Zack, am I supposed to believe that five years after Denny drowned, you called me—of all the travel writers in New York—out of the blue, by sheer coincidence?

How on earth was he going to answer that one?

Chapter Twenty-Seven

Sixteen Years Earlier: April 2003–July 2004

E ven though the television was turned down low, Zack heard her name loud and clear.

"And, now for those of you looking for a long weekend at an affordable price somewhere close to home, we have Jenna Sinclair, from the travel magazine Hither and Yon *to give us the lowdown on some terrific B and Bs. Good morning, Jenna."*

He turned away from the omelet sizzling in the pan to look at the TV screen. The TV was tuned to one of those local morning shows filled with fluff like cooking tips and celebrity gossip. Zack slid the omelet onto a plate, carried it through to the guests sitting on the patio and quickly returned to the TV screen. Yes, that was her, for sure, but obviously no longer working for that rag that had destroyed—or at least had tried to destroy—his life. He kept his eyes on her for the entirety of her time on camera, but he hardly heard what she was saying.

Instead, his thoughts churned with how he could get her to drive out to the North Fork to visit his inn. Why? he'd later ask himself. Why risk it? Why play with fire? His life was a piece of cake these days. As the grandson of the late Jeremiah King, he had it made.

But the idea took root, and he couldn't shake it. Maybe life had gotten a little too comfortable for him. Maybe he was looking to spice things up a bit. The minute he saw her on TV, he decided he had to meet Jenna Sinclair. He bought a copy of the travel magazine and found the short article she'd written about a Hudson Valley B and B. He picked up the phone and invited her to the inn. He discovered during their short conversation that she didn't play golf and she didn't like boats or being out on the water.

He stashed that tidbit at the back of his mind even as he wondered if there would be some flicker of recognition from her when they met; whether she might say, "Don't I know you from somewhere?" Of course, there was no real reason why that would happen. After all, they'd never met face to face. It was his mother who'd met Jenna and been bamboozled into spilling the big family secret.

And Jenna hadn't been there on the night the photographer from her shitty newspaper had crept up on him and Lisa and taken those awful photos.

Anyway, since then, he'd spent time in the islands, sailing as crew up and down the East Coast. That experience had toughened him up. He was no longer the pudgy dork he'd once been. No reason for Jenna Sinclair to make any connection between the "hunk" he'd turned into and the dweeb he'd been back then.

Still and all, he had his emergency plan, if worse came to worst: accidents happened on the water—especially to city folk who didn't have the foggiest notion about boating safety.

That nasty little idea flew straight out of his head the moment he laid eyes on Jenna Sinclair. There was one prickly moment when she stared at him for longer than would be considered polite by some folks, but then she blushed and asked him about his scar. In that moment, he decided he wanted Jenna more than he'd ever wanted any other woman.

At first, though, he wasn't sure what Jenna wanted from him. But he listened—he'd always been good at reading between the lines—and he eventually figured out that her live-in lover, McAllister, wasn't quite the dreamboat or soul mate Jenna made him sound. Sure, he had a big, important job, but there seemed to be another woman hovering in the background.

Jenna never spelled it out, of course, but he figured she made the trips to the inn to make McAllister sit up and pay attention—maybe make him jealous.

So, he made his moves slowly and carefully. "I like you, Zack," she said on her second weekend visit, "I really do, but, you know, I'm not really single." She said it as she stretched out on a chaise in a skimpy little two-piece bathing suit and let him apply sunscreen.

Sure enough, came the day—right after he assured her he always walked around the property after dark to check that all was safe— when she left the door of the cottage open. The lights were off in the room, but he saw her in bed by the light of the full moon.

"You've left the door open," he said, stating the obvious through the screen door before opening it and stepping into the room. "You need to lock it, Jenna. You may think it's safe out here, but never take chances."

She made a low, throaty sound as if she had been sleeping and he had just woken her. "Zack? What's up?"

He took a couple more steps into the room as she sat up in bed, pulling the sheet up to her chest. "I could have been someone dangerous," he told her.

He thought she said, "You are," but then she added, "I'm not scared. I can look after myself."

He laughed and took a few more steps toward the bed. "How exactly would you do that?"

"I have a gun."

"Really?"

"Yep," she sounded playful. "It's right here, in the nightstand." She moved toward the nightstand, clutching the sheet to her body, but then drew back against the headboard. He didn't know if she was joking or playacting. As he reached for her, she dodged to the other side of the bed, pulling the sheet around herself, but not before he noticed she was naked underneath.

He hesitated for a moment, then moved across the bed, slowly reaching for her hair, pulling her face close to his. "Naughty Jenna," he said softly. "Door open, naked in bed."

"What are you going to make me do?" she asked, breathing heavily, but not moving another inch.

He realized then what her game was. She wanted to pretend that he was the bad guy who was going to "force" her into things she shouldn't be doing so she could tell herself she wasn't really cheating on her editor boyfriend. Which was just fine with him. He could "play" the role of the bad guy if that's what it took. He pulled the sheet down and pulled her to him and kissed her and pushed apart her thighs, hesitating just a second to give her time to change her mind. Then he took her.

It was the way it worked for the rest of the summer. So long as he played the bad guy—whether he was a modern-day pirate boarding the sailboat while she was sunbathing, tying her wrists to the boat cleats with her silk scarves, a persistent inn guest finding her alone in the hot tub, or an overattentive waiter determined to give her the best service possible she always played along. And if playing those kinds of games made it easier for her to cheat on Ryan McAllister, that was just fine with him. He was having the best summer of his life.

———⟜〰⊱ ⟜〰⊱———

It was his buddies who got him thinking about marriage.

"Smart city chick and a writer. What's she doing with you?" Sol, another marina owner asked him after Jenna had spent a long weekend at the inn. Sol was right in a way. Zack knew he'd never be better than McAllister who was smooth and sophisticated, and a man about town who was also smart with words. But Zack was smart in other ways. He decided to go for it. He wasn't sure if he was in love with Jenna Sinclair, but he was definitely in love with the idea of Jenna becoming Mrs. King.

Marrying Jenna would be the icing on his cake. It would give him more respectability in the community. And she'd look great in the photos that he regularly submitted to the local newspapers as ads for the inn and marina.

She'd be there right alongside him. The Kings, proprietors of the Kings Inn and Marina: a fit, good-looking couple if ever there was one!

He also knew he'd be shoving it up McAllister's ass. Whatever else, Ryan McAllister was not going to like the idea of Jenna leaving him for a country hick. And, really, it was Ryan McAllister who'd been the editor pushing Jenna to write the slimy story about Denny Dennison. So, he deserved to suffer a little.

He wasn't surprised that Jenna tried to wriggle out of it at the very last minute. While he understood that maybe she'd never be truly happy with him, he laid it on thick, dredging up every bit of emotion he'd ever felt to more convincingly tell Jenna how she was the only woman who could replace his dead love.

He didn't care if the only reason she married him was pity, or guilt; he was sure he could make their marriage work one way or another. He'd keep the pool warm, keep the kitchen and wine cellar well stocked, give her time to herself to do her fact-checking assignments in the city. He would feed her and satisfy her, do all the things he did now when she came to visit.

He didn't think it would be difficult.

When they finally tied the knot a week after the original date, he was happy that his reckless impulse to meet Jenna was going to end as a happily ever after and not as an accident in the bay.

The feeling didn't last.

<hr />

A couple of weeks after the wedding Jenna told him she was pregnant. The news was so unexpected, he couldn't keep the shock off his face.

She laughed at his reaction. "Don't look so surprised," she said. "We've been screwing like rabbits for the last six months." Then she took his hands and placed them on her breasts. "I feel better than I ever thought I would—very horny."

Sitting on a big, flat rock on the beach, she spread her thighs to show she was not wearing underwear. He straddled her in seconds, faking a passion he didn't feel. Deep down inside, he was in a fury.

He thought about the stained wedding dress. She'd been so upset about spilling wine on it, but she'd never mentioned she was with McAllister when she'd done it. Now, he could picture it all: he no longer had any doubt that Jenna had spent her last night in the city with McAllister because that's how she'd gotten pregnant. That's how it had happened. There was no way the baby could be his because he'd had himself fixed. Like a dog. Right after Lisa's botched abortion, he'd gone into a doctor's office and had asked for the procedure so that he could never make another kid.

So, of course he was shocked and angry. It was all he could do to hide his rage when Jenna made the big announcement. He wondered if his thrusting could dislodge what was surely no bigger than a tiny seed at this point. He wanted to get rid of it. He wanted to get rid of Jenna that day. He was so angry he thought if he rammed into her hard enough she might fall backward and smash her head on the rocks. It would be no less than she deserved.

Chapter Twenty-Eight

June 2019
Week Two: Monday

J enna was breathing heavily as she reached the top of the wooden stairs that rose from the beach to the parking lot of the Horton Point Lighthouse. Going down was the easy part. She'd bounced down to the beach in a matter of minutes. Coming back up was slightly more challenging. There were 116 steps at this popular scenic spot, which, at this early hour of the day, was more like Jenna's personal StairMaster. Zack had brought her to this landmark years ago. The lighthouse was about a ten-minute drive from the inn; close enough for Jenna to make the round trip and take the steps twice down and up in less than an hour. It was such a high to get all that air into her lungs as she looked out from the top of the steps all the way across the Sound to the shores of Connecticut. So, of course, if anyone ever asked her, then yes, there were things she would miss about the North Fork once she'd be living in the city permanently. But you couldn't have everything, she thought, as her cell phone rang in her fanny pack.

She retrieved the phone as she started down the steps for the second time that morning. It was Hank from the marina forwarding a call. She had stopped at the marina to tell Hank where she was going, and to ask him to forward any phone calls to her before Ana arrived. The male on the other end introduced himself as Sam from Briny Breezes. Somewhere at the back of Jenna's mind, she recalled Zack mentioning the place as the trailer park where his mother had lived in Florida.

"So, Sam from Briny Breezes," Jenna responded, "what can I do for you?"

It turned out that Sam and his mother had been neighbors of Zack's mother, Miranda. Sam's mother had passed away a couple of months ago, so Sam had taken over from her in keeping an eye on Miranda's trailer. According to the young man, the trailer had been rented out till recently on a regular basis "as per Zachariah's instructions."

"Thing is, we had a huge storm a few days ago, and water got into Miranda's trailer through a leaky window and leaked into a padlocked closet. I got the padlock off to mop up the water and I found some stuff that Zachariah left here when he went north."

"Stuff?" Jenna had no idea what Sam from Briny Breezes was talking about.

"Well, it's a little leather travel bag that was in this closet. The bag got a little wet, but the stuff inside is fine. You know, it's old photos and knickknacks Zachariah didn't want to throw out immediately after his mom died. He locked everything up in the closet."

"A closet?" Jenna echoed.

"Yes. A lot of owners around here have stuff they lock in an owner's closet while they rent their homes out to other people," Sam said, "but Zachariah's never been back for it since."

Jenna giggled suddenly. "Zachariah? I've never heard anyone call my husband that. We all call him Zack."

"Well, Zack is definitely easier," Sam acknowledged. "But his mother never called him anything but Zachariah. It kind of stuck down here." A moment later he said: "I fixed the window where the rain got in. You don't have to worry about that."

Jenna thanked him. "Okay, Sam, I'll let Zachariah know," she said. She ascertained that the number that had shown up on her cell phone was the number where they could reach Sam again and hung up just as she reached the bottom step.

Feeling slightly winded from the conversation, she started up the steps again, and took each one staring down at her sneakers so as to not to trip. She was almost at the top of the stairs when she looked up and saw Brad.

W-T-F! Her heart thudded hard against her ribs in fear.

"I swung by the inn to pick up Bethany's phone. Hank told me you were here. He said you had the phone with you and were going to stop by the station later to drop it off."

"Yes, I have it in the car."

Jenna brushed past him and walked to her Jeep.

"I figured I'd save you the trip."

So you went totally out of your way, thought Jenna, when I have to drive right past the station on my way back anyway. Brad was creeping her out, no doubt about it.

She opened the passenger-side door and reached into her glove compartment for Bethany's phone.

"I have some additional news about Bethany." Brad cleared his throat. "A couple of things don't add up."

"Like?"

"Bethany didn't get on any jitney to Riverhead that Sunday. I checked with the bus line."

That fit, thought Jenna. If Zack had wanted her to stay, and if she was hiding out somewhere close like on the sailboat, then, of course, she hadn't boarded the jitney.

Jenna handed Brad the cell phone.

"Should tell you, there's something else that doesn't make any sense at all, but I thought maybe young Zack could weigh in? Should I stop by the inn later, perhaps?"

Jenna shook her head. "He's out on the boat with some inn guests."

He seemed to be deliberating with himself before he spoke again. "Thing is, she didn't even make a reservation for a jitney that Sunday. That's unusual not to have a rez for a Sunday. Busiest day of the week going back toward the city and so on."

"Huh." Jenna assumed a thoughtful expression. It was looking more and more like her hunch about Bethany was right.

"Jenna?" She realized Brad was staring at her.

"I don't know what to tell you, Brad."

"I'm sorry," he said. "I can see I caught you at the wrong time."

"No, it's okay," Jenna hurried to correct the impression that she wasn't paying attention. "It's just that I don't really have an answer for you, Chief. I wasn't here that weekend. Maybe you'll find something on her phone to solve the mystery. I did have a quick look. Couldn't really figure anything out. It has a whole bunch of her contacts on it though. One of them might know something."

Brad raised an eyebrow, looked as if he had another question, then held up the cell phone. "You're right. I'd better take a look at this. Might be a real good pointer on here as to what she did." He gave her a mini salute. "Enjoy the day, Jenna," he said, and then finally left, but not before giving her a long, lingering look and tapping her lightly on her forearm. "You should get some sunscreen on you. Sun's getting hot."

Jenna's skin felt itchy and hot as his eyes swept over her. Zack was right; there was something smarmy about Brad. She wished now she had not deleted the texts between Bethany and her friend. No reason why Bethany could not have deleted most of them herself, but the last three or four panicked ones from Sara had come in later in that week after Bethany had left the inn and left her cell phone behind. If Brad discovered that the texts had been deleted, it would be simple to deduce that Jenna was the one who'd deleted them. She could just picture how Brad would enjoy cornering her to accuse her of tampering with evidence.

Chapter Twenty-Nine

Zack heard Dollie gathering up the plates and flatware in the galley and washing them off in the little sink as he untied the lines and started up the motor. They had the best part of the day before they had to return to Coecles to pick up the Smiths and bring them back to the inn. As he pulled away from the dock, Dollie joined him. She was not wearing her inflatable flotation device.

She rolled her eyes when he told her to put it on. "Daaaad, look at the water. It's so calm."

He knew they were going to go through the same old nonsense. Dollie would tell him she didn't need to wear her flotation device because there was no law saying so now that she was older than thirteen;

he would retort, saying it was the law on his boats. Then she'd go below and return wearing a life vest because she knew he preferred her to wear the inflatable flotation device, and she'd leave the life vest unzipped, and he would tell her to zip it up.

"This is heavy . . ." Dollie whined as he navigated past a couple of small sailboats heading out of the harbor. She knew better. Wearing a flotation device or life vest, whether on the motorboat or the sailboat, was not negotiable. The accident that had claimed the real Zack King's life had taught him that a storm or squall could rise up from nowhere.

Dollie's grunting noises as she zipped up her vest broke into his thoughts. He made no comment as she moved to the bow to stare at the water. He knew she was sulking.

There were so many things he didn't understand. For one, why had she colored her golden hair jet black? Why the nose ring and the black fingernail polish? What was that all about? Was it some inner demonic character flaw, or just one of those fashion trends kids followed these days? Was she going to mature with time or spiral out of control one day? Of course, he understood that experimenting with weed and booze was normal these days. But there had been darker incidents with Dollie that seriously worried him.

He navigated around the island till he spotted a secluded cove where they could anchor and spend the day. Dollie immediately discarded her life vest and stripped down to a bathing suit.

"Dad? Shall I get you a beer?"

He shook his head. Then, because she was making an effort for him, he relented. "Okay, the Coors Light, please."

"What about a joint?" She laughed, quickly adding, "Just kidding."

Typical Dollie. Her moods changed like quicksilver from dark to bright and back again. In that way, she was a lot like him. But she wasn't as good at hiding the bad moods. At times like that, he was convinced she had to be his daughter after all, despite the odds. Doctors had told him that it could happen after his procedure, and there were things she did that made him think there were darker waters swirling beneath her surface. He'd never forgotten Lisa babbling on about genes skipping a generation. So, he'd made notes about all the little incidents that worried him. In the beginning, he'd wanted to share his concerns with some child therapist or psychologist, but he hadn't wanted Jenna to find out.

Then again, he'd tell himself he was overreacting, that she was just a normal teenager, and that she was most likely McAllister's after all. But he'd never really been sure one way or the other.

These days it didn't matter. It really hadn't mattered to him since the day she was born. His initial anger had evaporated well before then. His standing as a solid member of the community had grown. He'd even been invited to run for the town council just after Dollie turned one. Coincidental perhaps, but he figured that if Jenna was the icing on his cake, then Dollie was the sugar sprinkles on top. He was a husband and father. He had "gravitas" as Jenna had once said. He hadn't wanted to ask her what it meant, but it sounded good.

True, Jenna and McAllister had destroyed his first family, but they had made amends—and provided him with replacements. It all had a bit of a karmic touch about it.

He decided to join Dollie in the water. It was glorious, if a little on the cool side for him. He was soon back on deck, basking in a sun that was getting stronger by the hour. Definitely a joint would have made everything perfect. He had a feeling everything was going to be okay, after all.

Karma was on his side, and he was just being a nervous Nellie. Jenna's talk about tracking down Denny Dennison should not bother him. Nor should all her spouting about finding Adele and Rosie. For a start, his stepsister didn't know a thing. As for Rosie, well, she was a literal dead end.

So, how could Jenna possibly even come close to finding out that Denny was dead? Or that he had been dead for twenty years? Or that he had died on a sailing trip with Zack King? How would she even track him down to Florida? Why would she even think about checking death certificates? Why would she think of checking death certificates in Palm Beach County? In records that were twenty years old? They probably didn't even have them all computerized yet. She'd literally have to trip over Denny's gravestone to find out he was dead.

Chapter Thirty

Jenna returned to the inn to find an email from Gordon at *My World*. Her interview in Monte Carlo was a "go," he informed her. The editor-in-chief had approved three expenses-paid days in Monaco.

Jenna sighed. It would be difficult to leave while Bethany was missing, although she might be able to persuade Zack that it would be a new, eye-opening experience for Dollie to travel with her to the French Riviera. She would work on it when Zack and Dollie returned. Zack might even welcome the idea of time to himself—if, indeed, he had Bethany stashed away on his sailboat or elsewhere. In the meantime, she had work to do. First, to continue with her search for Adele and Rosie. Jenna googled the University of Arizona for the alumni association's contact number. She placed the call and left a message saying she wanted to get in touch with one of their alumnae, Adele Miller.

Next, she tried Ryan's cell phone, which, as she expected, went straight to voice mail. This time she didn't leave a message, but called his office at *CityMagazine*. His assistant, Cindy, told Jenna that Ryan was "making progress," according to Teddi. Cindy did not know any details or what "progress" meant, and she didn't have a clue as to what the cops were doing in their investigation. All she knew was that her boss was still alive.

Before Jenna could decide what to do next, the phone rang. It was from the alumni association. A polite woman with a pronounced twang asked for her, and Jenna explained she was trying to locate Adele Miller, who had graduated maybe twenty years before and had married the son of an Indian chief. She thought she heard a snicker at the other end and realized immediately that she'd used the term Indian chief carelessly and stupidly.

The polite woman came right back at her. "We don't call them Indian chiefs. It's tribal chairman or tribal president," she stated but didn't dwell on it. "May I ask why you're trying to contact Addie?"

Jenna had her story ready: "I've seen some of her jewelry designs. I'm trying to find out where I can buy them." She paused. "If you don't want to give out her information to me, perhaps you could contact her and pass on my message and my cell phone number. Please tell her it'll only take a few minutes of her time. I saw a piece she designed and it was beautiful."

"Of course, I can do that," the woman promised.

Feeling some small sense of accomplishment, Jenna retrieved the flash drive she'd hidden at the bottom of her purse, inserted it into her laptop, found the folder she'd labeled "Denny Search," accessed the document titled To-Do, and used the strikethrough key to draw a line through the first item on the list: *Call Alum Assoc.*

She sipped her iced coffee as her fingers hovered over the Dollie folder. She'd copied the whole folder from Zack's flash drive the day before, and now she was curious to read more. She clicked to open the folder and scrolled down to the entry below Dollie's disastrous kindergarten interview. It was another pdf document. This one was titled "Kittens."

July 23, 2009: (5 years)

Dollie was playing with Lenny on the dock today. They had a big bucket, one of those Hank uses for bait, and it was full of water. They showed me two feral kittens at the bottom of the bucket. I asked what happened. Lenny said they found them by the garage and put them in the bucket. Why? I asked Dollie, and she said, I heard you and Mummy talking about the cats and saying you had to do something about them, so Lenny and I did this to help. Lenny said his father did it all the time.

I didn't know what to say to her, so I said I thought she liked kittens. She shook her head, said, not when they upset you, Daddy. Haven't mentioned this to Jenna, or anyone. They didn't torture the kittens, but I don't know if I should ask someone about this, in case there's something wrong.

Jenna clicked out of the pdf, her finger stabbing at her track pad, wanting to erase the image of the dead kittens at the bottom of a bucket. What on earth had she said that had given Dollie the idea that she needed to drown the kittens? Whatever it was, it had been a poor choice of words if it had prompted Dollie to undertake such a task. Jenna couldn't recall even complaining about the feral cats although there was one spring when there had been more than the usual number prowling around the marina. And why had Zack used the word *torture*? Any parent who'd read a few books about raising kids knew that torturing small animals was one of three danger signs—which included bed-wetting and setting fires—of possible serious maladjustment. But Dollie had never wet the bed since getting out of diapers. Nor had she set any fires—at least, not until the barn-burning incident in Maine, and that had been accidental. Hadn't it?

Jenna felt a distinct chill as she turned to the next document. It was titled Marianna's Braids.

September 8, 2011 (7 years, 2 months)

> *School called today to say Dollie got a time out because she tied Marianna's braids to the chicken-wire fence and made her cry. Dollie went back into class and didn't say anything until teachers started looking for Marianna. Mrs. Jackson told me she was worried that it took Dollie so long to tell anyone. Mrs. Jackson said it showed a streak of meanness and nastiness that she has not seen in someone so young.*
>
> *Dollie told me the whole story on the way home. She said that Marianna had laughed at Dollie's hair because it was so short and she said Dollie must have had lice to have it cut so short. Dollie said she told Marianna that short hair was better because long hair could get caught in stuff. Marianna asked her what stuff? Dollie showed her by tying her braids to the fence. I asked her why she had left her tied up for a whole period, and she said I'm sorry Daddy. I forgot. I wonder how she could have forgotten?"*

Jenna scrolled down further to a pdf that didn't have a title.

June 22, 2016 (Dollie 12 years)

> *Dollie was picked up by Brad today. He brought her back in his car and said he had picked her up at Woods Creek horsing around with a group of boys. He said they were drinking beer and smoking, and he smelled pot. And, he said they had all waded into the creek and Dollie took off her T-shirt and had nothing on underneath. That's when he went over and said he was taking her home. I don't really like him around Dollie. I want him to stay away from her."*

Jenna clicked out of the folder and stared blankly out of the window. Why had Zack not shared these incidents and concerns with her? These were so much worse than the usual misbehavior that they argued and fretted over with Dollie. Why had Dollie not said anything? Why had they shut Jenna out?

All these incidents happened when she had been on work trips into the *Hither and Yon* offices in the city? Was it Dollie's way of acting out? Trying to tell Jenna that she didn't like it when Mommy was away from home? But then, why had Zack not hinted that their daughter turned into a "terror" whenever Jenna was away from home? Or had Zack truly thought that there was something seriously wrong with Dollie, and been too afraid to tell her?

Her heart ached as if someone had cinched it with a rubber band. She got to her feet and paced across the room and then back to her laptop. Sure, she'd been frustrated sometimes by Dollie's stubborn and reckless behavior back when she was little girl, but until Dollie's stunt on the sailboat earlier in the year, Jenna had never considered getting help for her daughter. Of course, had she known about the kittens, she might have thought differently. After all, drowning kittens was just as worrisome as slicing the fins off a fish like young Denny Dennison had done, according to Rosie's neighbor, Carol. Would she have arranged therapy sessions back then for Dollie just like Rosie and Norm had for Denny?

Of course, Rosie had had more reason to suspect something amiss with her son.

Jenna shuddered. These were talking points for a much longer conversation with Zack. They'd have to promise that, even if they divorced, neither would keep secrets about their daughter from the other.

They had to get a grip on Dollie's behavior before she got into serious trouble.

She ejected the flash drive and took a series of long, deep breaths before remembering that there were some contents she'd left unread among Rosie's papers. She walked over to her closet to retrieve the letters and envelopes at the bottom of the box.

They were mostly notifications from Nassau County utility companies confirming disconnection and payment of her last invoice. Rosie, apparently, had been methodical about severing her ties to her home in Seaford.

The envelope at the bottom of the pile, however, turned out to be more interesting. The sender's information was handwritten in the top left-hand corner. It was from a Manfred Greene at the US Coast Guard, Lake Worth Inlet Station. Looking at it more closely, she saw it was postmarked Riviera Beach, Florida, October 19, 2004. Only the name, Dennison, and the Seaford address was visible through the envelope window. She ripped it open and took the one-page letterhead out of the envelope.

The subject line stated: "Re: property of Denny Dennison." There was just one more line: "Please contact me at the above number re property." It was signed by a Lieutenant Manfred Greene.

Jenna frowned. It was a lead. Not much of one, true, but it seemed that Denny Dennison had been somewhere in the vicinity of Riviera Beach, Florida—wherever that was—in the summer of 2004. Which was just a couple of months after Dollie's birth. So, it looked like Denny had left and gone south after taking Dollie's photo in the Sutton Place park.

She wondered what kind of property the Coast Guard might have in its possession. What were the chances that the Coast Guard still had that property? How had they even gotten possession of it? Had Denny lost it? In Riviera Beach? What were the chances that there were any coast guards left who had worked there in 2004?

Yes, a long shot, but worth a phone call in the absence of any better leads. She dialed the number printed on the letterhead, and got a message informing her that unless she had an emergency to call back between nine and five. She was surprised to discover that it was already six o'clock. Late enough that she could pour herself a glass of wine and rummage for some leftovers, which Ana always left in the refrigerator before departing for the day.

She was on her way to the kitchen when her cell phone rang. Seeing Ryan's ID on the call caused her to stop dead in her tracks. As she slid her finger across the screen to respond, her heart pounded in her chest.

"Hi," she replied, and waited for the sound of his voice.

"Jenna, it's me, Teddi. I'm about ten minutes away from your inn. Can I see you?"

Jenna, caught off guard, heard herself mumbling something back at Teddi in a response that indicated sure, yes. Then, she sank down on the bottom step of the staircase. Why was Teddi coming to see her? Was it more likely she was coming in person to deliver good news—or bad news? Was Teddi coming to tell her that Ryan had asked to see Jenna? Or was she coming to tell her that Ryan was dead?

Chapter Thirty-One

Jenna showed Teddi into the inn's lounge when she arrived about a half hour after her phone call. The other woman's eyes were drawn immediately to the photos on the wall. They were big, black-framed photos telling the story of the inn's reconstruction by Zack and his grandfather, Jeremiah.

"Zack looks young," said Teddi.

"Well, he was back then. Those were taken about twenty years ago."

"Very strong too," Teddi added.

Jenna nodded. Teddi was too calm to be here to tell her that Ryan had passed away. "He's good with his hands. He and his grandfather rebuilt the inn, then added other structures. Our loft over the garage. The Miranda cottage." Jenna pointed out the photos. "It was a great bonding experience." She looked at Teddi. "What brings you all the way out here? How is Ryan doing?"

Teddi turned away from the photos. "Ryan and I will be spending some time out on the East End. The doctors decided to bring him out of the coma this morning. He'll be transferred to Southampton Hospital for a couple of days, and then we'll be at my mother's house so he can recuperate and build up his strength." Teddi's eyes filmed over. "It hasn't been easy to watch him try to make sense of what's happening."

Jenna moved toward her, but Teddi stepped back. "May I have a glass of water?" she asked.

Teddi followed her into the kitchen and took the bottled water that Jenna held out to her. "Oh wow! It's gorgeous out there."

Teddi was staring out across the back lawn to the bay, but Jenna knew that Teddi had not come for the view. She was evidently having trouble verbalizing whatever she had come about. "C'mon," Jenna urged her. "Let's walk out. It's a gorgeous evening."

They walked to the dock in silence. Then Teddi said: "I'm sorry, Jenna, I'll come to the point. I don't want you to visit Ryan while we are out here."

"*You* don't want me to." Jenna enunciated the *you*. "Then why bother to tell me he'll be out here?"

"You'd find out anyway. Ryan and I are the sort of couple the papers like to write about." That was a well-placed stab, Jenna had to admit that. "I know he was with you the night he was assaulted, and it's true that we were thinking about separating. My season in Palm Beach was a testing of the waters—well, partly that, partly I was working." She cleared her throat. "Ryan didn't know, but once I was down there, I decided to start gathering information about the winter White House. You know, what it's like at Mar-a-Lago, that sort of thing. I got to date a couple of guys who were members, so I hung out there a lot."

Jenna stared at Teddi, trying to keep her mouth from dropping open. Of course, it was a brilliant idea. Teddi would have fit right in. "Did you get what you needed?"

Teddi laughed. "And more. I couldn't wait to tell Ryan all the details. I wanted to give him all the info as soon as I got back to New York. He was supposed to pick me up at the airport."

"I know." Jenna nodded. "He told me."

Teddi's bright blue eyes narrowed. "I want to try again with Ryan. I can't let him go."

"Try again?"

"I love him. We went through a rough patch. Now, I guess I don't really care about a baby if he's so against doing the rounds of doctors and clinics. It's what we argued about. Ryan would never let me pin him down about going to see a doctor."

Jenna nodded. "I'm sure he wouldn't. Ryan wouldn't be interested in going to doctors or specialists. It never came up when we were together."

"You never got pregnant when you were with him?"

Jenna sensed that this was an underlying reason for Teddi's visit.

"No." Jenna told her.

"You never wanted a baby with him?"

"Honestly, I didn't know what I wanted back then."

"Yet you got pregnant so fast with Zack?"

Jenna laughed out loud. "No mystery about it. We'd been doing it every day, three times a day for months before the wedding, and then after the wedding probably more like four times a day." Jenna grinned. "Zack is quite a physical guy."

Teddi turned away and stared out across the water, maybe to hide her embarrassment at the sudden intimate revelation. Jenna had done it deliberately. Teddi's request to stay away from Ryan hit her hard and painfully, but she didn't want Teddi to realize just how much it hurt. She didn't want Teddi to think that she'd been pining for Ryan all these years. What's more, she wanted to drive home the point that Zack had given her what Ryan apparently couldn't give Teddi.

"So, we're agreed?" Teddi abruptly changed the subject. "You won't visit Ryan."

Jenna froze inside. Now Teddi was giving her orders. "Is that what Ryan wants too?"

"Ryan doesn't know what he wants. He needs me to get him back on his feet." A pause. "There's no room for the both of us, Jenna, regardless of what he told you. You know Ryan. He says a lot of things. You know he doesn't want to hurt feelings."

"Maybe Ryan should decide for himself." The words slipped out before Jenna could stop them.

"Maybe, but not for a while. I just want you to be clear about this, Jenna. You will not be welcome, or allowed into the house, or even past the gates should you decide to drive over for a visit. Stop trying to call him. I have all his devices. He doesn't need them right now. I'm doing what's best for him."

She took a sip of water from the bottle, then screwed the cap back on. "Thank you for understanding, Jenna," she said softly. "I'll walk myself out."

Jenna watched her leave. She moved so gracefully in her elegant little dress, her blonde hair swept back into a chignon where not one hair had come loose during their talk on the dock.

Oh, yes, Jenna understood. Teddi wanted Ryan back. If Jenna had thought there was even a glimmer of hope for her and Ryan,

Teddi had just killed it. No two ways about it. Not that it would stop Jenna's search for Denny Dennison. That's one thing she could do for Ryan that Teddi couldn't.

Jenna brought a bottle of cabernet back to her room along with a plate of antipasto and some crusty, fresh baguette. She picked up her iPad and settled in on the chaise on her deck, idly thumbing through her emails and Twitter account. She tried to focus on the work ahead of her and not think about Teddi or Ryan even though she felt like her heart was breaking. She couldn't blame Ryan for what he'd told her the last night they'd spent together. He'd obviously believed his marriage was over—till Teddi had decided otherwise.

Jenna focused intently on her Twitter feed. She'd had a small number of followers because of her blogs on the Inn website, but the number had really ballooned after her restaurant exposé for Ryan's magazine. She'd need to build a larger following as she worked on the Monte Carlo murder piece. But not tonight. Instead, she accessed Tripadvisor to search for a hotel in the principality.

At some time during the evening, she ventured down to the kitchen again to get some more antipasto, then back to her deck where she eventually fell into a deep sleep on the outside chaise. She woke with a stiff neck, surrounded by darkness. It was very quiet. There were faint lights dotted further along the shore, and she could see a glimmer of the light beyond the swimming pool on the pathway to the jetty where Zack usually docked his motor boat. But it was too dark beyond that spot to tell if the boat had returned with Zack, Dollie, and the Smiths.

It was so still and quiet, she suddenly felt a little uneasy. They had probably all stayed over on Shelter Island, like Zack had suggested earlier. She knew from experience that customers dictated a schedule. She pulled her wrap more closely around her although it was comfortably warm on her deck with just a hint of a light breeze coming in off the water.

Jenna wished she still smoked. She wasn't sure why she felt apprehensive. She would have liked to sink back in the chaise, holding a real, honest-to-goodness cigarette between her fingers, inhaling nicotine deep into her lungs. It would have relaxed her. Calmed some of her jitters.

The idea that Denny Dennison might have been in the vicinity of the inn—and could still be somewhere nearby—made her heart race uncomfortably. She wasn't usually such a scaredy cat, but the hairs on the back of her neck prickled as she tried to picture what she would do if Denny suddenly appeared on the deck.

Stop it, she admonished herself silently. Denny couldn't just materialize on her deck without making a noise. She'd hear the slightest footfall on the gravel below. She'd have time to run for the door. To her room. Anyway, who knew she was up here all on her own? No-one.

She set her glass down and leaned her head back against the chaise pillows. She felt herself nodding off again. It had to be the fresh air that was sapping her energy. She could have sworn she closed her eyes for only a couple of minutes, but when she jolted awake again, everything was pitch black around her. No light from downstairs, no light from her room, no lights from the jetty or from across the creek. Something had woken her though. She sensed she wasn't alone.

It was hard to describe, because it wasn't as if she could hear the breathing of another person; her nose hadn't picked up any strange smell or odor, but she felt the presence of something or someone nearby. Then she heard the creak on the steps to her deck. Then, another step. Someone was coming up the outside staircase to where she was sitting.

Chapter Thirty-Two

Week Two: Early Tuesday Morning

Jenna sat bolt upright on the chaise and listened. The steps halted as if the someone below was suddenly aware that she was awake and listening. She shivered and felt clammy at the same time. Had she really heard steps? Or was her imagination stronger than her senses? She was a foot away from her door. All she had to do was lunge for the door handle, hurl herself inside and slam it shut behind her. Then, she'd call the cops. They'd be here before the intruder could escape the property.

She listened for the sound of another footfall, but whoever was there had stopped climbing the stairs. It was as if he was listening for sounds from the deck, or from her room. She edged herself off the chaise. Still quiet. For sure, she'd imagined the noise of footsteps. Was she that spooked by her thoughts of Denny Dennison?

No, someone was there. Now she could smell the faint trace of stale smoke. Her thoughts raced. Denny? Or maybe it was Sonny? An image of the out-of-shape Sonny, who lived at Rosie's old home danced in front of her eyes. Or maybe it was Brad? Had she imagined him leering even more than he usually did when she'd mentioned that Zack was away? No, it couldn't be Brad. He was creepy, but he wouldn't risk his job like this.

Would he?

She was aware that she was trembling from head to foot. Now or never, she thought. One lunge and she'd be inside. She leaned forward and grabbed the door handle, tugged to open the door and in that moment felt hands on her shoulders pulling her back against a hard muscular body.

"Take it easy, lady."

Jenna felt hot breath against her neck and the hard, muscular body rigid against her.

"Zack?"

Strong arms and hands tightened around her, and she suddenly felt afraid. It couldn't be Zack, could it? She felt him pressing into her. Then, she smelled the tangy, sticky smell of salt air, the way Zack usually smelled after a day on the water.

"I heard you needed room service up here. Front desk sent me to see to it. Sorry you had to wait so long."

Zack.

"Cut it out, Zack, I wasn't waiting." She tried to wriggle free, but he had her pinned.

"Don't know about that." His breath was raspy. His fingers intertwined with her shoulder strap and he slid it off her shoulder.

She felt him pressing into her, his hand working its way under her camisole. "Seems like you were waiting for someone."

His mouth nuzzled her ear, moved down the back of her neck to her shoulder.

He groaned into her, then his mouth searched out her earlobe before moving down again to her bare shoulder.

Even as she wriggled to get free, her heart was suddenly beating faster.

He pinned her down more forcefully. "Don't struggle, lady. You know you want it."

"Zack, I don't want to play games." She said it quietly, almost in a whisper.

His mouth was back around her earlobe. "Just relax." His teeth nipped at her skin, little bites that would leave marks. She pulled her hand away from him but was aware of a warmth coursing between her own legs. Why did he always do this to her?

His hands were caressing her now, more insistently. She eased up against him, twisted around so they were face to face.

"That's right, you want it. I know you do." He brought his mouth down on hers as he thrust himself against her, and then into her. She sank down on him, her arms around his neck, wanting to push him away but hanging on tight.

Her back banged against the door, but she couldn't fight him. She'd forgotten how well he knew every inch of her. He moved rhythmically inside her until she moved with him. She couldn't help herself. She didn't care. He felt good inside her.

And then, they were sliding to the deck together, collapsing and gasping for air.

After a while, he got to his feet and held his hand out to her. "C'mon," he said.

She shook her head, turned away, and sat there till she heard him leave. She needed some time to recover, to let the throbbing inside her slow and stop—and then she would berate herself for being so weak.

Chapter Thirty-Three

Week Two: Tuesday

I
t was going to be a great day. Zack could feel it. He'd woken
alone but had replayed his lovemaking with Jenna before going
downstairs to make breakfast for the family. No doubt about it,
he and Jenna were good together. No, make that terrific, he thought.
She wouldn't be able to deny that. Why would she want to, anyway?
Even if she'd gotten it on with McAllister, she certainly wouldn't be
getting any more from the man-about-town for a while. Too long for
Jenna to go without.

   He arrived in the kitchen to see that Dollie was up too. He got
busy with waffles for her, and then started preparing Jenna's omelet.
He couldn't wait for her to come downstairs. She was always ravenous

the morning after they made love. It's not how he thought the night would end when he'd made his way up the staircase. He'd wanted to ask her how her search for Denny was going, but she'd lunged for the door and fought him as if he were some intruder. He'd thought momentarily about slamming her head into the door and ending everything right there. But then he'd felt her responding to his touch. He'd realized instantly what was happening.

Truth was, he'd never known Jenna to enjoy their lovemaking more than when Zack was playing someone who had to seduce her, okay, maybe sometimes force her. Either way, it seemed that he always had to work at making her want him. It was as if, in her mind, she'd never gotten over McAllister, or the idea that she was cheating on him when she was with Zack. It seemed like Zack had always played the other man in his own marriage.

It had stopped bothering him a long time ago. It could even be said that he enjoyed their games, and that Jenna and he were just two strange puppies who'd luckily found each other.

He got the eggs cracked and ready for scrambling, popped some thick slices of whole wheat into the toaster, retrieved bacon from the refrigerator, and cleaned and chopped tomatoes and mushrooms. Then, he went to the herb garden to pick some fresh chives. He heard the door above on the deck of Jenna's suite opening and, as he returned to the kitchen, motioned for Dollie to go upstairs.

"Tell your Mom I've got breakfast ready to go. Tell her I'm making her favorite omelet for her."

Dollie crossed to the patio doors, smiling broadly, obviously happy to see her parents getting along. But she was back in seconds. He watched Dollie reach for a large mug.

"Mom doesn't want breakfast. Just coffee."

"Wait," he stopped Dollie at the back door. "I'll take it."

He used the outside staircase, and saw Jenna on the chaise, her head resting against the cushions, big shades over her eyes. He couldn't tell if her eyes were open or shut. "Good morning, honey," he greeted her.

She didn't respond, but took the mug that he held out to her and sipped. No thank-you, no invitation for him to sit down beside her.

"You're not mad at me, are you?" he asked.

A long silence. Then: "Why should I be? Oh, you mean because you raped me last night?" Her words were clipped and angry.

He sat down abruptly on the chaise across from her. "C'mon Jenna, you know that's not true."

She pursed her lips together and shook her head. "What do you call it when a man forces himself on a woman who says no? In case you didn't know, husbands aren't allowed to do that anymore. If you'd come into my room, I could have blown your head off."

He was shocked at how angry she sounded. He tried to lighten the moment. "With that fake gun you have in the nightstand?" He knew she'd kept the silly .22 that she'd found among her mother's possessions years ago. "You know it's useless. It's loaded with blanks."

"Blanks can cause damage, even kill," she countered. "If they're right up against the head. I know that much."

He ignored her blathering about guns, but pointedly added: "You wouldn't have shot me. You weren't that angry."

"I said no. I didn't want it, Zack. You forced me. I'm going to be leaving as soon as we find out what's happening with Dollie's case in Maine, and I'm going to take her with me."

"No, you're not," he retorted, tasting bile at the back of his throat. "Not with some madman running around trying to harm her and you. Isn't that what you told me is going on? Why are you doing this, Jenna?"

"You're a liar and a cheat." She enunciated the words. "I saw the texts from Bethany to her friend about sleeping with you on your ride back from Maine, and how much you care about her, and how she was going to move into the master bedroom."

"What are you talking about? I told you Bethany paid for her own room in Maine."

Jenna fixed him with a look of pure hatred. "Sure, on a culinary-school stipend! You don't have to lie about it anymore. Bethany's texts to her friend go back quite a while."

He didn't respond immediately. What was in Bethany's texts? What had she said? Had she texted about the times when he'd driven her into town to catch the jitney? If she had, she obviously hadn't admitted that she had always started it. A woman didn't put her hand on a man's thigh and expect him not to react. Really, what was he supposed to have done about that?

He shook his head and assumed his most shocked tone of voice. "Jenna, honestly, Bethany was mistaken. She misread a lot of things I said to her. I never told her I cared about her. Or said anything about moving into the master bedroom. That's crazy, Jen. I wouldn't let her ruin our marriage. I love you, and I think you still love me. At least, you did last night."

"Huh?" She laughed abruptly. "Don't flatter yourself, I put up with you until you were done." She swung slowly back and forth on the chaise, her lips set in a thin line.

He wanted to grab her shoulders and shake her. "I don't think that's how it was at all. C'mon Jenna," he persisted.

She shook her head vehemently. "Just waiting till you got done. Couldn't you tell?" Her voice rose. "You forced me."

He got to his feet, paced to the edge of the deck and back as suddenly a better idea struck him. He pondered the wisdom of it for a couple of seconds. But what choice did he have? Jenna was lying. He knew it, and she knew it. He took his cell phone from his pocket.

"Why don't you make your calls downstairs. I need to get some rest." Jenna's tone remained clipped and hostile.

He stayed put, tapping the security system app for the inn. Another couple of taps and he was through to the video portion. He rewound and queued it to the segment he'd replayed for himself that morning.

Then he held it up in Jenna's face.

"Jeezus! What is that?" She shrieked, whipping off her shades to stare at the screen before making a grab for the phone.

He drew back a step. "Oh wait." He grinned. "I should turn up the volume."

Suddenly, they were both listening to the sound of Jenna's moans of pleasure and the deep intake of breaths that punctuated their lovemaking. He punched the double black lines and the tape stopped. "You're right," he said, "just waiting for me to be done?"

"You bastard," she spat out the words, lunged at him and this time succeeded in grabbing the phone out of his hands. Without hesitating, she flung it off the deck.

He laughed. "I can replay that tape on my iPad, or my laptop."

Jenna started to cry, probably because she was remembering how he'd set up security cameras all around the property several years ago. Her eyes traveled to the camera above the screen door. "You bastard," she repeated the words in a whisper. "You bastard."

She looked like she wanted to scratch his eyes out, but just then he heard someone on the patio below. He looked over the parapet and bile rose in his throat again. It was Brad. God only knew how long he'd been standing there, but now he was picking up Zack's cell phone.

"I'll bring it up," he said. "Dollie told me you were both up there. I have some answers"—he grimaced—"and more questions for you both."

As Brad made his way up the steps, Zack noticed he was staring at the screen of his phone.

Chapter Thirty-Four

Jenna flushed scarlet as Brad stepped onto the deck with Zack's iPhone in his hand.

"I think it's okay," he said, staring down at the screen and then pointedly across the deck at Jenna. "It landed on one of the chaises. Picture seems to be perfect."

His eyes stayed on her as Zack strode to his side.

"I'll take that." He snatched the phone from Brad's fingers, and his voice was quivering with anger when he spoke. "What do you want, Brad?"

Brad hesitated, turning his gaze to the chaise across from Jenna, but neither Jenna nor Zack asked him to sit.

"So, here's the thing: I drove to Riverhead to speak to Bethany's roommate. As y'all know by now, she didn't hear from Bethany on that Sunday at all. The jitney didn't hear from her. There was no reservation made in Bethany's name, and no one in the pharmacy at the bus stop remembers her coming in that Sunday afternoon or being dropped off at the bus stop."

Jenna was aware of Zack staring at her, raising an eyebrow. Then he turned to Brad.

"I'm sorry Brad, I should have told you before, I didn't drop Bethany off at the bus stop, I didn't give her a ride to the jitney that Sunday. I told Jenna that after she found Bethany's cell phone in her room. I wasn't exactly truthful about it first time around because I was kinda embarrassed I didn't go after her, but Bethany was gone by the time I got back to the house from the boat. I figured Jenna would have told you that when you came for the cell phone."

Jenna gulped her coffee and narrowly avoided sputtering it all over herself. Why was Zack making it sound as if she was the dishonest one? As if she was the one hiding something?

Sure enough, Brad was staring right at her when he said: "So, okay, which one of you erased Bethany's texts?"

Jenna put down her coffee mug before it slipped out of her fingers. She was aware that her hand was trembling. She'd been afraid it might come to this, since Bethany's roommate still had those texts on her phone.

Her face was aflame. "I checked the phone. I was curious to see if there was anything on it, some clue. If I erased the texts, it was by mistake."

Jenna glanced at Zack. He looked as if he didn't believe her. Brad wasn't buying it either. He paced across the deck between them. "Look, you two, the roommate kept all the texts and they were kinda revealing about what was going on here."

Jenna was aware that Brad hadn't taken his eyes off her. "She told her roommate you walked out on Zack because you found out that she and he were having an affair."

Zack was shaking his head before Brad finished speaking. "Swear to God, Chief." He held up his hands as if in mock surrender. "Not an ounce of truth to that. An affair? Are you kidding me? She may have wanted it, but I didn't do anything to encourage her. I told you the truth the other day, she offered to stay, I told her no."

Brad had not taken his eyes off Jenna. "You had a fight over her, didn't you? You didn't believe there was nothing to it?" He shook his head. "Look, kids, I'm trying to be helpful. You really don't want to have to come to the station to talk about this, do you? But something is not adding up. You, Jenna, you're away in the city for a couple of weeks, now you're back, but phones are flying around, texts have been erased. Dammit, I wasn't born yesterday."

Jenna shrank back in her chaise. She wondered if she was doing the right thing talking to Brad at all without a lawyer. On the other hand, she didn't want to be facing these questions at the police station.

"You're right, Brad," she finally admitted in a small voice. "I thought there was something going on, but Zack and I are working things out."

Zack nodded in agreement.

"However, Bethany is still missing," Brad said. "Where were you that Sunday, Jenna?"

"In the city." Jenna spoke before realizing what he might be driving at. "Where's this going, Chief?"

He sighed. "Just trying to cover all the bases. Look at it from my point of view. The girl created trouble between the two of you. Jenna, you left, but then maybe you decided you weren't going to let her break up your marriage and you came back from the city. You had the motive, Jenna. And you erased the texts."

"What? The motive for what?" Jenna's voice rose, and she was aware from the look on his face that Zack was puzzled by this turn in the conversation but seemed to be enjoying her discomfort.

Brad cleared his throat. "Have you got someone who can vouch for you being in the city?"

Jenna laughed. It was a short burst of laughter, but she realized Brad was serious. "I'm sorry, I don't know what to tell you. I can't give you any names of friends in the city. It was Sunday. I slept in and had a very slow, relaxing day."

Jenna squinted to give the impression she was trying hard to recollect the day. It had been the weekend before Ryan was assaulted. "I know I didn't use the car. I left it parked on the street. You could talk to the doormen at my apartment building," she declared. "You don't seriously think I harmed Bethany?"

"Maybe not, but maybe you ordered her to leave and not come back." He shook his head. "I really don't know, maybe you told her to go back home and threatened to turn her in to Immigration. It doesn't seem like she had a green card or a current work permit." He allowed himself a halfhearted grin. "I feel I know both of you, and I want to believe you both, but one of you isn't telling me the whole story."

Jenna ignored the queasy feeling she always had when Brad tried to make it look as if he was doing them a favor—as if to show them how important he was in the town. "Give a man a uniform, and you've got yourself a general"—that's the phrase that always bounced into her head when she was in Brad's presence.

She wondered about the strange, smug look on Zack's face when Brad was questioning her. Maybe Jenna was right in her suspicion that Zack had told Bethany she needed to lie low, and that he knew exactly where she was. But then again, would he keep up the pretense while the Southold Police Department launched a full-scale search for the girl?

Jenna simply didn't know what to think and was relieved when her cell phone rang. She glanced at the number that appeared on the screen. It was not identified and she didn't recognize it. She answered it anyway, turning away from the two men on her deck.

The voice on the other end sounded friendly: "Hi, this is Adele Barnett." There was a short pause, then she added: "I used to be Adele Miller. Are you the person trying to reach me?"

Chapter Thirty-Five

Zack wasn't happy when Jenna disappeared into her room. It meant he was alone with Brad. He didn't want to be, even though it seemed he wasn't the one under suspicion. The deputy had focused more on Jenna and on the fact that Jenna had more reason to want Bethany gone than he had. It was a surprising turn of events.

"You cannot possibly think that Jenna has anything to do with Bethany's disappearance," he finally said, breaking the silence.

Brad's face set in a serious expression. "Honestly, I don't know. But in my line of work, strange things happen. I can't see why she'd try to erase the texts if not for trying to erase a motive."

Zack had to suppress a smirk.

It would serve Jen right if Brad focused on her for a while. She'd been a bitch about their lovemaking the previous night. Maybe it would do her good to discover what it felt like to be accused of a crime. Still and all, he had to make a little bit of a show of being the good husband.

"Listen, Brad, I know it seems like Jenna and I are going through a rough patch, but I'd find it really hard to believe that Jenna could do anything criminal."

"Yeah, me too, pal. But I gotta check her out now," he responded, taking a step closer to Zack and glancing at the door that had closed behind Jenna. He lowered his voice. "You can level with me, son. Just between us, you and Bethany were having a fling, right? C'mon, I saw her here a couple of times. If she was coming on to you, she'd be a tough one to kick to the curb."

Zack wanted to laugh in his face. He had an urge to say something like, "Well, that's because you're a dirty old man." But he resisted the impulse. He thought it was a hoot that Brad imagined he was going to get him to admit anything by pretending they were buddies, or worse, related? It seemed Brad was using *son* in a casual way, in the same way he probably addressed most younger men around these parts as *son*. Zack didn't like it; he felt like Brad was putting one over on him, making him feel like he should trust the deputy when that was really the last thing he should be doing.

He didn't want Brad snooping around, making pointed remarks about Bethany. It was difficult enough to keep the girl out of his thoughts whenever her name came up; he certainly didn't want to think about her while Brad was staring at him, waiting for some response.

"Honestly, Brad," he said finally. "I can't say I don't notice her, but for God's sake, she's very young, and she works for me. So, no Brad, there was nothing going on between us."

"So her texts and what she told her roommate was what?"

Zack shook his head. "Imagination. Wishful thinking. I don't know, Brad."

Brad looked like he was finally going to leave, and Zack stepped up behind him. He wanted to see him off the property. Suddenly, Jenna's door opened. She looked pleased with herself, and he was curious about her phone call.

After Brad finally left, Jenna insisted on knowing what else Brad had said behind her back.

"He's going to check out your alibi," Zack told her.

"He's an idiot," she burst out.

"I know. I know. It's a bitch when you're being accused of something you didn't do."

Jenna stared at him, biting her lower lip. He wasn't sure how to read her expression. It seemed to soften as he stared at her and he wondered if she was sorry she'd accused him of raping her. But he wasn't going to bring the subject up again.

Instead, he lied. "I told him there's no way you would have come back to talk to Bethany. I told him you'd never drive all that way out from the city just for an airhead like Bethany."

Jenna laughed. "You got that right."

"How come you didn't mention your suspicion about the spawn to him? You could have diverted attention from yourself."

Jenna sighed and rolled her eyes as if he'd missed the point. "It would have just made me sound guiltier." Then, suddenly her face brightened. "I've found Denny's stepsister," she announced, holding up her phone. "That was her. She totally told a different story from Carol, the neighbor. Carol said Rosie Miller moved to Arizona to look after Adele's baby . . ."

"Yeah?" His tone was cautious.

"Well, she doesn't have one. A baby, I mean. She hasn't seen or spoken to Rosie since Rosie moved from Seaford, and the last time she saw Denny was when he returned from the islands for Christmas, a few months after my article. It just seems like Rosie wanted to disappear."

"What did you tell the sister?"

"I told her the truth. I said I was the reporter on the exposé about Denny, and that I wanted to know how his life had turned out. She'd like to find Denny too. She wants to know that he's okay."

"Where is this sister?" he asked as calmly as he could. He'd dismissed the possibility of Jenna tracking down Adele when she'd started prattling about a reservation in Arizona. He knew Adele had returned to New York years ago.

"Well, she's not in Arizona," said Jenna. "She's here in New York. She divorced the son of the tribal chief. She's on the Shinnecock reservation in Southampton. And listen to this: while we were on the phone, she went to her photo albums and found a photo of Denny from that last Christmas. She said she was putting it in her purse, and I could come over anytime to see it for myself. She works at the Big Joe Smoke Shop."

He barely heard the rest of what Jenna was saying. All he could think about was the Christmas photo.

Fuck. He tried to recall that Christmas. He'd returned briefly from the islands, so he'd probably already looked fitter. Not quite the way he'd looked when he met Jenna, but still and all, not like the dork that had appeared in the photos after the *Sun* photographer jumped out at him and Lisa.

"You're a helluva reporter, Jen," he finally said.

"I am, aren't I?" she replied, a triumphant note in her voice.

He nodded. "Do you want me to take the boat over there and pick up the photo? I'll get Rick to drive me from the marina to the smoke shop. I could be back in an hour. Save you taking the ferry and driving across."

"Gosh no." She laughed.

Of course not, he thought. That would have made it too easy for him to get his hands on the photo to see exactly what it showed.

"I want to meet Adele," Jenna said. "She says she doesn't know anything, but if I sit down with her, something else might shake loose when I start prodding. I'll drive over tomorrow morning. She says the mornings are slower for her. So, maybe she'll remember what Denny's plans were. I'm pretty sure there'll be some clue if she puts her mind to it."

He made a last effort. "Do you really need to do this? Don't you have better assignments to work on?" He grinned to lighten the moment.

Jenna smiled. "Sure, but you know what? Now that I've found Adele, I need to talk to her. Look, even if it turns out that Denny had nothing to do with Ryan's assault or Bethany's disappearance, I still want to know how his life turned out," Jenna said. "It's something I need to put to rest, once and for all."

"Okay." He nodded, making his way toward the staircase. "I'm going over to the marina," he added although Jenna looked as if she couldn't care less. "I need to check out the bookings for next week with Hank."

It was another lie. What he really needed to do was focus and come up with some plan either to stop Jenna meeting Adele or to stop Jenna from getting her hands on the Christmas photo.

Chapter Thirty-Six

Jenna took a deep breath as she watched him go. She needed to slow the pace. The morning had been hectic, but she was buoyed by making contact with Denny Dennison's stepsister. She'd make a day of the trip to Southampton tomorrow. She'd suggest that Dollie come with her. Dollie could visit the Shinnecock Nation Museum while Jenna was talking to Adele, and then they could have lunch together. Maybe look at the shops. She would make it a mother-daughter day. In the meantime, she would call the Coast Guard in Florida. The sooner she could get a sense of Denny's whereabouts, the sooner she'd be able to get on with her Monte Carlo assignment and the rest of her life.

She dialed the number of the Coast Guard. The phone connected with a gruff male voice.

"I'm trying to find someone who worked for you in 2004. He sent a letter to a friend of mine. I'm going through her belongings, and this letter was unopened in her stuff. It refers to some property you have that belongs to her son. Just wondering if you still have the property."

"Are you kidding, lady?"

"I'm holding the letter in my hand. I could scan it and email it."

"Look miss, I'm sorry, that won't help. We don't have a lost and found department, so I'm not sure what the letter is referring to. Really, I wish I could be more helpful."

"If I fly down to Riviera Beach, is there someone who could help me? It's really, really important."

She must have sounded desperate, because the voice on the other end asked: "Who signed the letter?"

"Lieutenant Manfred Greene."

There was a momentary hesitation, and then: "He's retired."

Jenna's reaction was so loud and pitiful, the voice at the other end added: "But he's still around these parts. I could maybe track him down. But it won't be for a few weeks. We're really undermanned."

Jenna decided to give it her all. "So, if I come down there, would you point me in his direction?"

"Wow, what's this about? Was there a stash of diamonds in this property?"

"It's more important than that."

The male at the other end was silent for a moment, as if trying to figure out what Jenna meant. Then he said: "Well, okay. If you're coming this way, stop by. There might be some other guys here who'll know where Manny is hanging out these days."

Jenna hung up, annoyed that she hadn't been more persistent about getting a phone number for Manny. Perhaps she'd try later, get a different coast guard on the phone. Maybe he'd find a phone number for Manny. Meanwhile, she'd check Google, Facebook, and Twitter for Lieutenant Manfred Greene. She didn't want to fly to Florida. She really, truly hoped that Adele would dredge up some useful memory.

Dollie burst into her room as Jenna was fashioning an email reply to Gordon at *My World*. *Gordon: Am finishing up a prior assignment and will be making reservations for Monte Carlo shortly. Ttyl.* None of it was true, but it couldn't be helped. She was juggling her life as best she could. She hit send without giving the email another glance because Dollie seemed frantic.

"Dad said he'd be back in time to take me into town. I need a new charger for my phone. He's late."

"I'll take you." Jenna didn't even question why her daughter needed a new charger, although she wanted to.

But Dollie seemed not to hear Jenna's offer. "I can't reach him. He said he'd be at the marina with Hank. But he's not there." There was a note of panic in her voice. "I tried to call him, but his phone goes to voice mail. Something's happened to him."

Jenna sighed, noting Dollie's panic-stricken tone at the thought that something had happened to her father. It was difficult not to feel a little jealous of the bond between them.

"C'mon sweetheart. If you're ready, I'll get the car. I said I'd take you."

Dollie climbed into the passenger seat a few minutes later but seemed preoccupied, looking over her shoulder as Jenna pulled out of the driveway as if expecting Zack to come walking into view. She slumped down in her seat, frowning. "His phone never goes to voice mail," she said in a small voice. "Not when he sees it's me."

Chapter Thirty-Seven

Week Two: Wednesday

Thomas here are two routes from the North Fork to the South Fork where the tony Hamptons are located. Neither of them is direct. The first goes west to Riverhead, then south on Route 24 to Sunrise Highway, and then back towards the east and the Southampton exit. Or one can take Route 25 east on the North Fork to Greenport for a ferry to Shelter Island. Then it's a short drive across the island to the ferry for Sag Harbor, and from there through Noyac and into Southampton. Jenna had allowed Dollie to choose the route the previous evening when they'd returned from their successful trip into town for Dollie's charger, and she had told Dollie about her appointment on the Shinnecock reservation.

"Let's take the ferries. Then, we can have lunch at the American Hotel," Dollie said with an enthusiasm Jenna had not seen in a while. "Don't you remember, Mom, we used to do that all the time. I love the American Hotel."

In fact, they had eaten lunch at the hotel only three or four times one summer when Jenna had enrolled Dollie in a dance class in Sag Harbor. Jenna was gratified, nevertheless, that Dollie appeared to have stored it as a happy-childhood-with-Mom recollection. "Sure, we can take the ferry. We'll have lunch on the way back from the reservation."

Of course, Zack spoiled the whole idea of a mom-daughter day. He appeared in the doorway as Dollie was getting in the car. "Hey, you guys! Where are you off to?"

Dollie squealed, beaming with pleasure. "Daaad! Where have you been? We're going to Southampton. To the Shinnecock Museum and to the American Hotel for lunch. Wanna come?"

"I'm sure Dad's busy," Jenna interjected immediately. Their paths had crossed the previous night in the kitchen, where Jenna had taken some small delight in telling Zack how he'd disappointed his daughter with his disappearing act earlier in the evening. "Well, then I shouldn't disappoint two gorgeous women on the same night," he'd retorted immediately. "How about I cook us up a great supper. I got some delicious fresh fish. Just caught this afternoon." Jenna had declined the invitation.

Now he was looking decidedly cheery. "Nah. I'm not busy. My day's wide open today," he replied. "I'd love to make it a family day. Just the three of us."

Dollie had turned to Jenna, eyes wide and imploring. "Oh yes, Mom, let's make it a family day. Pleeez."

Jenna sighed, and her lips set in a thin line when she threw the keys to Zack. "You drive, then." She saw the smile playing on his lips.

She couldn't figure out if he was truly happy to be along for the ride with his family, or because he knew he was foisting himself on Jenna when she didn't want to be near him.

"Roof open or closed?" he asked.

Jenna shrugged. She didn't care, and she wasn't going to let herself engage in conversation. But it was difficult with Zack sitting so close to her, his right arm brushing against hers on the armrest. She focused on his hands on the steering wheel, momentarily flashing back to their coupling on her deck. Whatever else she thought of him right now, she had to admit that he certainly knew how to use those hands. He knew every inch of her body, knew just how to make her respond to him. He'd always been able to do that, right from the very beginning. He'd never forgotten anything she told him about how she liked to be touched or caressed.

There was something very basic about him and his determination to satisfy her. It was almost impossible to fight him when he made up his mind to seduce her.

Jenna wondered where Bethany figured in Zack's plans now. She didn't know what to believe about Bethany or how Zack felt about the girl. He certainly didn't act like a husband wanting a divorce. So, maybe the disappearing act, and leaving her cell phone behind with all the incriminating little texts for Jenna to find, was Bethany's way of forcing Zack's hand. In which case, what if Jenna took a leaf out of Teddi's book, and simply informed Bethany—when she eventually surfaced—that Jenna was giving her husband a second chance, and taking him back?

Would that be such a terrible prospect?

It was true that the farm-to-table fraud story had whetted her appetite for bigger, more important stories, and for being back in the center of the universe, but as much of a city girl that she was, she had adapted to life on the North Fork quite comfortably over the last sixteen years. She had gotten to enjoy writing a weekly blog about the inn and marina, and the North Fork, and that had led to regular opinion pieces for the weekly newspaper. Eventually, she'd even gotten involved with some local issues when they came up for discussion and votes at the town board meetings.

People in the town liked her. How bad would it be if she just stayed on the North Fork as Mrs. King?

Zack turned to her minutes after pulling out of their driveway, his eyes signaling at Dollie in the backseat. "You're taking her to meet the spawn's sister?"

"The spawn!" Dollie piped up. "What are you guys talking about?"

Zack shushed her. "Nothing Dollie, it's a joke. We're just joking." He drove in silence for a while, then started up the conversation again as they were rolling off the ferry in North Haven.

"So, do I get to meet her too?"

Jenna threw her hands up. "Give it a rest, Zack. You can take Dollie into the Museum, and I'll join you when I'm done."

"Mom, Dad, what are you going on about?"

Both Jenna and Zack turned around to stare at their daughter. "Nothing Dollie," Jenna said.

"Not your business, sweetheart," Zack added more gently.

Minutes later, as Jenna nudged Zack to make the right turn for the Noyac Road to Southampton, Dollie yelled out, "Hey, let's have lunch first!"

"Oh, jeez," Jenna whispered under her breath. She really wanted to get her hands on whatever photos Adele had as soon as she could.

Zack reached for her hand. "Tell you what, why don't you drop us off on Main Street? We'll walk down, look at the shops, get a table and chew on some breadsticks while you zip over to the smoke shop."

"Yeah," Dollie chimed in. "Mom, I really don't want to look at some stinky museum."

Jenna shook her head, exasperated, but knew it was no contest. Zack had hijacked her day with Dollie. "I'll be back as soon as I can," she said, dropping them off at the corner of Main.

It took her just twenty minutes through the center of Sag Harbor and along the North Road, then into the center of Southampton to reach that stretch of Montauk Highway that borders the Shinnecock reservation.

It was a one-mile hodgepodge of little kiosks, smoke shops—one almost on top of another (to accommodate the volume of customers who didn't want to pay tax on their smokes)—a log cabin that was the Shinnecock Museum, and deli-style stores, one with a big chalkboard held by a cardboard cutout of a Native American in a headdress stating there were fresh eggs and spinach on the premises.

She saw two state-trooper cars parked on the side of the road as she approached the museum. Adele had told her the smoke shop was three doors down from there. But now she couldn't see a parking spot on that side of the road.

She pulled over across the street, eyeing the yellow "Do Not Cross" tape strung across the front of the smoke shop.

Her heartbeat quickened as she swung open the car door and waited for traffic to pass before she crossed the highway.

"Ma'am, you can't walk here," said a young officer standing next to one of the state-trooper cars. He motioned for her to back away.

"Officer, what's going on? I have an appointment with someone at the shop there."

"I'm sorry, ma'am, no one is allowed back there."

Jenna stopped. "Officer, could you please tell me what's going on? I came from the North Fork to meet with Adele Miller, Adele Barnett,

I mean. Can you ask someone if she's around? I don't want to get in your way."

She realized she suddenly had the officer's attention. "Did you say Adele Barnett? You came to see her?"

"Yep, all the way across from the North Fork. Please don't make me have to come back. I only came to pick up a photo."

"Wait here."

Jenna watched him walk over to two uniformed state troopers, and then watched as one of them came toward her.

"Ma'am, I'm going to need your name and phone number."

Jenna swallowed. "Jenna King," she replied, adding her cell phone number. "Look, Officer, I was supposed to meet Ms. Barnett here, this afternoon. I'm here to pick up a photo she had for me."

He was shaking his head as she spoke. "Sorry, ma'am. That won't be possible. Not today. Are you a friend, relative?"

"No." Jenna shook her head. "I don't know her personally."

"Ma'am, I'm afraid there's been an accident. You'll have to go back."

Jenna looked around. There was no sign of any ambulance or EMS vehicle. "Please, Officer, just give me an idea of what's going on, and I'll come back another time."

The state trooper shook his head, reached for a card in his breast pocket and handed it to Jenna. "Call us later, we might be able to tell you more then." Jenna nodded and took the card just as a man wearing hospital booties and latex gloves emerged from behind the smoke shop pushing a gurney. There was a black body bag lying on top of it.

Jenna stared blankly as he stopped and removed his booties and gloves and then continued pushing the gurney toward a low-slung, white station wagon parked next to the state troopers' cars.

PART THREE

Chapter Thirty-Eight

Zack had never seen Jenna look so shaken. Twenty minutes after arriving on the veranda of The American Hotel she still hadn't regained any color in her cheeks. Nor had she said a word, other than ordering an iced tea.

"What's up, honey? You look like you've seen a ghost?"

She glared at him, then shook her head and rolled her eyes toward Dollie, who was scrolling through her iPhone. He gave Dollie some coins and told her to go and feed the meter.

Jenna took a long sip of her iced tea. "She's dead," she said, her voice cracking. "I know she's dead."

He let out a low whistle. "The sister?"

Jenna nodded.

"How?"

"I don't know. They wouldn't tell me anything except that there was an accident, but there weren't any ambulances or EMS vehicles." Jenna shuddered. "There was just a body bag zipped all the way up on the gurney."

"Who's they?"

"The state troopers." She took out her iPhone and started thumbing away, probably looking for her news apps. He tried to take the phone from her. But she held on to it tightly.

"We'll find out at home, okay?"

"It's on the 27east app. It says the owner of the smoke shop, Adele Barnett, was attacked."

He didn't want to think about Adele. He'd never really gotten along with her when they'd lived in the same house with Norm and his mom. He'd always felt she was spying on him. She was surprisingly quiet when she moved around the house, and she'd had a habit of creeping up on him and scaring the shit out of him, staring at him with her big, unblinking, dark eyes.

As Jenna now frantically scrolled through her various news apps on the cell phone, he surmised that it had been a stupid idea to go to Adele's smoke shop the previous evening. He'd not even had any sort of plan—although he'd brought Jenna's "little gun" with him—as to what he'd do when he got there. But he'd seen Adele's purse hanging on a hook by the cash register, and she'd told Jenna she was putting the photo in her purse.

He'd kept his baseball cap down low over his brow and asked for a carton of cigarettes. Then he'd left and walked around the back to figure out a way to get his hands on the envelope. His best plan, he figured, was to wait till Adele was closing up the shop, then to go back in and cause a commotion—knock over some magazine racks he'd seen near the front of the shop, and while she was dealing with that lift her purse off the hook and walk out the store. Stupid. Stupid. Stupid. A seventh grader could have come up with a better plan.

Jenna gasped suddenly without looking up from her cell phone. "She's dead. She was stabbed," Jenna whispered across the table just as Dollie returned to the veranda.

It wasn't till they were back in the car, waiting in line to board the ferry back to Greenport, and after Dollie fixed her air pods in place that Jenna was able to fill him in on some more information. "They found her body just by the door. They think she was closing up when it happened."

"That's terrible," he said, casting a glance at Dollie in the backseat. "Where are you reading that?"

"*Newsday* breaking news. The state police are looking for some kids who were seen in the area just around the time she usually closed. Apparently, there's some surveillance tape from a neighboring smoke shop that shows them all drunk, or high, leaving after harassing the shopkeeper there. Cops think they may have been trying to buy drugs."

"Could be," he said, remembering the kids who had pulled into the front parking lot as he was waiting out back. He hadn't seen them, but had heard the music from their car, and their yelling and hollering.

As they pulled onto the ferry, Jenna was breathing harder, and once they were in position with the emergency brake on, she rolled down the window and gulped for air as if she was drowning. She looked as if she was in pain when she turned toward him. "Maybe it wasn't those kids," she said softly. "Maybe this isn't a coincidence." She paused. "Ryan was beaten up, Bethany's disappeared, and now Adele . . ." She left the words hanging.

He reached for her hand. "Stop it, Jenna," he said. "Stop it. That's crazy talk. This has nothing to do with the spawn." He air-quoted with one hand.

Jenna looked away, out of her window.

"Listen to me," he lowered his voice as the ferry docked with a slight bump against the pilings. "How would he know you spoke to Adele? He would have to have NSA-type equipment to listen in on phones on our property." He started the engine. "Also, just so you know, I asked Hank a couple of days ago to check around the property every couple of hours for any strangers hanging out."

He couldn't quite read the expression on Jenna's face. *Really?* it seemed to be saying.

So, you're taking this seriously?

He squeezed her hand. "Jenna, I'm not going to let anything happen to you or Dollie. However crazy the whole thing sounds to me, I'm not going to take the chance, okay?"

Jenna sighed but didn't withdraw her hand from his. "Shit," she swore suddenly. "The photo, I really wanted to see it." She paused. "Do you think they found it in the shop? Do you think they'd turn it over to me if I asked them?"

"I don't know. Jen. It's a crime scene. You don't even know if she had the photo with her. Did you speak to her again?"

Jenna shook her head. "No." Then she swore again, more vehemently. "Shit, shit, shit. I really wanted to talk to her. I really thought she'd remember something if we talked."

"I know." He tried to sound sympathetic, but he didn't know what else to say, and they drove in silence till they reached their driveway.

"What the hell!" Jenna's voice rose as they came through the rhododendrons, and she spotted the parked police car outside the front doors. Brad was leaning against the driver-side door. "I'm sick of him," she whispered under her breath. "I'm going to tell him he'll need a warrant next time he wants to drive in here."

"Steady." He placed a hand on her forearm. "Let's keep the law on our side."

Her lips twisted into a half smile, no doubt recognizing her own words coming back at her as she exited the car. Striding toward Brad, he heard her greet him with a smile and a bantering note in her voice: "Chief Brad! We're going to have put up a permanent 'reserved' sign here just for your car."

As Zack got out of the car, he noticed Brad wasn't returning her smile. "I'm sorry, you two," he said, "but I don't have good news."

Chapter Thirty-Nine

J enna waited for Dollie to head for the pool before beckoning to Brad to follow her into the inn. Zack stopped in the doorway. "I'm getting a beer. Jenna? Brad?"

Brad shook his head. "Just hold off a mo," he beckoned Zack into the room. "Perhaps you want to close the door. We'll keep this private."

Jenna didn't like what she was hearing. Her heart started beating harder. Was it bad news about Bethany? She fervently hoped not. One death was enough for the afternoon.

"I'm giving you a heads-up, kids. Got a call from NYPD," Brad stared hard at Zack as he spoke. "They wanted some info on you. What did I know about you? That kind of thing. Seems they're heading out here sometime soon to have a chat with you."

"About?" Zack leaned against the doorjamb. He had ignored Brad's suggestion to close the door.

Brad reached into his pants pocket, brought out a small notebook. "About a Ryan McAllister. Apparently, he was assaulted last week."

Jenna felt her face flush red. "Yeah. We know what this is about. I had dinner with Ryan McAllister the night he was assaulted. Zack wasn't in the city."

Brad nodded, looked at Jenna, then at Zack. "Well, all I know is that they're coming to chat with Zack." Then: "I shouldn't be telling you this, maybe, but . . ." He shrugged. "Apparently, it took them a while to find, but they seem to have some CCTV tape that shows Zack's car, the Jag, in the vicinity just prior to the assault."

"What!" Jenna couldn't mask her shock at Brad's revelation. "Brad, how's that possible? Zack was on his way to pick up Dollie in Maine."

Brad's eyes stayed on Zack, his demeanor suggesting he was waiting for an answer. "They got make, model and license plate." He consulted his little notebook again. "Jaguar, 2016 model. And your license plate. I just checked it on my way down the driveway."

Jenna turned on her husband, waiting for him to protest or give Brad some explanation. Zack just shrugged.

Brad put away his notebook and appeared to study Zack intently. Then he stepped toward the door. "I'll level with both of you: I don't think they have anything besides your car on CCTV. If they had anything, they'd be swarming all over you right now without calling me first." Brad shook his head. "I hope you kids get this straightened out. First it's Zack messing around with the help—or not. Now it's Jenna out to dinner with some guy who gets mugged outside your building in the early hours of the morning. Of course the husband is going to be a suspect, CCTV or not." He shook his head again with a look of disbelief on his face. "Don't know why you're doing this to each other."

Jenna felt nauseous. She hated the way Brad was suddenly front and center in their lives, knowing every detail, and making it look as if he was doing them a favor every time he came down their driveway. She didn't even want to think what he might want in return.

"Oh"—he paused in the entrance hall—"I'd get a lawyer for when the NYPD arrive."

Jenna followed Brad to the front door, unease and anger swirling inside her. She was afraid she'd let it all spill if Brad didn't leave immediately. "We do appreciate you giving us the heads-up," she said, surprised by how calm she sounded. "We really do."

Brad patted her on the shoulder. "See if the two of you can sort things out between yourselves. You don't want NYPD to start adding two and two and coming up with five."

Jenna watched to make sure he got in his car, then strode back into the inn to confront Zack. "What the hell, Zack? W-T-F! You were in the city the night Ryan got his head kicked in?" She felt as if she was about to explode, but Zack did not seem embarrassed or uncomfortable by being put on the spot.

"Yeah, I was. I came to pick you up so we could both drive to Maine to pick up Dollie."

"And?" Suddenly, she remembered the photos of her and Ryan that she'd received by FedEx, the kinds of photos an estranged husband might take.

"You weren't there. Lights were off in the apartment. I called your cell phone. No answer. I didn't have time to hang out. Remember, one of Dollie's parents needed to show up before they handed her over to

Child Protective Services. Do you think I was going to leave Dollie sitting in a police cell for the night?"

Jenna processed the information even as Zack moved toward her. "C'mon, Jen, this is stupid shit. Anyway, you can't possibly believe I beat up McAllister? The cops are grasping at straws. I'm not bothered if they want to come all the way out to talk to me."

Jenna backed away from him. "Why didn't you tell me you were in the city?"

Zack shrugged. "I don't know, Jen. It didn't seem important. Anyway, you were so convinced that this "spawn" character had come after McAllister. Does this change your mind about the spawn? Maybe now you think it's me who mugged McAllister and made Bethany disappear? Oh, and stabbed Adele to death?"

Jenna chewed on her lower lip.

She knew Zack was making fun of the way she'd lumped all the incidents into one big conspiracy. But why had he not told her that he'd come to the city to pick her up?

"So, you're saying you drove into the city. You called me. You didn't get a reply, so you drove to Maine from the city?"

"Yes."

Jenna made a show of retrieving her phone and scrolling down the "recents" in her calls. There they were, on 6/20/19. One incoming call from Zack. Around 8:30 pm—which was the time she'd arrived at Neary's. How long had Zack waited outside her apartment building? Had he seen her and Ryan walk into the building? That would have made him angry for sure. But then, if he was the one who'd taken the photos and assaulted Ryan, and then mailed the photos from the all-night FedEx center, it meant he'd been in the city till 4:00 am. She couldn't picture it.

Not with Dollie waiting in a police precinct.

He stood a couple of inches away from her. "Honestly, Jen, look at me. Do you honestly think I could mug someone?" A pause. "There's plenty of better suspects before you get to me."

"Yeah? Like?"

"What about all those chefs you mentioned in your article? They'd have it in for McAllister as much as they'd have it in for you, since he ran your article in his magazine. I'd have certainly been mad if someone wrote about my inn that way. I wouldn't have resorted to physical violence, but those Hamptons restaurants are huge businesses. Any one of them could have come to the city to punch McAllister's lights out."

Jenna was well aware of the other suspects in Ryan's assault. Although Zack hadn't mentioned him just now, Denny Dennison was still number one on her list, and she'd already made a reservation—on her cell phone in the car returning from Sag Harbor—to fly to Florida to check out the Coast Guard connection to Denny. "I'm not sure what to think right now except you should listen to Brad and get a lawyer to sit in with you when the cops come."

Zack nodded. "Fine, I'll alert Fran."

"Fran!" Jenna blurted out the name in a gasp. "Fran does real estate and wills. I think Brad meant someone who can deal with NYPD detectives."

Zack shook his head and laughed. "I appreciate your concern, Jen, but I wasn't going to get a lawyer at all. Really, I have nothing to hide. Fran will be fine." He changed the subject. "Now, how about I start some dinner? I've got gazpacho made, chilling in the refrigerator. It'll wash out the taste of Brad." He winked at Jenna as she grimaced, her thoughts churning.

The one thing she didn't want was for Zack to be hauled off by the cops in front of Dollie. She didn't want to explain to her daughter about Ryan McAllister, and how Ryan had gotten beaten up outside Jenna's apartment building in the early hours of the morning, and why the cops suspected her dad in the assault.

Chapter Forty

Week Two: Thursday

Zack called Fran the moment the two NYPD detectives arrived to question him in the late afternoon. She was there within twenty minutes. It had been a little tough since Brad had given them the heads-up about the cops. He'd wanted to be out on the water but hadn't wanted to leave in case they turned up and decided he was avoiding them, obstructing justice, resisting interrogation, or anything else that would give them an excuse to make an arrest and take him in for fingerprinting.

No sirree. He didn't want any of that kind of trouble. He didn't need that sort of grief. He'd made every effort to stay on the right side of the law for the last twenty years. He'd never even gotten a speeding ticket. He was on the dock, cleaning out a dock box when they finally arrived. He walked them back to the patio where Ana had set up a carafe of water and a jug of iced tea under the umbrella. The duo sat down and he let them sip their water while he waited for Fran to arrive. When she did, they got right down to it. Martins led the questioning, asking where Zack had been on the Thursday night when McAllister got assaulted.

"More specific please, detectives," Fran interjected. "What time are you talking about?

"We're investigating an assault on a Mr. McAllister," replied Martins, turning momentarily to stare at Fran before bringing his penetrating glare back to settle on Zack. "He's a friend of your wife's. We need to know where you were late Thursday night, early hours of Friday morning, Mr. King. It's a formality."

For sure.

A formality based on a CCTV image. For the first time in his life as Zack King, he found himself warming up to Brad for giving them a heads-up about these cops. It had given him time to prepare, and he was going to be as polite and helpful as he could be.

"I was on my way to Maine, detectives, to pick up my daughter, who was in summer camp up there." He wondered whether to add any details about Dollie, but Fran had warned him against answering more than he needed to, so he waited instead for the next question.

"Could you give us a better idea of your time line?" Martins looked impatient. "When did you set out for Maine? What time did you get there?"

He nodded, pretending he was thinking carefully about the time line and other details, as if he hadn't been preparing his answers since Brad had informed him and Jenna that the cops were coming. "I left here about six. Got to the city about eight thirty."

He realized his answer had caught them off guard. They obviously had not expected him to admit so readily that he'd been in the city. They obviously had no suspicion at all that Brad might have tipped off Zack as to what evidence they had.

"You went by way of the city?"

"Of course. I wanted to swing through and pick up my wife." He gave them his best half-cocked smile. "It's a long trip to Bethel and we had things to discuss about our daughter."

"But you didn't pick up your wife?"

"No, she wasn't at the apartment. I called her, but she didn't pick up. I waited for a while, and then had to get moving to get to Maine in time to pick up my daughter."

"Do you know what time you left the city?"

"Approximately, yes."

They glanced at each other. Then, Martins asked, "So, what time was that?"

"Around midnight. Maybe a little later. Not much later though. I had to be in Maine early for my daughter."

The cops appeared to be so surprised by his answer they didn't bother following up with a question as to how early, or what he meant by early.

"You waited all those hours? But not in the apartment?"

"No, I didn't go in. Didn't want to have to park the car in a garage. Very expensive in that part of town. I circled around and called my wife. Figured she'd call me back when she got in."

"But she didn't."

"No. I parked in a couple of different spots, kept moving so as not to get a ticket. I may have dozed off at one point."

Tuby leaned forward, almost spilling his glass of water. "Were you and your wife having problems?"

"What marriage doesn't?"

"Care to explain the problems in yours?"

He shrugged. "Not really. We were going through a bit of a rough patch, that's all. She was working in the city."

"So, you weren't separated? Didn't your wife tell you she was leaving you?"

He rolled his eyes. "Yes. In the middle of an argument. You can probably see, she's back now."

"Do you know about her relationship with Mr. McAllister?"

"I know she had one before we were married, and I know he bought the most recent article she wrote for his magazine."

"That's it?"

"Pretty much what I know."

"But you dislike Mr. McAllister, don't you?"

He grimaced, then shook his head. "I don't know him."

"You didn't see him and your wife return to her apartment?"

"Nope. All I know is what my wife told me; that he was assaulted, found in the street, and that you would probably want to talk to me."

"So, you didn't speak to either your wife or Mr. McAllister outside the building?"

"No."

Tuby asked for a refill of iced tea.

Martins took a chug from his bottled water and looked out toward the dock and the bay beyond. Then he reached into his pocket for a notebook.

"Okay, the thing is, Mr. King, we have CCTV of you in the city in the approximate time frame for the assault. So, right now, we can place you at the scene of the assault, approximately at the time of the assault, with a possible motive for the assault."

"You're not arresting him, are you?" Fran interjected.

"No." Tuby agreed. "Thing is, we'd like Mr. King to appear in an audio lineup."

"An audio lineup?" Fran looked puzzled.

"Yes, ma'am," Tuby nodded. "It's like a lineup using people to parade in front of a victim, but using voice recordings instead."

"So, he's out of his coma?" Zack interjected.

Tuby gave a curt nod.

Fran's mouth parted in a half smile. "Mr. McAllister didn't see his assailant?"

The detectives didn't reply. Zack had to hand it to Fran; she wasn't doing half badly for an attorney who wasn't into criminal defense.

Fran continued: "You realize that Mr. McAllister and my client have met, have socialized on at least one occasion." She turned to Zack for confirmation

"Years ago," he said, remembering the occasion. It was just after Jenna and he had married, when she probably still had some idea that they could all be buddies together. "It was a holiday party at the mother-in-law's house in Southampton. McAllister's mother-in-law, that is. Jenna and I didn't stay long."

"Maybe, a while back," Fran added, "but it means Mr. McAllister may recognize my client's voice and not realize it's because he heard it way back then."

The detectives looked uncertain for a moment.

"It's okay," Zack said finally. "I'll do the lineup. Whatever kind of lineup. I'm good with that, Fran. I just want this over and done with." He turned to Martins. "Are you going to take me back to the city?"

Martins shook his head. "No. In fact, Mr. McAllister was brought out to that house in Southampton yesterday, so we can do this at the Southampton police station. Monday, three in the afternoon?" He took out a card and scribbled down the address and handed Zack the card.

"That's it?" He must have looked perplexed at the thought that they were trusting him to turn up.

Martins nodded. "Just be aware Mr. King, if you fail to show, we'll put out a warrant for your arrest, okay?"

Zack held up his hands in mock surrender. "I'll be there. Don't worry, Detectives. I want this cleared up asap."

"They've got nothing," Fran said, when the duo was eventually out of earshot. "Maybe they've got the CCTV of your car on the street. But that's about it. Even I know it's not enough."

He grinned. He was fine with the audio lineup, whatever it entailed.

Lola, of course, had a different take on it, throwing up her hands in horror, saying he should never have agreed to it. He didn't argue with her; he was grateful to Jenna for asking Lola to drive out to prep him, and he was grateful to Lola for turning up the evening before the lineup.

"You shouldn't have volunteered so readily," she said over dinner.

The dinner was delicious. He'd grilled a whole branzino and tiny, buttered potatoes in their jackets with a salsa made of nectarines, tomatillos, and red onions in lime juice. He joked about the last meal of a condemned man, which prompted Lola's remark—and her annoyance.

Then, Jenna voiced her concern. "The lineup sounds hokey," she said quietly.

He wondered if she was genuinely concerned for him, or because she didn't want Dollie finding out and asking awkward questions.

Chapter Forty-One

Week Three: Monday

H e drove to Southampton with Fran and Jenna while Lola followed in her own Jaguar. Lola had spoken to the Southampton cops before they left the inn, and it seemed that they were all going to be welcome. Lola had also given Fran some specific instructions as well as tips on everything she knew about audio lineups. It had all sounded very legal and technical.

Lola had said something about "foils" which she explained would be four or five other male voices (probably of cops and detectives at the precinct) who were of Zack's age and ethnic background "blah, blah, blah," and who would be speaking the exact same phrases that he'd have to record before the lineup. Lola said it would include the phrase or sentence that the perp had said to McAllister—as he remembered it—during the assault. Then, they would all watch McAllister try to pick the one that sounded like the guy who assaulted him.

Lola suggested that Fran take detailed notes about the foils and about the procedure. She said if, "God forbid" (her words) it came to charges or a trial based on the results of the audio lineup, a good criminal defense attorney would still stand a chance of getting the audio lineup result thrown out. Audio lineups were highly unusual, she'd said, but she knew of at least one conviction on Long Island that had been based solely on such a lineup.

Anyway, she'd added, echoing Fran, an audio lineup meant Ryan McAllister obviously didn't see who assaulted him. "This is all very shaky ground for the cops," she said. "It means they have nothing other than the CCTV of your car on the street."

Lola was being a rock, he thought. Which wasn't surprising. She'd always liked him. He knew she was the one who'd taken his side when Jenna was dithering over getting married. As they were getting ready to leave for the ferry, he mentioned his one niggling fear to her: What if McAllister recognized his voice from when they'd met years before and identified him out of spite or for his own purposes?

Lola raised one perfectly groomed eyebrow. "You mean if he wants you out of the way so he can pursue Jenna?"

He nodded as Lola shook her head vehemently. "I don't think that's a consideration right now." She looked to see if Jenna was anywhere in earshot. "Teddi is the one nursing him back to health, and she's doing it in the luxury of all her homes. I don't think Ryan is in any shape to fight that."

It was pretty much the way he'd figured it. He didn't really think McAllister wanted to break up with his wife. He also didn't figure McAllister for the sort of guy who wanted the news to get out that he'd gotten beaten to a pulp by an angry husband for messing around with that husband's wife. That would have put a real dent in his image.

He was feeling quite relaxed when the cops led him into the room to record the key phrases they would play for McAllister. One of the phrases was, "Take that, you motherfucker!" He sat down at a long conference table just as five other guys walked in. Sure enough, they all looked like cops or detectives: All short hair, polished faces, and ties with button-down shirts. They were given numbers, and Zack was handed a small index card with the number 2 printed on it. Then, they all took turns recording the couple of phrases also printed out on the index cards, once without a mic, and the second time using a microphone. Martins, who was supervising, asked Zack to pull the microphone closer to his mouth, like the others had done.

Then, they waited in a poky, windowless office. Tuby and Martins told Fran they'd be waiting till McAllister arrived and was seated so that he didn't accidentally bump into Zack. It would compromise the lineup, they said, if McAllister knew he was in it. For the same reason, they didn't want Jenna hanging outside either.

It didn't take long before Martins was leading them all into the witness room. Jenna and Fran and Lola were allowed into the witness room along with him. Obviously, Lola had some pull. She explained that the room was the one they used for regular lineups where witnesses got to see perps standing in front of them. Only now it was reversed. They would get to see the victim, but he wouldn't be able to see the suspect who was witnessing the lineup.

Fran, who'd detoured as they were being led into the witness room, returned to inform them that McAllister had arrived. "He was helped into a wheelchair," she said.

Zack avoided looking at Jenna, knowing she probably wasn't taking this news well. She looked white when McAllister wheeled himself into the room on the other side of the two-way mirror. He was alone—without his wife or an attorney. There was a row of five chairs on their side of the mirror, and Zack sat down on the middle chair. Jenna let Fran and Lola sit on either side of him and then perched herself on the end of the row. Out of the corner of his eye, Zack saw her staring at McAllister as if she was trying to drink in every little detail about him.

McAllister moved stiffly, with his head bandaged and a big, yellowing bruise on his cheek and temple. His fingers clutched the arms of the chair. He leaned back in his chair as the operator of the lineup, in the room with McAllister, explained how the process worked: McAllister was to call a number from one to six and the operator would play that numbered recording. McAllister could call the numbers in any order so long as he called all of them at least once. He could then ask for any of the numbers as many times as he needed to hear the recordings.

He began by calling the number five first, then number one, then three, then four, then two—which was Zack— and finally, six. Then he sat for a while, staring down at the notes he'd scribbled on a notepad, holding the pencil awkwardly between two fingers. He asked to hear three again, then two again. Then, the number two recording again. He sat in silence again, as if listening to some sound in his head. He asked for five, then two—Zack's recorded phrases—again.

Zack felt a bead of sweat erupt on his upper lip as McAllister asked for the number five and two recordings to be replayed. Whatever the cops thought, Zack was sure that McAllister knew that Zack was the main suspect and the witness behind the mirror of the audio lineup. So, the thought crossed his mind that McAllister was toying with him, dragging things out, picking up the glass of water that had been poured for him, fidgeting with his pencil.

It was what Zack would have done had their roles been reversed.

He noticed McAllister's hand shaking as he brought the glass of water to his mouth. He stared at the other man's bruised fingers, and caught himself wondering what kind of a lover McAllister was. Damn it, he really hadn't wanted to go there, but suddenly he couldn't stop himself: What was it that Jenna found so fucking irresistible about the guy?

Zack turned to look at her and wished he could fathom what was going on in her head. She was staring hard at McAllister, who now looked simply perplexed. He was asking for all the recordings to be replayed.

Then he sat back. Waited. Asked for four, then for two again. Then, he looked down at his notes, studying them for what seemed like an eternity.

Zack felt a bead of sweat roll down his cheek and onto his shirt collar.

Chapter Forty-Two

They were shunted out through a back door so that they could get away without crossing paths with McAllister. Zack blinked as they all walked out into sunlight. Jenna kept looking over her shoulder as if she was hoping to catch a glimpse of her former lover. He tugged at her hand. "Told you it wasn't me."

When McAllister had finally shaken his head and told the operator, "No, I don't hear him on any of these," Fran and Lola had grinned broadly, but when Zack had looked over at Jenna, she was wiping her eyes with the back of her hand and her cheeks were wet with tears.

He didn't know whether the tears were from relief that McAllister hadn't identified Zack, or from the sight of McAllister all bruised and beaten up. He held on to her hand as they walked a couple of paces behind Fran and Lola. "Thank you," he said softly. "Thank you for being here."

Before Jenna could respond, they reached their cars and Lola threw her arms around both of them. "Well, all's well that ends well," she announced breezily. "Bet that's a huge relief, Zack." She grinned before announcing she had to get going back to the city.

They pulled out behind her, Zack's hands steady on the wheel. Fran gave one of her raspy laughs from the backseat. "I'm happy for you, Zack."

"I'm happy for me too," he replied.

Another raspy laugh from Fran. "I wasn't quite sure what I'd have done if they'd detained you. I had no idea."

He laughed too. He liked Fran. She was a friend as well as his attorney—and the type who had no time for bullshit.

She leaned forward from the backseat and put a hand on Zack's shoulder, squeezing it. "And, speaking as a friend rather than an attorney, I would have been totally distraught if they locked you up." She cast a sideways glance at Jenna. "Your husband is probably the most decent guy I know. The first time I met him, he and Jeremiah were fixing the roof on the inn. He really put you through a bit of torture, didn't he?" She looked back at Zack. "Sometimes, I wondered how long you'd stick it out." A moment later she said: "You were the best thing that happened to him."

Zack could hear the emotion in Fran's voice, and he realized that the lineup had been more of an ordeal for her than she'd bargained for. He grinned at her, hoping to put her at ease. "He was a tough taskmaster, that's for sure." He paused to laugh out loud at the memory, then glanced over at Jenna. "He'd knock on my door at six every morning and off we'd go to the lumberyard for new planks for the porch, or to get new trim to replace the rotting eaves, or to get sheetrock up or pour the concrete for the floors." Zack glanced across at Jenna. "You should have seen this place. It was falling apart around him."

"Yes," Fran interrupted. "You gave the old man a whole new lease on life."

"That worked both ways," Zack nodded. "He let me run with it when it came to the kitchen renovations. I told him I had an idea for turning the house into an inn with a small restaurant, and he just said, go ahead. You don't get that sort of opportunity every day."

Zack fell silent. Jeremiah had been the grandfather he'd always wanted, just as Zack had evidently turned out to be the grandson Jeremiah had always wanted. He had genuinely loved the old man, but had been shocked, nevertheless, after Jeremiah's death when Fran told him he'd inherited the entire property.

Jenna intruded on his thoughts as they approached Cutchogue after dropping off Fran, reminding him they needed to pick up Dollie from Cath's house. They'd both decided to let Dollie sleep at Cath's over the weekend so that she wouldn't wonder why Fran and Lola and her parents were talking about cops and audio lineups. Jenna had gone to great lengths to ask Cath's mother to keep an eye on Dollie, and not to let the girls roam around town in the evening. She'd given Cath's mother some hokey explanation, which Zack hadn't even listened to. He knew Jenna was still looking over her shoulder for Denny Dennison to materialize and snatch Dollie.

"I'd like to take Dollie with me to Palm Beach tomorrow," Jenna added as they pulled up in front of Cath's house. "I have a reservation for tomorrow morning. I can add Dollie to it. I'm sure there's plenty of seats on the flight, what with it being summer. Not too many people going to Florida."

"Florida?" he echoed, not masking the surprise in his voice.

Jenna cleared her throat. "It's for my Monte Carlo story," she said. "I'm sorry, but what with this whole audio lineup going on, I didn't want to mention it." She cleared her throat again. "Thing is, there's a Palm Beach angle to the story. You know how these rich people bounce around all the swanky resorts. The magazine will reimburse me for expenses . . . but obviously not Dollie's plane fare. I just think it would be good for her to see other places."

Before he could tell her what he thought of the idea, Jenna continued: "And I thought I'd swing by your mother's old place in Briny Breezes. I could pick up whatever stuff that neighbor is holding on to for you."

"No!" He was startled by how loud and adamant that one word sounded in the car. So loud and adamant that Jenna snapped her head to stare pointedly at him. He remembered she'd mentioned the phone call from the neighbor's son who'd rescued some of Miranda's stuff from a leak in the roof, but he'd told Jenna he would take care of it when he had more time.

"No, don't go out of your way," he added, a little more calmly. "Don't waste your time. You have enough on your plate with your assignment."

Jenna laid a hand on his arm. "Don't get upset, Zack. I know your Mom lived in a trailer park. You told me that when I met you. I thought it might be good for Dollie to see where her grandmother lived. Even to spend the night there. Apparently, there isn't a tenant in there at the moment."

He took a deep breath and then shrugged. There was one way to make Jenna more determined to do something and that was by trying to argue her out of it. He focused, instead, on trying to remember the day he'd gone along with the real Zack to the trailer that had been his mother's home before she died. It was a week or so before they were due to sail the *Manny Boy* up to Block Island. Zack had told him he wanted to clean out the trailer so he could turn it over to the local realtor for renting. He remembered Zack tossing a lot of stuff into trash bags, which he then threw into a dumpster in a mall parking lot, but he'd gathered up all the photos of himself and Miranda and pocketed them. "I'll need something to show the old geezer I'm his grandson," he'd said. Then he'd put some other items into a small leather traveling bag and stuffed it into a closet, which he padlocked. "I'll come back for this other stuff," he'd said.

Try as hard as he could, Zack couldn't remember now what was in the bag, and that meant he didn't know if he should be worried about Jenna looking through it.

As it turned out, after lunch (which both he and Jenna refrained from calling a celebration lunch in front of Dollie) their daughter made it very clear she wasn't interested in visiting some "smelly trailer park" where her grandmother had lived, or even stopping in glamorous Palm Beach.

"Florida is full of old people." Dollie frowned at Jenna across the table as she fiddled with her cell phone and suddenly shrieked: "Look at this! It's about a hundred degrees there right now and pouring rain." She looked up from the iPhone. "Thanks, but no thanks, Mom."

"Oh, Dollie, I'm so disappointed." Jenna sounded genuinely upset. "I think you would have loved window shopping on Worth Avenue."

Zack didn't comment. He realized Jenna was doing her best to find a way through to Dollie, but he suspected she would have quickly gotten impatient when she realized she had a sulky teenager accompanying her on a work assignment. He also had a feeling that after Jenna did whatever she needed to do in Palm Beach, she'd rethink driving to a trailer park to pick up an old bag of useless garbage.

Chapter Forty-Three

Week Three: Wednesday

Jenna was outside the gates of the Coast Guard station just after nine in the morning. She knew there were coast guards on duty 24/7, but she also knew the office kept regular business hours, otherwise she would have been at the gates much earlier. She had woken early, around six, with the sun streaming in right through her eyelids. She'd reached the Palm Beach Shores and Vacation Villas on Singer Island late the previous night and had left the blinds in her room open. Big mistake. No hiding from the sun in her ocean-view room.

She'd aimed to find a hotel on the other side of the Intracoastal Waterway near the Coast Guard station, but someone on the plane had dissuaded her. Riviera Beach sounded more glamorous than it was, he'd said, and Singer Island was just three minutes over the Blue Heron Boulevard Bridge.

In a way, she was relieved Dollie had chosen to stay home. She had to admit it hadn't been a very wise choice, anyway, to bring Dollie on a trip that might have placed her in the path of a stalker. Certainly, her daughter was right about the weather. The humidity was debilitating, even this early in the morning. She couldn't wait to be done with Florida.

But it was the only lead she had left. She couldn't leave it be. Even if her search ended with finding Denny all settled down in some sunny beach shack with hardly any memory of her or her story, it would be worth it. More than worth it. She'd have closure. She would finally know that she hadn't done him any lasting damage.

Now, outside the gates to the Coast Guard station, she pressed the buzzer on the keypad, and checked her hair in the rearview mirror. A voice came through the intercom asking her business.

"I have a letter from you guys about stuff that you found . . ." The gates swung open. Two minutes later she was handing over the letter to the first coast guard she encountered.

He looked as if he was reading it over twice. "This letter is fifteen years old. Do you know that?"

"I know," Jenna chewed on her bottom lip. "Look, it's a long story, but it's addressed to a guy I need to find. I just found the letter among his things, and I'm hoping that the coast guard who signed this letter might have more information. Or that there might be a clue in this property that's mentioned here."

The coast guard shrugged and exhaled with a long, low whistle. "Good luck with that. I'm pretty sure his stuff is no longer here. We don't have a lost and found. If it was property from a rescue we would turn it over to the EMS guys. And, if it was from an apprehension on the water, it would go with the law enforcement agency. Say like drugs, those would go with the DEA. Even if we did store anything, and I can't imagine what that would be, we'd toss it if it was unclaimed after five years. Definitely after ten. I don't know what to tell you."

"It's really vital," Jenna interrupted. "How about Lieutenant Manfred Greene? The guy who signed this letter?"

"Manny?" He turned to another coast guard who entered the office behind him. "Hey, Bernie? Where's Manny hanging out these days?"

"Where he's been hanging out since he retired. At the old place."

The coast guard, whose name was Larry, smiled at her. "That means he's not too far away. The old place is the old Coast Guard HQ on Peanut Island."

"An island?" Jenna echoed. "How would I get to it?"

"There are water taxis that'll take you there." He reached for a white sheet of paper. "Here." He drew a big X. "You're here. Turn left out of the gates. Take the road a mile or two. The marina for the water taxi is just the other side of the bridge. Once you're on the island, just start walking. You'll eventually hit the old place. Ask the guy on the taxi for the shortest route."

"How will I recognize Manny?"

Larry looked at his buddy. Then shrugged. "You know what? I'm off duty in fifteen minutes. I'll take you there. If Manny's there, he'll be messing around, or napping on the porch. He'll be easy to find."

Larry did not mention that he'd be taking Jenna there by boat, but two minutes later she was clinging to the armrests as his little Boston whaler left the dock. "Won't take long," he yelled at her cheerfully as the boat gathered speed. She had never been on a boat so small. It seemed smaller than the dinghy that hung off the end of the *Dollie Too*. She wished she hadn't eaten such a big breakfast.

As they bounced over the waves, Larry kept up a steady chatter like a tour guide. Peanut Island was now a Palm Beach County Park, but it had once been the home of the Lake Worth Inlet Coast Guard. It was also the place where an underground bunker had once been maintained for President Kennedy, who had visited his Palm Beach winter home frequently during the short time he was president, in the sixties. The bunker was there in case of a nuclear war.

Jenna was about to ask if there was a bunker at Mar-a-Lago when a sandy beach and some rotting pilings rolled into view. Larry cut the motor and coasted onto the sand. He helped her down onto the beach and set off striding toward a squat white building.

"Hey Manny?" he yelled as they approached the front doors. "Come on out, brought you a visitor here."

Manny was not at all what Jenna had expected, which was some wild man with disheveled hair and a weather-beaten face. Instead, his gray hair was neatly slicked back, his cargo pants were tan and clean and pressed, and his eyes were behind an expensive pair of Ray Bans.

Jenna handed over the letter Manny had sent to the house in Seaford. "I'm following up on this, Manny. I'm trying to find Mr. Dennison. Does this stir any memory for you? At all?"

Manny stared at the page for a while. "Yeah, sure." He looked slightly embarrassed. "Sure. Sure."

Jenna stared at him expectantly.

He cleared his throat. "We don't keep lost and found stuff as a rule. But I fished out one of the life preservers of the *Manny Boy* from the ocean, and well, it was knocking around and I kept it. See, my name is Manfred, Manny for short, so I hung *Manny Boy* on my wall at the coast guard station."

"You fished it out of the water?" Jenna frowned. "You just found it floating in the water? I don't get it."

Manny shook his head forcefully. "No, what happened, we got a Mayday from the *Manny Boy*. It was a sloop. A beauty. The kids that were sailing it were caught in a squall and stuff got tossed around and overboard and we fished it out."

Jenna held out the letter he'd sent to Denny Dennison. "So why this?"

"Yeah, Dennison. He was one of the two kids that were sailing it. The one that went overboard."

"You fished him out too?"

"Yes. Yes, we did. He was wearing a flotation device but wasn't strapped to a safety harness like the other kid."

Jenna stared at Manny, aware that her mouth was hanging open. "You're saying he drowned!" Even as she mouthed the words, she couldn't quite process what Manny was saying. "Are you telling me he was dead when you got him out of the water?" She heard her voice rise shrilly.

Manny suddenly looked startled. "I'm sorry. I didn't realize you were close to this gentleman. I mean, we tried our best to revive him. We always do our best . . . I'm really sorry to have upset you."

Jenna brushed her hair off her face as a sudden gust of wind whipped around them. Then she placed a hand on Manny's arm. "No, it's okay." She took a deep breath. "It's okay, Manny. I didn't know him. It's just that this is not what I expected to hear."

An understatement if ever there was one, thought Jenna. She took another deep breath. She had not expected this kind of closure, or such an abrupt end to her search for Denny Dennison.

"I just need a moment," she said quietly to the two men who were now staring at her with perplexed expressions on their faces. She held out her hand to retrieve the letter from Manny. She took a couple of steps toward the water as she stared at the words on the page.

She wanted to feel relief. Wanted to be glad that her worry about Dennison coming for her and Dollie was unfounded. He was dead. And yet, something niggled.

"You recall what year this happened, Manny?"

He shook his head. "Not exactly, but I had the preserver on my wall a few years before I wrote this letter. Could have been about five years."

"Five *years*?" That didn't make sense. The letter was dated September 2004. If the accident had happened five years earlier, in 1999, then Dennison had been dead five years before Dollie was born. Then who had taken the photos of Dollie as a baby?

Manny shook his head again. "Honestly, I can't be sure of the year. I remember the sloop and the drowning; that's not something you forget in a hurry, but the actual year? That's a tough one. It'll be somewhere in our records. We make a note of the incident, but usually we turn everything else, you know IDs and contact info, over to the EMS guys when they meet us at the pier. They would definitely have it, or in this case the medical examiner would have it, for sure." He nodded quickly. "Yup, that's where I got the Dennison address when I decided to write this letter." He looked at Larry. "Lucas is still out there, isn't he? Working a couple of days a week?"

Larry nodded, and Manny turned his attention back to Jenna. "Your best bet is the ME's office. They'll have all the details. They're on Gun Club Road, out by the airport. They've got autopsy reports computerized these days. Going back several decades. If you ask for Lucas, and tell him Manny sent you, he'll dig a little deeper. He'll probably have the date, the name of the sailing buddy who made the formal identification, the funeral home where they transported the body, and so on. They're a tad better organized than we are. Have to be, when it's human remains you're dealing with."

Jenna turned to go, then hesitated a moment longer. "So, why did you send this letter about the life preserver to Denny's family?"

Manny ran his hand over his hair. "When I retired and was clearing out my office, I thought I should return it to the family. I don't know why, it seemed like a good idea at the time, something they'd have of him and his last voyage . . ." Manny looked sheepish, but Jenna nodded as if the explanation made perfect sense. It made as much sense as anything else she had heard this morning.

Less than an hour later, she was walking through the doors of the ME's offices. It took staff a while to locate Lucas, and then a little while longer for Lucas to find the records in the office computer.

"June 1999." Lucas rubbed the side of his nose as he stared at the screen. "Guess they were sailing the boat back before hurricane season hit, but didn't quite miss stormy weather."

"The year was 1999?" Jenna's voice rose a notch. So, Manny had been right about how long he'd kept the life preserver on his wall, and Denny had been dead for almost five years when the photos of Dollie as a newborn were taken.

"Yes, ma'am. No mystery. Death by drowning. Body retrieved by the Coast Guard, identified by his mother, Rosie Miller of Seaford, Long Island. Transported to a West Palm Beach funeral home for burial." He swiveled the screen so that Jenna could take a look.

Identified by his mother? Jenna stared at the screen, her thoughts churning. Rosie had known of her son's death but had never told her friend Carol about it? *He's gone*, she'd told her neighbor, as if she meant that Denny had simply upped and left. So, was it Rosie who'd stalked her and taken the photos of Dollie? Was it possible that Rosie had become unhinged by her son's death? Maybe it hadn't taken much to unhinge Rosie completely. After all, what kind of a woman falls in love with a serial killer? But how likely was it that Rosie had anything to do with Ryan's assault or Bethany's disappearance so many years later? Not very, thought Jenna. An older woman like Rosie would have found it difficult to overpower Ryan, or even a girl like Bethany, no matter how unhinged she'd become.

Still, it was difficult to let go of the idea. She should find Rosie: To be positive that the old lady had had nothing to do with Ryan or Bethany. The question was, How? Jenna was back to square one. The address on the screen in front of her was Rosie's old Seaford address.

"What about the sailing buddy?" Jenna asked Lucas, grasping at a straw. "Do you have his name and contact information?"

"Not on here." Lucas sighed. "How important is this?"

"I can't even begin to answer that."

Lucas got to his feet. "Okay, okay, as a favor to Manny, I'll go and see if there's anything more in my notes. They'll be somewhere in my filing cabinet in the basement."

He didn't suggest she go with him, but Jenna followed the old man out of his office and down two floors to a freezing basement where the hallway was lined with empty gurneys. It took Lucas about ten minutes to locate the filing cabinet in a storage room and another five minutes before he held up a folder with a smile. Perching on a stool, he riffled though the pages of notes. Jenna thought she was going to have to leave empty-handed, when Lucas grunted and looked up, beaming.

"Well, lookee here." He peered at handwritten squiggles over the top of his glasses. "But the only name I've got is the name of the marina from which the crew sailed." Jenna waited for more as Lucas brought the page closer to his face. "I've also got the name of an FBI agent who called me about Dennison about a year after the drowning," he said. "He said he wanted confirmation of the drowning. Said he'd been looking for Dennison and had tracked him as far as the marina."

Lucas looked at Jenna and shrugged in response to her startled look. *What interest could the FBI have had in Denny Dennison?*

"I can give you the name and phone number of the G-man, and the address of the Cozy Cove Marina in Fort Lauderdale," Lucas said. "But don't ask me why the G-man was looking for Dennison. He didn't tell me." Lucas snapped the folder shut. "And I didn't ask."

Chapter Forty-Four

Week Three: Wednesday Evening / Thursday Morning

A s soon as she saw the mobile homes on both sides of A1A, Jenna knew she had arrived in Briny Breezes. On her way down from the ME's office and her meeting with Lucas, she had called the airline to change the following day's reservation for her return trip to New York. She'd noticed Cozy Cove Marina was almost next door to the airport in Fort Lauderdale, so there was no point in trekking all the way back to West Palm Beach for her flight home. She needed to visit the marina in person to explain why she was looking for the crew of a boat that had sailed out of the marina almost twenty years ago. She didn't want anyone hanging up on the long-winded explanation she had readied. She had also called the

FBI agent, Jonathan Vickery, and left her name and phone number with his office. Now, as she drove slowly down the street where Zack's mother had lived, she saw Sam waving her down. She'd texted him that she was on her way, and now he was waiting for her outside his trailer, standing next to a tiny grill that was belching out smoke. He was a good-looking man with what she was beginning to think of as a Florida complexion: heavily tanned and a little weather-beaten, with premature wrinkles around the eyes. He checked under the grill hood before producing a set of keys and beckoning her next door into what had been home for Zack and his mother.

When Zack had finally calmed down after she'd told him she intended to swing by Briny Breezes to meet Sam, he'd warned her not to expect too much. He didn't even know the condition of Miranda's old home. The realtor's office had continued to rent it out, but God knows, some people would pay rent to sleep in a dock box by the beach.

He was essentially biding his time, holding on to the property in case a developer came along and offered all the current owners a mega deal for the prime piece of land on the ocean. It had happened once before, and now there were fresh rumors about a developer making similar offers so that he could dedicate the land to a Trump Presidential Library.

Jenna followed Sam into the trailer. A ceiling fan was whirring at top speed in the main room and all the windows were flung open.

"It was a little musty in here," Sam explained. "But I'm not sure that letting in all this heat helps." He showed her how the stove worked, and that the refrigerator was running and the water was on. Jenna smiled and didn't bother telling him she wasn't going to stay long enough to need a stove or refrigerator. He pointed to some bedding and blankets on the bed in the one bedroom. "They're clean.

I threw them in with my laundry when I thought Zachariah might fly down."

Jenna cleared her throat. "He's sorry he couldn't make it. Right now, he's gearing up for our busy season. I was flying down this way for a work assignment, so, two birds with one stone."

Sam grinned in reply. "No problem. I'll let you throw some cold water on your face, then please come and join me. I got ribeye going on the grill, and some sliders."

Jenna joined him less than ten minutes later. The ocean air made her ravenous, and she devoured a couple of sliders and immediately washed them down with a tumbler of vodka on the rocks.

"Did you know Zack's mother?" Jenna asked Sam as he turned off the grill and set the ribeye aside under foil.

"Not that well. I was ten when she died, but she and my mom were friends for years."

"So what do you remember about her?"

Sam laughed. "Back then, I would have described her as totally batty. My mom said she was only batty when she went off her meds. I think today she'd be diagnosed bipolar. Although she was also a big drinker so you couldn't say whether it was too much booze or too little medication that caused her issues."

Jenna allowed Sam to fill her tumbler again with vodka rocks as he launched into another memory of Miranda. Gradually, she heard all about Miranda's wild mood swings, her vicious temper when she was drinking, and how she'd knifed one of her abusive boyfriends. "Zachariah got involved in that one, and the cops initially charged him with the knifing. I think he spent a night in jail before the boyfriend recovered and pointed the finger at Miranda."

Jenna sipped her vodka, took a small bite of the ribeye and wondered why Zack had never mentioned any of this. His mother's history of bipolar behavior was surely why he had kept the diary focusing on Dollie's behavior. It was something he should have shared with her years ago when Dollie was born. Jenna promised herself she'd confront Zack about it when she got home.

Sam filled up his own vodka glass. "Miranda was allowed to plead guilty to disorderly conduct. She was a bit of a charmer when she wanted to be. I'm sure she sweet-talked her way out of that one." He got to his feet, retreating inside his trailer for a couple of minutes before emerging with the leather bag holding Miranda's belongings. "I brought it over here, had it out in the sun to dry off the outside. Like I said, the stuff inside is okay, pretty well preserved, considering."

They went through the contents together. There were some handwritten recipes, a list of books to read by Carl Hiaasen and Edna O'Brien; a receipt from the Boca Raton hospital for Zack's delivery by C-section. Jenna wondered if Zack had seen it. She placed that document in her tote as she picked up a bunch of photo-booth strips of a young Miranda with a guy. Same guy in all the strips, from the type of photo booths that used to be popular in shopping malls before iPhones and selfies knocked them out of business.

She stared at the male face in the strips. Then, she realized it was a younger-looking Chief Brad. In the photos he had long hair, sideburns, a mustache. They had obviously been taken before Zack's birth, before Miranda had been kicked out of her father's house on the North Fork for getting pregnant. In another photo—taken with a real camera—Brad was sitting on a motorbike.

Very seventies, thought Jenna as she recalled Brad's efforts to establish a connection with Zack.

Zack had explained it to her once, saying that Brad had wanted Miranda to have a blood test for her baby before he agreed to marry her. Implying, as Zack had pointed out, that he didn't believe he was her only boyfriend. "Well, I'm not going to let him take a test now to prove he was," Zack had said emphatically. "Don't need him now."

So, maybe Brad really was Zack's father, thought Jenna. That would explain why Miranda had kept the photos. Whatever happened, you'd surely keep a photo of your baby's father, wouldn't you?

She didn't tell Sam why she was taking the photos. Instead, she said, "I guess Miranda wasn't big on using a camera. There aren't any photos of Zack."

"I think there were, but Zachariah probably took those to show his grandfather. You know, to show himself with Miranda."

Jenna wondered idly where those photos were now. She had never seen any of Zack's baby photos. The only photos or albums she had ever seen at the inn were those taken of him and his grandfather renovating the inn.

"Did you know Zachariah?"

Sam shook his head. "Not really. I was a kid when his mom died, and I never really saw him again after. He only came by that one time to clean out the trailer, but I must have been at school. He'd moved out of her home a few years before. I don't really know where he was or what he did. A bit of everything, my mom said."

A couple of hours later, Jenna stumbled getting to her feet, and Sam helped her across the strip of concrete separating their trailers. She was asleep minutes after her head touched the pillow. She slept deeply but not long, waking in a sweat that bathed her whole body. Since it was already getting light, she got out of bed, threw on shorts and a T-shirt over a bathing suit, and walked down to the beach.

Sam was up, with the door to his trailer standing open, when she returned after her swim. She'd also found a cold-water shower on the beach, where she'd rinsed off the salt water. "I feel like a human being again," she announced. "That was a delicious shower on the beach."

"Probably much more refreshing than the one in your trailer," Sam agreed, adding that he'd have breakfast ready in about a half hour.

Florida hospitality, thought Jenna. Sam was so helpful. He had googled the Fort Lauderdale marina the previous evening and input directions into her rental car's GPS even though she could see on her iPhone that it was a straight run down I-95. She was crossing to Sam's trailer when her phone pinged with a breaking news alert from *Newsday*. She opened the message as she sat down in the folding chair on Sam's deck. It carried a Cutchogue dateline. It was just one line: *Body Washes Up on Robins Island. Feared to be Missing Local Woman.*

Chapter Forty-Five

Z ack slipped his cell phone into his pants pocket and watched Brad's police car pull up outside the front doors. He'd been dreading this ever since word among the locals got out in the early hours of the morning that a couple of kids on a Sunfish had seen a body wedged in between the rocks on the west side of Robins Island.

Brad had called first thing. He said he thought Zack might be of some help in a preliminary identification. He didn't have to spell it out; it was a good bet it was Bethany.

Brad stepped through the front doors into the lobby, and Zack beckoned him through into the lounge. "News travels fast," he told Brad. "Jenna just saw the alert on her *Newsday* app."

Brad didn't respond. Instead, he pulled something out of his pocket, then opened his hand to show Zack a bracelet.

It was silver that had tarnished.

Zack nodded to indicate that he recognized it. Of course he did. It had been a Christmas present for Bethany from him and Jenna, although Jenna had never seen it.

He'd picked it out, bought it and wrapped it up. Jenna couldn't have cared less. He groaned as if someone had just punched him in the stomach.

"You recognize it?"

"Yes. It was a Christmas gift from Jenna and me." He felt the color draining from his face. "It was on the body?"

Brad nodded. "Sorry, son."

Zack turned away quickly and rushed to the bathroom down the hallway, where he retched violently, bringing up his morning coffee. His eyes teared up from the retching and Brad acknowledged the shock of it when Zack returned to the lounge.

"Honestly, I thought she'd turn up okay sooner or later," the deputy said, looking helpless. His usual I'll-take-charge-of-everything attitude seemed to have evaporated.

Zack sank down into one of the sturdy oak chairs by the door. His forehead and face felt clammy. "Brad, I . . ." he started, but couldn't finish the sentence.

Brad gripped his shoulder. "Take a deep breath. Yep, and again," he said. "Where's Jenna?"

"She's in Florida on a work assignment. That was her on the cell phone as you pulled up. She'll probably be back later today," Zack added, although Jenna hadn't said anything about coming back just yet.

"Okay," Brad nodded. "I'll keep you posted. This is just a preliminary ID. We're getting dental records from Riverhead. We've got to be positive before we give the info to the press." He prepared to leave.

"I expect TV reporters and media will come barging in here within the hour. We had a missing girl—now that it's a drowned body, they're already putting two and two together. I could put up some police tape at the end of the driveway."

"Yeah," Zack said, "that would be a good thing." He took a deep breath. "Do you know what happened to her? Did she drown?"

Brad shook his head. "Won't know for sure till the ME finishes his autopsy. All he's got so far is an indication of trauma to the head. But he can't tell yet if that happened on the rocks after she went in the water, maybe accidentally, or whether someone did that to her and then dumped her in the water."

Zack took another deep breath and exhaled slowly. "Jeez, Brad. If he decides someone killed her, I'll be the prime suspect, right?"

There was a long, awkward pause before Brad replied. "Well, let's not go there just yet . . ."

"Just give me some idea," Zack interrupted. "I mean, let's say she was murdered; say someone picked her up on her way into town that Sunday and then killed her, maybe raped her and killed her, you guys are going to start by looking at me? Isn't that right?"

Brad shook his head. "For a start, if the ME decides it's homicide, it won't be Southold PD that's investigating. It will be the Suffolk County homicide squad. We'll have to share our information with them, but they'll take the lead. And then . . ."

"Then, what?" Zack felt beads of sweat erupting at his hairline.

Brad nodded. "Yes, okay, they'll probably want to speak to you. You were the last known person to see her alive. You admitted that you and she had words on the boat; that she wanted to stay and you told her to go back to Riverhead; her roommate will tell them that according to Bethany, the two of you were having an affair." Brad stopped and sighed. "On top of that, Jenna found her cell phone here. That might look like she never got off your boat."

There was another long moment of silence between them before Brad added: "I probably don't have to tell you that if the ME finds any DNA on her . . . or in her . . . then the homicide guys will almost certainly ask for your DNA."

"But . . ."

Brad held his hand up. "If you're a person of interest and you don't consent, they'll get a court order." Suddenly, his face brightened. "But you could volunteer before they ask. It would be one sure way to clear things up and get them off your back."

Zack exhaled loudly as Brad took a step toward him and laid a beefy hand on his shoulder

"Look, I know you refused to take a DNA test to determine if I'm your father. I know you're touchy about that, so I got to assure you, if you let the county guys take a swab, there's no way I could get my hands on that. Don't be pigheaded about it. I'm giving you my best advice."

Zack nodded, barely listening to the end of Brad's little speech. He had to get out of the house, he told Brad. Go out on the water, where he could breathe. He'd need to take Dollie. He didn't want her finding out about Bethany on her phone. He'd need to break the news to her gently. She'd been very fond of Bethany.

Brad muttered that he understood and agreed it was probably a good move to get away from the reporters.

Definitely. Zack knew they'd find a way to get close to the house. They'd probably want to charter a boat to ride out to Robins Island. Zack knew he just wouldn't be able to deal with that.

"Just don't go too far, son," Brad said, walking to the main doors of the inn and out to his car.

After Brad was gone, Zack checked with Ana, who told him they had one guest arriving. He'd booked the day before; before they'd found Beth's body, Ana assured him. She was pretty sure he wasn't a reporter.

He nodded, fine. "But don't take anyone else, or we'll be swarming with reporters. Tell everyone else we're full."

She nodded.

Of course, Ana was a rock. Nothing much fazed her. She'd hold the fort till Jenna arrived.

Then he texted Jenna to fill her in.

Looks like it's Bethany. Brad was here with her bracelet.

OMG!!!!! Jenna responded immediately.

Brad says it's a good idea to get away, he texted back, as if it was Brad's idea, not his. *TV news vans gathering at end of driveway. I need to get Dollie out of here.*

It was a few minutes before Jenna replied. "*Of course. Where u going?*"

Across the Sound, maybe Block Island, he texted.

Although when he and Dollie finally pushed away from the dock, he steered the boat in the opposite direction.

Chapter Forty-Six

By the time she left Briny Breezes heading for I-95 to Fort Lauderdale, Jenna had checked the website of every local paper on Long Island for any additional news. There was none. There was only speculation linking the news of the body to the missing persons report Bethany's roommate had filed. A North Fork news website had added a line about Bethany interning at the Kings Inn. Way to go, thought Jenna. For sure, TV news vans would be pulling up outside the inn, right this minute.

She was relieved that Zack was taking Dollie out of that scene; he wouldn't know how to deal with it. Once Jenna was back on the North Fork, however, she wanted Dollie home and with her. With both her and Zack. If it was indeed Bethany who'd been found in the water, Dollie would be inconsolable.

If there was a way Jenna could have gotten home faster, she'd have taken it. As it was, her flight from Fort Lauderdale was the first available from the Palm Beach County area to Long Island.

It took her almost an hour to drive from Briny Breezes to the Cozy Cove Marina. She was impressed that I-95 had five lanes each way. Even so, traffic was as bumper-to-bumper bad in some spots as it was on the LIE in New York. As she neared the marina, she hoped she'd get an answer to her question about Denny Dennison's sailing buddy. But what were the chances that anyone at the marina would be able to easily and quickly unearth information about a sailing trip in 1999?

Jenna parked and walked across the tarmac to the marina office, which was signposted with a blinking red neon arrow. A thirty-something woman with blonde hair tied back in a ponytail looked up as she pushed open the door.

"Good morning." Jenna approached the desk, where a nameplate stated the young woman's name was Stefanie Fuller. "I'm looking for some information about a boat that set sail from here a while back." Jenna bit her lip. "Quite a while back."

"Okay." Stefanie smiled at her.

Jenna took a moment to give her the briefest of explanations. She was looking for the name and contact info of a captain who had sailed the *Manny Boy* from Florida to Block Island in 1999. Jenna looked embarrassed. "I know it's so long ago. It's just that the guy who was sailing with him, Denny Dennison, drowned and his mother never really got the whole story." Jenna shrugged. "We have a mutual friend, and the mother knows I used to be a reporter. She thought maybe I could track down the captain since I was coming to Florida to visit."

It was as hokey an explanation as she had ever cooked up, but Stefanie didn't look puzzled.

"I know the trip you're talking about. Who doesn't around here. The *Manny Boy* docked here every season for years. I was a kid back then but I know there was a drowning. It doesn't happen often, so you tend to remember things like that."

Jenna beamed, not bothering to hide her amazement. "So, you remember the name of the captain?"

Stefanie laughed. "Goodness, no. I just remember the story about the *Manny Boy*. The crew was caught in a sudden squall a little further up the coast. The boat wasn't damaged. Not that it was our first concern, you understand?"

"Do you have records for that year?"

Stefanie grimaced, but hit a couple of keys on her computer. Then she shook her head. "I didn't think they'd be in here. Our digital records only go back to 2005. We're working on the rest." Suddenly she brightened up. "Got something better than records in a computer though. We've got Dale. He's one of the family members here, so he's been around here for centuries." Stefanie laughed. "He doesn't always remember what happened yesterday, but get him talking about the old days, and he can reel off all the names of the boats that docked here, stories about the owners, and so on."

Jenna laughed. Did every marina have a stock old timer like their own Hank at Kings Marina? It sounded more hopeful than Jenna had anticipated. Still, she glanced at her watch, hoping Dale could be summoned up swiftly.

Stefanie suggested Jenna walk through to the snack bar while she looked for Dale. He'd meet her at the lunch counter.

Sure enough. Less than fifteen minutes later, Dale was following Stefanie into the snack bar. He was breathing heavily as he sat down across the table from Jenna and reached for an inhaler. "COPD," he explained. "Not as young as I was."

Stefanie patted his hand. "This lady's here about the *Manny Boy.*"

Dale's eyes brightened. "Yeah, Commander Graver's sloop. I remember her crystal clear. Ran into a squall on one of her trips back north. A few miles up the coast from here. One of the kids drowned."

"Yes," Jenna nodded. "Kid by the name of Denny Dennison."

"That's right." Dale fiddled with his inhaler. "Probably a mistake to have taken him on."

"A mistake?"

"The kid looked okay, but there must have been something shady about him. There was an FBI agent came here asking questions about him one day." Dale shook his head again. "Kid was already dead a couple of years by that time."

Jenna nodded quickly. This was ancient history so far as she was concerned. "I'm actually looking for the captain from that trip, Dale. I heard he carried on with the trip up to Block Island."

"That's right. Picked up another crew member in Lake Worth. Zachariah. That was his name."

"The crew member's name?"

"Nah," said Dale. "Nah. The captain."

"Zachariah is my husband's name, too. Everyone calls him Zack." Jenna smiled.

Dale shook his head vehemently. "Why would you shorten a good solid name like Zachariah?" He reached for his inhaler again. "Nah, I always called him Zachariah. He was a good sailor too. A little bit of a know-it-all sometimes, but solid on the water." Dale paused, but before Jenna could prod him for any more information, he added. "Yeah, not a bad kid at all. Came from that trailer park, north of here. Briny Breezes." Jenna's ears pricked up. "Maybe you heard of it."

Jenna nodded, aware of her pounding heartbeat.

"King. That's it. That was his last name. Of course. How could I forget, a King from a trailer park?" Dale chortled.

King? Zachariah King? Her Zachariah King? Of course her Zachariah King. How many different Zachariah Kings could have lived in Briny Breezes?

Jenna's stomach clenched.

"Are you okay?" Stefanie was staring quizzically at Jenna.

Jenna nodded. "Might be the diesel oil," she lied. "It's making me feel queasy." She got to her feet. "I don't suppose you have an address for him?" She didn't really need it, but she had nothing else to ask.

Dale shook his head. "He won't be at the trailer park. He said he was quitting after he delivered the *Manny Boy.* Said he had plans up north. Commander Graver may know where he fetched up. We got his address somewhere."

Jenna waited while Stefanie found the address, knowing she'd never need to follow up on it. She knew exactly where Zachariah King had fetched up.

There couldn't be any doubt about it, Jenna told herself as she made her way to the airport. Her Zachariah King had sailed up the coast with her Denny Dennison almost twenty years ago—and this was the first she was hearing of it. She felt like her head was going to explode. Zack had never told her about sailing up the coast from Florida. She'd always had some image of him packing up his things after his mother died and hitching his way up I-95 to Long Island to meet his grandfather. He certainly had never mentioned a sailing buddy who'd drowned, much less a sailing buddy named Denny Dennison.

Once she was at the gate waiting for her flight, she ordered a wine and tried to organize her thoughts in a more orderly fashion. She tried to picture Zack meeting Denny Dennison almost twenty years before. Denny would probably not have volunteered any information about his father, the serial killer, or the fact that he'd been exposed as a "spawn of evil" in a supermarket tabloid. It's why he had left home, after all: to shake off his past and get away from pointing fingers.

So, when she first mentioned her ill-fated scoop to Zack, he'd had no reason to think that the spawn in the story was his sailing buddy. For back then, she had never mentioned Denny Dennison by name. Never. Not even to Lola. She had wanted to expunge the name and the story from her memory. And, if she mentioned it at all, she had always described the serial killer's bastard son as "the spawn" or "the kid" distancing herself from the idea that there was a real, thinking, feeling person behind the epithet.

So, yes, it was possible that Zack had called her without knowing of her connection to his dead crew member. And, yes, it was possible that he subscribed to and read travel magazines like *Hither and Yon* because he was in the hospitality business. And sure, it was possible that he had simply found her name looking for articles that featured inns like his, even though Jenna's article had been no more than a tiny snippet. But if that was how he'd found her, thought Jenna, it just had to be the biggest, hugest coincidence in the world.

Okay, so a coincidence. A gigantic coincidence. But they did happen. Sometimes.

Jenna took a deep breath. And, then another. What was totally inexplicable, however, was that Zack had not said a single word when she'd mentioned Denny Dennison's name just days ago. She had definitely mentioned the name then. She remembered it clearly. They'd been on the *Dollie Too* just before Zack and Dollie took off with the guests from the inn, and she had voiced her suspicions about Denny Dennison to warn Zack about him. So, surely he should have had some reaction like: "Wow, I once knew a guy named Denny Dennison." Or "Dennison? That's weird. He was a sailing buddy of mine way back."

And then, Jenna would have said, "That's quite possible. He took off after the story broke. His mother said he'd gone to the islands."

So, why had Zack not said something like, "If he's the same guy, nothing to worry about now. He's dead."

Chapter Forty-Seven

He skirted the shoreline through the narrow channel between shore and Robins Island. Out on the water, he was able to breathe again without feeling as if there was a giant hand tightening around his lungs. He tried not to stare at the spot where they'd found Bethany. How the hell had she washed up there? There was one police boat anchored by the rocks, but fortunately Dollie didn't seem interested.

He hugged the shore for a little longer until he had a clear run straight toward Meschutt and the Shinnecock Canal. It would take twenty minutes to cross the bay once they left Robins Island behind.

It was impossible not to think about Bethany.

Or more to the point, about the DNA the medical examiner might find on her and in her. Brad had mind-fucked him; had taken just a little too much pleasure in giving him the heads-up, reminding Zack of his reluctance to match his DNA with Brad's all those years ago. And what was that crap about volunteering? Who would ever volunteer to give their DNA to the cops?

Sure as shit, it wasn't going to clear anything up. Any trace of his DNA on her clothes or arms or legs could be explained by the fact that they'd been together on the boat. But then they'd find semen in her mouth and vagina, and if that DNA was good enough to be tested, well, that was just going to make things a whole lot more complicated for him.

Not less.

He knew he should have admitted to Brad that Bethany and he had screwed around that morning. Brad had prodded him on it before and had seemed ready to understand. He could have told Brad that he'd tried his best to resist her. It would have been the truth.

He could have leveled with Brad, said something about feeling depressed with Jenna gone to the city, and Bethany being right there, offering to comfort him. Any man would have understood that.

"You sure you told her to go back to school after the two of you had intercourse?" Brad would ask. "Really?"

"Yes," he could have said. Even after screwing her, he'd told her she had to go back to school. He'd been adamant about that, he could have told Brad. And, then the idea that Bethany had stormed out of the inn, upset and on foot, would make more sense. It's probably how she had run straight into some stranger who'd ended up harming her, he could have suggested. He could have persuaded Brad that screwing around with Bethany did not make him a murderer.

But now that ship had sailed.

Dollie's thin little voice suddenly interrupted his thoughts. "Dad? Where are we going?"

"The islands," he replied without thinking.

"No, c'mon Dad, really, where are we going?"

He slowed down and motioned for her to come and sit beside him. "We're going across to the beach club at Meschutt," he said, knowing it would cheer her up. She'd been pestering to go since some of her friends had gone the previous summer. Apparently, it was a bit of a wild scene on summer nights. Maybe it would help her get through what he was about to tell her.

The idea of just sailing away was tempting, however. He could do it. Easily. The *Good Times* was on its way to Barnegat Bay. He had his emergency stash of money in the Caymans account which the owner of the *Manny Boy* had set up for the real Zack and him all those years ago. He could text the kids who were sailing the boat down the coast to dock there, and leave. It would take him a couple of days to motor to Barnegat Bay so he could switch boats. Then he—and Dollie—could be gone before everything started turning to shit.

Chapter Forty-Eight

Week Three: Thursday Evening

Jenna was so exhausted by the time she landed at the Islip airport, all she wanted to do was crawl into bed and sleep for six weeks. The flight from Fort Lauderdale had been delayed, and they had not made up the time in the air, even though the plane was one of the new super 737s. She'd tried not to let her thoughts twist themselves anymore, but it was difficult to escape the obvious conclusion: Zack had not said anything about Denny because Denny was a convenient scapegoat for the attack on Ryan.

He had thought her idea that Denny was behind Ryan's assault and Bethany's disappearance was a "waste of time," and yet he'd suggested she share her suspicions with Brad and the city cops. Why? So, that there was another suspect beside himself? Why would he want to divert attention from himself, if he was innocent? Obviously, he had never expected Jenna's discovering that Denny Dennison had drowned. Which she'd done only because she'd followed up on the Coast Guard letter.

A chance in a million.

By the time they landed on Long Island, Jenna knew what she had to do. Still, her hands shook as she sat in her car in the airport parking lot and dialed Ryan's cell phone number. She let the phone ring out. She knew that Teddi had told her she would not let Ryan pick up a call from Jenna, but surely Teddi would pick up, eventually.

When she did, Teddi sounded angry. "Jenna, I told you not to call. I'm not going to let Ryan talk to you. He needs to focus on getting better, and talking to you isn't going to help him. If you call again, I'll block your number."

Jenna's breath caught at the back of her throat. "Teddi, please. Don't hang up. Please hear me out." Jenna was aware of a pleading note in her words. "I have to ask him . . ."

"Ask him what?" Teddi's words were clipped and cold.

"About that night. Does he remember anything?"

There was a very long silence at the other end. Then, Teddi finally spoke. "Ryan has nothing more to tell you, Jenna. I'm sorry, but you need to ask your husband about that night."

"Please, tell me, Teddi. This is not the time to be cryptic. I need to know what happened."

"Ask your husband." When she spoke again after a moment, her words were hardly more than a whisper: "Ryan's sorry he got involved with you again, Jenna. If you must know, he feels you misled him about your marriage; he's sorry he found himself in the middle of it. Let this be an end to it, and we can all move on. So, stay away from

Ryan. Stay away from us. Okay?" Then she hung up without waiting for Jenna's answer.

Jenna laid her head on the steering wheel and felt tears stinging the back of her eyelids. The thought that Ryan blamed her for what had happened was more than she could bear. Was Ryan even certain that Zack had attacked him? Teddi hadn't confirmed it, but if it was Zack who'd attacked him, why hadn't Ryan picked out Zack's voice in the lineup? In any event, the conversation with Teddi hadn't provided Jenna with any kind of answer at all.

She dabbed at her eyes and clicked on the Google icon on her phone to search for the website and phone number for the police department in Bethel, Maine. Introducing herself, she asked to speak to the detective or police officer who'd been on duty when her daughter Dollie King was brought in after a barn-burning incident two weeks ago.

She thought at one point that her call was disconnected, but the timer was still running, and continued to run for several minutes until a female who identified herself as Detective Laura Sanders introduced herself on the phone. "I brought your daughter in, Mrs. King. How can I help you?"

"I'm . . . I'm trying to establish a time line, Detective. Our lawyers in New York would like to know who interviewed my daughter while she was in custody, how long she was in custody . . . and so on . . ." Jenna was rambling, trying to figure out how she could come straight out and ask what time Zack had arrived at the police precinct.

"In custody?" Detective Sanders sounded puzzled. "Your daughter was never in custody, Mrs. King. She's a minor. At least, in Maine, she is. We delivered her safely to the camp where she was enrolled after she called her father and he told us he would be there as soon as possible."

"So, she spent the night at camp?"

"So far as we know. Your daughter returned to the police station with your husband to meet with the JCCO the following morning."

Jenna swallowed. "Were you there, Detective?"

"Yes, I was. "

There was no way around this, Jenna thought. She knew the question would sound weird to the detective, but she had to ask. "What time did my husband and daughter arrive at the station?"

Sure enough, there was a short pause before Detective Sanders replied: "They arrived just after I got here." She stopped and laughed abruptly. "That was close to noon." Another short pause. Then: "Mrs. King, if you're trying to determine how long your daughter was at our station, I can assure you it was an hour or two at most. She was never interviewed without an adult present. Okay?"

Jenna thanked the detective and hung up. She placed her phone on the passenger seat and switched on the engine. She felt numb.

So, Zack had outright lied about having to pick up Dollie from the police station early that morning. In fact, he'd had plenty of time to get to Maine. Plenty of time to hang outside Jenna's apartment building, watch her and Ryan, take photos, and assault Ryan. He'd have had plenty of time, too, to send the photos at 4 am from the all-night FedEx center on Lexington Avenue. Everything he'd told her about that night was a big, fat lie.

She texted Zack:

On my way to the inn. Will deal with the reporters. Please come back ASAP.

She wanted answers. Lots of them. She needed to hear Zack's side of the story. There had to be one.

Chapter Forty-Nine

It took her another hour to reach the inn, but it was still light when she drove past the media vans at the end of the driveway. A couple of reporters tumbled out of the vans as her car approached. Someone had strung yellow *Do Not Cross* police tape across the gravel road, and she had to produce her identification and wait while a local cop in uniform unfastened the tape and waved her through.

Cameras flashed in her face. "Can you tell us anything about the girl?" a woman yelled at her.

Jenna stopped and rolled down her window.

"Please," she addressed the woman. "Please leave. You're wasting your time here. We have nothing to say." She rolled up her window and proceeded along the driveway, her knees shaking as much as her hands.

Ana opened the front door immediately and ushered her in. "Come." She took Jenna's hand, leading her into the kitchen. "I'm preparing dinner for our one guest this evening, but you must be starving too."

Jenna noticed the guest as soon as she walked into the kitchen. He had chosen the table by the doors onto the patio. Jenna immediately walked over to him. "Are you a reporter?" she asked, not bothering to disguise the hostility in her voice as Ana placed a small plate of burrata and sliced tomato in front of him.

"Most certainly not, ma'am." It was obvious he was pretending to be insulted. He stood. "I'm Jonathan Vickery."

She struggled for a moment to recall where she'd heard the name, just as he added, "I'm the FBI agent you called yesterday. I guess the reporters are here because of the body they fished out of the bay."

"The body has a name. It's Bethany," Jenna retorted stiffly, trying to mask her surprise at the agent's appearance at the inn. "She was a Culinary Institute student. She was an intern here at the inn."

"Of course. I'm sorry, ma'am."

Jenna realized she sounded unnecessarily harsh. "Please, cut the 'ma'am' crap—I'm Jenna," she said, brushing off his apology. She motioned for him to sit and eat. "Did you drive all the way here from the FBI because of my phone call?"

Jenna recalled leaving only the barest details in her voice mail, identifying herself as the reporter who'd covered the "original" story about Ed Haynes's son, and letting Agent Vickery know she'd just left the Palm Beach County ME, who'd given her Vickery's name and contact info. But she'd identified herself as Jenna Sinclair, and she hadn't left a phone number for the inn or its location.

He nodded. "I was curious." He paused, dipping a torn piece of baguette in the delicious, swirling mess of olive oil and balsamic on his plate. "It sounded like you'd only just found out Dennison had drowned. That made me curious. Because when I checked you out, I discovered that you're now married to the captain of the boat that Dennison was sailing on when he drowned. That seemed odd. Made me wonder about a lot of things. Didn't your husband ever tell you about Dennison?"

"You checked me out?"

He smiled. "Not really. I just googled you. It wasn't difficult to find your most recent article or your bio with information about this inn and your husband."

Jenna didn't respond. Alarm bells sounded inside her head. Why would an FBI agent care when she'd found out about Denny Dennison's drowning? Or care about what Zack had told her or hadn't told her about knowing Denny? She perched on the chair facing Vickery.

"What's so interesting to you about all that, Agent Vickery? Why are you asking questions now?"

Jonathan Vickery grinned at her. "I'm not really asking any questions," he said. "I told you I was just curious about you reappearing to ask about Denny Dennison after all these years. Idle curiosity, if you like. I'm not investigating anything for the FBI." Then: "Look, I was in Connecticut on an assignment. Since I was so close, I decided to stop here in person."

That didn't sound so reassuring to Jenna either. "So, how about you tell me why you *were* investigating Denny Dennison all those years ago?"

Vickery waited while Ana set down a glass of merlot in front of Jenna together with a small plate of shrimp and cocktail sauce. Then he said: "No problem. I can level with you. I'm assigned to a behavioral science unit in Quantico. Have been for about twenty years. We were initially tasked with finding the children of psychopaths who were known to us."

"Known to you because they'd murdered people?"

"Yes."

"Like Ted Bundy?"

"Yes. Our objective was to see if we could establish any behavioral patterns that would point to some sort of a genetic link or influence between those fathers and children, to establish if there really is a killer gene or a psycho gene. A junior *Mindhunter* unit, if you like."

"And Ed Haynes," she added as if he hadn't spoken.

"Yes. Although we didn't know there was a child in Ed Haynes's case until your exposé. By the time I turned up on his mother's doorstep, he was no longer there. He'd left, she said. The last she'd heard, he was somewhere in the Keys. By the time I got around to his case again and traced him to the marina in Fort Lauderdale, he'd already been dead for about a year. I called the ME's office to confirm it and to ascertain that there hadn't been any drugs or alcohol, or criminal activity involved—which there hadn't—and then I closed his file. I pretty much forgot about it. And then you called the other day. So, what renewed your interest in Denny?"

Jenna had no intention of sharing that with Agent Vickery. It was bad enough having Brad and the New York cops snooping around in their lives without getting the FBI into the mix. She shrugged. "I guess a similar interest to yours, Agent Vickery. I wanted to know how his life had turned out after my exposé."

"I get that," he nodded. "But please, not Agent Vickery. Call me Jonathan."

Jenna felt herself relaxing a little. "Only if you lose the blazer and tie," she said, smiling. "You don't need them in our restaurant. We're very casual here."

It seemed Jonathan didn't need to be told twice; he immediately loosened his tie and undid the top buttons of his shirt. He took off his blazer and rolled up his sleeves to expose muscular, tanned arms. "Is that better?"

It was, but Jenna wasn't going to make any such comment. Instead, she said, "So, what did you find out about the children of other serial killers, Jonathan?"

"Have we come to any conclusions, you mean? Not yet. Look, it's not a cut-and-dried science. Genes are important, of course. They're the itty-bitty little things that make all the decisions." He grinned suddenly. "Not my description. Someone said that on TV the other day, but there's a lot of truth to it. On the other hand, a lot also seems to depend on the other influences you have growing up. Genes give you the potential for certain behavior, but that doesn't mean you're going to fulfill that potential unless your environment helps to make you that way."

"So?"

"In the cases we looked at, we haven't found any bad seeds where the fathers were known serial killers. Not in this country, and definitely not in the cases of children that weren't raised by those fathers. Say, like Ted Bundy's daughter. She was born while Bundy was on death row. Never knew him, never met him. Turns out she's a lovely woman, but her mother changed their names so that no one would know who she is.

"When we conclude our study, hopefully, we'll be able to dispel that kind of prejudice."

"What do you mean?"

Vickery pushed away his plate and reached for his cell phone, clicked on an icon before handing it to Jenna. "That's from iBooks, and specifically it's an excerpt from a book by BTK's daughter. BTK, you know, stands for bind, torture, kill? He's a serial killer we caught up with in 2005."

Jenna nodded and took the phone as Vickery added, "She didn't change her name, so she was pretty much in the media spotlight when her father was arrested and tried. She got a lot of flak on social media. You can tell."

Jenna scrolled through the excerpt. It was titled "Things Not To Ask a Serial Killer's Daughter." It referred to questions that had come up on Kerri Rawson's Facebook page. Things like, "Do you think you will murder anyone? Do you have a serial killer gene? They say traits skip a generation. Aren't you worried about your kids?"

Jenna handed the phone back to Jonathan, who fiddled around with it for a moment before passing it to her again. "Here's an article written by the daughter of another serial killer. She wrote it last year for *Huffpost*."

Jenna focused on the screen. "I wondered if I had the monster gene," Jenna read. "Two family members told me to keep the murders a secret or no one would ever marry me . . . Another boyfriend broke up with me because he didn't want his children to have a serial killer as a grandfather."

Jenna shivered and handed the phone back.

"Did you know that Dennison's wife aborted their baby when she found out that Ed Haynes was Denny's father? When she read it in my—"

Vickery touched her hand gently to interrupt her. "I know," he said. "I know you must have felt really bad about that. I can only imagine." He paused as Ana set down a plate of shrimp and scallops over angel hair for him and placed a new bottle of merlot on the table. Addressing Jenna, she said, "If you can manage now, I'm done. But I'll be upstairs if you need me."

"Thank you, Ana." Jenna nodded and turned her attention back to Jonathan. "Yes. Bad enough to quit my job and run and marry the guy who apparently saw Denny drown."

She laughed.

A short, humorless laugh followed by silence between them, until Jonathan laid down his fork and stared pointedly at her.

"So, your turn now, Jenna. Why do you think your husband never told you about Denny drowning?"

Jenna sighed. "We never talked about Denny."

Jonathan looked surprised. "What do you mean?"

"I mean, Denny's name never came up. Zack never told me about any sailing accident or about anyone drowning, and when I told Zack the story about my big scoop, I never mentioned Denny's name. I never used it in my article. I was careful about that, back then. I felt we'd done enough damage to him. I would also assume that Denny never shared the information about his father with Zack. I mean, it's why he took off for the islands. Why would he ever share that with anyone in his new life?"

"So, Denny's name never came up between the two of you?" Jonathan's face was a picture of incredulity.

Jenna shook her head. "Never." It had been the truth until just a few days ago. And it didn't seem like this was a good time to admit that the only time she'd mentioned Denny's name to Zack was in connection with the assault on her ex-lover.

"Not even when you told him you'd be chasing this story a second time?"

"I don't discuss my stories with anyone. No journalist does." Jenna struggled for composure. She needed to get out of this conversation.

"So, how did you meet? I assumed it had something to do with Denny?"

"No." Jenna took a deep breath. "He called me about writing an article about his inn. He said he'd seen a piece I wrote about an inn in Hudson Valley and he invited me out."

"So, a humongous coincidence?" Jonathan's eyes bore into her like a laser.

Jenna bit her lower lip.

"Just called you out of the blue? Of all the reporters on all the magazines in all the world . . ." He let the line hang unfinished.

"Yeah, something like that." Jenna nodded, suddenly feeling a little stupid.

Jonathan sipped his wine. "Sorry for sounding skeptical, but we're not really big on coincidences at the FBI."

Although his voice had dropped a notch, Jenna suddenly felt as if he was needling her, mocking her. The fact that he was confirming her own niggling concern about coincidences upset her. She suspected the grin on his face was supposed to soften the meaning of his words, but it just made everything worse.

She pushed back her chair and stood. "I don't really care what you're big on in the FBI," she erupted, feeling all the anger and frustration of the day bubbling up in one big geyser of emotion. "I don't care what my husband knew or when he knew it. Or what he told me or didn't tell me. None of it is relevant anymore. We're getting a divorce. I shouldn't even be here."

She felt tears pricking at her eyelids as she threw down her napkin and brushed past Jonathan to make her exit through the patio doors.

"Please, Miss Sinclair . . . Jenna." He stood and followed her onto the patio. "Please, I'm sorry . . ." He reached out and caught her forearm. "Don't go."

Jenna stopped in her tracks, let her eyes rest on his hand where he was holding her. "Don't touch me." She spat the words at him, and even as he released his grip, she lashed out with her other hand and slapped him across the face with all the force of her pent-up anger.

And then, because she realized that, on top of everything else that had happened, she had just assaulted an FBI agent, she burst into tears and ran.

Chapter Fifty

S he didn't know where she was going until she'd skirted the
patio and pool and found herself on the back path that led to
the adjoining vineyard once owned by Zack's grandfather. She
knew the path led to the vineyard outbuildings and the tasting room.
Perfect, she thought. A spot where she'd be able to sit and sip a glass of
wine without worrying about reporters or FBI agents who asked too
many questions. She needed to pull herself together before she faced
Jonathan again.

She'd have to apologize, of course. Offer him the room at a
discount. Hell, never mind discount, she'd tell him there was no
charge—even though he had checked in to the $500-a-night Miranda

cottage. Not for the cottage, and not for dinner—which she'd probably ruined for him.

"Evening, Mrs. King." The young barmaid greeted her as Jenna perched on a stool at the long bar. She wasn't surprised the girl knew her name. Her photo was on the inn website, which Jenna knew their neighbors read regularly. "A pinot noir?"

Jenna nodded. The vineyard bottled a good, solid pinot noir. "Thank you," she said. She did not recognize the girl. It was a long time since she, or Zack, had come to the tasting room for a glass of wine. She could hardly remember when they'd last visited, although she remembered that, oddly enough, on that occasion too, she had stormed out of the inn and walked over, following the back path to the tasting room.

Jenna figured it had to have been at least four, maybe five years before. She and Zack had been arguing about Dollie. Who else? Zack had set her off with some stupid remark. Their fight had started in the bedroom. She'd been in the middle of dressing for an evening out. For date night. Of course, the argument over Dollie ensured that the evening was spoiled before it had begun. Zack had said something about Jenna being tough on Dollie and never giving her a break.

"I get it," Zack said as Jenna paced across their bedroom to her closet. "You see Dollie growing up all young and beautiful, while you're losing your allure. You're just jealous."

"Allure?" Jenna repeated the word as she reached for a scarf in case the evening turned chilly. It sounded like some sort of bullshit he'd read or heard on some morning show.

"Really? Losing my allure, am I?" She smoothed down her blouse. One of her favorite tops. A pleated white silk blouse that was cut low. She swept her car keys off the dresser. "In that

case, you needn't bother going out with me. I wouldn't want to embarrass you."

Zack stopped her at the door. *"Give me the car keys. You can't go out drinking and then drive home."*

Not bothering to argue, she tossed the keys at him and strode out the door, walking to the path that led to the tasting room next door.

There was a small crowd at the bar. Mostly couples: No one drove to a vineyard tasting room to meet other singles. But Jenna recognized Natasha, one of the salesgirls, who slid her a pinot noir across the bar as soon as Jenna sat down. She downed it quite quickly, and Natasha poured another.

"And one for me, please," said a man walking up behind her. With a distinct Southern drawl, he added: *"It's a long time since I've enjoyed a glass of wine with a pretty lady. Are you from around these parts, pretty lady?"*

Jenna didn't acknowledge the voice or the compliment. She didn't even turn around to look at the man. She didn't need to. If Zack thought she was just going to play some dumb game with him and forget everything he'd said to her, he was mistaken. Instead, she finished her wine and headed for the door. She was turning toward the path leading back to the inn when she heard the car behind her, slowing, and a window rolling down.

"Hey, pretty lady can I give you a ride?"

Before Jenna could reply, he added: *"How come you're out here on your own? Doesn't your husband worry about you being in the middle of nowhere like this?"*

Jenna stopped then and waited for him to draw level. *"My husband's an asshole,"* she said. *"I don't care what he thinks."* She heard rather than saw him grinning as he rolled along behind *her. "I'm sure you do care. Pretty lady like you must have a helluva fine-looking man for a husband."*

Jenna laughed shrilly and turned toward him as he drew level with her again and stopped. She rested her arms on the open window, leaning in so he could see she had nothing on under her blouse.

"You know mister, I don't really want to talk about my husband right now." She leaned in farther. "He really pissed me off."

"Can I give you a ride?"

Jenna pretended to think about it. Then, "Sure, why not?"

They drove in silence. Jenna wondered if maybe they could talk things over in a calmer way now. But Zack didn't seem too interested in talking as he drove past the inn entrance.

"Hey, mister, that's my turn, right there."

"You didn't say." He kept driving, making a couple of turns. Jenna saw the moon shining down on a stretch of grass when he finally stopped and switched off the engine.

"What are you doing?"

"You said your husband pissed you off. I'm trying to take your mind off it." He turned and slid his hand down into her blouse.

She shrank back in her seat. This was not what she'd had in mind. "Don't!" She pushed him away. "I want to talk."

"You want to talk, lady? That's not the vibe I'm getting." He grabbed at her again. "You get into my car. You got nuttin' on under that nuttin' blouse there. I don't think you want to talk."

"Zack, c'mon stop it. We need to talk."

He thrust himself at her, pinning her back in the seat. Then, she heard the click of the locks on the doors.

"Stop it! I'm not playing, you hear me?" She grabbed for the door handle as he grabbed for her blouse. She heard a ripping sound and exploded.

"Asshole! Now look what you've done." She knew the blouse was ruined. *"Open this goddam door!"* She lashed out at him with the palm of her hand. *"Open it."*

As soon as she heard the locks spring open, she grabbed for the door handle and stumbled out of the car.

He was beside her in seconds, pushing her down on the grass as his knee forced her legs apart. *"You don't slap me, bitch,"* he breathed into her ear, his mouth moving down into the hollow of her throat as he unzipped his pants.

She screamed, and tried to bite his hand, but he forced his elbow against her throat. *"I'll choke you,"* he threatened, making her gag.

"Don't, Zack. Please." He was scaring her now. She'd never seen him this angry.

"Don't call me Zack. I ain't Zack," he yelled at her, covering her mouth with his hand. Then, just as suddenly as he'd forced her to the ground, the fight seemed to go out of him and he rolled off her, letting her struggle to her feet.

"Wait, Jenna, I'm sorry." In a second, he was on his feet too, reaching for her hand.

Too late.

———

"Another one, Mrs. King?"

Jenna looked blankly at the girl behind the bar, trying desperately to gather her thoughts back into the present. She'd been so terrified that night with Zack, she'd refused to get back in the car and had walked the half mile home from where Zack had parked on the grounds of the North Fork Country Club.

A wave of nausea suddenly washed over Jenna.

"Mrs. King, are you all right?"

Jenna gasped, as if someone had stabbed her in the ribs and she couldn't get any words out. She felt a sudden rush of air into her lungs. For a moment she thought she might faint or throw up, but she held herself together as she walked unsteadily to the door and out into the dark, stumbling on the gravel before setting off back along the path back to the inn.

She noticed the lights were off in the kitchen as she ran toward the staircase leading to her room. Fuzzy as her head felt, she took the stairs two at a time. Inside the room, she flung open the closet doors, pulled out the box she'd brought from Rosie Miller's house, and overturned it, spilling the contents onto the floor.

The map, she thought to herself. *Where's the map?* That crudely drawn map of where Evil Ed had buried the bodies of his victims.

There it was. She snatched it up off the floor and stared at it. Only a week or so ago, she'd glanced at all the locations. But she hadn't given it much more thought. Evil Ed had skulked around about twenty years before either she or Zack had even known the North Fork existed. But there it was, the dot marking the location with NFCC—North Fork Country Club—in black above it.

She doubled over, wrapping her arms around herself. *Don't call me Zack. I ain't Zack.* Back then, Jenna had thought he was playacting, that it was just one of their games gone sadly wrong. Now, realization hit her like so many blows thundering down on her. How could she not have realized it instantly at the Cozy Cove Marina? How could she have missed the most obvious explanation for Zack's failure to tell her about Denny?

Zack had never mentioned his drowned buddy, Denny Dennison, because Denny Dennison hadn't drowned off the Florida coast. It was

Zack King who had drowned, and Denny had simply taken Zack's place.

She tasted bile in her mouth, felt more of it rising in her throat. She stood to make her way to the bathroom, but instantly doubled over and vomited onto the floor. On her hands and knees, she crawled to the cool tile of the bathroom floor and hunched over the toilet bowl. She vomited again and again, until there was nothing left to vomit except a thin streak of saliva.

Chapter Fifty-One

Week Three: Friday Sunrise

He loved watching the sun rise. He loved to see the sun coming up over the ocean and glancing off the water in the bay. He wanted Dollie to see the sunrise too, but she was grumpy when he went to wake her. She turned over, pulling the covers closer around herself. He hoped she wasn't sick with a hangover. He'd let her have a half glass of rosé wine the previous evening at the Beach Hut. The bartender hadn't asked for ID.

Dollie had ended up giggling all the way back to the boat over some girl who had attached herself to him. He'd nicknamed the girl Scrawny, causing Dollie to erupt in a fit of giggles as she remembered Scrawny telling him that he should leave girls like Dollie alone.

"She's young enough to be your daughter," Scrawny had said, linking her bony arm through his as Dollie laughed so hard that tears ran down her cheeks. It was good to see her laugh after the outburst of tears when he'd told her about Bethany being found in the water. "They don't know how it happened. It was probably an accident," he'd told her.

Now, standing over his daughter's bundled form, he said, "I'm going for a run on the beach." Then he texted the same information to her phone just in case she hadn't heard him and woke panicked over where he'd disappeared to.

Out on the dock, he wondered if Jenna was already awake this morning, and if she was wondering why he hadn't texted. She'd texted last night asking him to come back ASAP. He was sure it wasn't very pleasant, having all those reporters on the doorstep, but if anyone could deal with them, it was Jenna. He didn't expect her to start worrying about him and Dollie just yet. It'd been less than twenty-four hours since they'd left the inn. Jenna knew not to expect a barrage of texts or phone calls when he was out on the boat.

He jogged through the marina toward the beach. He saw Robins Island on the horizon, or at least the tip of it through the early morning mist. It was hopeless. Wherever he went, he was reminded of Bethany.

Jogging along the beach, Zack was aware that he'd broken out in a sweat. He wasn't sure whether it was the memory of Bethany or the warmth of the sand already beating up from the beach that caused him to feel so hot and clammy. He jogged down to the water's edge, where the waves were lapping onto the sand and stopped to take some deep breaths before turning around and heading back to the boat.

Dollie was up when he came aboard. She was stirring what looked like a smoothie and staring down at her phone. "There was something on here about Bethany," she said without looking at him.

He drew a sharp breath. "What?"

"Hold on, let me find it.

"What did it say, Dollie? Dammit!"

"Jeez Dad, just chill. I'm looking."

Chapter Fifty-Two

Week Three: Friday

J enna did not remember climbing into bed or waking during the night. At some point, she must have stepped into the shower in her vomit-stained clothes because they were lying wet and crumpled on the bathroom floor, and she was naked in bed when she woke in the morning.

Through the night, the memory of her realization had made her bury her head under the sheets to pretend it was all just a bad dream. But as the light crept into her room, she couldn't escape the fact that she was married to Denny Dennison. That he was Dollie's father. That Dollie was the flesh and blood of a convicted, executed, sadistic serial killer.

Denny's first wife had chosen to abort his child. Would Jenna have made the same choice had she known the truth all those years ago? But there was no point at all thinking like that. Dollie was not a seed, but a real person, a child she loved and cared for and worried about. Not a monster, but a little girl. Her little girl.

So, how could Zack . . . no, Denny . . . no, Zack. She couldn't call him Denny.

How could Zack not have shared this secret with her?

She tried to imagine how she would have taken the news if he had told her the truth years ago. Had he been trying to tell her that night at the North Fork Country Club? Had he decided that it was time to share the secret of Dollie's real paternity? It was almost funny that she had thought of taking him to task for keeping secret Miranda's bipolar mood swings when she'd still believed—was it only a day ago?—that he was Miranda's son.

Darker thoughts penetrated as the night wore on. Why had he done this to her? Why had he pursued her? Married her? Impregnated her? To punish her? For revenge? By morning, her thoughts turned from wondering how it had happened to how she and Dollie were going to get away.

If Zack was not Zack but was Denny Dennison, did that mean they weren't legally married? Did it mean he didn't really own the inn and marina and restaurant? She understood now why Zack had resisted Brad's efforts to match their DNA. And where was Rosie in all of this? She had obviously conspired with Denny in identifying a stranger's body as that of her son. Where was she now? Was she lurking somewhere close? Watching them? Watching her granddaughter?

And then back again her thoughts went: How had Zack pulled this off? How had he managed to make her a unwitting partner in this gigantic sham marriage?

She turned on the TV just in time to catch the end of a report on Bethany. She turned to her cell phone and the *Newsday* app to get the full story. The medical examiner was calling Bethany's drowning a homicide. Murder by blunt-force trauma to the head. She was dead before she went into the water, said the medical examiner.

The memory of the night on the golf course penetrated Jenna's thoughts again. Zack had forced her to the ground, and her head had slammed down on the grass. Maybe he'd played games with Bethany too. Maybe he'd done the same thing to Bethany, only her head had made contact with something more solid than grass. Had he accidentally killed her? Then there was Adele. Zack's, no, Denny's stepsister. Had Jenna sealed her fate by telling Zack that Adele had a photo of him?

She checked her phone. Still no reply from Zack. *Calm down*, she told herself. She could not allow herself to think about Zack as a cold-blooded killer while he was out on the water with their daughter. Zack had no idea that she knew anything. He had texted her to tell her he was taking Dollie away from the reporters camped at the end of their driveway. It was less than twenty-four hours ago that she'd agreed it was a good idea. It was like any other time he and Dollie had taken off on the boat.

He couldn't have a clue as to what Jenna knew. She tried not to think what might happen if he suspected that she'd discovered the truth. God forbid. After all, it was a well-known fact that husbands and fathers who got backed into a corner in fraught situations sometimes turned on their wives and children . . .

No, she could not go there. There was no way he could possibly know about her realization. He would know only when she decided to reveal it to him, when he was back, safe with Dollie. Then she would tell him what needed to be done: that she was leaving and taking Dollie.

She would promise not to tell anyone about his big scam so long as he let her and Dollie go. Of course she wouldn't tell anyone. She didn't want herself and Dollie to be at the center of some media shitstorm like all those other children and grandchildren of serial killers that Jonathan had talked about. Or, she realized bitterly, the kind of media frenzy she'd brought about with her own exposé of Denny so many years ago.

She got out of bed, splashed cold water on her face, brushed her teeth, and went to the loft. She wanted to piece together what Denny had done all those years ago when he'd come to the North Fork to meet Jeremiah King. The two had never met, so it had probably been easy to fake his way into Jeremiah's home with the real Zack's driver's license, passport, or whatever documents the real Zack had carried with him. But maybe there was something in the computer files that would give her some concrete evidence of how he had stolen another man's identity and inherited a vast property by doing so. She'd need to present him with some evidence of his wrongdoing so he couldn't gaslight her and tell her she was acting like a crazy woman.

She looked at the folders. She began to access their bank accounts (the password for all of them was *Dollie*): the checking account in their joint names, an account for the inn and restaurant, one for the marina, a savings account in their joint names, and the Caymans account—in his name only—which she could not access. He had told her he never used the account.

She clicked into their savings account. The most recent transaction was a wire transfer from the account of $150,000 into his Caymans account. It was the day after she'd stormed out and driven to the city. But where had the $150,000 come from in the first place? It wasn't profits saved from the running of the inn and marina. She knew all those went into their joint account for their living expenses.

Jenna drummed her fingers on the desk as her thoughts spun. If Zack was going to cheat the IRS (which of course he'd never do) he would have had that amount deposited directly in the Caymans account, surely? That kind of amount in a savings account would have to be accounted for in their tax returns. She cursed herself for not paying attention to boring tax returns when Zack had attempted to involve her. She had left all of that up to him.

She opened a filing cabinet under the desk, then a couple of drawers in the cabinet. The thick gray folders with their accountant's business card clipped to the front of them took up the entire bottom two drawers. There had to be ten years' worth of tax return copies in the drawers. That made sense. You only had to keep tax returns and receipts for seven years, but that would not have been sufficient for Zack. She scrolled back through the savings account. That amount of $150,000 had first shown up in the savings account back in 2015, so the income, if it was income, would have appeared in the tax return filed in 2016. It took her a couple of minutes to locate the folder, and then another ten minutes to look through the pages. She found an amount of $520,000 listed as sales income from depreciated rental property in Greenport. She recognized the address.

Zack had told her many years ago about the cottage, the very first home Jeremiah King had bought on the North Fork. She recalled how Zack had invested in a new boat, the *Dollie Too*, the spiffy forty-two-foot Carver Super Sport, after selling the cottage because the tenant had died. So, apparently $150,000 had remained after he'd purchased the boat with the proceeds from the sale of the cottage.

She remembered the cottage. Zack told her it was rented out to an old "witch." Over the years, she remembered him taking calls from the "witch" because stuff in the cottage always needed fixing. Jenna had never been interested in the tales of woe. Leaking pipes, burst boilers, and garden fences that needed painting were of no interest to her. Anyway, the "witch" didn't seem so bad, according to Dollie, who often went along with her father to fix things at the "witch's" house. She had toys and coloring books for her own grandchildren that she let Dollie use.

Jenna suddenly felt hot and clammy as the obvious conclusion hit her: the tenant had not been any old "witch" but Rosie, Denny's mother who had moved into the cottage after selling her house in Seaford. And Jenna would bet that the only child who had ever visited and played with the toys and coloring books in that Greenport cottage was the only grandchild Rosie had: Dollie.

She closed the IRS folders, threw them back in the drawers, and clicked out of the bank accounts. Her head pounded with a dull, throbbing pain as she crossed the yard to the kitchen, where Ana sat at the counter rolling out pie dough. A big bowl of sliced fresh peaches sat at the other end of the counter. Jenna helped herself to a couple of slices. She thought of all the questions she could ask Ana. She thought that Ana probably knew more about Zack's life on the North Fork than Jenna did. But Jenna had run out of steam.

"Did our guest leave?" she asked Ana.

Ana shook her head. "No, but he said he'd eat in Riverhead this evening. He said he's checking out tomorrow morning."

Good, thought Jenna. She wouldn't have to deal with the embarrassment of seeing Jonathan again. She checked her phone. Still no texts from Zack. She told herself to stay calm. But it was difficult. Her concern for Dollie threatened to turn into a panic attack. She had to keep reminding herself that Zack had absolutely no idea she knew everything. She had to sit tight. There wasn't an alternative. She couldn't summon Brad or the Coast Guard to help her track him down and bring him back to the inn. Why would they?

She picked up her phone again and texted Zack:

When u guys coming bk? Missing u . . .

She hesitated for just a moment; wondered if Zack would believe her, then added the word *both* before tapping the send arrow.

It was difficult to get through the rest of the day without constantly looking out to the water, watching for the *Dollie Too* to appear. She took a long walk on the bay beach, keeping her eyes on the horizon. She swam laps in the pool. She exchanged pleasantries with Hank in the marina. She should have been exhausted by bedtime, but it took her a long time to fall asleep, and she woke several times in the night to check her phone for texts. It wasn't till dawn was breaking that she heard the ping of a new text.

It was not from Zack, but from a number she didn't recognize.

"It's Jonathan," the text said. *"Pls call me asap. We need to talk."*

Chapter Fifty-Three

Week Three: Saturday Dawn

Dollie was still sleeping below when Zack stepped out onto the deck and lit a cigarette. His daughter had noticed the carton he'd stashed in a drawer in the galley after buying them in Adele's smoke shop. Dollie had thrown him a disapproving look, and he'd told her he didn't intend to smoke any of them; he was simply keeping them on board for guests. He hardly ever smoked since Jenna and he had quit years ago. But he needed one now as he prowled back and forth, knowing he had to make the decision of his life.

He hadn't been able to get his thoughts straight since he'd heard that the medical examiner had ruled Bethany's death a homicide. It was official. He'd tried to put it out of his mind when Dollie and he had returned to the Beach Hut the previous evening. He'd even looked around for Scrawny. Anything to take his mind off the news—and the realization that he was about to become a prime suspect.

He tried to picture how it might all go down. They probably wouldn't come for him straightaway. They'd want to nail down the forensic evidence first. He'd seen it on shows like *Forensic Files*. That's how they solved most murders these days. With DNA. They would run the DNA found inside Bethany through various criminal databases where they'd be looking for a match with a criminal offender before they came for a fine, upstanding business owner like Zack with a court order.

So, first they'd get a hit with the DNA they'd taken from him as Denny Dennison, after he'd bitten and punched out the *Sun* photographer. He hadn't known any better back then, so stupidly, he'd let them take a swab of saliva from his mouth along with his fingerprints when they'd arrested and charged him.

His attorney, the public defender in his case, had assured him that his record was automatically sealed, and all evidence and fingerprints and DNA samples destroyed when the DA dropped the charges. He'd believed it, and all those years ago, he'd thought nothing of submitting his fingerprints as Zack King with his liquor license application for the inn. The application hadn't thrown up any red flags, and he'd gotten the license, no problem. But DNA profiles had to be a different story. Anyone who watched those TV crime shows knew that the FBI had millions of DNA profiles in its databases. So, no, he didn't believe any of those got expunged or sealed. Ever. They were all there somewhere, floating around in a giant database in cyberspace.

Zack tried to imagine the expression on Jenna's face when they told her the DNA evidence from Bethany had matched up with one Denny Dennison. She'd hardly be able to contain her excitement, because that would prove her right about Denny Dennison all along. Then things would get really sticky.

The detectives from the county homicide squad were a tad brighter than Brad, so they would eventually discover that Denny had drowned on a boat trip captained by Zack King, and then they'd descend on him like a ton of bricks. They'd interrogate him, probably find some sneaky way to get his saliva from a glass or water bottle or a cigarette butt . . . and then—*oops!* Surprise. They'd find a perfect match between his and Denny's DNA.

His life would never be the same again. He'd not only be charged with murder, but exposed as an imposter and fraud. It wouldn't even matter if there was no other evidence connecting him to Bethany's murder, they'd pin it on him anyway. Game over. He'd be back to square one as Denny Dennison, spawn of Evil Ed, savage serial slayer, and facing a murder rap, to boot.

He took a couple of deep drags on his cigarette, and wished he had a joint to calm his jangling nerves. For sure, he still had time to get clear of the New York shoreline, and once he was out in the ocean, he was as good as free. He didn't want to do it. He really didn't want to leave. He loved his life, loved owning the inn and the restaurant and getting all those *Dan's Papers* awards for being the Best Brunch on the North Fork. He knew he could have died happy at his inn.

But there was really no point in hanging out till they declared him a person of interest. Right now he had a head start. It wasn't the way he'd ever thought it would end, but he couldn't see an alternative. He could reach Barnegat Bay in a day or so and switch to the sailboat. Once he got further south, it would be even more difficult to find him.

He'd have to start all over again, of course, but it was better than sitting in jail for the rest of his life. No contest. Once he and Dollie were in the islands, they'd be safe and free. No one was going to find them there. All those coves and bays. No one was going to even look for them down there.

He had to take Dollie with him. If they found out about his past, Dollie's life would become hell as Evil Ed's granddaughter. He'd rather she was dead than have her face that kind of shame and finger-pointing. Dollie would live like the island children, carefree on the beach, eating fruit and fish, and so what if she didn't show up to face the music for her barn burning in Maine? She'd be a fugitive just like him.

Chapter Fifty-Four

Week Three: Saturday Morning

Jenna's spirits lifted a little when she arrived at the Miranda cottage. Jonathan was waiting for her on the small brick patio. There was a pot of coffee on the table to the right of the front door, and a plate of croissants.

Two cups.

She reflected that Jonathan probably wouldn't have ordered breakfast for her if he was going to arrest her for assaulting a federal agent. Still, he looked all buttoned up again; dressed to go, in his blazer, collared shirt, and a tie.

A big, official-looking black briefcase lay to one side of the tray holding the coffee and croissants.

Jenna wrapped her cashmere shawl more tightly around herself. "Hi." She smiled hesitantly, noticing that her slap had left a scratch above his left eyebrow. "I'm sorry I slapped you the other night."

He laughed, brushing the scratch with his fingers. "It didn't hurt, and I touched you first. I shouldn't have done that. Anyway, I understand. You had a rough day." He beckoned her over. "Come on, Jenna, come and have some coffee with me."

"You said we need to talk. What about?"

He didn't respond immediately. Instead, he poured coffee into their cups, and then clicked open the locks on his briefcase. Finally, he looked up and there was an odd expression in his eyes. "I'm so sorry about this, Jenna. I'm sorry I couldn't let it go. But I just got this hunch when you told me that Zack had called you out of the blue and never once mentioned Denny. It just sounded so off. I don't know how else to put it. I had to check things out."

Jenna suddenly had a feeling she knew what was coming.

She didn't say a word but watched as Jonathan brought a laptop out of his briefcase and opened it. They both stared as the laptop powered up and revealed a screen that looked like a whole bunch of swirls. He reduced the size and she realized she was looking at a fingerprint. It made sense

What else would an FBI agent have as his screensaver? Only it wasn't a screensaver.

"This is your husband's fingerprint, Jenna," Jonathan told her. "Zack King's print from his liquor-license application. They keep those on file so that if you're arrested and fingerprinted, say for DWI, the State Liquor Authority gets to find out about it, pronto."

"Okay." Jenna kept her eyes fixed on the laptop screen.

Jonathan clicked on another fingerprint in the series that ran down the side of the screen. He overlaid it on the one he'd said was Zack's.

He moved the print till it sat precisely over the first one, matching it whorl for whorl, ridge for ridge.

"That's also Zack's, right?"

Jonathan nodded. "But it comes from a twenty-year-old arrest file," he said. "From Denny Dennison's file when he was charged with aggravated assault for what he did to your photographer."

Jenna dug her fingernails into the palms of her hands. If she'd had any doubts at all as to Zack's real identity, this was solid proof. But why had it taken this long for anyone in law enforcement to discover it?

"So why didn't his liquor license fingerprints get matched with the Denny Dennison prints when he first applied for the license?"

"Because his record was automatically sealed when the charges were dropped—which means that all fingerprints, DNA samples, photographs, and so on are either destroyed or returned to the accused or his attorney. That's how it's supposed to be done in New York."

Jenna took a deep breath. "So why do you have that information? And the fingerprints."

"I had a copy of his arrest file transferred to the FBI database before the charges were dropped." Jonathan took a bite of his croissant.

There was a short silence between them as Jenna stared blankly at him. "Didn't the FBI have to seal his record after the charges were dropped?"

Jonathan looked embarrassed. He cleared his throat. "Technically yes, but . . ." He cleared his throat again. "We're a research unit in the FBI, and Denny's DNA profile . . . the DNA profiles we've collected from other children of serial killers, usually with their consent, by the way, give us potentially useful information."

"Like?" Jenna was aware that her tone was cold and clipped as she continued to stare at Jonathan.

"Like if one of the kids we've researched turns into a homicidal maniac, and his/her fingerprints or DNA pop up as a possible match with those we find at a crime scene," Jonathan replied. "Then we'd have a basis for assuming genetic influences were at play. It would be a starting point for further research of course, not a scientific conclusion."

Jonathan loosened the knot of his tie and rested his hand on the table, his fingers almost brushing Jenna's. He looked concerned. "I know this is a lot to comprehend, Jenna, but believe me, there's no mistake about your husband's fingerprints."

Jenna realized he'd taken her questions to mean she doubted what he was saying about Zack as he added, "You understand what I'm telling you, right?"

Jenna put down her coffee cup on the table and nodded. Of course she understood, but she wasn't going to admit to Jonathan that she'd already worked everything out for herself. She buried her face in her hands and rocked back and forth. She was not going to tell him anything more. She'd already decided how she was going to deal with the situation. Now, it seemed, the FBI was going to mess up her plans.

Chapter Fifty-Five

She tried to ignore the panicky feeling rising in her chest as she stared at Jonathan. "So, you're here to arrest my husband?"

Jonathan closed his laptop. "No," he replied. "Why would I? I just felt if my hunch was right, then I had an obligation to let you know."

Jenna made a visible double-take. "Isn't it a crime to impersonate a dead person? Isn't that fraud?"

"Not per se. To be prosecuted under federal law, you'd have to be impersonating someone and using their identity with the intent to commit another crime, like bank fraud or securities fraud. Something like that. He'd have to have stolen the real Zack King's identity with the intent of doing so for financial gain."

Jenna laughed abruptly. "Like impersonating the grandson of a rich old man with the intent to inherit all his property?"

Jonathan ran a hand over his head. "Yes, well that's just it, there doesn't seem to be any evidence of fraudulent intent there. It's the first thing I looked into, yesterday.

"Let me back up a little. I have to confess I drove here after you left your message not just because I was curious, but because your message raised red flags all around when I realized you'd married Denny's sailing buddy. I can't explain it all, but it's just something . . . you get a sixth sense about these things, and I just felt something was a little off. Then, when you told me the other night that Zack had never mentioned Denny to you, and that his call to you was just coincidence, I decided I had to dig some more."

Jonathan took a sip of coffee before continuing. "After I got his prints from the SLA application, I drove to Surrogate's Court in Riverhead to check Jeremiah King's will. Thing is, Jeremiah didn't die intestate. Might have been a different matter if he had died without a will and your husband had stepped up with his stolen ID to claim the inheritance. But that's not how it went down. He actually named your husband as his beneficiary."

"Of course he did. He thought Zack was his real grandson."

"No. It's worded almost as if grandpa had his doubts, but didn't care. The wording is, 'the man I've come to know and accept as my grandson Zachariah since 1999.' It was so unusual, it stuck in my head. The old guy apparently couldn't have cared less if Zack was Denny Dennison or Jack the Ripper."

Jenna pursed her lips, recalling Fran's story in the car about Jeremiah and Zack bonding over the renovation of the inn. "That's all you're interested in?" she finally asked.

Jonathan got to his feet and paced across the tiny patio.

"That's all the FBI is interested in. There's nothing really to prosecute, or I should say, to *successfully* prosecute, since Jeremiah is dead. Zack's story could well be that he didn't defraud his grandfather; that he confessed everything to him and the grandfather didn't care. The way the will is written supports that.

"Listen, Jenna, this may sound weird, but I totally understand why Denny took Zack King's identity. When King drowned, I'm sure Denny saw an opportunity for making a fresh start without the burden of his history. Look, I made some inquiries about him, around town with people he's done business with and socialized with . . ."

Jenna's face must have registered her horror at the thought of Jonathan making inquiries because he quickly added: "Trust me, I was very discreet. I said a local tourist board in upstate New York was considering him for an award. Anyway, no one had anything bad to say about him. I don't know what else to tell you except that I'm not here to make life difficult for kids who had no say or choice as to who their parents are or were. I'm not here to make this public knowledge."

With tears suddenly threatening the backs of her eyelids, she said, "I feel stupid and pathetic. How could I not see or suspect anything?"

"Why would you? There are women who have been married to actual serial killers and they had no idea that their husbands were out at night killing and raping."

"What about Bethany?" Jenna suddenly blurted out the question before she could stop herself. She didn't want to put any ideas in Jonathan's head, but she had to know if he'd shared his knowledge with anyone else. "Will this make Zack a suspect in Bethany's murder? Have you told Brad Halsey about this?"

Jonathan shook his head. "Hell, no! Why would I do that? I don't intend to interfere with any local investigation. Everything you've ever seen on TV about local cops hating it when the FBI interferes is true. If they find that Zack—Denny—had anything to do with her murder, well, then I'll obviously be interested in that for our research. But right now, what would I tell them? That your husband is the son of a serial killer?"

Jonathan paused, looking amused. "I wouldn't dare put that idea in anyone's head. Can you imagine what a defense attorney would do with that? 'He wasn't a suspect, Your Honor, till cops found out about his father.' Anyway, the latest I read, or maybe I heard it on the radio, is that the detectives have named her boyfriend as a person of interest. They have a search warrant for his apartment. They said her skull was dented with something like a child's baseball bat. Apparently, the boyfriend has a kid who plays baseball."

Jenna momentarily reflected that at least no one would find an object like that in their home. Dollie had never expressed an interest in any team sports. She smiled weakly. "So, you're saying you don't think Zack is a psychopath, even though his father was?"

Jonathan smiled back at her, probably to soften his reply. "Well, that's a whole different question. Fact is, there are more psychopaths out there than most people know. Not all of them are serial killers. Not all of them are criminals. It's difficult to pick them out of a crowd."

Jenna felt the taste of her coffee turn bitter in her mouth. "How difficult can it be?"

"I've never met your husband, so I couldn't tell you with certainty one way or another. But even though psychopaths are usually cold and calculating and totally unemotional, they can fake it. They can be extremely manipulative and smart, and they just learn to walk the walk, talk the talk of normal people to get what they want."

"Like stealing lines from movies to tell you they love you?"

Jonathan looked perplexed for a moment, then shrugged, closing his briefcase. "Yeah, maybe."

"That's what he did with me. He was very determined to marry me." She hesitated, aware that her lower lip was trembling. "Do you think he did it for revenge? Or to punish me?"

Jonathan shrugged. "I really can't begin to know what was in his mind, Jenna. Only he knows the answer to that. But it doesn't seem that his motive was to punish you. Or hurt you. From what I see, you have a rather nice life here." He stood to go.

Jenna said nothing as she waited for him to gather up his briefcase and dust the croissant crumbs off his pants. She walked him to the inn and watched as he left through the main doors.

"Jenna!" Brad's too-familiar voice stopped her in her tracks as she was making her way to the kitchen.

Oh, dear God, she mouthed the words to herself. What was he doing here? Would there never be an end to his visits? She turned toward the front doors to face him, forcing a bright smile to her lips. "Chief Brad, what's brought you here?"

The look on Brad's face suggested it was something discomfiting. He looked embarrassed. "I have a message for young Zack," he said, without asking to speak to Zack himself.

"Sure," Jenna replied. "What is it?"

"Well, I was here a couple of days ago, you know, after they found Bethany." He hesitated, his Adam's apple bobbing. "I was a little heavy-handed with your husband. Told him that he'd probably become a person of interest if the medical examiner determined she'd been murdered. I advised him they'd probably get a court order for his DNA. I told him it would be better for him to consent to it so he could clear things up, asap."

Brad paused again and before Jenna could prod him to spit out what was on his mind, he added: "Just wanted to tell him I got ahead of myself . . ."

"Meaning?" Jenna's tone was sharp. She needed Brad to come to the point before she screamed.

"Turns out the DNA on . . ." he looked flustered ". . . in the girl is too degraded to use. Too long in the elements, in the water." Brad shuffled his feet before adding: "I'd hate for Zack to think I was intimidating him or trying to coerce him into doing something he didn't have to do."

Jenna nodded and turned away abruptly, leaving Brad standing in the hallway. She made her way out to the patio, where she sank down on a lounge chair, her heart pounding. She checked her phone. Still no text or any response from Zack.

Her unease was about to turn into a full-blown panic. Brad had told Zack that detectives would come for his DNA. That had probably freaked him out just as he'd freaked when Brad had suggested matching their DNA profiles to determine if Zack was his son.

Her husband would never surrender to a DNA test that would prove him to be a liar, fraud, and a serial killer's spawn. There was no point in waiting to confront him; no point in waiting for him to return her texts—or return to the inn. With a sinking feeling in the pit of her stomach, Jenna realized that Zack was on the run.

And he'd taken Dollie with him.

Without another moment's hesitation, she ran for her room, threw on jeans, and layered up. She took the .22 revolver from her nightstand drawer and retrieved the bullets she'd bought, the real thing, not the blanks that Zack had made fun of. Then, she went in search of Hank. He knew all the public and private marinas all the way down to Atlantic City, and up north to Bar Harbor. He had some sophisticated ship-to-shore equipment too. He would find them, and then they would go together to get Dollie.

It didn't take long.

Hank reached her through the house intercom a half hour later. "They were at the public marina at Meschutt last night. They went through the locks to Shinnecock Bay around lunchtime. They're stopped at Sundays for lunch. I think they'll be there for a while. There's a bit of a storm brewing offshore . . . Are you sure you want to go and join them? I could contact him from here."

"No, Hank," Jenna answered firmly. "Please do not contact him. I need to get Dollie. Will you help me?"

Chapter Fifty-Six

Week Three: Saturday Noon

Zack tied off the lines where the dockmaster had shown him to a guest berth and followed Dollie along the dock to the restaurant. Sundays had a nice, wide outside deck that overlooked the boat slips. At this time of year, the slips were well filled, but there were plenty of tables available in the main dining room. Dollie picked a table in the corner away from the water and the dock. She said she'd had enough of boats. She wanted to do some people watching for a change.

Not a good omen for the little speech he was about to give her. The one where he was going to tell her that, after lunch, they were going to carry on through the inlet and along the coast of Long Island,

and then on down the Jersey Shore and so on, all the way to the Islands. He wouldn't tell her just yet that it was a permanent move. The way he saw it, there really was no alternative. He'd been flipping back and forth between the local news websites trying to find more news about the medical examiner's report. The *New York Post* had an exclusive. The medical examiner had told the *Post* reporter that the murder weapon was something like a child's baseball bat.

Interesting because his angler's priest looked exactly like a child's baseball bat. It was something that he used to finish off fish if they weren't dead when he brought them in. Jeremiah had told him that it was called a "priest" because it administered last rites to dying fish. Most times, though, he just called it a fish bat.

If he'd had any intention of returning to the inn, then, of course, he'd have had to dump the fish bat in the water. He was happy he wouldn't have to now. It had belonged to Jeremiah. So, it wasn't any old angler's priest but an antique he had carried with him on all his fishing trips.

He wouldn't have to dump Adele's hunting knife overboard either, now that he'd decided to keep moving. A knife like that would be useful in the islands for chopping up mangoes or water melons, maybe even spearing fish in shallow water. He hoped that it wouldn't always remind him of Adele because that was such a bad memory. His stepsister had gotten the hunting knife right in her neck because she'd attacked him first. Pure self-defense on his part. She should never have crept up on him out back of that smoke shop. She should never have given him that crap about "one move, buster, and Mama's hunting knife goes right in your jugular."

His reaction had been purely instinctive, and before he knew it, her Mama's hunting knife was in his gloved hand, and then it was in her jugular and her big body was sliding to the ground in a pool of blood.

"Another beer, sir?" A pretty, young barmaid interrupted his thoughts, hovering at their table as they finished eating. "That young lady at the bar wants to buy you a beer."

He looked across the table at Dollie. She was looking fed up, not amused the way she'd looked the other night when Scrawny had refused to take no for an answer.

The chick sitting at the bar was waving to him. God knows, he wasn't even trying. He imagined that life was going to get even better in the islands so far as hooking up went. The thought cheered him, made him feel less stricken by the idea of leaving the North Fork forever. For sure, Jenna would be better off without him. She'd made it clear she planned to leave him, anyway. And, she would have taken Dollie, and he'd never have seen his daughter again. It was going to be better this way—for everyone.

"I'm not hungry." Dollie interrupted his thoughts.

"So, why don't you go back to the boat? Check the weather. Watch a movie. I'll bring you takeout when I'm done here."

"Yeah, fine," she said, but the expression on her face said something completely different. He knew there would be a hundred more moments like these: Dollie getting bored, pissed off, angry with him—especially when she started missing her mother. She would blame him, resent him, and she'd be hard work. He knew those would be the days he'd regret that he hadn't taken off on his own.

He made his way to the outside bar. He had some time. He'd wait till the dark clouds passed. The least he could do was exchange a few words with the lady who was buying him a beer. Hell, he should buy her one in return. She was a stunner.

As he crossed the dining-room floor toward her, he entertained a short fantasy about persuading her to join him and Dollie on their trip south. Yeah, right! Like she'd just pick up and jump on a boat with him and his sullen teenage daughter. She'd have to be a carefree spirit like Bethany to go along with a wild idea like that.

Zack groaned quietly. Bethany. There she was again. In his thoughts. How could he have messed things up so badly with her?

Chapter Fifty-Seven

Three Weeks Earlier

B y eight in the morning, the sun was already a brilliant yellow ball rising over the glass-smooth waters of Peconic Bay. There was no breeze from either the Ocean or the Sound, so belowdecks the temperature had risen quickly. Zack never heard Bethany step onto the deck; never heard her footsteps till she was almost on top of him in the tiny bathroom stall where he was working to replace the hose for the shower. He had no idea why she had followed him onto the boat. He'd told her he'd be back in time to take her to the jitney.

"Zack?"

"What do you want, Bethany?" He turned to face her, wiping his hands on an oily washcloth and dabbing at the sweat trickling down his neck and onto his bare chest. He wished he hadn't taken off his T-shirt as Bethany stared at his chest with her lips parted.

He motioned for her to back up into the main cabin. She was standing way too close. She did as he asked, and he thought she had left. But ten minutes later, after he'd cleaned up the shower, he realized she was still there. And how?

Naked. Well, almost naked. Her little top barely covered any flesh, and she'd taken off her skirt. Her tiny panties weren't covering anything as she stretched out on one of the banquettes, propping herself up on an elbow.

"Come on Bethany," he said, reaching for her hand to pull her off the cushions. "You can't do this to me."

"I think you like it," she whispered, reaching playfully between his legs.

He groaned, wishing he could walk away. But she had proved herself to be a willing and ready playmate, seducing him rather than making him work at it, the way he usually had to with Jenna. No playing games with Bethany. She was never any work at all. She brought him to the edge again not five minutes later with her mouth. When he was done, she looked up at him with her big brown eyes.

"Zack, please let me stay. I can help. You know I'm good, like in the kitchen, and with, like, you know, guests. Don't make me leave."

She was so eager to please him, and yet he was annoyed with her. She was to blame for causing the argument between himself and Jenna and for Jenna's angry departure. It had all started unraveling after the trip to Maine. Bethany had become more possessive, more demanding. He hadn't intended for it to get so out of hand.

As for Bethany's offer to stay the whole week? No way!

As he zippered up, he waited for her to slide back into her shorts, but she grabbed his hand as he was heading for the cabin steps. "Zack, you don't have to be such a fuddy-duddy about school. I really don't need to be there. This experience here at the inn is worth so much more than sitting in a classroom. It's like, real. I could run the website, too. I know all that stuff. I could be a real help. I'd be here all the time."

It was suddenly all too clear to him what Bethany meant. He couldn't believe it. The nerve of her. He could hardly stop himself from laughing in her face. Stupid, stupid girl. Did she really think she could step into Jenna's shoes just like that? Step into the shoes of his smart wife who looked picture perfect next to him on the "Welcome" page of the Kings Inn website?

"Zack and Jenna King," the caption read. "Proprietors of the Kings Inn." Those were Jenna's words, of course. It was Jenna who'd set up the website and started the weekly foodie blog in the days when websites and blogs were just starting up.

His smart wife. *My smart wife.* Sometimes, he'd whisper those words in her ear, padding up behind her as she was writing. When she was in the right mood, she'd laugh and say he made her sound like all the other "smart" devices he owned.

He'd never had any intention of replacing her with the kitchen help. A number of his buddies who had restaurants on the North Fork had married their kitchen help. Jenna had always been different. A step above. So much classier.

"You're going to need me, Zack," Bethany said a little more insistently as she tugged on his hand. "You know Jenna's not coming back anytime soon. Didn't you read that Page Six item about her and her ex-lover?"

He stared at Bethany, suddenly hating the sight of her. *Lover?* Why had Bethany used a word that would deliberately infuriate him? But yes, of course, he'd seen the item. It had only been one line mixed in with other VIP Sightings in the city, but how could he have missed it, when Bethany had left it right there, on the kitchen counter, for him to see?

"Come on, Zack," Bethany said as he stopped in midstep to stare at her. "You're not angry with me are you?" She reached out to touch him, but of course he was so angry with her that before he could stop himself he shoved her aside.

As her head hit the top step of the little stairway leading from the galley to the deck, the expression on her face turned to shock and disbelief. "Oh my God, Zack," she whimpered.

Then, just as quickly, she seemed to pull herself together and reached for him again, her face breaking into a smile even though there were tears glistening in her eyes. "It's okay. I'm okay," she said hoarsely. "Don't worry. Maybe I deserve to be punished. Do you want to punish me, Zack?"

With that stupid little smile on her face, he knew she had something else in mind. But he was done with her. He didn't want her. She'd caused enough trouble between him and Jenna.

So, he pushed her again; shoved her backwards so hard she crumpled onto the steps.

Suddenly, her eyes were blazing. "Asshole, you asshole! You're going to be sorry for this!"

All at once, he remembered everything Jenna had said about playing with fire, how Bethany was an intern and an employee and how, if he was messing around with her, she could report him to the culinary school—and the cops. He'd never stand a chance in these #MeToo times.

He took a step toward her. "Sorry, Beth. I'm sorry. I didn't mean . . ."

But she wasn't in any mood now to accept an apology. "Get away from me, you jerk. Just get away." She started crying, softly at first, and then more loudly, sobbing harder and harder. "You asshole," she repeated, over and over, her voice rising. "You're an asshole."

He needed to stop the screaming. His hands tightening around her throat, he pinned her against the stairway with such force that the back of her skull smacked against the top step. Her bare heels, trying to gain traction, slid away from her on the polished teak floor. He could feel rather than see her arms and hands flailing, trying to gain a grip on something, but she couldn't find anything to grasp. Her useless flapping suddenly resurrected the memory of Adele's goldfish, which had flopped around without its fins or tail on his mother's cutting board.

He stood there with his thumbs pressing into Bethany's windpipe. He knew if he let her get off the boat, she'd go running to the cops. So, he stood there, wondering how long before her arms stopped flapping. He could hardly bear to look at her face turning purple, her eyes rolling back behind her lids; her mouth opening and shutting. He wondered how long before he could lay her down on the floor of the galley and go start up the engine so he could motor out into the ocean. He wondered why it was taking so long.

Then he saw the angler's priest in the sink in the little galley alongside the steps.

Chapter Fifty-Eight

Week Three: Saturday Afternoon

J enna did not like the look of the clouds or the way the wind was beginning to whip up as they pulled away from the marina. Hank had said that there was a storm brewing offshore, which she interpreted to mean on the ocean. She tried not to dwell on the information Hank had gleaned about the *Dollie Too* going through the locks into Shinnecock Bay for lunch at Sundays. She hoped they were still there. She didn't even want to think about Zack going through the Shinnecock Inlet out into the ocean. How would she and Hank ever find him out there?

It took them about twenty minutes to cross Peconic Bay, making a straight run south of Robins Island, and then another ten or so minutes to go through the locks into Shinnecock Bay. Hank headed for the docks at Sundays while Jenna kept her eyes open for the boat. It didn't take her long to spot the *Dollie Too* docked at one of the guest berths at the furthest point from the restaurant. Hank trained his binoculars on it.

"Don't see Zack. They're probably still at lunch. Wait. Dollie's on deck. Looks like she's on a cell phone. What do you want to do, Jenna?"

"Pull up alongside." She had concocted a story for Hank. She'd told him about an argument with Zack and how she needed to talk to him without Dollie in the way. "If Zack is on the boat, I'll tell him I need to speak to him urgently and privately and that you'll take Dollie home."

She called out to her daughter as Hank docked the boat.

Dollie looked shocked to see her and then unexpectedly happy. Jenna relaxed a little. "Where's your dad?"

Dollie nodded toward the restaurant. "He's having a couple of beers with someone."

"Come on sweetheart, step over here. Hank is going to take you home. I'll wait for your dad. I need to talk to him. Leave him a note so he knows you're safe. Tell him Mom came with Hank to pick you up."

Jenna thought Dollie looked relieved at the thought of going home, but for a moment she eyed Jenna suspiciously as she looked around to find paper and pen. "Why should I leave him a note—won't you be here to tell him?" Dollie said. "Oh, never mind, I'll leave a note."

Then she looked at Jenna again. "You won't fight with Dad, will you? He said we were going to the islands. Did you know that?"

"No, honey, I didn't know. I'm sure he didn't mean today." Jenna fingered the .22 stuck in the back of her waistband. No reason to alarm Dollie, but it confirmed her gut feeling. She hugged Dollie and held her till her daughter squirmed.

"You're hurting me, Mom."

"I love you, Dollie."

"Yeah, love you too," Dollie called over her shoulder as she jumped onto the deck of Hank's boat. Jenna watched them pull away and then went below, positioning herself in the cabin with the .22 at her side on the banquette.

She didn't have long to wait. Within a half hour, she heard voices and footsteps and the sound of a woman giggling. Jenna moved quickly and slid into the head off the main cabin. She held the door a little ajar as Zack told the woman to make herself comfortable on deck while he fetched a couple of beers from below for them. "Don't think we'll be heading out today," he told her. "Relax. I'll just check on Dollie."

Through the crack in the door, she saw him come down the stairs for the beers, but he stopped when he saw the note Dollie had written. Jenna watched him pick it up.

"Shit. Shit. Shit." Zack muttered the words loudly enough for Jenna to hear as he returned above. "You have to go, Sue," Jenna heard him say. "My daughter . . . Look, you just have to go."

Jenna wondered what he was going to do as she heard the engine roaring to life. Was he going to give chase to Hank and Dollie? Or was he going to hightail it out through the inlet before the storm hit? Jenna hoped sincerely that it was the former. She had absolutely no idea what she would do if he chose to go through the inlet. She'd probably get seasick before she could confront him.

She heard the boat scraping against a piling. Five minutes later, she heard him bump through the locks. She breathed a long sigh of relief. So, he was heading back toward home, not the ocean. She realized he was slowing down, navigating his way through the canal and the no-wake zone at five miles per hour. She relaxed, easing her way out of the shower stall. Through the portholes she saw they were passing the public marina and Canal Cafe on the left. They'd be out on Peconic Bay in minutes.

She let him pick up speed on the open water, counted to ten, and made her way up the steps to the bridge, clutching the handrail so tightly she saw her knuckles go white. Zack couldn't hear a thing. She stood far enough behind him that he couldn't reach out and grab her.

Then she said, "Lovely night for a boat ride."

He looked over his shoulder. He appeared startled, then amused. "Wow, Jenna. What's going on?"

"Just keep your hands on the wheel," she said. "We're going to talk. I'll tell you when to cut the engine."

He looked over his shoulder again. "What is this?" She could tell by the look on his face, he had no idea.

Jenna felt cool and comfortable and totally in control for the first time in days. She knew exactly where she was going with this. She brought her gun out of her waistband and prodded him in the back with the barrel. "No games. This is my little gun you can feel, but the bullets in it are real."

She gripped the side of the boat. "I'll tell you when to stop." She paused. "Then we can have our chat, and you can tell me everything." She paused again. "And this time it had better be the truth." She paused once more before spitting out the name: "The whole truth, Denny."

PART
FOUR

Chapter Fifty-Nine

enny? He stood ramrod still at the wheel even as he felt the hairs on his neck bristling.

His thoughts raced. How the hell had she put that together? Had they already put the DNA from Bethany into the database? Had they lifted his DNA from something at the inn? Had they matched it to him in that criminal database where it was supposed to have been expunged?

He waited for Jenna to say something more, but she was very quiet, standing behind him as they approached Robins Island. If she'd figured out he was Denny, then no doubt she was angry enough to use that gun. He had to fix that immediately.

He slowed down as they rounded the spit of sand at the southern tip of the island. Suddenly he cut the engine and elbowed backward, knocking the gun out of Jenna's hand and throwing her off balance. He let the boat drift as he spun around and grabbed her and pinned her against the instrument panel.

Her face flashed furious. "You liar! Let go!"

"So you can shoot me?"

She kneed him hard and he yelled in pain, loosening his grip on her. She wriggled free but he was on her, catching hold of her arms and pinning them back behind her, pushing her toward the seats. The boat rocked. He thrust her onto a seat, scooped up the gun off the deck, and held it at his side.

"Now, why don't you tell me what this is about?" If looks could kill, he thought, Jenna wouldn't need a gun.

"Are you just going to let her drift?"

He didn't reply.

First, he needed to know what was going on back at the inn. If they were already onto him, he had some tough decisions to make in the next few moments. He'd have to get moving. With or without Dollie. Definitely without Jenna. He pointed the gun at her and took a step forward till the barrel was almost touching her chest.

"How did you find out, Jenna?"

There was a terrified look on her face, as if she actually believed he might shoot her. He reached out and grabbed her hair and pulled her face closer to his.

"In Florida," she stammered, her eyes narrowing. "I found the marina where you and the real Zack King set sail from. Did you really think I wouldn't figure it out?" Her mouth twisted into a weird smile. "Oh, and an FBI agent who turned up at the inn confirmed it all."

An FBI agent? Fuck. He didn't like the sound of that.

"Why?" He tightened his grip on her hair, and saw she was barely holding it together. Her eyes were glistening. Maybe with tears, maybe from the salt air. "Because of Adele?"

He yanked on her hair.

"No."

"Then why? Because of Bethany?"

Jenna pursed her lips.

He needed an answer. He yanked again.

"No. They don't have anything." Jenna stared at him pointedly. "Brad said any evidence on Bethany, or in Bethany, was too degraded to use."

He eased up on his grip. "Then what's the FBI agent doing?"

"Let go of me. I'll tell you."

He thrust her away from him and stepped back, easing into the captain's chair, but still with the gun aimed at Jenna.

In short, breathless half-sentences, she began talking, telling him how she'd tracked down Denny Dennison to Riviera Beach and found out there was an FBI agent who had tried to track down Denny years ago. And, how the same agent had appeared at the inn with Denny's prints from the arrest for the run-in with the photographer.

Well, he'd always suspected that would come back and bite him in the ass. "Why was he tracking me?"

"For nothing. He was collecting information, that's all, for some behavioral science unit."

"Where is he now, this agent?"

"He left. He said you haven't done anything wrong."

That sounded about right. He would have come for him with Jenna if they'd really wanted him for some crime. He noticed tears running down Jenna's face as she continued without waiting for him to say anything.

"But you lied and cheated and deceived me. Made our marriage a sham from day one." Her words come out like little spitballs. "Why? Why did you do it? To punish me? Take revenge? Impregnate me? To get even? You're a monster, Zack, Denny . . . I don't even know what to call you, but I know what you are, you're a psycho, just like your father."

He silently counted to ten. Jenna was wrong. He wasn't a monster. Or a psycho. It was simply unfair of Jenna to turn on him before she'd heard his side of the story.

He moved towards her and she shrank back. He couldn't bear to see that look of fear and revulsion in her eyes. He thrust the gun at her, holding it out for her to take. "Here," he said. "Take it and shoot me. If you really think I'm a monster. Shoot me. But if you really want to know how all this happened, I'll tell you."

Jenna didn't take the gun. He knew she wasn't going to. He knew that normal people like Jenna couldn't shoot someone in cold blood. Besides, she wanted to know why he'd done what he'd done. She wanted to hear an explanation that made sense to her and wouldn't frighten her. He wanted to tell her what she wanted to hear.

"Jenna, I never meant to hurt you like this. That first time I called you, all I wanted was to meet you, see what kind of a person you really were. That's all. Think back. I didn't expect to see you again after that first time. But you came out to the inn again and I got to know you and . . ." His eyes swept over her face. "I fell in love with you."

Jenna sat very still. He could tell she was thinking back, remembering how it had been between them. "But your life was a lie already back then. You conned me. You conned Jeremiah King," she said, a fresh look of dread creeping into her eyes. "You killed Zack King."

"No. Absolutely not. Let me tell you Jenna, the real Zack King was a shithead. He was an arrogant shithead. He fell overboard because he refused to strap himself to a safety harness. I did my best. That's how I got the scar." He ran his finger down the length of it. "I brought some joy into that old man's life. The real Zack never would have."

"Oh yes, and then you inherited his estate."

"I worked to build it. The real Zack wouldn't have done that either. He was out for what he could get. He told me he was going to 'fleece the old man.' Zack King was a douchebag. I was the grandson Jeremiah wanted and loved." Zack lowered his voice. "And I tried to be the best husband I could for you. When you agreed to marry me, it was like I got a second chance at life."

It was difficult now to tell what Jenna was thinking. He couldn't quite figure out the look in her eyes, possibly because it was getting darker as the gray clouds blew in. It seemed like they would see some weather from the offshore storm. He noticed the water getting choppier.

Jenna's mouth suddenly set in a hard, thin line. "Don't give me that crap. All that lovey-dovey bullshit, mouthing lines from movies. I should have seen it back then. You're just a good actor," she said. "Apparently, all psychopaths are. You just wanted to punish me."

He really didn't like it when she called him a psychopath. He wished she would stop it. He took a step toward her. "Sure, and I did that so well, didn't I? Oh yeah, I punished you, for sure. I beat you and abused you every chance I got, right, Jenna?" He knew she had no answer to his sarcasm. "C'mon, give me just one day when I wasn't the best damn husband any woman could wish for."

She turned her head and looked out over the waves. "You got me pregnant. You did that out of spite. Because your wife aborted your baby. You were getting even. Laughing behind my back that you were going to get your baby and I was going to make it happen as my punishment."

"That's crazy talk, Jenna."

"Why did you get me pregnant?"

He took a deep breath, pondered the wisdom of throwing her own words—*we've been screwing like rabbits*—back in her face, but instead said, "Dollie was a mistake."

"Like hell she was. You wanted her to prove that you are normal, that your child would be normal. I read the diary. Except that Dollie—"

"I mean Dollie wasn't supposed to happen."

Jenna laughed shrilly.

He took another deep breath. "I got myself fixed after Lisa died. Do you really think I was going to inflict that kind of horror on any other woman? Or myself? Is that what you think of me?"

Jenna leaped to her feet, and for a moment he thought she was going to hurl herself onto him with both fists pounding into his head. "You liar! You damn liar!" She pushed him and made a grab for the gun, but there was no way she was going to get it now.

He kept her at arm's length. "I can prove it, Jenna. Sorry to get technical, but my vasectomy was done in a way that would make it easier to reverse. I didn't ask for that, but I think the doctor decided I was maybe too young to know my own mind. Only trouble is, when the procedure is done like that, with clips, it can fail. That's what the doctor told me after you got pregnant."

The look on Jenna's face was one of pure horror, and then suddenly she was wiping tears off her face, taking in long deep breaths. He had no clue as to what was going through her head. She was gasping, and then it sounded as if she was laughing or hiccupping. When she finally spoke, there was a note of triumph in her voice: "Or maybe Dollie isn't yours?"

There was a long silence between them as the words sank in, and he realized it was going to take all the mental strength he had to keep it together. "Yeah, Jenna, I wondered about that," he said softly. "I thought about that scumbag McAllister. I know you spent the night before our wedding with him. That bastard's been hovering over my life for the last twenty years, but he's not Dollie's father."

Chapter Sixty

J enna sank down on the seat, her thoughts racing. Some of what
the lying, cheating scumbag was saying to her rang true. She
remembered his reaction when she'd told him she was pregnant.
He had been genuinely shocked.

Sure, it would have been a shock if he'd had a vasectomy. If he'd
told her that back then however, she would have thought harder about
her last night with Ryan.

They'd both woken disheveled, and Ryan had assured her he'd
been too drunk to make love to her, "if that's what you're worried
about"—and that's not what she'd been worried about because she'd
been more upset over her ruined dress.

"Did you have Dollie tested?" Jenna finally allowed herself to speak, although her words came out in a strangled whisper.

Zack shook his head. "I didn't."

"Then how the hell do you know Ryan's not her father?"

"I didn't want to know. Still don't. When Dollie was born, I just told myself I'd gotten a second chance. That this was my chance to make amends, to have a family, be a normal person, and not make a mess of it."

"What about me? What about Dollie?"

He carried on speaking as if he hadn't heard her. "After a while it didn't seem to matter anyway. I was Dollie's father. I am Dollie's father, and she is my daughter. I've taken care of her, supported her, and loved her for all of her life. It really doesn't matter now whose sperm it was."

Bile rose in Jenna's throat. She leaped to her feet and lunged at Zack. "Doesn't matter? Are you crazy? We had a right to know. Dollie and I had a right to know. Dollie has a right to know if she's the granddaughter of a serial killer—or the daughter of a man I really loved."

Jenna fell silent, feeling stricken at the enormity of this latest revelation. Tears welled up in her eyes. She was overwhelmed with such anger, she pushed Zack with all the ferocity that was coursing through her. He lost his balance and stumbled backwards. Jenna took advantage of his momentary surprise to grab the gun from his hand. Without hesitating, she flung it across the deck, saw it bump down the steps and then sail off the deck only to land in the dinghy that Zack pulled behind the boat.

"There now," she screamed. "Now, neither of us has it. And you can take me back. Right now. I'm going to put this right. We're going to do this the right way. Get Dollie tested and then—"

"Then what?" Zack interrupted, standing and blocking her way as she tried to get to the wheel. "What are you going to do, Jenna?"

"You watch me," she screamed at him. "You've stolen enough of our lives. Ryan has a right to know. If he's Dollie's father, he needs to know, and Dollie has the right to know who her real father is."

Jenna felt her fury rising with every word. "Get this boat moving, Zack . . . Denny . . . you lying bastard!"

"Wait, Jenna," he caught her hands in his and gripped them. "Please think this through. You're not thinking clearly."

"Oh, yes. Yes, I am thinking clearly. For the first time since I married you!" She wrenched her wrists free and stumbled backward. "Take me back," she told him.

"Not till we've talked about this."

Jenna shook her head and backed away. She looked out across the water, saw the waves had gotten higher as they were talking. She blinked, swallowed, and backed away, down the steps onto the aft deck before jumping onto the diving platform and from there leaping straight into the water.

The shock of its coldness was like a punch to her gut. She gasped and heard Zack yelling at her as she started swimming for the island. Then, she heard the anchor unspooling into the water.

She swam harder toward the island. She wasn't a strong swimmer at the best of times, and now she realized that while the shore had looked close enough from the boat, from where she was floundering in the waves, the island looked like it had suddenly gotten a whole lot farther away.

Chapter Sixty-One

er fury gave her the strength to keep going. Occasionally, a wave washed over her head getting water in her eyes and nose and mouth. Keep going, she told herself, spluttering. She was not going to let Zack fish her out of the water. She heard the sound of the dinghy motor somewhere behind her as she kept going toward the beach, and then it seemed like it was almost on top of her.

Oh God, oh God. Her mind seemed to freeze on the sudden, graphic image of the dinghy's propeller slicing through the water—and through her. Zack could kill her out here and tell everyone it was an accident. She closed her eyes and dove deeper into the water, even as she heard Zack's voice and heard him pleading with her to stop and to come on board the dinghy. Keeping her eyes closed tightly, she pushed herself forward in the direction of what she hoped was the beach.

And then, just as her lungs felt they'd reached the bursting point, her outstretched fists hit something. She opened her eyes to see sand in front of her, and then, summoning another burst of strength, she dragged herself onto the beach.

She looked back to see Zack sitting in the dinghy, obviously waiting for her to surface in his vicinity. In that same moment, he spotted her, and pointing the dinghy in her direction, revved up toward the beach.

Jenna scrambled to her feet and stumbled across the sand toward the bluffs. She ignored the pine needles and shrubs hurting her bare feet. Keep going, she told herself. She knew her best bet was to make a beeline for the main house once she was at the top of the bluffs. If she could make it to the house, there would be staff there, even if the owner wasn't home.

She'd get the staff to help her.

She looked behind her to see Zack steering the dinghy onto the beach just as her foot slid. She grabbed for a shrub to steady herself, but succeeded only in pulling it out by its roots. She started slipping down the bluff.

Zack was on top of her before she even realized he'd made up the distance between them. "Stop, Jenna," he mouthed into her ear as the weight of his body forced her into the sand. "There's nowhere to go."

Jenna allowed herself to go limp under the weight of his body. There was no point in struggling now. There was sand in her mouth, and it felt as if she'd sprained her wrist.

"Let me go."

"I can't do that—until you listen."

Jenna felt his heart pounding against her shoulder blades. "You have to listen to me, Jenna. If you don't listen, I'm going to tie you up and leave you in the woods. All the way back here."

"Like your psycho serial killer father buried women in the woods?"

Zack's voice was cold and clipped when he replied. "No, I'm not going to hurt you. You're not going to die, but by the time anyone finds you, Dollie and I will be gone. We'll be out in international waters, where no one can touch us. You will never find us."

Jenna didn't believe he wouldn't kill her. She knew now that Zack could be violent, even though he'd spent their whole marriage hiding this side of himself. She wasn't sure what had happened to Bethany, but she was sure now that he'd stabbed Adele to stop her from meeting with Jenna. She struggled to turn her head. "What can you possibly say to make me listen?"

He loosened his hold on her and let her sit up till they were face to face.

"I just want you to think it all through carefully, Jen. You don't want the world to know about me, or that Dollie's grandfather was a serial rapist and killer. You don't want anyone to know that you were duped and married the man you exposed as the secret spawn of evil, do you?"

Jenna pursed her lips.

"Don't you understand, Jen? The reason you're not with McAllister playing happy family is because he never wanted it. Did he ever ask if Dollie is his? Did he care enough to ask?"

Zack reached for her hand, but she shrank back.

He shook his head as if in disbelief. "But you know what, go ahead. Tell him. Then, if it all pans out, tell Dollie she's Ryan McAllister's daughter. Do you want to take the chance they'll both hate you?"

"Dollie will need to know."

"What? Need to know what?"

"Who her real father is."

"I'm her real father. I am the only father she's ever known. I guarantee it will be less of a trauma for her to find out that her grandfather was a serial killer than to find out that the man who raised her and has loved her all her life is not her father because her slut of a mother cheated on him on the night before her wedding. Sure you want that, Jenna?"

Jenna's thoughts were beginning to jumble as Zack talked at her.

"McAllister doesn't care, Jenna."

"Why did you hurt him?"

Zack took a deep breath. "I saw you both returning to the building. I saw him go inside with you, and I decided to wait. It was a long wait, Jenna, and then I saw him come out of the building and you came running after him. I could see you were upset. I lost it. Here I am loving you with all my heart while he treats you poorly, and it's still him you want. I just couldn't stop myself from kicking the shit out of him. I knew he wouldn't ID me. You know why? Because, for one, he'd look like a pussy, getting beaten up by an angry husband."

"You took the photos."

"Yes, I took the photos. I thought if you saw them in the cold light of day, you might come to your senses—especially if you saw how angry you were with him that night."

Jenna didn't want to hear any more. She wanted him to stop talking about Ryan. Otherwise, she'd have to think about what he was saying.

Why had Ryan never asked her if Dollie was his?

"What happened to Bethany? Tell me the truth."

"Jenna, I swear I don't know. I promise you. There wasn't a single reason why I would hurt her. Why would I harm Bethany?"

"Because maybe she thought you were serious about her, and when you told her she couldn't stay, she threatened to report you for raping her."

Zack laughed. "Bethany wasn't going to report me. Not in a million years. She had a boyfriend who was going to marry her and that's what she needed. She needed a husband so she could stay here legally. But know what I think? I think for some reason her boyfriend got jealous that she was spending so much time at the inn, and he's the one who hurt her."

Jenna wondered for a second if Zack was making up this story off the top of his head. He certainly seemed to know more about Bethany now than when Brad had first told them Bethany had disappeared.

He reached over and brushed the sand off Jenna's clothes. "You must be freezing. Sitting there in wet clothes."

Jenna had hardly noticed, not with the big drops of rain starting to fall.

"What about Adele? Why was she suddenly stabbed after I told you I was going to meet her?"

"Oh, Jenna, that's nuts. C'mon, when was I supposed to do that? After you told me you were meeting her? Did I race over there to get her before you met her?"

"You could have."

Jenna thought back and remembered how upset Dollie had been that Zack had gone missing that day. But he had been back later that evening. She shook her head, she couldn't remember exactly how the evening had gone, but he hadn't appeared as if . . . as if what? As if he'd stabbed someone? No, he'd offered to cook supper for the two of them. Could he have done that if he'd stabbed someone to death? Surely, he would have seemed a little . . . what? Upset? Nervous? Not in the mood for cooking?

Zack intruded into her thoughts. "I've always loved you Jenna, tried my very best, but you've always clung to some fantasy about Ryan McAllister. I don't know why. You accuse me of living a lie. What about you?"

Jenna turned her head away. She didn't want to hear it.

"I know you'd rather be with McAllister, but I'm still prepared to make a go of it, Jenna. It's not like we've had a bad life together. Whoever I am, whatever I did all those years ago to become Zack King can't matter as much as the life we made together with Dollie."

Jenna heard the nagging voice at the back of her mind. She didn't know what to believe, what to think. Hadn't Jonathan said that psychopaths were manipulative? Wasn't Zack—Denny—manipulating her now?

She blinked away a tear. Make a go of it? It sounded lame. But maybe it was the only thing to do. Hadn't her thoughts already drifted in this direction? Anyway, Dollie had to come first. What would it do to her if she found out that Zack wasn't her father? It would surely shatter her. What would it do to her if she found out that Zack wasn't really Zack King, but the son of a serial killer who had been executed? Wasn't it just better to close her eyes to this whole sorry mess and pretend that the last few weeks hadn't happened? But how could she pretend? She, at least, would have to know whether Zack or Ryan was Dollie's father.

She took a deep breath. She was too cold to think about it all now. If she refused to go along, he would leave her here and take Dollie, and the two of them would sail away. Disappear. Forever.

"You're shivering." His voice cut through her misery. "Come on, let's get back to the boat. You need a blanket. And maybe a shot of whiskey."

She let him help her to her feet. He swung her up in his arms and held her tightly as he steadily made his way down the dunes.

Chapter Sixty-Two

July 2019: One Month Later

Zack spotted Brad Halsey lumbering up the sidewalk toward them before Jenna did. They were sipping coffees in to-go cups at a wooden trestle table in a small courtyard next door to a cafe that was open for breakfast. It was across the street from where they'd dropped Dollie off at her therapist's office. Zack felt sick the minute he saw Brad. He was happy he hadn't ordered anything to eat.

He didn't know why a sudden fear gripped him. He knew that if the cops were going to ask him any questions about Bethany, detectives from the Suffolk County squad would take the lead in the interrogation. They were the ones handling Bethany's homicide. But one never knew with Brad; perhaps he was coming to give Zack a heads-up that the county homicide squad was about to descend on him with search warrants for the inn and his boats.

He cursed himself silently for not disposing of the angler's priest. He'd stopped thinking about running off to the islands after Jenna had told him that, according to Brad, any DNA evidence on Bethany was too degraded to use. He'd lulled himself into a false sense of security and been careless with the angler's priest. He had no idea why he'd transferred it to the motorboat in the first place. He hadn't even properly cleaned it before hiding it under all the crap in the dock box at the end of the jetty.

It would have been better if he'd left it to sail away on the *Good Times* to Barnegat Bay.

"Hi, kids." Brad's voice boomed, visibly startling Jenna. Immediately, Zack saw her take a deep breath as Brad loomed into her view, planting his hands on his hips and rocking back on his heels. "I'm glad I bumped into you. Was wondering how things are working out for the two of you."

Before Zack could respond, Jenna jumped in. "How are things working out for *you*, Chief? Hear anything from the detectives investigating Bethany's murder?"

Brad shook his head. "No progress as of yesterday. But the county guys have cleared the boyfriend. Don't know the details, but they've eliminated him as a suspect, apparently."

"That's a relief," Jenna interjected.

Zack stared at Jenna, narrowing his eyes. "A relief?" he echoed, turning the phrase into a question. What was she talking about?

"I mean, it would have been tough on his little boy," she added, looking at Brad. "Isn't he a single dad?"

"Yep, something like that, I believe." Brad shrugged. "Anyway, not an easy case. Lots of strangers around these parts this time of year. She could have gone off with anyone who offered her a ride that Sunday afternoon."

He seemed to be waiting for a reaction.

"Not an easy one at all," Brad repeated when none came, and gave them a mini salute. "Have a great day, kids," he added before ambling away.

Zack took a gulp of coffee and said nothing. But Jenna's words niggled. It was an odd thing for her to say: as if it was a relief the boyfriend had been eliminated because she knew the boyfriend was innocent—because she knew it was Zack who had killed Bethany.

Why would she be thinking that?

Hadn't he convinced her that day on the island that Bethany's boyfriend had more of a motive to kill her than Zack did? Hadn't she let Zack carry her back in his arms to the dinghy, and let him wrap her in blankets on the boat, and tuck her in on the banquette?

True, there'd been one scary moment while he was back on deck raising the anchor and starting the engine. Hearing a loud crash below, he'd run back down to see that Jenna had pulled one of the galley drawers right out.

"Sorry." She looked up, trying to sweep everything back into the drawer with her hands. "I need to find some Advil. My head feels like it's going to explode."

He'd almost had a heart attack seeing the entire contents of the drawer on the floor. The angler's priest and the hunting knife that Adele had held to his throat were lying right there. But they were in the middle of a whole mess of twine and fishing reel and other knives and tools for shucking and cleaning fish. Jenna would not have known what she was looking at in those few seconds before Zack helped her to her feet and led her back to the banquette.

He was overreacting now.

There was no way she could have been harboring suspicions like that about him these past few weeks without letting it show.

Not that she'd been overly warm towards him. Sometimes she looked as if she could barely stand him. She'd moved from her suite at the top of the staircase into the Miranda cottage, signaling that their estrangement might last a whole lot longer. She'd also asked him to return her gun to her after he retrieved it from the bottom of the dinghy.

He'd catch her staring at him as he worked in the kitchen. He wondered if she was wishing him dead, or if she was trying hard to persuade herself that sixteen years of a darn good marriage were more important than her discovery that he'd stolen another man's name.

There were some hopeful signs. She'd blown off her Monte Carlo trip. She said Dollie was more important. She was planning to take Dollie back to Maine to sort out the mess up there. In the meantime, she'd found a therapist for her. She said Lola had told her it would be points in Dollie's favor if Dollie could tell the district attorney in Maine that she was in therapy. In any event, given what she now knew about Dollie's paternity, she'd said therapy for Dollie wouldn't go amiss.

As he'd suspected, she had gone ahead with an attempt to determine who was Dollie's biological father. It didn't matter that she couldn't officially do what they call a "peace of mind" DNA test in New York. He knew from Google that she couldn't just take hair from a comb or brush or anything else that could yield DNA (and he was sure there was still plenty of McAllister's DNA lying around in her apartment) and send it off with Dollie's sample. Swabs in New York had to be submitted by a physician or a lawyer and tested by a legitimate lab.

But not if Jenna enlisted Lola's help.

Lola knew medical people in morgues and labs all over the city; she probably knew plenty of people who would do that sort of test on the quiet.

So, when Jenna drove to the city with Dollie, he figured that's what she was going to do. It had been a nasty couple of weeks while he waited for the hammer to drop. He'd even planned different scenarios of how he could stop Jenna from telling McAllister—if the test determined that McAllister was Dollie's father.

As it turned out, he didn't need to resort to any of the scenarios. Jenna had told him just the other morning that, yes, a test that Lola had arranged had shown that McAllister was not Dollie's father. "I owe you the truth," she'd said, holding out the paper with the result as her eyes brimmed with tears.

He'd felt sorry for Jenna in that moment, so he'd been generous. "I know you probably wanted a different result, Jen, and I'm sorry for you, but I think you know deep down that McAllister would never have been the kind of father—or husband—you fantasized he would be."

Jenna had nodded, biting her lower lip. "I know," she said. "He wouldn't have been half the father you've been for Dollie." Then, she'd turned away abruptly, without adding anything about him being a better husband than McAllister would have been.

It had hurt, but that day, he felt, had been a small turning point in their relationship. So, he'd made some bolder attempts to regain her interest. He'd invited her out to dinner— just the two of them—at a couple of new restaurants that had opened in their area.

He'd been happy to see that after a couple of drinks, Jenna loosened up with him, and they'd spent the evenings comparing menus and discussing possible new dishes Zack could add to the menu at the inn.

He'd also broached the subject of their future. Did she intend to return to the city? Or could she imagine staying with him on the North Fork?

"I'll do whatever is best for Dollie," she'd said, adding that she had a lot to process.

Now, waiting for Dollie to finish her therapy session, and with Brad having departed, Zack squeezed her hand and was heartened that she didn't snatch it away from him. The best thing for Dollie would be her two parents living together under the same roof. Jenna would come around to seeing that, he was sure. She'd come around eventually because she'd see past that little detail of a name because he was a good guy, a good husband, and a good father. Even the FBI agent had told Jenna that Zack had done nothing criminal in taking the real Zack King's name, hadn't he?

The deaths of Bethany and Adele hadn't really been criminal either but purely accidental; nothing at all to do with the sort of impulses his father had been unable to control. He had not killed Bethany or Adele for sick self-gratification. So, no, he wasn't a psycho. A psycho would have killed Jenna when he had the chance on Robins Island. Right there, he'd had the chance to kill her and bury her where her body might never have been found. The island was part nature preserve; her grave could have gone undisturbed forever. But he hadn't done it, had he? ·

He'd thrown Adele's hunting knife overboard the very next day, right after returning with Jenna from the island. Now, he made a mental note to get rid of the angler's priest next time he went out on the ocean. He was sorry at the thought of parting with it, but he couldn't leave it in the dock box. So long as Bethany's murder remained an open case—and it seemed like it would for a while—he had to get rid of the last little bit of evidence; the only thing that tied him to the crime.

Chapter Sixty-Three

Jenna watched from the kitchen windows as Zack unloaded the dock box at the end of the jetty. He'd already done it once this morning. Then he had thrown everything back haphazardly. Now, he was unloading the fishing rods, life preservers, and folding deck chairs again; opening and reopening the side pockets on the deck chairs, opening all the little boxes that carried the hooks and other small paraphernalia for fishing.

He was searching for something. He was getting frantic about it. She waited in the kitchen till he walked back from the jetty to join her.

"What are you looking for?" she asked, nodding toward the jetty as he walked over to the big kitchen sink to wash his hands.

He blinked. "If you must know, I'm looking for the angler's priest. You know, the fish bat, the one that belonged to Jeremiah."

"In the dock box? I thought you kept that on the boat."

Zack stared at her, looking momentarily startled. "Well, it's not on the fucking boat, is it?" He turned away and soaped his hands slowly.

The image of the angler's priest lying next to a fancy hunting knife flashed in front of Jenna's eyes. The two weapons had caught her eye when they'd fallen out of a galley-kitchen drawer on board the boat. If she'd just seen the angler's priest, it might have escaped her attention, but the hunting knife with its fancy inlaid blue handle and a blade accented with silver scrollwork had made no sense to Jenna. It was not anything she'd ever seen used for filleting fish or for cutting through twine.

She'd turned over the image in her mind, again and again, piecing it together with the news stories about Adele's stabbing until she was in no doubt that the knife used to murder Adele was lying in the drawer on the *Dollie Too*. In turn, this had prompted the thought that the murder weapon described in Bethany's case as something "like a child's small baseball bat" fit the description of the angler's priest.

The realization had caused a dull ache in the pit of her stomach, but not shock. Nothing she discovered about Zack could shock her anymore. From that day, it had just been a question of timing; of when she'd be able to extricate herself from a husband who was a cheat, an imposter, and a murderer. She'd mulled over her options, knowing that her first step was to retrieve the evidence.

She'd had to wait a couple of days after the return from Robins Island for Zack to leave the inn for a business lunch so that she could board the boat without raising his suspicion. Neither item had been in the drawer into which Zack had hurriedly swept everything off the floor that day she'd spilled its contents.

She'd eventually found the angler's priest hidden in the folds of an old sun umbrella in the dock box, but she could not find the hunting knife anywhere. She assumed that he'd simply tossed the knife into the water.

In any event, his attempt to conceal his possession of the two weapons had confirmed her suspicions, and with the angler's priest in her hands, she'd called Jonathan.

He would know how to determine if there was any evidence on it to prove that it had been used to kill Bethany. If there was, he would also know how to get Zack to confess that he had killed her—and that he had stabbed Adele to death. Maybe he would persuade Zack that in return for his confession, the FBI would close the cases without revealing his true identity. Wouldn't Zack agree to that to protect his wife and daughter?

It would be devastating enough for Dollie to see her father hauled away as a murderer without the added tragedy of discovering she was a serial killer's granddaughter.

The message on Jonathan's direct line, however, informed her that he was out of the office for six weeks attending seminars and conferences in London, Dublin, and Brussels. If it was an emergency, he'd left another number to call. Until this morning, however, she hadn't felt any urgency to call anyone else at the FBI. It had seemed to her that Zack had buried the angler's priest in the dock box and forgotten about it.

Now, as he wiped off his hands, he turned to her and said, "I'm sorry I got angry with you just now. I was looking in the dock box because I figured maybe Dollie stowed it in there by mistake when she cleaned up after the last fishing trip. I'm sure she'll know where it is." He took a step toward her. "Will you forgive me?"

She nodded. "Of course."

"How about a date night, tonight? Tommy's having a clambake at his restaurant. It'll be a blast."

She nodded again. "Sure. What time?"

"Six-ish."

"Fine. I've got a few errands to run in town. I'll be back by five. Shorts and T-shirt okay, I assume." She smiled. Then, hesitating in the doorway, she added, "Just don't get mad at Dollie over the fish bat, okay?"

She didn't even wait for Zack's response, but hurried toward her Jeep, her heart thumping. She couldn't believe that Zack was acting as if they could just pick up and go on as before. Date nights? Did he really think she was going to join him in living the lie he'd lived for the last twenty years? Could he not see the revulsion in her eyes whenever she looked at him?

As soon as she was on the main road, she reached for her phone and dialed the number Jonathan had left for emergencies.

"Is it an emergency?"

Jenna took a deep breath. The woman who'd answered the call had picked up on the first ring. Jenna didn't know what to say. Obviously, the sooner she could hand the angler's priest over to Jonathan the better, but was this really an emergency? Probably not the kind the FBI would consider an emergency. Zack hadn't given any indication that he suspected Jenna of taking it.

"He'll be back in the office soon," the woman continued. "I can take a message for him."

Jenna left her name and cell phone number and hung up.

Several hours later, seated at a candlelit table in Tommy's bay-front restaurant, she let Tommy fill and refill her glass as she and Zack dove into the clambake feast.

"All locally harvested," Tommy assured her with a knowing grin.

Jenna smiled at Tommy's acknowledgment of her restaurant exposé, and Zack gave her a thumbs-up too. She let him reach over and stroke her cheek as Tommy poured another glass of wine for them.

She was relaxed by the time they were finished, and let Zack walk her from his car through the inn—where they checked on Dollie to find her asleep in front of the TV—to the door of the cottage, where he paused.

"Are you going to invite me in?" he asked.

Her heart sank at the thought that Jonathan had still not called her back. How many more date nights would she have to spend fighting off Zack?

She shook her head. "Not a good idea," she said. "I'm too buzzed to think straight. I'll be asleep before my head touches the pillow."

"Okay. I don't want to take advantage of you." He took a step back. "It was a great evening. Thank you for coming out to dinner."

As she slid into bed with her iPad to check on the next day's weather, she was a little puzzled that he'd given up so easily. He hadn't even tried to kiss her on the cheek. She stared blankly at her screen wondering why it was taking so long to access the weather app. Then she noticed there were no internet bars. Accessing her settings, she saw she had no internet connection at all. She tried again to join the inn network. Nothing. The little circle just kept spinning around.

Immediately, she rejected the thought of calling Zack to tell him the internet was down. He'd probably disconnected the modem and router himself and was, even now, waiting for her call so he had an excuse to come back to the cottage. Was that his plan? To play some stupid role as a cable guy? Or an internet repairman? Was he hoping to seduce her by playing one of their stupid games?

She sat up abruptly.

No, that wasn't it at all.

Her heart slammed against her rib cage. How stupid was *she*? She'd gotten it wrong. Plying her with wine and a great dinner was not a prelude to seducing her. That had just been an act for Tommy and anyone else who'd seen them at the restaurant: See, everybody. My wife and me. All lovey-dovey.

No, Zack had something different planned.

She jackknifed out of bed and yanked one of the drawers in her lingerie chest so hard that it came right out. She took it back to the bed and swept the underside with her hand, realizing instantly that the angler's priest she'd taped to it was gone.

Somehow, she'd alerted Zack to her suspicions about him. Probably when she'd told Brad it was a relief that the cops had eliminated Bethany's boyfriend as a suspect in her murder. That had not been a clever thing to say, she'd realized almost immediately. Zack was too smart not to have picked up on the subtext. From there, it would have been a simple step to figure that if the angler's priest was missing, Jenna had it.

Her thoughts raced. No internet meant no surveillance cameras.

No surveillance cameras meant Zack could break into the cottage—and blame it on an intruder. Why had she thought that a man who had killed two other women was going to play games with her?

Zack wasn't coming to seduce her. He was coming to kill her.

Chapter Sixty-Four

T he adrenaline kicked in hard as Jenna raced around the room, her hands shaking, her heart pounding as she grabbed for her jeans, a T-shirt, and her sneakers. She had to get out. She had to get Dollie.

She hoped Dollie was still in the main house, asleep in front of the big-screen TV in the lounge. Zack had switched off the lights and TV, leaving her on the couch.

Jenna moved swiftly to retrieve her gun from the nightstand and threw the covers back over the bed and pillows. It looked like she was still under the sheets. She tried to imagine what Zack would do. Would he try to wake her before killing her?

Would he fling back the sheets and cover? Or not?

Would he just plunge a knife into where he thought she was under the bedclothes?

She shuddered and stepped into the bathroom. The windows by the jacuzzi tub were low to the ground and looked out the back of the cottage. From there, she could run through the rose garden to the inn.

She unlatched the window just as she heard a scraping noise at the screen door, the low whirring sound of some battery-operated gadget, and the jiggling metal as he picked the flimsy lock.

She was right.

He was going to make it look as if an intruder had broken in. She moved swiftly behind the bathroom door and looked through the space between the door and the jamb.

Zack, dressed all in black, stepped into the room. He was wearing a ski mask, as if he didn't want Jenna to know, in her last moments on earth, that he was the scumbag who'd come to kill her. He walked toward the bedroom. He hesitated in the doorway.

Jenna felt beads of sweat roll down her face. Was he listening for the sound of her breathing? She heard herself swallow as Zack stepped toward the bed, and then stared in horror as he raised his gloved hand. He was holding the angler's priest, raising it high above his head. He held it there for just a second before bringing it down full force, right on the spot where her head would have been.

Jenna wasn't sure if the gasp came from her or her husband, but she saw him look over his shoulder, his eyes nothing more than narrow slits as he took a stride toward the bathroom. She pulled the door wide open and aimed her gun at him. "Stop right there. Or I'll shoot you."

He hesitated. Then laughed abruptly as he took another step toward her.

She cocked the hammer and fired.

"What the fuck?" He was still coming at her, his voice angry now, "Drop that stupid little gun, Jenna. You know you're not going to kill me."

He was swinging the fish bat in a circle over his head. Getting closer to her.

She cocked the hammer again, her hand shaking violently, her teeth chattering, her heart pounding, her eyes brimming with tears. She couldn't miss this time. She pointed the gun at his chest. She closed her eyes. And then she pulled the trigger.

Chapter Sixty-Five

July 2020: One Year Later

The tables for two were arranged around the pool to show that the inn was following the rules of social distancing for outside dining. Even though New York's governor had lifted his "stay home" order for Long Island, people were still nervous about the coronavirus. Everybody was wearing masks. Inside the inn, plexiglass partitions separated the tables.

However, if reservations for rooms and brunches were anything to go by, everyone was raring to get out of their houses and apartments; they'd had enough of sheltering in place and quarantining.

Jenna crossed the patio holding her iPad and a glass of ice-cold pinot grigio. She made her way to one of the little tables set up by the pool, studying the iPad and noticing that just this morning a writers' group had booked all the rooms at the inn for a two-day seminar over the Labor Day weekend.

Things were looking up, she thought, happy that she'd decided to stay and run the inn on her own.

"Is this seat taken?" She looked up to see Jonathan hovering over the seat across the table.

"You made it."

He nodded, adjusting his mask over his nose. "I thought I'd never get here. Traffic is brutal. Like the whole of New York is heading out to wine country."

She smiled to cover the sudden apprehension she felt. She'd felt it since his phone call a couple of days before. He hadn't really given her a specific reason for his visit, and Jenna hadn't asked, afraid to hear his answer. She was terrified he was coming to tie up the only loose end left.

It was his second visit to the inn since the shooting the previous summer.

When he'd arrived the first time—the day after Zack's funeral— the yellow police tape was still strung across the doors of the Miranda cottage, and the media vultures were still trying to get more information about the night that Jenna Sinclair King had shot her husband, the owner of the Kings Inn ("voted Best Brunch on North Fork 2017").

Over a period of several days following the shooting, with Lola at her side, Jenna had talked to the cops. Then, the Suffolk County homicide detectives had released short, terse statements to the media: Jenna Sinclair had shot her husband in self-defense; her husband had tried to kill her to silence her after she found the fish bat with which he'd killed his girlfriend, Bethany Smithers.

The detectives subsequently confirmed that forensics had found microscopic traces of Bethany's blood and skin cells on the head of the fish bat. They had also found traces of her blood on Zack King's sailboat after sending two detectives to Barnegat Bay, where the sailboat was moored.

Of course, the media had gone crazy over what they naturally and immediately labeled "the fish bat murder." The *Daily News* had secured an interview with Bethany's roommate and parlayed her insights into the headline AFFABLE INNKEEPER BLUDGEONS GIRLFRIEND TO DEATH, THEN TURNS ON HIS WIFE.

The *New York Post*—with the headline FISH BAT WAS LOVE'S LAST RITES FOR NORTH FORK COUPLE—had interviewed Tommy and others who'd attended the clambake on the last evening the Kings had spent together. Everyone professed shock because the couple had seemed so happy together that night.

Star Magazine had a huge cover photo of Dollie at the funeral, with her two middle fingers aimed at the camera, her father's casket behind her, and a headline shrieking LEAVE US ALONE!

In the end, the media had wrung every last drop of news and nuance from the deadly love-triangle tragedy—and then moved on after Zack's funeral.

Teddi had called Jenna the day after. "We're sorry for your troubles, Jen," she'd said, then come to the point immediately. "I suggested that Ryan snap up your story, in your own words, for *CityMagazine*. He thinks that's a good idea."

Jenna had been tempted to answer that if Ryan thought it was a good idea, he should call her himself and she might consider it. But she knew that would be a lie. She wasn't going to tell her story to anyone. And anyway, she didn't believe Ryan had said anything about it. It was probably all Teddi's idea. So Jenna had hung up on her.

Jonathan had shown up the next day. "I could have come sooner, but I didn't think you needed questions as to why the FBI was here."

"I guess not," Jenna had replied. She'd been relieved to see him, knowing he was the one person with whom she could share her worst fear: that the medical examiner had taken Zack's prints postmortem and somehow would get a match from the FBI database. "And then they'll name Zack as Bethany's killer—and as Evil Ed's son."

Jonathan had held her hand and said: "That's not going to happen. No reason why it should."

"Yes, but Denny Dennison's prints are in your FBI file, along with your findings, which I'm sure now say that he didn't drown but was living as an imposter—as Zack King, who then bludgeoned his mistress to death and tried to murder his wife. Isn't that what your unit was set up to find: the psycho children of psycho parents?"

"Jenna, please. We're not a tabloid newspaper, and we're not going to give out that information to any tabloid newspapers or any media. It's ongoing research, and it will probably be years before we reach any conclusions—if we ever come to any conclusions," he asserted. "And even then it will probably be a dense, incomprehensible scientific report that no one will understand and in which we won't even identify all subjects by their full names."

"Meaning?"

"Well, we wouldn't have to spell out that he was living under the name Zack King, just that he was living under an assumed name when he murdered his mistress and tried to murder his wife."

Jenna was not reassured.

All she understood was that nothing was ever truly expunged from an FBI file, and whoever said differently was lying. Jonathan was going to be holding her and Dollie's future in his hands, in his files forever. There was no way she was going to confide in him now about the hunting knife, or her suspicion that Zack had also murdered his step-sister, Adele.

Fuck him. Fuck the FBI, she thought. She was glad when Jonathan had left. The funeral had been exhausting for her and Dollie. With everybody gone, they could share their grief, just the two of them.

Dollie had slept long hours since her father's death, first in a seemingly catatonic state, then fitfully, waking every hour or so to make sure that Jenna was beside her, as if fearing that her mother might disappear too. Jenna had welcomed her daughter's closeness; she had expected accusations and recriminations and questions that she could not have answered with any ease. Instead, Dollie had apologized. "I'm sorry, Mom. I blamed you for everything. I shouldn't have." Finally, with tears spilling from her eyes, she had asked Jenna, "Mom, what happened to Dad? He just went crazy. Why?"

Jenna had not been able to answer her daughter. Her grief was genuine too. As was her second-guessing. She wondered if things could have turned out any other way, How much of it was her fault? She had felt bitter and angry about Zack's deception, but there were moments when she had to acknowledge her own culpability. She'd retraced her life to what she had written all those years ago and knew that if she had not exposed Rosie's secret, Denny would not have felt compelled to steal another man's identity. She had set the chain of events in motion and then resurrected the whole sorry mess with her determination to find Denny. She had unwittingly stirred up whatever bad blood had flowed into his veins from his father till he had turned into the evil spawn of her ill-fated headline.

Jenna had not heard from Jonathan again—until his phone call a few days ago. "I'd like to see you, Jenna," he'd said.

Now, she tried to read the expression on his face as he sat down at the table and removed his mask. He looked relaxed. Maybe he wasn't here to tie up the loose end of Adele's stabbing. Maybe it wasn't because federal investigators had uncovered prints or DNA evidence at Adele's crime scene that had led back to Jonathan's Denny/Zack files. If there was a chance of that, surely it would have happened already? Even so, she'd worried about it for days, and dreaded the thought that Jonathan was coming to shatter their world and to tell her there was nothing he could do to stop their secret from getting out now.

"I stayed away longer than I meant to," he said, as he sat down at their little table.

Jenna nodded. "I'm happy to see you, Jonathan," she said in her best mistress-of-the-inn voice. "How long do you think you'll stay?"

"I could stay a while. Is the Miranda cottage available?"

"It's available and all cleaned up." She smiled hesitantly.

"I'm not squeamish." He smiled back at her, and suddenly she wondered if he'd come with a different aim. Not to tell her about Adele. Maybe her death would remain unsolved, a cold case, forever.

Maybe Jonathan was here for a different reason entirely. Maybe he was here because he thought she was ready for a new man in her life. Maybe he thought he could worm his way into her life because he knew about Zack and Denny and Dollie. As the keeper of their secrets, maybe he thought she owed him.

Stop it, she told herself. It was one thing to feel that she wouldn't be able to trust another man anytime soon. It was another to impute the worst possible motives to Jonathan.

He was not an ogre. He of all people would understand that Dollie came first now. That she needed all of Jenna's care and love and attention. It was one way of guarding against any of Dollie's father's or grandfather's bad blood bubbling to the surface. Jenna could help her. She knew she could.

Dollie was already turning into a sunnier, warmer teenager.

She took a deep breath and noticed that Dollie was making her way across the patio with a tray of soft drinks in her hands. She watched as Dollie deposited the drinks at one of the tables and then approached their table. She tucked the empty tray under her arm and adjusted her colorful mask. "How are you, sir?" She addressed Jonathan. "Can I get you a drink?"

"A beer would be terrific." Jonathan grinned at Dollie. "Anything you have on tap is just fine."

"Sure," Dollie smiled. "I'll get Ana to bring that for you. I'm not allowed to serve alcohol yet."

Jenna noticed that Dollie had retouched her nail polish and had chosen to wear a clean white blouse with clean, pressed shorts like she had every day since agreeing to help out at the inn. What's more, Jenna was amazed that after a day's work, Dollie still had the enthusiasm to update the inn's website with photos and a blog that documented her experiments in the kitchen. She'd titled it *Dallies with Dollie*.

"Looks like she's doing really well," Jonathan observed as Dollie walked back to the kitchen.

Jenna nodded and suppressed the hysterical giggle that rose to her lips. Maybe Jonathan was here to check on the next generation of the serial-killer gene pool. Immediately, she regretted being so cynical. Maybe Jonathan simply wanted to know that she and Dollie were okay.

She allowed herself the smallest hint of a smile. "Yes. Dollie's doing really well." She watched her daughter weaving her way around the tables, stopping at one to ask if they needed refills, at another to ask if they needed appetizers. She knew Jonathan was watching, too.

"Definitely a trouper." Jonathan turned his attention back to Jenna, staring at her over the tops of his sunglasses. "Just like her mom."

Jenna's heart beat a little faster and this time she laughed out loud. "Yes," she nodded. "I guess she is. Exactly like her mom."

Acknowledgments

For helping guide this third novel from its scrappy beginnings through to publication, I am indebted to:

My husband, Joe, my rock and my #1 fan. He has encouraged and supported me in everything I ever wanted to achieve. I couldn't wish or hope for—or even dream up—a better partner.

Helga Schier, who was my editor before she joined CamCat Books as Editorial Director. I could not have made it out of the gate nor across the finish line without her support, her words of encouragement at the lowest of times—and the "red pen" that helped turn *Fool Her Once* into the very best book it could be.

My brother, Michael Patyna who was the first reader of my first draft and who went through my manuscript with an editor's insight and with an astounding eye for detail. His rates are reasonable and he can be reached at mjpatyna@yahoo.co.uk.

The best of the best beta readers: my stepson, Sean Elm whose support has been unwavering since he read one of my earliest drafts; my besties, Julie Johnstone in the U.K. and Judy Calixto Goldman in New York for their critiques and support since the very beginning; Annmarie Magliocco, as avid a reader as any author could find; my former editor at Star Magazine, Phil Bunton, and Cathy Helowicz, who had the final look-see and who as former executive director of the Palm Beach Writers Group brought me into the fold.

Gavin D. Silver who set up my website, www.joannaelm.com out of the goodness of his heart, when I was totally clueless; and James M. Catterson, who jumped on board as my assistant to help steer me through the complexities of book marketing and promotion.

The Gonks aka the writers I met in St Augustine at the Algonkian Author-Mentor Workshop (Class of 2017): To this day, we share our successes and setbacks, and support each other's projects. Thank you Gregory Renz, Doug Spak, Paula Zimlicki, Noreene Storrie, Mandi Bean, Lunka Dinwiddie and Chris Capstraw Pappas.

Sue Arroyo, publisher of CamCat Books, Laura Wooffitt, marketing guru, Gabe Schier, social media expert, Maryann Appel, cover artist extraordinaire, and the rest of the team at CamCat Books who have the most amazing energy and commitment to making every CamCat book a success. Thank you for including me in the CamCat family.

For Further Discussion

1. Should Jenna Sinclair have blamed herself for the tragic consequences of her first scoop when she outed the secret son of a serial killer? Why? Why not?

2. Do you blame her for wanting to revive her relationship with Ryan McAllister?

3. Do you believe that genetic influences are stronger than environmental ones? Can a child really be a "bad seed?" And if there is a predisposition towards evil, do you think that child can be saved by loving parenting?

4. Is Zack King a sympathetic character? Is he a good husband? Father?

5. Should Zack be punished for trying to hide his past/lying about it to Jenna?

6. Do you think the serial killer's son was a psychopath himself, or did you agree with the way he explained his actions?

7. Do you think that tabloid newspapers provide any service beyond sensational reporting? What would you have done in Jenna's place? Would you have included information about the serial killer's secret son, or left it out of the interview with the serial killer's fiancée? Why? Or, why not?

8. Do you think the interview with Rosie, the serial killer's fiancée, would have looked any different in the New York Times or your local hometown newspaper compared to the tabloid newspaper?

9. Do you think reporters have an obligation to think about the possible consequences of their reporting? Why? Why not?

10. What goes around, comes around could be seen as one theme of this story. Do you think that's fair in Jenna's case? Why? Why not? Are you apprehensive for Jenna's and Dollie's future? Do you wish they could have had a happier ending?

About the Author

Joanna Elm is an author, journalist, blogger and an attorney. Before publication of her first two suspense novels (*Scandal*/Tor/ Forge 1996); (*Delusion* Tor/Forge/1997), she was an investigative journalist on the *London Evening News* on Fleet Street in the U.K. She also wrote for British magazines like *Woman's Own*.

She moved to New York in the late 1970s where she worked as a writer/producer for television news and for the tabloid TV show *A Current Affair*. She was also the researcher/writer for WNEW-TV's Emmy-award winning documentary *Irish Eyes*. After she joined the *Star* as a reporter, she became the magazine's news editor and managing editor before moving to Philadelphia as editor of the news/

features section of *TV Guide*. After completing her first two novels while living in South Florida, Joanna returned to New York, enrolled in law school, graduated summa cum laude, passed the NY Bar exam and worked as principal law clerk for an appellate division justice in the prestigious First Department. She has been married to husband Joe for 35 years. They have one son, Daniel.

Check out Joanna's website
www.joannaelm.com.

Follow her on twitter and Instagram @authorjoannaelm.

Author Q&A

Q: Are there real-life models to your characters?

A: To a certain extent, Jenna Sinclair is based on myself. Thankfully, there have never been any deadly consequences to the stories I investigated. But Jenna's style is similar to mine. When her husband observes that, "he could hear her circling back, zeroing in on the tricky question in that way she had of making everything sound like an interrogation," I tend to do the same even in non-professional settings. As my son, Daniel says, "You ask too many questions, Mom." I like to think it's because I am genuinely interested and insanely curious about you, about how stuff works, and why things are the way they are.

Q: How do you research your books?

A: Whenever I can, I like to research by actually going to the location where I'm setting my story and by meeting the people who are experts in the questions I need answered. For example, in researching one particular scene in *Fool Her Once*, I was lucky enough to spend time with U.S. coast guards, Rachael Greene and Jeremiah Jacobs at the Lake Worth Inlet Coast Guard station. Sometimes, however, I'll just pick up the phone, say to the medical examiner's office in the county where a death scene is set, or to the New York State Liquor Authority to ask about fingerprints on license applications. It's wonderful that most people are more than happy to share their expertise when they hear you're writing a novel.

Otherwise, these days, there's an abundance of information on the internet and in books. Although I love sailing, I've never been in a severe squall or storm, but I gleaned what it might be like from an excellent article by Robin Urquart in sailmagazine.com

As for inside knowledge about psychopaths, there's no better manual than Robert D. Hare's Without Conscience.

Although I've read a lot about the FBI, and its work, I've never seen anything to suggest there is a unit that investigates possible genetic influences of serial killer parents on their offspring. Like TV's X-files unit investigating paranormal events for the FBI, the behavioral science unit in *Fool Her Once* is a figment of my imagination. I think.

Q: What was most fun about writing this book?

A: I've always loved plotting out a book and outlining the chapters. That didn't change with *Fool Her Once*. I loved (almost) everything about returning to writing fiction after 25 years.

I found a lot of changes. Mostly for the better. I love Scrivener, the new software for authors. It makes the actual mechanics of writing a novel a delight. I loved attending writers' workshops and seminars and online courses that allow authors to get great advice and tips on writing in whatever their genre is. I loved networking in writers' groups, and meeting other authors at events like the annual Palm Beach Book Festival. The two-to-three day festival was founded by Lois Cahall in 2015 and, in my humble opinion, is the best thing that's ever happened to Palm Beach.

Q: What was the greatest challenge in writing this book?

A: Getting to the finish line. Even after CamCat Books offered me a contract, there were edits and revisions to be made. That's always where the hard work is: in the editing and revising. There was a point (isn't there always for an author?) when I thought of throwing everything in the garbage. I told my husband: "I'm never going through this again. I'm never writing another novel," His response? "I'll give you two months before you get back to your next one."

Q: What is your super power?

A: My super power is my husband, Joe. Authors are, mostly, very difficult people to live with. Even when we're there, we're often not quite present because our minds are in our fictional worlds. And, if a scene or chapter is not working, watch out!

You need a spouse or partner who understands all that, who understands what makes a writer tick, and who will pick up the slack. Joe is that partner. Because he's always been very secure in his own accomplishments, he has given me the space and freedom to satisfy my ambitions—and has always had more confidence in my abilities than I have.

He has always encouraged and supported me in everything I wanted to do from publishing my first novel in 1996 to becoming a lawyer of the New York Bar in 2005. More recently, he took a back seat while I worked on *Fool Her Once* even though he's always looking for us to spend more time together.

If you liked *Fool Her Once*
by Joanna Elm,
you'll like
The Disappearance of Trudy Solomon
by Marcy McCreary.

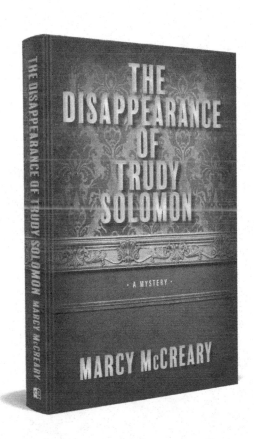

Chapter One

MY PALMS were sweatier than usual. I glanced around before reaching into my desk drawer to rub Secret on them. Yes, that Secret. The anti-perspirant. There was going to be lots of handshaking today and I wasn't sure I could avoid it. They finally solved the case. Missing August 6, 1978. Found October 22, 2018. Forty years, two months, and sixteen days. And the answer . . . right under their noses the entire time. Dad didn't know yet. My plan was to stop by Horizon Meadows Residences after my shift to break the news.

Sally McIver strode across the precinct floor and planted herself on the edge of my desk. "Hey Susan, can you believe it? Wait until your dad hears the story."

The story. The one that consumed my life forty years ago. A case my mother derisively referred to as a "Big F-ing Deal." Emphasis on the F. For years, the disappearance of Trudy Solomon confounded my father—the lead detective on the case—until it faded away, yet not completely. Like a chalkboard where you can see remnants of math equations long erased. The cold case of Trudy Solomon. No strong suspect. No obvious motive. No forensics to test. No computer databases to mine. Just gumshoe detective work that yielded few leads and no resolution. Until now—until this fluky stroke of luck.

Someone leaked the story to the press. That didn't take long. Trudy was found only a few hours ago. An unruly group of reporters swarmed the police station. I held no animus against reporters—like locusts, they were harmless when just a handful were flitting around the halls, but they had a way of causing damage when they got all riled up around a potentially juicy story. I had been dodging them all morning. I wasn't sure how much more I could offer up than what Ray Gorman, the detective (and the guy who shares my bed), had told them. He's the one who connected the dots and found her. I could only assume I was the human interest side of the story. They'd want to know how Dad reacts to the news. They'd want to know if I knew about this case back when I was thirteen and if so, how it impacted me and how I felt now. But that was my story. Not theirs.

⟞∿⟞ ⟞∿⟞

FOUR WEEKS ago, Monticello Police Chief Cliff Eldridge called me into his office. A day like any other day. A day stuck at my desk while Internal Affairs reviewed my case. A day with my gun locked away. A day feeling spasms of pain in my right thigh, a throbbing reminder of the bullet lodged in fatty tissue. I had returned to the station exactly one week earlier, on September 17, cleared for desk duty and not much else. Shuffling papers. Watching surveillance tapes. Answering phones. Monitoring police vehicles. They called it restricted duty. Felt more like purgatory—am I in or am I out? My future as a detective resting in the hands of others.

"We just got a call from a senior investigator with the New York State Police." Eldridge glanced at a piece of paper on his desk. "John Minot. Ever hear of him?"

"No, sir."

"His unit found skeletal remains along Route 9W in Ulster County. He ran up against a wall trying to identify the body, so he started going through regional missing person reports." Eldridge paused and peered over his cheaters. "Do you know where I am going with this?"

"Are you saying this could be Trudy Solomon? Are the bones forty years old?"

"They've been there for some time, but they haven't determined how long yet. Detective Minot claims they roughly match the description of Trudy Solomon. Female. Caucasian. Late twenties, early thirties."

"Holy shit. And cause of death? Is that known?"

"Gunshot to the head. Close range."

"Jeez."

"Minot is looking for a relative of Trudy's so he can run a DNA test to confirm or rule out that it's her. He thought we might have something in the files, people we can contact. But this case has been dormant for so long, we'll have to do a little digging on the relative front." Eldridge shifted slightly in his chair, then cleared his throat. Two short grunts. "I know you, Susan. You're gonna want this case. I can see the gears turning in your head right now. But you know the situation. You're on desk duty until you are cleared by Internal Affairs, the department shrink, and your doctor. If it were up to me, I'd hand this to you to follow up. But it's not up to me."

"Who are you assigning this to?"

"Ray and Marty. I told them to keep you apprised, and if they need help, the kind you can do from a desk, they'll let you know. Okay? That's the best I can do right now."

"And my dad? Can I let him know?"

"That's up to you, Susan. But I would keep it to myself until we know more. No need to get his hopes up—then dashed. Probably best not to replay 1978 again. You were too young to remember, but I'm not."

Oh, I remembered.

When the world is crashing down around you during your preteen years, you remember everything. F U Mother. With an emphasis on the F. I decided not to tell Dad until there was a definitive answer. Eldridge was right.

No need to dredge this up prematurely.

In the weeks that followed, Ray and Marty sifted through local and national databases to find a living relative of Trudy Solomon. Not a soul emerged.

But Ray did hit upon something odd. When he did a search on Trudy Solomon's social security number he found it was still in use, associated with a medical bill for a patient in Massachusetts. That patient was a woman named Gertrude Resnick who had the same birth date, February 16, 1951, as Gertrude (aka Trudy) Solomon. Eldridge gave them the go-ahead to travel 250 miles east to a hospital in Lowell, Massachusetts, to question her.

In the early-morning hours of October 22, Ray awoke early to make the trip. "Wish you could come with us," he whispered in my ear. Then he leaned over and kissed my forehead before I had a chance to draw the blankets over my face. "Y'know, you're kinda cute when you're mad."

"Then I must be cute all the time."

—ᔆᔆᔆ— —ᔆᔆᔆ—

BY MIDAFTERNOON I was getting antsy waiting to hear from Ray as to whether the Trudy in Lowell was in fact our Trudy. From the moment the body was found until now—what felt like the longest four weeks of my life—I had been in a constant state of agitation. Between keeping this discovery from my dad and awaiting clearance from IA, I couldn't remember a time in my adult life that sucked more. Well, except for being shot . . . and almost dying.

I was in the police-station bathroom, trousers at my ankles, when Ray finally called me.

"Hey. Did you talk to her yet?" My voice echoed around me in the little stall.

"Gertrude Resnick? Not yet. We're about to go in. Did you get your gun and badge back?"

"Yeah. A half hour ago."

"Super. We'll celebrate tonight."

I stared at the inked heart on the stall door. The initials SM and EP scribbled in its center. Sally still refused to use this stall after Elaine Pellman broke up with her nearly two years ago. I suggested she paint over it, but Sally insisted it should live on, like her pain.

"Susan. You there?"

"Yeah. Sure."

"You okay?"

"Yeah. It's just been a long morning. Lots of paperwork and shit."

I was definitely not in a celebratory mood. Sure, IA exonerated me, but many folks in this town certainly hadn't. In the end, it came down to my word, an officer in good standing, against a criminal's word. The fact I was shot probably helped my case. Thing is, I shot and killed the person who wasn't holding the gun. And Calvin Barnes's family still wanted answers.

I splashed cold water on my face. I tried not to look in the mirror, dreading what I would see staring back at me. But I glanced up anyway. I'd seen better days. A recent botched dye job turned my curls from chocolate brown to bluish black. Which would have been cool thirty years ago when I was going through my punk-rock phase. The concealer I applied this morning was doing little to mask the charcoal-tinged bags under my eyes. Even my blue eyes seemed dingier. No longer bright as cornflower, they were murky like an oil-slicked ocean. I grabbed a couple of paper towels and patted my face dry. Then I scrounged around my bag and removed some essentials—concealer, lipstick, eyeshadow, blush. Ah, the wonders of makeup. A dab here and there, and voilà, I didn't look half bad for a been-through-the-wringer, fifty-three-year-old detective.

A NEW sign greeted me at the entrance to Dad's digs: Welcome to Horizon Meadows Residences. What I wanted to know is who came up with the name Horizon Meadows. Did they just pick two random words and throw them together? The place was literally in the woods. You could barely imagine a horizon. And anything that might once have been a meadow had been subdivided and built on. So why not call it Forest Haven or Sylvan Acres? Maybe because, for the residents of places like this, the horizon was a metaphor for what awaits them all.

After his second heart attack, Dad relented, but not without complaint. Claimed he would die within six months of moving, as he put it, to an old-age home. He was convinced he would be reduced to a drooling, blithering, incapable clod. That was two years ago. Then a few old guys from the police force moved in. At seventy-seven, Dad was the reigning Horizon Meadows bridge and shuffleboard champion. He and most of his buddies were in Level One. Independent living. A decently appointed one-bedroom apartment with an emergency call button in the bathroom. Bud was in Level Three, a floor in the building that featured a nurse on duty at all times. And poor Andy. Level Four. Dementia got the best of him, but he joined them in the dining hall on his better days. A few months ago, he asked my father to put a pillow over his head when he reached Level Six. I doubt Dad would oblige. But, then again, I wouldn't bet on it.

As I made my way through the lobby to the computer room, I wondered if Dad had gotten wind of the Trudy Solomon story. If he had, I was pretty sure I would have heard from him. I spotted Dad on the far side of the computer room helping Agnes navigate her granddaughter's Facebook page. "Hey, Dad. Hi ,Agnes."

Agnes leaned toward Dad like a lion protecting her cub. "Hi Susan," Agnes purred. "Will told me about your brush with death, I prayed for you every night. And well, here you are, looking wonderful. Prayers answered. God is looking out for you."

"He must have heard you." I glanced at Dad—eyebrows raised, admonishing my sarcasm. "Thank you, Agnes . . . I'll take all the help I can get."

"Well, well, well. The prodigal daughter has returned. How's the bullet wound?"

"Dad, I'm fine. I've got some news for you." I glanced sideways at Agnes. "Can we find a quiet place to talk?"

Agnes patted Dad's arm. "We can do this later. I'll be right here when you return."

It was unseasonably warm for late October, the temperature hovering around seventy degrees, so we headed out to the benches behind the main building.

"There's been a break in the Trudy Solomon case." I paused to study his reaction. Skepticism. "She's alive. Ray found her."

His mouth twitched and one eyebrow lifted ever so slightly, signaling a shift from incredulous to unconvinced. "Are you sure it's her?"

"One hundred percent sure."

"What happened to her? Where's she been all these years?"

"That's still not clear. She has Alzheimer's. Has had it for a while now."

"Then how do you know it's her?"

I told him how they found skeletal remains that jogged the case open, then traced the social security number to Gertrude Resnick. I told him that she'd identified herself from a Cuttman Hotel work ID photo, proclaiming "me," and then verbally identifying her husband, Ben Solomon, when shown a picture of him.

"Holy shit. Holy . . ." He paused and shook his head. "Where is she?"

"In an Alzheimer's care facility in Lowell, Massachusetts."

"Well, I'll be damned. A social-security-number trace. Seems so simple."

"Dad, things were different back then. You couldn't just plug a social security number into a computer. Don't second-guess yourself."

Dad shifted his attention to his shoes and poked at the dirt with the tip of his worn loafers. "And the remains that were found? Has she been identified?"

"Nope."

"So now what? Is Ray going to find out what happened to Trudy? I mean, maybe she was kidnapped? There could still be a criminal element to this."

"I think you know the answer to that. Eldridge is not going to put any more resources on this."

"Did he say that?"

"Well, no. But where's the crime? She's been found."

"Don't you want to know what happened to her?"

"Sure, I'm curious. But—"

"Ask Eldridge to reopen the case. Or take a leave of absence. Help me figure this out. We had the beginning. We now have the ending. Let's figure out the middle."

"Are you kidding? For what reason?"

"Do I sound like I'm kidding? This has haunted me for decades. I deserve to know what happened. We finally have a break we can work with."

What was with this we shit? Nineteen seventy-eight was one of the worst years in my life. Grandpa died. Mom and Dad separated. My best friend dumped me for a new best friend. Mother hit the bottle hard. And a woman who went missing pulled Dad out of my orbit. The funny thing was, I'd been obsessed with this case too. But looking back, it was hard to discern if it was the mysterious nature of the case itself that intrigued me, or my desire to bond with my father over something, anything. I pestered him incessantly about leads, suspects, witnesses. He was so sure she was kidnapped or murdered. But there was also a theory floating around that she simply wanted to walk away from her life. And I just wanted to know how that was even possible. How did she do it? Why did she do it? Where did she go? Did anyone help her? Trudy captured my imagination. I imprinted on her at a time when I wanted to disappear, reinvent myself. But I was thirteen—what did I know about how to do such a thing?

"I'll think about it." My palms started sweating profusely again. Palmar hyperhidrosis—the clinical term for excessive, uncontrollable sweating of the hands or palms. The bane of my existence.

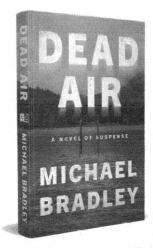